MW01026315

COMBAT
INEFFECTIVE

A Jock Miles-Moon Brothers
Korean War Story

A Novel By
William Peter Grasso

Novels by William Peter Grasso:

Jock Miles-Moon Brothers Korean War Story
Combat Ineffective, *Book 1*

Moon Brothers WW2 Adventure Series
Moon Above, Moon Below, *Book 1*
Fortress Falling, *Book 2*
Our Ally, Our Enemy, *Book 3*
This Fog of Peace, *Book 4*

Jock Miles WW2 Adventure Series
Long Walk to the Sun, *Book 1*
Operation Long Jump, *Book 2*
Operation Easy Street, *Book 3*
Operation Blind Spot, *Book 4*
Operation Fishwrapper, *Book 5*

Unpunished

East Wind Returns

Cover design by Alyson Aversa
Photo courtesy of Olive-Drab.Com

Combat Ineffective is a work of historical fiction. Events that are common historical knowledge may not occur at their actual point in time or may not occur at all. Apart from the well-known actual people, events, and locales that figure in the narrative, all names, characters, places, and incidents are products of the author's imagination and are used fictitiously. Any resemblance to current events or locales or to living persons is purely coincidental.

Contact the Author Online
Email: *wpgrasso@cox.net*

Connect with the Author on Facebook
https://www.facebook.com/AuthorWilliamPeterGrasso

Follow the Author on Amazon
https://amazon.com/author/williampetergrasso

Dedication

Henry J. Van Der Waarden
1930-2018

To Henry John Van Der Waarden
My wife's father
A Navy man who, after eighty-eight years,
has embarked on his final voyage
May the heavenly seas offer him eternal peace

SUMMER 1950

NORTH KOREA ATTACKS

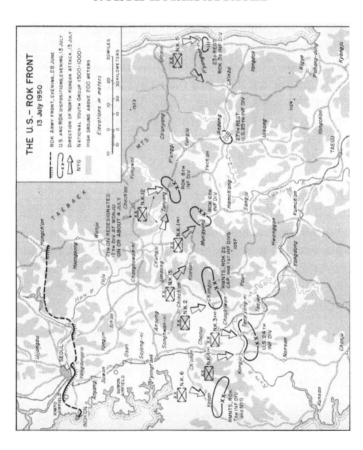

Author's Note

Often called the "forgotten war," the Korean War of 1950 to 1953 remains overshadowed by the vastness of WW2. Yet it marked an escalation of America's military misadventures on the Asian mainland, where US domestic politics continued to distort foreign realities, provoking disaster and an ultimate stalemate on the battlefield. In no way, however, does the fictional story presented here mean to denigrate the hardships and sacrifices of the individual American soldiers forced to fight an enemy they did not understand and for whom they were woefully ill prepared.

Korea marked the first time the American military fought as a racially desegregated organization. The stresses of combat, coupled with lingering racial animus in both the ranks and the high command, forced a limited return to segregation for some units. Derogatory terms for people of color used in dialogue serve no other intent than to accurately represent this animus in the contemporary setting of 1950.

Chapter One

9 July 1950

Travis Slocum wanted to be back in Japan. Life was good there; so good, in fact, that being a corporal in an American army that might actually be expected to fight seemed an afterthought. Once he showed up for morning formation—more a *route step* gaggle of milling GIs in and out of uniform—he could get lost for the rest of the day and, as a rule, nobody would come looking for him. Off post, there were countless women for the taking, plenty of booze to be consumed, and fat black market profits to be made, whether it be from American cigarettes or any government property you could pilfer for resale.

If some overzealous lieutenant or sergeant did catch a GI in some misdeed, his punishment was usually whittled down to next to nothing once the C.O. got involved because nobody was looking to make waves in MacArthur's postwar fiefdom of Japan. A unit with an abundance of disciplinary problems reflected poorly on its C.O. If he expected to get promoted in the severely shrunken postwar US Army, he'd put a lid on his problems.

But Travis Slocum wasn't in Japan now. A week ago, his infantry unit had been jerked from their comfortable accommodations on Kyushu, the southernmost of the Home Islands, and stuffed onto USAF transport planes for the two-hundred-mile flight across the Tsushima Strait to the Republic of Korea; South Korea, as the GIs knew it. They traded their cushy, off-base apartments for two-man tents and their pillow-soft mattresses for the rock-hard ground outside the town of Suwon, just twenty miles south of Seoul, South Korea's capital.

It's only temporary, Slocum assured himself. *They might've pushed the South Korean Army around without hardly breaking a sweat, but those North Korean gooks will run like scared rabbits when they come up against good ol' Uncle Sam's boys. We'll be back in Japan in a week or two. All the officers will tell you that.*

"Set up your *reckless rifle* over there on that ridge," the platoon sergeant told Slocum, pointing to a spot over one hundred yards away. "Target that road that's below us. And why the hell are you still wearing those stupid galoshes, boy? It ain't raining."

"They keep my feet warm, Sarge."

"That's a crock of shit, and you know it, Slocum. You're just too damn lazy to shine your boots. How many times I gotta tell you that they'll fall apart if you don't take care of them? Now get that weapon set up on the double."

"Can't we hitch a ride over there, Sarge? That's a long way to hump this heavy son of a bitch."

"No, you cannot hitch a ride, Corporal. The company's only got one damn jeep, and it's got better things to do than haul your sorry asses around. I know that thing's heavy, but that's why there's four of you. Now, why are you goldbricks still here?"

By the time the crew of the 75-millimeter recoilless rifle—the *reckless rifle*—had carried the 114-pound weapon and six rounds of its anti-tank ammunition, each weighing twenty pounds, to the designated firing point, the four out-of-shape GIs were exhausted, gasping for breath. That trek was probably the only physical exercise short of sexual intercourse, hoisting a beer bottle, and walking the chow line any of them had had in months.

"Ain't this a bad position?" a PFC named Owens asked Slocum. "We're sorta skylined on this ridge, ain't we?"

"We can't be on the front slope, dummy," the corporal replied. "This thing won't have enough rear-end clearance. The backblast will pick up rocks and shit and send them flying. Probably kill us all. You forgot already that a *reckless rifle* has two wrong ends?"

"No, I didn't forget nothing. I just—"

"Can it, Owens," Slocum interrupted, pointing to the two stripes on his sleeve. "When you've got enough of these, then maybe one day you can be section chief. Now, where's the damn sight box?"

"It's right here."

But when Slocum opened it, the box was empty.

"For fuck's sake, Owens, where's the fucking gunsight?"

"Gee, I don't know," was his flustered reply. "We had it when we were on the truck coming up from the airfield. It must've fell out."

"Well then, go back and find it, you moron. You

had one damn job, for cryin' out loud."

As Owens skittered off, Corporal Slocum sagged to the ground, lying flat on his back to take the load off his aching legs. Trying to walk around in the galoshes was taking its toll. He'd lied to the sergeant why he was wearing them; it had nothing to do with keeping his feet warm. He'd lost his GI boots—both pairs. When he'd packed his gear in that great rush for the flight to Korea, they were nowhere to be found. His Japanese houseboy, who he hadn't seen for a day or two, must've taken them to be shined...

Or had simply stolen them.

Either way, Slocum's only remaining GI footwear was his low quarter shoes, oxfords you wore with dress greens or khakis but never combat fatigues, which they'd be wearing until their upcoming victory parade through the streets of Seoul. The galoshes were just a flimsy attempt to keep from being caught out of uniform.

But his legs were paying the price. If he had to walk anywhere else—or worse, run—he didn't think he'd be able to do it.

If we were shipping out of anywhere but Japan, I'd have never gotten away with it. The top sergeant would've inspected every piece of gear for every swinging dick, Slocum told himself. *But we're in MacArthur's Army, and he has his own set of rules. Nobody bothers to check shit. It just turns up problems when you do.*

Other commanders have problems, not MacArthur. Everything's always hunky-dory in his house.

PFC Luckinbill was hovering over him now. "Hey, Travis," he said, "how the hell are we gonna aim this *shit tube* without the sight?"

Still flat on his back, Slocum replied, "First off, that's *corporal* to you. Secondly, were you dozing off when they told you about boresighting?"

"You mean looking down the barrel through the breech?"

"Right. See? You weren't asleep after all."

"But we ain't gonna have to do that, anyway, right, *Corporal*?" Luckinbill said. "Those gooks ain't gonna take us on. But talking about *boresighting*—don't they have to be pretty damn close for that to even work? I mean, the tube's gonna move a little when we load a round and close the breech. That'll knock the aim off, won't it?"

Slocum knew that was correct, but he didn't want to think about it. "Relax," he said. "Owens will probably be back any second with the sight."

"But the gooks," Luckinbill persisted, a smug confidence in his voice, "they're not going to take us on, right?"

"That's what all the brass say, Private."

Something made Travis Slocum sit up. He didn't hear it, he sensed it—that dull, low-frequency vibration of mechanized power, like the constant, menacing rumble that seeped from the foundries of his hometown—punctuated by the clanks and squeals of metal in motion. He didn't see its source on his first scan with binoculars.

But then some GIs on the ridge to his right were shouting, pointing into the distance like terrified spectators of an unfolding calamity. He couldn't hear what they were yelling at first, but then the sheer repetitiveness made its meaning obvious:

Tanks! Gook tanks!

Slocum's first thought was that *gook* was an unnecessary adjective. Tanks could only belong to the *KPA*: the *Korean People's Army*, the North Koreans. The South Korean Army—the *ROKs*—didn't have any; American tanks were scarce and hadn't been deployed this far forward.

He could see them now: four dark green hulks in column emerging from a shroud of dust and diesel smoke, rumbling down the road toward him. Luckinbill and PFC Lopez—the two men left in his crew—saw them, too. Their expressions shifted from amusement, to disbelief, to terror in a matter of seconds. Owens still had not returned from his quest for the missing gunsight.

"They're too far, right?" Luckinbill asked. His trembling voice sounded like it was making a wish rather than a statement of fact.

"Get a round ready to load," Slocum ordered. He knelt behind the recoilless rifle, his face pressed against the breech, sighting the weapon on the lead tank.

"I don't see any infantry with them," Lopez said hopefully as he fumbled with his M1 rifle.

"That don't mean they're not there," Slocum replied. "They don't have to be on the road. Maybe we just don't see them yet."

"We're gonna shoot as soon as they're in range, right?" Luckinbill asked.

"Unless somebody orders us different," Slocum replied.

When he looked back to the tanks, they seemed to

have gotten impossibly closer. He'd seen pictures of T-34 tanks, Soviet weapons that cut their teeth against the Germans in the last war. US Army doctrine said they were reliable tanks, proven in battle, but far from perfect; the American soldier more than possessed the firepower to kill them.

Private Owens came bounding up to the gun position. "I found it!" he yelled. He thrust the gunsight into Slocum's hands, who wasted no time mounting it on the recoilless rifle.

"Load the round," he commanded, his eye pressed against the sight as he tracked the T-34s.

There was no point in firing yet. Slocum reckoned they were about nine hundred yards away, technically within range but still too far for a probable first-round hit.

Luckinbill pleaded, "Shoot them, already!"

"Keep your drawers on," Slocum replied.

But farther down the ridgeline, another 75 millimeter fired.

Slocum watched the streaking black dot fly toward the T-34s, counting the seconds to impact for confirmation of his own range estimate.

Three seconds had never seemed so long.

The shot missed, impacting the ground well short of the lead T-34.

The 75 millimeter was recoilless but not smokeless. One thing their crewmen knew for certain: *you'd better get a first-round hit against a tank because you'll never get a second one; the act of shooting gives your position away.*

If you miss, you'd better run like hell.

And that's exactly what they did.

But not fast enough. The lead tank's reply blew them and their weapon to pieces.

A 75 millimeter to Slocum's left took another shot at the lead tank.

It was a direct hit...

But completely ineffective. Striking the T-34's sloped front armor, it bounced off before exploding, causing the tank crew little more than headaches and bleeding ears.

The second tank in line pulled off the road so it was no longer masked by the leader. Within a moment of stopping, it fired back, scoring a hit that sent the unlucky 75 millimeter tumbling through the air like a matchstick. The GIs manning her escaped the carnage; they'd fled the second they realized they'd missed.

Slocum pulled his head away from the gunsight, turning to tell his crew to have another round ready to load the moment he fired.

It was wasted effort. They'd run away, too.

So he waited, telling himself, *At least I can try and kill one of these bastards before I take off myself. But they've got to get closer. Come on...give me five hundred yards.*

He never got it. His eyes glued to the gunsight, he didn't see the North Korean soldiers who'd crept up on him from behind.

His first hint was a glint off the steel of a thrusting bayonet...

And then nothing would ever matter for Travis Slocum again.

Chapter Two

Colonel Jock Miles sat on the front porch of his new home in Monterey, California. It was a sprawling, Spanish-style ranch he'd never laid eyes on until the car bringing him from San Francisco International Airport arrived at its door just three days ago. Like a visitor to a strange new universe, he was still learning the place.

A briefcase sat open at his feet, containing folders full of notes he needed to condense into an after-action report, but he couldn't bring himself to begin that task. Still trying to reset his disoriented body clock after that bone-rattling, thirty-hour flight from Tokyo, with stops at Wake Island and Honolulu, it was far more pleasant to watch his two young children play on the lawn of their new home than write that damn report.

The overseas tour he'd just completed had been with KMAG: the Korean Military Advisory Group of the US Army. In that frustrating eight-month charade, what he'd witnessed as a senior advisor to ROK Army Headquarters was enough to shatter a soldier's confidence in the wisdom of the US Army and the government it served.

But if he put that frustration and the reasons behind it into writing, he knew he could kiss what was left of his career goodbye. Nobody—not in MacArthur's Tokyo headquarters or the halls of government in Washington—was interested in being told their policies for ensuring the safety of South Korea were delusional and headed for disaster.

He saw the olive green sedan making its way up the winding road to the house. Once it turned into the circular driveway, there was no mistaking where it had come from and who was in it: the Army staff car had a Fort Ord ID tag on the front bumper and flew a small flag with two silver stars from its front fender.

It's got to be General Whitelaw, Jock told himself, *and he's showing up unannounced.*

This smells to high heaven already.

From inside the house, Jock's wife Jillian saw the car coming, too. Cursing under her breath, she dropped what she was doing and stormed out to the porch. The car was coming to a stop at the front walk as she said to Jock, "That's Whitelaw, isn't it? What in bloody hell does he want?"

"Whatever it is, Jill, I'm pretty sure we're not going to like it. I doubt he's just dropping by to say hello."

Major General Jarvis Whitelaw didn't wait for his driver to open the sedan's rear door for him. He sprang from the car unassisted and strode purposefully up the walk to the porch.

"I hope I'm not interrupting anything important," Whitelaw said. "Jillian, I must say you look lovely as ever. Absolutely radiant." He took her hand and kissed it. Then he added, "I need to steal a few minutes of your husband's time if you don't mind, dear."

"Very well, General," she replied, covering her just-kissed hand with the other as if she couldn't wait to cleanse it. "Can I get you something to drink?"

"Coffee would be wonderful, dear. Cream, two sugars."

She disappeared into the house.

Jock and Whitelaw exchanged a perfunctory handshake and settled into deck chairs. The two curious children—five-year-old Jif and his sister, three-year-old Jane—had sidled up to the porch railing close to the men. They were playing a shy game of peek-a-boo through the bars with this stranger wearing the stars on his shoulders.

Jock told his son, "Jif, take your sister and go help your mom."

"Can't we stay here with you?" the boy asked. His conspicuous Australian accent startled the general.

"No, mate," Jock replied. "Be a good soldier and do as you're told."

Reluctantly, Jif took his sister by the hand. Together, they marched into the house, a platoon of two.

Once they were inside, Whitelaw said, "You *are* going to teach that boy to speak proper American, aren't you?"

"Give him a little time, sir. He was born and raised in Brisbane, remember? With a very Australian mother. And he's only been in this country a couple of months."

"We were all a little afraid you were going Aussie on us, too, Jock. You spent too long *down under* in that attaché's post, my boy. The little stint with KMAG you just wrapped up has gone a long way in getting you back into the fold, though."

As he said that, Whitelaw was scanning the opulent home and its spacious grounds. His survey done, he said, "Such a lovely house you've got here, Colonel."

Jock got the implied inquiry immediately: *How the hell does a li'l ol' bird colonel in Uncle Sam's Army afford a spread like this?*

Before he could reply, Whitelaw answered his own question: "You certainly married well, son. Very well, indeed. But what did you call that young man of yours? *Jip?*"

"No, sir, it's *Jif.* We named him John Forbes, after Jill's father. When he first learned to talk, he shortened it all by himself and took to calling himself Jif."

The housekeeper appeared and set a tray of coffee on the end table between the men.

"Thank you, Juanita," Jock said.

Once she was gone, Whitelaw observed, "You've got *beaner* help, too. I must say I'm impressed, Colonel. But don't let on to my wife or she'll be so jealous."

Jock suppressed a pained smile. Then he said, "With all due respect, sir, you didn't come here to talk about my house or my kids. If it's got something to do with this after-action report I'm writing—"

"Oh, hell…no, Colonel. I don't give a damn about that report. Neither does Washington. Not anymore."

Jock looked surprised to hear that.

"We've been keeping it out of the news for the time being, Jock, but Korea's gone to hell in a handbasket in the last forty-eight hours. We've got an absolute shambles on our hands. The ROKs have already crumbled. Our own troops—the few we've got there—are collapsing right behind them. Give those North Korean commies a couple of weeks more and they'll swallow us all up. It's looking like Corregidor all over again."

Jock slumped in his chair and let out a disgusted sigh. But he couldn't say he was surprised. The ROKs might have talked a good game, but he was well aware they didn't have the training, leadership, or equipment to be more than a parade ground army.

And it seems that no GI who joined up after the last war believes that the US Army might actually be expected to fight. It's like they're all on one big, exotic vacation. You can't blame them, though...MacArthur's been too busy playing the king of Japan to worry much about soldiering anymore.

Jock asked, "Can I speak frankly, sir?"

"Please do."

"Everything I saw over there tells me we'd need a massive infusion of American troops—*combat-ready* troops, not those *tourists* in GI uniforms under MacArthur's flag—to defend Korea. But I'm not sure there's any stomach for that sort of commitment in Washington."

"So what are you saying, Jock? It's a lost cause?"

"Affirmative, sir."

"Well, Colonel, you know damn well we just can't let that happen. Especially since we let China slip away to the commies."

"That was another lost cause, sir. We backed the wrong horse again."

Whitelaw pretended he didn't hear that. Shifting to a fatherly tone, he asked, "How's that leg of yours doing, Jock?"

There could only be one reason Whitelaw was asking that question. He wanted to know if Jock was fit enough for a field command again.

"The leg's fine, General."

As lies go, it was a whopper. The leg that had been injured—and then reinjured—during the New Guinea campaign of the last war, that same leg that had escaped amputation only through the act of one surgeon willing to take a chance and buck the Army's combat medical protocols, had been flaring up again. Its intermittent dull ache and subversive weakness was something he was trying very hard to mask.

Not sure who I'm fooling, though.

Whitelaw said, "I'm glad to hear it, Colonel, because what good is a regimental commander without his legs?"

"You're offering me a regiment, sir?"

"Damn right, Jock. Twenty-Sixth Regiment needs itself a new C.O. The man in the job now just isn't cutting the mustard."

"Isn't that regiment already in Korea, sir?"

"Damn right again, Colonel. But if we're going to turn that mess around, we need our best talent in place."

"I'm flattered, sir, but I'm a little surprised. I've never exactly been one of MacArthur's favorites."

"Things have changed, my boy. MacArthur's used to having an emperor for an errand boy nowadays, which in his mind makes him God. So he doesn't trouble himself with the little things anymore. When it comes to the workings of his own command, he doesn't get into the nuts and bolts of any organization run by somebody wearing less than three stars. But we're hurting for experienced combat leaders...and you need a job. Sounds like a match made in Heaven to me."

From Jock's perspective, it sounded more like a match made in Hell.

But it also sounded like a done deal.

He asked Whitelaw, "When do I need to leave, sir?"

"How about yesterday, Jock?"

★ ★ ★

He didn't have to break the news to Jillian. The entire conversation with Whitelaw had been heard through the open windows.

As soon as the general left, she'd retreated to her piano without so much as a word. Jock instantly recognized the piece into which she was pouring her heart: *Consolation Number Three* by Liszt.

He knew better than to interrupt her.

She'll talk when she's good and ready.

She was ready more quickly than he'd expected. Ten minutes later, after playing the piece twice, the second rendition far more melancholy than the first, she found him in the kitchen.

"Just remind me why you stay in the bloody Army, Jock," she said. There was no hint of anger in her voice, just the steely composure of a woman who'd survived the journey to Hell and back several times during the last war.

"Do I really need to say it out loud, Jill?"

"Yes, you do. I need to be reminded why I uprooted our children and moved halfway around the world just so we could watch you leave again."

He knew she hadn't meant to wound him. Still, her words were like a stab from a knife so sharp you didn't feel it pierce your flesh. He gathered his words and spoke them slowly.

"I stay because I still haven't figured out a better way to repay all those men who spilled their blood doing my bidding, Jill."

A child's footsteps broke the silence that had fallen between them. Jif was now standing in the kitchen entryway.

"Are you going away, Daddy?" the boy asked.

"Yes, Jif. I've been ordered back to Korea."

"When will you come home?"

"As soon as I can, mate. It won't be long, I'm sure."

"But then you'll leave again, won't you?"

Jock thought his heart might break right then and there.

But his son demanded no answer. Climbing onto a stool, he took an apple from a bowl on the table. Then he walked out without another word, renewing the silence he'd interrupted.

It was Jillian who broke it this time.

"They learn so bloody quickly, don't they, Jock?"

Wiping away a solitary tear, she added, "Too bloody quickly."

Chapter Three

Seventy-two hours later, Jock stepped off a USAF C-54 from Tokyo at K-2, an airfield near Taegu, South Korea. There was an air of urgency to the operations there but not panic. He'd expected something much worse; from all the loose talk on the flight across the Pacific, he wouldn't have been surprised if Taegu had already been overrun. But the leading elements of the North Korean Army—the KPA—were still some one hundred miles to the north. He had the choice of waiting around for a courier flight to K-5 at Taejon— whenever that *puddle jumper* might show up—or be chauffeured in a waiting jeep. He picked the jeep for the eighty-mile trip to 26th Regiment outside Chongju.

He could tell so much about a combat unit from his first contact with it. A half mile from the regiment's command post, he encountered its first sentry post. It was occupied by three GIs, none of whom emerged from beneath the ramshackle tarp they'd strung up as cover from the midday sun.

"Stop the vehicle," Jock told his driver.

Approaching the shelter, he asked, "Who's in charge here?"

A young PFC stepped forward reluctantly, eyeing the silver eagle on Jock's collar. He replied with a question of his own: "Aren't you, sir?"

"That wasn't my question, Private. Who is in charge of this outpost?"

"I guess that's me, sir."

"You guess, Private? You're not sure?"

"Nobody's real sure about anything around here,

sir."

"Are you sure about what unit you belong to?"

"Yes, sir. Headquarters Company, Twenty-Sixth Infantry."

"Well, that's a start, Private. Now, why didn't you challenge me for the password?"

The GI looked dumbfounded for a moment. Then he replied, "Why, sir? You're not a gook, are you?"

"No, I'm not a gook, Private, just your new commanding officer. My name's Miles. And your name's going to be at the top of my shit list if you don't challenge anyone approaching this perimeter, whether they look like a gook or not. Is that clear?"

"Yes, sir…but we don't have the password. Nobody told us one."

As first impressions go, Jock thought, *this one couldn't get much worse.*

The second impression didn't improve things. As the jeep drew closer to the deuce-and-a-half vans that housed the regimental CP, it was apparent that there'd been no serious attempt to conceal most of the vehicles and equipment. As a monument to poor terrain appreciation, a water trailer—adorned with big white stars on all sides—was perched on a hilltop, acting as a marker for the military installation surrounding it. Anyone with a cheap set of binoculars would be able to see it from miles away.

And if you can see it, you can direct fire on it.

The capper came as Jock walked into the commander's van. The colonel he was about to relieve, a much older man, far from physically fit, was sitting in a corner, oblivious to the confusion swirling around him. It was obvious he'd mentally checked out of this command already; the minute his relief arrived, he'd be out the door, straight to the aircraft that would deliver him to the safety of Japan.

As if that wasn't plain enough, his seat was a large civilian suitcase, not a GI duffel, travel bag, or field pack like Jock was carrying. It was no different than what someone might pack for a pleasure trip with the wife and kids. This one had been used for such trips, too; it still bore the stickers from an assortment of resort locales. In a combat zone, the suitcase stuck out like a square peg in a round hole.

"You're Miles, right?" the colonel said as he struggled to his feet. "Really glad to see you." Pointing to a harried officer with a telephone in each ear, he added, "Colonel Lewis here can fill you in on whatever you need to know."

And then he hurried out of the van to the waiting jeep, lugging that incongruous suitcase. Jock was right on his heels.

"Before you run off, Ed...it is Ed, right?...how about you fill me in on your estimate of the situation?"

The departing colonel had already made himself comfortable in the jeep. He replied, "My estimate? It's simple. We're fucked. There are a million gooks streaming south who're going to push us right into the Sea of Japan...unless MacArthur convinces that idiot Truman to drop the A-bomb on them."

"That doesn't sound like much of a solution, Ed, considering dropping that bomb just might kill us and a whole bunch of friendlies, too. If that's what you're waiting for, you've been singing from the wrong hymnal."

"Not my problem anymore, Miles. But where the

---

hell did you come from, anyway? You're not one of those pinheads from Washington, are you?"

Jock laughed. "Hardly. Except for a few days home with my family, I've been right here in lovely Korea for the better part of a year."

The departing colonel shook his head. "Then you should know better, Miles. A lot better."

As the jeep drove off, Jock told himself, *Let's hope I do know better...at least better than you, you over-the-hill sack of shit.*

Back in the command van, Lieutenant Colonel Lewis—the regimental XO—gave Jock a bleak picture of what was confronting the regiment. "The KPA just keep pushing us back down this highway toward Taejon. We don't have enough armor to stop them. Hell, we hardly have *any* armor, and the little we've got—mostly *Chaffees*—don't have the punch to stop a T-34. We pulled back to this position two days ago to gain a little breathing space. In all likelihood, they'll hit us again tonight."

Jock asked, "How's our artillery support?"

"Spotty, sir. Their accuracy is pathetic. And they're chronically short of ammunition, too."

"Air support?"

"Fair to middling in daylight and clear weather, sir. Nonexistent at night, of course, when the gooks usually attack."

Jock was no stranger to this rugged terrain; he'd traveled it during ROK training exercises a number of times while with KMAG. On the flight from Tokyo, he'd been able to read a folder full of after-action reports from the regiment. In each case, it seemed an armored force advancing along a narrow, confining road wasn't the main problem; enemy infantry enveloping the Americans over mountains and through passes was the real reason for the retreats. From what he could tell on Lewis' situation map, they were setting themselves up to be enveloped again.

Jock touched his pencil to several points on the map, each point a gap between the high ground on their flanks. He asked, "Who's covering these passes, Colonel?"

"Those areas are the responsibility of Second Battalion, sir."

"Wait a minute...you've *split* a battalion to cover our flanks? And if I'm reading this map correctly, the two halves of that battalion are over five miles away from each other."

"Yes, sir, that's true."

"Doesn't that make *command and control* a little difficult, Colonel?"

"We do have the radios, sir, and—"

Jock cut him off. "Radios don't *see*, Colonel. That poor battalion commander is blind to what at least half his unit is doing. We're going to fix that right now, while we've still got enough daylight to pull it off."

"But we'll have to move all three of the battalions, sir. That'll be chaos."

"From the looks of things," Jock replied, "you've already got nothing but chaos going on here. It would be pretty hard to make it much worse. And you won't have to slide all your battalions—just one. Pull Second Battalion back as the regimental reserve. First and Third Battalions will adjust to cover their own flanks."

"A reserve, sir? In defense?"

"Damn right, Colonel Lewis. We're going to need

one to plug holes in this shaky line of ours while providing an all-around defense of the position. From what I've seen so far, this regiment seems to be forgetting the enemy can come at you from behind, too."

Lewis looked crestfallen, like a man about to get fired. Apparently, this unorthodox—and to this point, unsuccessful—defensive disposition had been his idea. He asked Jock, "Do you plan to bring in your own staff officers, sir?"

"To be honest, Colonel, I would if I could. But MacArthur's Tokyo headquarters keeps skimming off the cream of the crop as soon as they show up from the States. I wasn't much interested in what was left, so whoever's here will be staying. But I was able to bag a couple of senior NCOs—*fighting* NCOs—to fill out this regiment's staff. With any luck at all, they'll both be here before supper."

Jock's luck must've been good because the first of his two *fighting NCOs*—Master Sergeant Melvin Patchett—strolled into the CP van at 1430 hours. When he saw Jock at the commander's desk, a tight-lipped smile crossed his weathered face. "As I live and breathe," Patchett called out, "if it ain't ol' MacArthur's worst nightmare, complete with a brand new chicken on his collar, too."

Their vigorous handshake turned into a mutual backslap and then a manly hug. "I didn't know they let old folks out of the home to come and fight," Jock said, still with a grip on Patchett's shoulders. "How the hell old are you now, Top? You've got to be at least eighty."

"With all due respect, sir, you mind your tongue now. I just turned fifty years young."

Even at fifty, Patchett looked more fit than soldiers less than half his age.

He continued, "And I figure, hell…any damn fool can do two wars. Why not go for three? And at least we won't be fighting in no damn jungle this time. By the way, thanks for pulling me out of that replacement pool in Tokyo. Lord knows what shithole outfit this li'l ol' country boy would've ended up in. But first things first…how's Miss Jillian and them kids of yours?"

"They're all fine, Top. Settling into Monterey pretty well, I think."

"You *think*? You don't know?"

"I was only there with them for a few days. Next thing I knew, I was on a plane back to Korea. But what about you? You ever think about settling down? You ain't getting any younger, you know. See much of Miss Ginny these days?"

"Nah, we don't cross paths no more, not with her life being on Papua and mine wherever *Uncle Sugar* decides to send me. But you know the drill, sir…if the Army wanted me to have a wife, they would've issued me one. Been thirty-two years and they ain't got around to it, so…"

Despite the indifference Patchett was trying so hard to project, Jock could still see the pain of loss in the man's eyes. He and Ginny Beech had made quite a pair.

But deep personal conversations would have to wait. They stepped outside the van.

"We've got a seriously fucked-up situation here,

Top."

"Don't I know it, sir. I got me a good look at some of these dipshits that pass for soldiers on the way in. Where do you need me?"

"I want you as regimental sergeant major. I need you to be out in the field with me, real *hands on*. Let some clerks handle the paperwork. We've got bigger fish to fry."

"Understood, sir. But one question…"

"Shoot."

"How's your leg?"

"I'll be honest with you…it's not one hundred percent."

Patchett smiled. "No sweat, sir. I carried you all over those damn islands when I had to. I can do it in Korea, too."

"Thanks, Top. I appreciate that. Now I'm sure that between you and me we've got our infantry tactics down to a science. But nobody in this regiment, including us, knows a whole hell of a lot about armored warfare, and we're going to be seeing a lot of it here. So I'm bringing in a master sergeant with heavy armor experience. I worked with him at KMAG and he knows his shit cold. He was all over North Africa and Europe with Patton in the last one. We're going to need him…bad."

"What's this tanker's name, sir?"

"Moon. Sergeant Sean Moon."

"Where's he from?"

"Brooklyn, Patch. That's part of New—"

"I know damn well where Brooklyn is, sir. Been there once, didn't leave nothing behind, so I ain't never gotta go back. But you're telling me I've got to put up with not one but two of y'all damn Yankees now?"

He quickly added, "With all due respect, sir," since Jock was one of those *damn Yankees.*

Jock and Patchett spent the next two hours touring the regiment's positions. Everything they saw required some degree of correction. "It's like these youngsters ain't never learned nothing about interlocking fields of fire," Patchett observed. "A couple of dozen gooks could've walked line abreast through their fire lanes without ever getting themselves a scratch. You thinking what I'm thinking, sir?"

"If you're thinking they're going to buckle at the slightest pressure, then yeah…we're thinking the same damn thing. We're going to have to get a handle on that real quick."

The other *damn Yankee*—Master Sergeant Sean Moon—was jumping down from an ammo truck when Jock and Patchett returned to the CP. "These dummies were lost as hell and I needed a ride," he called out. "Figured I'd kill two birds with one stone, sir. It wasn't coming here, but I'm pretty sure we could use this ammo, anyway."

"Damn right we could use the ammo," Jock replied. "Good to see you again, Sergeant Moon. Glad to have you aboard."

Patchett nudged Jock and said, "I'm liking the way this Moon fella thinks already. Every good NCO's gotta have *hisself* a set of sticky fingers."

Pointing to Patchett, Jock told Sean, "This man here is none other than Master Sergeant Melvin

Patchett. He's the *top* here, this outfit's new sergeant major."

"No shit? The great Master Sergeant Patchett, in the flesh?" Sean said as the two NCOs shook hands. "I've heard a lot about you from the colonel here. The way he tells it, the sun rises straight out of your asshole."

Patchett appraised the much younger sergeant coolly. "Only when it's facing east, son. I *hear tell* you're gonna teach us how not to get run over by those commie *spam cans*. You've been up against T-34s before?"

"Yeah. Had to face down a bunch of them in Germany, Austria, and Czechoslovakia at the end of the last big show. They're tough...but they ain't *that* tough. And from what I'm seeing, the gooks don't know how to use 'em any better than the Russians did."

"Try telling that to the dogfaces in these parts," Patchett replied. "Near as I can tell, most of these touch-holes left their balls in some Japanese whorehouse."

He pointed toward the ammo truck and added, "What'd y'all bring us, anyway?"

"Mostly thirty cal," Sean replied. "But there's fifty cal and grenades, too...plus the trailer's got HE and illum rounds for one-oh-five howitzers. That one-oh-five battery I passed about a mile back...that's our direct support, right?"

"Affirmative," Patchett replied. Then he asked Jock, "If it's okay with you, sir, why don't I escort this vehicle to each of our units and distribute Sergeant Moon's li'l ol' housewarming gift? I'll be back way before your commanders' meeting at 1800 hours."

"Sounds like an excellent plan, Top. Do it."

As they watched Patchett climb into the truck's cab, Sean said, "Watch this, sir. That driver and his assistant ain't gonna like this one bit. They're typical ammo humps...they just wanna dump all that shit in one big pile and get their asses back home before dark."

He was right; in the cab, a vigorous protest erupted. Patchett seemed totally unruffled; his response couldn't be heard. But whatever that response was, the two fell immediately silent, looking like they'd just had the fear of God instilled in them. Without further delay, the truck drove off on its new mission.

Smiling, Jock said, "I figured it would be like that. Top can be real persuasive."

"No kidding," Sean replied. Though trying to hide it, he sounded crestfallen as he added, "But I got a question, sir. If he's the *top*, what do you need me for? I mean, where do I fit in with this outfit?"

"I need you to wear two very important hats, Sergeant Moon—operations sergeant and NCO-in-charge of training."

"You know, sir...a wise man once told me that a guy trying to do two jobs won't get to do either of them worth a damn."

"Well, Sergeant, that wise man probably didn't get to see you working with the ROKs like I did. I think you can handle it. I've seen your personnel jacket, so I know your commanders back in Patton's Third Army thought you could, too."

Chapter Four

As the regiment's commanders and staff filed into the CP at 1800 hours, there wasn't a doubt in Jock's mind that aside from himself and Sergeants Patchett and Moon, they were a beaten-down lot. They'd presided over two weeks of deadly, unrelenting rout, being steadily pushed back by an enemy that MacArthur's headquarters kept insisting was nothing more than a collection of primitives, incapable of prevailing on the modern battlefield.

Yet these *primitives* were prevailing, extracting a terrible toll in American lives, equipment, and prestige in the process.

Jock knew that in their desperate state, his leaders would be skeptical of any plan he proposed, at least until that plan had borne some positive result. It would be no different in any other regiment of the three American and five ROK divisions that currently comprised 8th US Army; collectively, they had all failed to hold back the North Korean onslaught.

One of the battalion commanders, a lieutenant colonel named Brand, was particularly unhappy about Jock's plan to employ a regimental reserve. "We can't afford to do that, sir," Brand said. "All our troops need to be up on the line. Every rifle's going to count when the gooks come at us again. We can't be holding any men back."

"That hasn't worked for this regiment so far," Jock replied. "What makes you think it's going to work now?"

Brand sputtered a few words in response, but they

didn't qualify as a coherent answer.

"Let me put it this way," Jock said. "From what Sergeant Patchett and I observed this afternoon, none of you were employing proper fields of fire. If that's the way you've been doing battle in the past, it's no wonder they keep penetrating your positions. And when they do break through, you've got no reserve to throw them back."

He stepped to the big tactical map and continued, "Now, I'm not saying we're going to stop the North Koreans in their tracks. They're a clever fighting force—regardless of the nonsense being pumped out by Tokyo—and for the moment, they've got superior firepower, especially in armor. But that doesn't mean we can't make them pay a heavy price for every foot of ground we have to yield before we get enough manpower and weaponry shipped in here to start pushing them back. The way I see our current position, as long as we hold the hills on either side of the highway, their armor will have a very difficult time breaking through." Pointing those hills out on the map, he added, "The trick, of course, will be holding them against pressure from North Korean infantry—in the dark, at that. First and Third Battalion will remain on their respective hills. Second Battalion is now our regimental reserve."

Then he asked the nine officers and two NCOs assembled before him, "How many of you fought in Europe in the last war? And by *fought*, I mean you earned combat stars."

Two officers and one NCO—Sean Moon—raised their hands.

"Okay, good. Now how many fought the Japs

anywhere in the Pacific or Asia?"

Only Jock and Patchett raised a hand.

Noticing Brand was among the officers who hadn't responded either time, Jock asked, "What about you, Colonel? Where'd you serve?"

"The Canal Zone, sir."

Jock couldn't resist a glance at Patchett. He was expecting to see the sergeant's trademark smirk. Instead, with a straight face, Patchett, like a preacher from the pulpit, called out, "An underappreciated campaign, Colonel. Crucial to the war effort, by God."

He made it sound like he was deadly serious, too.

Patch can still blow smoke up your ass with the best of them.

"Okay," Jock said, "we can swap war stories some other time. Let's get back to the problem at hand. As we just found out, a few of us have a great deal of combat experience, which we're going to share with you and your men, beginning tonight. Sergeant Moon— a highly experienced tank commander—will be working with the anti-tank teams. Sergeant Patchett and I will be sharing some infantry defensive techniques you probably haven't had the opportunity to pick up yet. Are there any further questions?"

Another battalion commander—Lieutenant Colonel Eliason—had one: "Since my battalion is in reserve, Colonel, just what exactly is it supposed to do when the gook tanks break through again?"

Jock pointed to Sean. "You want to take that one, Sergeant Moon?"

"I'd be glad to, sir. Let me answer it like this…any tank that's rolling past you is showing you her most vulnerable parts. If you don't take advantage of that and kill that bitch right then and there, either with a rocket up her ass or a grenade down her throat, then shame on you, sir."

Colonel Eliason then asked, "But what if there's infantry accompanying the tanks, Sergeant? How are we supposed to get close enough to kill their armor then?"

"The gooks operate their armor just like the Russians do, sir. Ain't no surprise since that's who taught 'em all they know. But that means they've got shit for communication between their armor and infantry—especially in the dark—so any protection the infantry might offer the tanks is gonna be a fucked-up, uncoordinated mess once the shit starts flying. And a tank taking on infantry without its own infantry in support is still dead meat."

Whether Sean Moon's explanations had swayed any minds, Jock couldn't tell.

It was nearly dark as Patchett joined up with 1st Battalion, the unit holding down the left sector of the regiment's defensive line. It was time to see if they'd followed through with the instructions he and Jock had given during their afternoon inspection tour.

"Show me your listening posts, sir," he told a lieutenant whose platoon was positioned on a ridge covering the flank.

"Why, Sergeant? We're not going to be manning those LPs. Too risky."

"Well, sir...I don't think much of that plan, but

those empty holes can still work for us. You ran the
commo wire down to the LPs like I told you earlier?"

"Yes. It's all there."

"Outstanding, Lieutenant. Now where's that box of
grenades and ball of string I asked for?"

"These two men right here have them, Sergeant."

"Very fine. You two come with me."

Reluctantly, the PFCs followed Patchett down the
slope. He used the commo wire already on the ground
as a guide, lifting it almost waist high and letting it slide
through the curled fingers of one hand as he walked.
When they reached the empty hole that had been dug
for the LP, one of the PFCs said, "Here's that foxhole. I
made the dummy machine gun out of a broomstick
myself."

"Nice work, son, but that ain't no foxhole,"
Patchett replied. "A foxhole's something a useless
numbnuts hides *hisself* in. In this regiment, we call
them *fighting holes*. Got that?"

"Yes, Sergeant."

"Good. Now you boys turn around and follow that
wire back up the hill about ten paces."

When they got there, Patchett said, "Now take one
of them grenades and tie a string to the loop of that
safety pin. Hold onto that *pineapple* for dear life now,
you hear?"

That task done, he continued, "Now measure that
string against your forearm and cut the other end at
your elbow. Y'all see where I'm going with this?"

"I think so," the other man replied. "We're going to
tie it off to the commo wire, right?"

"Correct," Patchett said. "Now hang onto that
grenade real good while your buddy does the tying."

The knot was made. Patchett took the grenade and placed it on the ground with the loop of the safety pin pointing straight up and the handle clear to fly off once that pin was gone. Then he set a rock on top of it to hold it in place.

"Now in case you hadn't already figured this out," Patchett explained, "the gooks'll try to follow this wire up to your position just like we followed it down. When they lift the wire off the ground right here, the pin'll get pulled and the handle'll fly off all by itself because nothing's holding the damn thing on no more. Before they know what the hell's going on, they blow themselves to kingdom come...and y'all up on the ridge'll know exactly where they're coming from. We call that *recon by grenade*."

One of the PFCs sounded skeptical as he asked, "You ever done this before, Sarge? I mean, does it really work?"

"The answer to your first question is *affirmative*. The answer to the second one is *I wouldn't be standing here still drawing breath if it didn't*. Am I making myself clear?"

"Yeah, Sarge. Real clear."

"Good. Now move another twenty paces up this hill and hook yourselves up another one."

"Why, Sarge? Won't one be enough?"

"Son, you think them damn gooks gonna quit just because a couple of their buddies just got *pureed*? The Japs wouldn't quit, and that's who taught 'em their infantry tactics, seeing how they occupied this country for years. Besides, it's gonna be dark, and they ain't gonna have the faintest fucking idea what just happened. So, yeah, y'all are gonna set out another grenade on this wire, and then y'all are gonna do the same to every damn wire from every other damn LP."

There were only three tanks at Sean's disposal, lightweight M24 Chaffees that were designed as infantry support vehicles and never intended to fight other tanks. Sean asked the tank platoon sergeant, "What the hell happened to the rest of you?"

"All shot to hell, Sarge. We're all that's left of a twenty-tank company. Eighteen KIA...I lost track of how many wounded."

Sean asked, "Got any officers left?"

"Nope. All dead, Sarge."

"Well, my friend, you'll have to do, then. Now, what the fuck is your platoon doing down on this road like sitting ducks? You looking to get them all KIA, too?"

"Where the hell else are we supposed to be?"

Sean asked, "Did the engineers bulldoze you any indirect fire ramps so you could at least lob some rounds over those hills?"

"Are you kidding? The engineers have been all tied up fighting as infantry. What's left of them, anyway."

"All right then, I tell you what you're gonna do. Take your platoon down the road, where the terrain flattens out on both sides of the highway. I know it's getting dark, but you'll still be able to see the outlines of the hilltops for a while yet, so use them to get oriented. Put yourself in the best hull-down positions you can find off the side of the road."

The platoon sergeant asked, "What the hell good is

that going to do?"

"The first *good* it's gonna do is keep you from going head to head with T-34s and getting your asses blown up right off the bat. The second *good* is that if any gook tanks do get through, you can ambush them with flank shots. You might stand a chance of actually knocking one or two out that way. The third *good* is that Second Battalion—the reserve battalion—will be all around you, covering your ass. And last but not least, should we actually beat off this next attack, you're in position to pursue and exploit. Your radios do work, right?"

"Affirmative. We've got good commo, but we can only talk to each other and Regiment. Frequency incompatibility with the battalion radios, you know?"

"Yeah, I know all about it. Get with the infantry once you're in position so they can be a relay for you. Now, what're you still doing here? Get your vehicles moving."

Sean's next task was to check on the four-gun platoon of 75-millimeter recoilless rifles. As head-to-head anti-tank weapons, they'd be useless; so, after some heated debate, he'd convinced the battalion commanders to deploy them at the pass through the hills where the highway crossed the regiment's defensive line. Positioned high in those hills, the 75s would be able to engage tanks from the flanks rather than head-on. That would be the only chance they'd have of a kill, striking the softer armor of the sides and rear deck.

The battalion commanders' main objection: they'd be letting the tanks actually reach the regiment's line before being able to engage them.

Sean's rebuttal: "The seventy-fives ain't gonna stop them tanks before they get to us, anyway. At least with a flank shot, they've got a chance of knocking one out. And if the poor bastards miss, maybe they can get their asses to the other side of that hill before they get cut to shreds."

Satisfied with the recoilless rifle platoon's positioning, Sean asked its sergeant, "What happened to this regiment's other two *reckless rifle* platoons? Each battalion's supposed to have one, right?"

"Yeah, but we had to leave pieces behind like crazy every time we pulled back. Some of the guys couldn't run away fast enough after they missed their shot, too. We cobbled together this platoon from the survivors."

"Figured it was something like that," Sean replied. "These fucking things are too damn heavy for a moving fight. They're only worth a shit when they're mounted on a jeep. At least then they've got a chance to get out of town when it all goes to hell."

"I think there's only about half a dozen working jeeps left in this whole regiment," the platoon sergeant said. "The brass have them all tied up."

"Yeah, I've noticed," Sean replied. "Is your ammo count still four rounds per gun?"

"Affirmative."

As he turned to leave, Sean said, "Let's hope you get to fire more than once."

It was completely dark now. Sean was glad he'd told the rocket teams to meet him at 3rd Battalion's CP.

They might never have found each other at a less prominent location.

But something was wrong right off the bat. The three teams—each with four men—had brought the wrong weapons.

"What's with the little bazookas?" Sean asked. "I told your commanders I wanted nothing but *three point five-inch* rocket launchers for this operation."

"Nobody told us shit about that, Sarge," a corporal named Dowd replied.

"Well, go get the goddamn launchers I asked for, on the fucking double. You shoulda learned by now that those peashooters you got won't stop nothing. Load up with six rockets per weapon, too."

"But we're not trained on the *three point five*, Sarge," Corporal Dowd protested.

"Well, then, you're gonna have your first class right fucking now. Move it. You got three minutes."

"Six rockets per tube?" Dowd asked. "I don't think we've got six rounds for the *three point fives* in the whole regiment, Sarge."

"Two minutes, fifty seconds, Corporal."

To Sean's surprise, they returned with six seconds to spare. But they were hardly combat ready. The rocket launchers—two cylindrical sections that locked together to form a five-foot-long aluminum tube— hadn't been assembled. The rockets themselves were still in sealed ammo boxes, which the GIs were dragging behind them.

Sean asked, "While you muttonheads are screwing those things together, I gotta ask one question...they do have the shipping grease cleaned off 'em, don't they?"

In reply, he got nothing but blank looks.

"Give me one of those fucking things," he said, grabbing a launcher.

He wiped his fingers over the spring contacts for the igniter wires at the rear of the tube. Satisfied they were dry, he then inspected the trigger housing with his blackout flashlight.

"Okay, this one's good," Sean told the men. "Now check the other three the same way. We don't want one of these babies hanging fire when the shit hits the fan."

That task done, Sean asked, "That's all the rockets you've got? Nine?"

"That's all we could find, Sarge," Corporal Dowd replied.

"That stinks to high heaven, but three rounds per tube's better than nothing. Unpack them."

"But Sarge, we've been told not to take a rocket out of its shipping container until you're ready to fire it."

"Believe me, Corporal…you're ready to fire it. Do it now."

As their crews unpacked the rockets, Sean told the section chiefs, "While we're waiting, I'll check you guys out on this baby's sight picture."

✯ ✯ ✯

The real shock for the 3.5-inch rocket launcher crews came when Sean told them where they'd be setting up: in the broad, flat rice paddies that lined the highway *well in front of* the regiment's defensive line in the hills.

Horrified, Dowd said, "We're going out there? That's *Indian country*!"

"That's where our best fields of fire are gonna be," Sean replied. "And there's a thousand places to hide from the *Indians* in those rice paddies, provided you don't mind getting a little wet."

He let them process that for a moment and then added, "And I assume you'd rather be wet than dead, right?"

"But it smells like shit something awful down in the paddies, Sarge."

"That's because they use shit for fertilizer, dumbass. This whole fucking country smells like shit."

Chapter Five

It was no surprise when they first heard the rumbling and creaking of approaching T-34s. Sean and his rocket launcher teams were waiting in a ditch alongside a trail through the rice paddies, out of range to hit moving targets on the highway. They'd move closer to the road—two hundred yards or less—once they were sure that North Korean infantrymen were not providing close support for the slow-moving tanks.

Corporal Dowd said, "Let's have the artillery hit those tanks with HE."

"Oh, that'd be swell, wouldn't it?" Sean replied. "Then we could just get the hell out of here, right?"

Dowd nodded eagerly; that was exactly his intention.

"Negative, Corporal," Sean said. "It would take a direct hit with a one-oh-five round to knock out a T-34, and the odds of that happening while they're lobbing rounds over them hills is about zip. Now pay attention, boys, because you're about to learn something."

Keying the walkie-talkie, he called the artillery forward observer on his hilltop observation post. "Fire mission," Sean told the FO. He gave the coordinates of a point on the road just ahead of where he estimated the tanks would be in one minute.

His call for fire came with special instructions: "Shell *illum*, burst height *fifty yards*. I say again, burst height *fifty yards*."

Sean could hear the question in the FO's voice as he requested, "Say again burst height."

After Sean repeated it yet again, the FO replied,

"Roger. Relaying your fire mission now."

"Fifty-yard burst height for an illum round, Sarge?" a surprised GI asked. "Ain't that a little low to pop the flare? It'll be burning on the ground."

"That's the idea, jughead," Sean replied. "We'll put a few flares on the ground around those gook tanks. It'll blind the shit out of them and silhouette 'em real good for us. We used to do it to the Krauts sometimes when they had numbers on us."

"But what if a flare starts a grass fire?" another GI asked. "We could get caught in it. Get our asses barbecued."

"You don't start grass fires in rice paddies, dummy. Too fucking wet."

But a whole minute had gone by since the FO acknowledged receiving the call for fire. It was taking much too long for the confirmation that rounds were on the way to spill from the radio: the words *shot, over.*

The artillery battery commander—a captain named Swanson five years out of West Point—had missed WW2 entirely. But he was familiar with an expression from that war: *If your infantry doesn't like you, artilleryman, you did a crappy job giving them fire support.*

Captain Swanson had little doubt that, so far, the infantrymen of 26th Regiment didn't think much of his battery and the fire support they had—or *hadn't*—provided.

He'd heard the gripes aimed at his gunners by frazzled riflemen who felt they'd been let down: *Hey, you cannon-cocking sons of bitches! A day late and a dollar short again, dammit. Wanna switch jobs?*

But he'd vowed tonight would be different: *If I have to supervise every gun crew myself, by God, I'll do it if that's what it takes...because that new regimental commander is looking to kick ass and take names.*

The first fire mission of the night, however, hit a snag right off the bat.

"That FO is all fucked up, Captain," his fire direction chief moaned. "The flares are going to be bouncing on the ground, dammit."

"But that's what they asked for," one of the chart operators said. "We've got to give them what they want. That's the way it works, isn't it?"

"What's it going to be, Captain?" the chief grumbled. "Are we going to shoot this the right way or are we going to waste rounds?"

Swanson's solution was a stall to mask his indecisiveness: "Tell the FO to give us the call for fire again."

An angry voice boomed out of the darkness: "We don't have time for that, Captain. Give them *something*, dammit, and give it to them right now."

Then the man who'd spoken those words stepped into the dim light of the fire direction center's tent. It took the battery commander a moment to recognize him: *Colonel Miles.* The briefing at 1800 hours had been the one and only time he'd ever seen the regimental commander, a man who'd only arrived that very afternoon.

"Sir," Swanson said, "there seems to be some discrepancy in the request for fire and—"

"Bullshit, Captain," Jock Miles replied. "Don't

second guess them. Just shoot what they ask for. You don't know what they're up against."

"But sir, this is a clear case of—"

"There's nothing *clear* about it, Captain, so give them what they say they want. And do it NOW, for the love of God. Lives are depending on it."

The lives of Sergeant Moon and his men, Jock suspected.

"Well, it's going to take a minute, Colonel," the section chief said. "I'll have to recompute the whole damn mission and—"

"No, you don't," the chart operator interrupted. "I've already worked it out."

He called the firing data down the landline to the guns.

Twenty seconds later, the words Sean had been waiting to hear finally spilled from the radio: "Shot, over."

Sean's men were frantically counting the North Korean tanks, their dark outlines now close enough to be visible in the moonlight. "They're keeping a good tactical interval," Sean said. "Let's see how long they can maintain it when the shit starts flying."

"There's got to be fifty of them!" one GI whispered, his panic obvious even in those hushed tones.

Sean replied, "Simmer down, okay? Ain't no more than a dozen tanks on that road. Just looks like more because they're spread out pretty good."

To the frightened troopers, a dozen might as well

have been a thousand.

The column of T-34s had slowed almost to a stop. Sean thought he knew why: "They're waiting for some sign that their infantry is hitting our guys up on the hills," he said. "They won't try to run the pass until they get it, neither. Too much chance of shit getting dropped on their heads. Now where the hell are those illum rounds?"

He'd barely gotten the words out when the first flare popped. Its parachute didn't even have a chance to fully open before the brilliant ball of light was bouncing along the highway right in front of the lead tank. Each hop of the flare threw sharp-edged shadows that danced crazily across the paddies. The first few tanks in the column were silhouetted harshly in its glare.

Then the second flare popped and dropped quickly to the ground. It took one bounce before coming to rest on the foredeck of the third tank in line.

"Whoa," Sean said. "The gooks in that tank ain't just blind...they're getting a *hot foot,* too."

With two flares burning at ground level now, it was like daylight on the road.

All that illumination told Sean something he desperately needed to know: there was no North Korean infantry around the tanks. He called in his adjustment to the FO: "Left one hundred, repeat." That would put the next two rounds one hundred yards farther down the column of tanks.

He told his rocket teams, "Okay, you know the plan. Move out."

The plan: the three teams would spread out and close to within two hundred yards of the road. With their first rocket, the middle team would engage the third tank in the column; the right team would engage the second tank; the left team the fourth tank.

They'd let the first tank go for now. As Sean explained, "Standard ambush practice. It adds to their confusion when the shit hits the fan."

If they got a second shot, Sean would call the targets.

As they rushed through the rice paddy, he had only one worry: *Those bastards better not shut their engines down so they can listen for a fight up in the hills. If they do that, they'll be able to hear the whoosh of the rockets coming at 'em...and they'll know exactly where we are.*

They're already blind from the flares. Let 'em stay deaf, too.

The tanks had stopped. That was a break Sean hadn't expected; you could hit a target from farther away if it wasn't moving.

"Hold it up right here," he said as he ran from team to team. "Range two hundred fifty yards. Take your shot, right fucking now."

Corporal Dowd asked, "Should we aim for those fuel tanks on the aft deck?"

"Negative," Sean replied. "Too small a target...and they got diesel in 'em, anyway. Might not burn even with a bullseye. Go for the hull side, just below the turret, where all their ammo is."

Within seconds, the three rockets were ready to fire. In rapid sequence, each left its launch tube with a roar and a flash of flame.

One rocket missed completely; it flew right over the second tank's foredeck.

Another rocket struck the edge of the third tank's

aft deck, rupturing one of the external fuel tanks. There was a brief flash as a spray of diesel fuel ignited for just a moment.

But there was no sustained fire as the bulk of the liquid fuel refused to ignite.

The rocket shot at the fourth tank found its mark perfectly. A heart-stopping instant after it penetrated her hull, she *brewed up*, with long tongues of flame spewing from her hatches.

Then she exploded with a violence no one in those teams but Sean had ever known before. The shock wave passed through the prone GIs like a blow from a giant fist. When the startled men opened their eyes again, the tank was a turretless, flaming shell.

A smoldering leg, still with a leather boot on its foot, fell back to earth just yards in front of them with a dull *plop*. The GIs stared at it in horror.

"Stop gawking, for cryin' out loud," Sean told them. "Reload, dammit!"

Just as the first two flares were nearly extinguished, the next two arrived and began their crazed dance along the ground near the middle of the tank column.

The first T-34 in line began to move forward down the road, away from the rocket teams. None of the other tanks followed her. Sean told them, "So much for their tactical discipline...but forget her. It's her lucky night. Take out the two we missed the first time around."

The second tank was still stationary, but her turret was slowly traversing toward the GIs, spewing machine gun fire blindly into the night...

Until a rocket pierced her hull.

She didn't blow up like her sister but seemed

stricken just the same. A series of muted explosions began from deep within her as ammo cooked off like corn in a popper. The GIs couldn't tell if any of her crew escaped.

The flare had finally burned out on the deck of the third tank. She didn't move, either, but her turret began to slowly traverse their way.

Two rockets struck her in rapid sequence, one shattering the drive sprocket for the right track.

The other exploded harmlessly against her turret's tough armor.

"I got her!" one of the GIs said.

"Don't think so," Sean replied. "You gave 'em a headache, that's all. At least she can't move with that busted track."

But she could still shoot.

And after a few anxious seconds, she did just that, spraying machine gun bullets from her turret that chewed up the sodden dirt of the paddy but came nowhere near the GIs.

The T-34s farther back in the line were still blinded by the flares. But that was only temporary. Perhaps in coordination with the second tank—or just in their own confusion and fear—a few of the farther ones began pumping machine gun rounds across the rice paddies, too.

Even if the GIs hadn't been spotted, it didn't matter: a bullet that hits you by sheer luck kills you just as dead as a well-aimed one.

"Time to *cut a chogie*, boys," Sean yelled. "Fall back to those sheds on the far side of the paddy."

It took longer than Sean figured to get to the sheds. The sweeping fire from the tanks' machine guns came perilously close a few times, forcing him and his men to low crawl through the watery slime of the paddy's troughs, using the dikes for cover as bullets *hissed* above them. But they all made it unscathed.

The sheds weren't meant for habitation; they were there to house the tools and supplies used in cultivating the rice. Their only advantage to the GIs was concealment. They provided no cover from bullets or shell fragments and were hundreds of yards from the base of the hills on which the regiment was perched. The machine gun fire from the T-34s never reached the sheds. Then it stopped.

"They sure wasted a lot of rounds shooting at nothing," Sean whispered.

"So what do we do now, Sarge?" Corporal Dowd asked.

"We wait and see what those tanks decide to do, then we tell the boys up on the hill all about it. We still got three rockets left, so we might get ourselves another T-34 or two before this is all over."

Dowd replied, "We don't have three rockets, Sarge. We must've lost some crawling through that damn paddy."

"How many is *some*?"

A GI held up one rocket. It was wet and coated with sludge from the crawl through the troughs.

"All right," Sean replied, "we've got *one* rocket left. Let's not waste it." He grabbed an empty burlap sack from a pile and tossed it to the GI. "Here," he said, "dry the damn thing off…and try not to lose it, too, okay? And nobody throws their tube away, neither. They ain't expendable. You got me?"

Twelve heads nodded in the darkness.

Then Dowd asked, "Why aren't those tanks moving?"

"Because they're confused, probably," Sean replied. "They're lucky if they got one or two radios between the whole bunch. And who knows? Maybe we knocked those radios out already."

A GI at the far corner of the shed started waving his arms wildly. At first, everyone thought that maybe he'd been attacked by a squadron of flies; there were certainly enough of them around the paddies. They'd been swatting them away all night.

But then the GI whispered, "We've got company. Lots of it."

As they looked across the moonlit rice paddies, they could see the outlines of human shapes coming from the north toward the sheds and the hills beyond, where the rest of their regiment was.

"How many do you figure, Sarge?" Dowd asked.

"Couple of platoons' worth…maybe a company," Sean replied.

Even at a whisper, the panic in the corporal's voice was unmistakable: "What the fuck do we do?"

"We lay low and hope they walk right the hell by," Sean said. "Everybody down, *now*. And if anyone makes a fucking sound, I'll kill you myself."

The shapes drew closer, becoming silhouettes of well-dispersed soldiers advancing cautiously with weapons at the ready...

And they sure as hell ain't carrying GI rifles like

our guys or the ROKs would, Sean thought.

But the sheds didn't hold any interest to the North Korean infantrymen. They stole past on either side, their objective apparently farther in the distance.

The hill, Sean told himself. *They must be headed for Hill 142, where First Battalion's dug in. It's right behind us.*

This is some of the infantry support those T-34s are waiting for.

And then they'd moved past without so much as a peek inside the sheds.

The GIs were about to let out their collective breath when they noticed two more men approaching from the same direction as the others. They didn't appear to be in any hurry; if anything, they were dawdling, hanging back.

Stragglers, Sean thought, *looking to make themselves scarce. Like goldbricking GIs.*

Or maybe they're just officers.

The two stopped about ten yards away, as if trying to decide what to do next. After exchanging a few words, they headed for the sheds.

Sean wondered if any of the GIs with him knew how to kill quietly.

The odds are real good they don't.

Dammit. That's all we need—gunfire and screaming with a whole bunch of gooks a stone's throw away.

The two North Koreans walked into the shed where Sean and one rocket team were hiding. There was nothing between them and the GIs but some crates, stacks of straw baskets and burlap sacks, and the darkness.

One of the Koreans stepped back outside the shed, gazing into the distance as if following the progress of their comrades headed for the hill. The other poked around inside, stopping about ten feet from Sean, who was lying on the ground behind a pile of crates.

The Korean seemed curious—and then fascinated with something. It took Sean a moment to realize what it was:

Ah, shit! He's staring at the muzzle end of a three point five. It's propped up on a pile of something. Dammit!

The Korean called to his partner while pointing excitedly at the launcher. But the man wouldn't come; a dismissive gesture accompanied his verbal response.

I need something long and sharp, Sean told himself.

Then he realized he had such a tool within his grasp. On the ground an arm's length away were several long, thin poles sharpened to a point.

I bet the gook farmers must use these to plant seeds or something.

The poles looked sturdy enough to be used as a lance. Whether they'd penetrate flesh was another matter.

The Korean put his face right up to the muzzle, as if needing a better look in the dark. Then he pulled his face away. He called to his partner again.

But he still wouldn't come.

The curious soldier had placed his rifle on a crate, and with his hands free now, reached out to pick up the rocket launcher. As he did, he put his face up to the muzzle one more time...

And Sean thrust the *lance* through the empty tube,

straight into the Korean's eye.

His *yelp* of shock and pain brought his partner running back into the shed. As he bent over the groaning man, Sean grabbed him from behind in a one arm choke hold. With his free hand, he wrenched the rifle away from his startled captive.

Corporal Dowd was now standing over the wounded Korean, pointing his carbine at him, frantically looking back and forth between his captive and Sean as if seeking instructions.

Though the struggling man was inescapably in his grasp, it still took some effort for Sean to say, "Wrong weapon. No noise. No prisoners."

"Then what am I supposed to do, Sarge?"

"Slit his fucking throat."

The corporal took a sudden step back. It was obvious he wasn't up to the task.

The choke hold had taken effect. The captive was losing his fight—and consciousness—quickly now. The incomprehensible string of words he'd been hissing as his air supply was throttled had finally ceased.

"Do me a favor," Sean told Dowd. "At least stick a sock in *One-Eye's* mouth. And if he tries to get up, butt-stroke him in the head until I'm done with this clown."

Grabbing a burlap sack, Dowd tried using a corner of it to gag *One-Eye*. But the Korean still had plenty of fight in him. Thrashing wildly, he bit the American's hand and shoved him back with a violent thrust of his foot.

While still holding the nearly unconscious man in the choke hold, Sean kicked *One-Eye* squarely in the side of his head. He fell back to the ground, stunned and silent.

In a few quick motions, Sean rid himself of his captive's weapon, pulled his GI bayonet from his belt, and slit the man's throat.

Then he squatted behind *One-Eye*, propped the man's head against his thigh, and slit his throat, too.

"That wasn't so hard, was it?" he told the four GIs in the shed. Even in the darkness, their eyes shone with the horror of what they'd just witnessed.

Then Sean added, "Next time, though, a little help would be greatly appreciated."

The GI with the walkie-talkie was in another shed. Sean found him and said, "Gimme that squawk box. Gotta warn the guys up on the hill they got gooks coming their way."

But when he keyed the transmitter, he knew he'd be delivering no warning.

The radio was dead.

"Ah, shit," he mumbled. "Don't tell me this thing went into that sewer water, too."

Then he heard a sound that told him more bad news was on the way: the revving engine and squeaking tracks of a T-34. It was coming from the direction of the highway and getting closer.

Back in the shed with the two dead North Koreans, Sean had a good view of the tank. She'd left the highway and was coming toward the GIs on one of the dikes that crisscrossed the paddies. Her tracks were nearly too wide for the narrow, earthen path. There was someone walking in front of her, giving signals to the driver.

"They need that guide to keep them on the dike," Sean said. "If she slips off, it's all over. She'll sink so deep into that mush they may never pull her out."

"What are we going to do, Sarge?" Dowd asked.

"Give me one guy and a three point five with that last rocket," Sean replied. "Take everyone else about fifty yards west, to the other side of the sheds. Give yourself good fields of fire at that tank."

"But rifles aren't going to stop a T-34, Sarge."

"No shit. But they can sure stop anybody climbing out of it or walking in front of it. I'll take the three point five and put this lady out of her misery. But if I don't knock her out with the rocket, you'd better skedaddle west, and quick. Don't even think about engaging. Just beat it into the night. You hear me?"

Corporal Dowd didn't need to be told twice.

Sean asked the man assigned to him, a PFC named Curran, "You ready to get down in the stink again?"

"We already smell like shit, Sarge. What's it gonna matter?"

"I like your attitude, pal. Just keep that fucking rocket dry."

Using an adjacent dike for cover and concealment, Sean and Curran quickly got behind the T-34 without being seen. They were only fifty yards away from her when Sean said, "Load that baby."

The rear end of the tank seemed to fill Sean's sight picture. "I can't miss," he whispered. "Not from this close."

He squeezed the trigger.

Nothing happened.

"Something's wet," Sean said. "Unhook the igniter wires and pull the rocket out."

He said it so calmly, so casually—as if this was just some minor malfunction and not a matter of life or death—that Curran forgot for just a moment how terrified he was. As he did what Sean told him, he was surprised how steady his hands were, despite the fact that at any second the malfunctioning rocket motor could ignite and burn those hands right off.

But, somehow, he knew Master Sergeant Moon would never allow that to happen.

Sean took the rocket from him the moment it was out of the tube. "It ain't trying to burn," he said. "It never lit off. Dry the contacts real quick and we'll try again."

Curran really wanted to do that. But he couldn't think of *how* he could dry them. Every piece of cloth they wore or carried was soaking wet.

When Sean saw his confusion, he said, with that same casual air, "Use the shit paper under your steel pot. I bet that ain't wet yet."

Those three sheets of toilet paper—the ones the first sergeant always made you store there—was for more than just wiping your ass, apparently.

The contacts now dry, Curran slid the rocket back into the tube. Gingerly, he reconnected the igniter wires.

The T-34 was twice as far away from them now, some one hundred yards distant.

But it was still an easy shot. When Sean squeezed the trigger again, the weapon fired.

The shaped charge on the rocket's head penetrated her aft hull like a knife through butter, tearing into the engine compartment.

She faltered and then stopped. A pregnant silence seemed to go on for an agonizingly long time, although it was only a matter of seconds.

Then they heard an explosion from within her hull like a brief clap of thunder. All her hatches blew open.

But none of her crew were escaping through those hatches.

They couldn't see the guide who'd been in front of the tank; their view was blocked by the iron beast they'd just killed.

They heard a rifle shot, though, and then another. And then there was nothing but that silence again.

"You think the crew's dead?" Curran asked.

"Probably."

"How about we have a look inside, then, Sarge?"

"Not yet," Sean replied. "She may have some more blowing up to do...and if we start wandering around her, the rest of the team'll probably shoot our asses. Let's get back with them first."

Working their way down a trough past the inert tank, they stumbled over the body of a North Korean. "I guess we found the ground guide," Sean said.

When they reached the rest of the team, Sean told them, "Whichever one of you clowns did the shooting...well, you did a good job. Real nice shot."

"You mean we got him?" a surprised GI asked.

"Deader than a doornail, pal," Sean replied. Then he told the group, "C'mon...let's steal the machine guns outta that tank. If she ain't brewed up by now, she ain't gonna."

Corporal Dowd asked, "I don't know, Sarge...you sure those guys inside are all dead?"

"If they didn't come out by now, they ain't never coming out. The way she blew, they're probably just pink stains on the walls. Now let's get those MGs. We might need an automatic weapon or two to get back inside our lines. I've got a bad feeling there's a whole bunch of gooks between us and home."

The silence in the air was broken once more. The sounds of explosions and gunfire were rolling down from Hill 142.

Chapter Six

It was near midnight when Jock and Patchett linked up at the OP on Hill 142. The FO had an interesting tale to tell them.

"It started out with a dozen or so T-34s coming down the highway, sir," he said. "Whoever we've got down there in those paddies took out three of them. Couldn't tell if it was *reckless rifles* or three point fives that did it. I did the radio relay for them when they wanted illum rounds."

"It was three point fives," Jock replied. "Sergeant Moon's team, I suspect. That was *Montana Four-Six* who engaged the tanks, right?"

"Affirmative, sir."

"Then that's Sergeant Moon. Have you heard from him lately?"

"Not in about two hours, sir."

In unison, Jock and Patchett mumbled, "Shit."

The FO added, "But it was a good thirty minutes after his last transmission that the last T-34 got knocked out, sir." He was pointing to the inert tank sitting in the rice paddy.

"Maybe Moon's radio crapped out, sir," Patchett offered.

"Let's hope that's all it is, Top."

Except for the other two dead T-34s, there were no vehicles on the highway. Jock asked the FO, "What were those tanks doing all that time, Lieutenant?"

"They sat still on the highway for a good hour after they showed up, sir. The one that's laying in the paddy, I think she was the one who went all by her lonesome toward the pass between Hills One-Four-Two and One-Two-Seven. But then she came back, drove into the paddy, and ended up getting killed right there. It wasn't long after that, maybe just a couple of minutes, that the rest turned tail and went back the way they came."

"I reckon we ain't seen the last of them, sir," Patchett said. "Everything that's happened so far tonight is probably just a feint. Even the gook infantry coming up *One-Four-Two* got discouraged a little too easy to suit me. Tripped a couple of our grenade traps, took some fire, and vanished. Don't expect we'll find too many of their bodies on the upslope come sunup. And I ain't heard a bit of artillery fire from our flank regiments, neither. What do you hear from Division?"

"Not a damn thing, Top," Jock replied. "It's like everyone but us is off the air. For all we know, the rest of the whole damn Twenty-Fourth Division is on a boat back to Japan."

"Let's hope not, sir. Where do you need me next?"

Before Jock could answer, the distant chatter of machine guns erupted. It was coming from the rear of the regiment's defensive perimeter, where 2nd Battalion—the regimental reserve—was emplaced.

Jock's driver called out, "Second Battalion needs you on frequency, sir. Sounds like he's in a big pile of shit."

As they ran to the jeep, Jock told Patchett, "I guess that answers your question about where I need you, Top."

✯ ✯ ✯

It took less than five minutes to drive to 2nd Battalion's CP. Jock and Patchett found Colonel

Eliason, the battalion commander, shouting frantic instructions to his companies over the radio. The sounds of gunfire had become sporadic, more random potshots than a coordinated assault.

From the state of the chaos in the CP, Patchett came to a quick conclusion about 2nd Battalion. He pulled Jock aside so they wouldn't be overheard.

"Looks to me like they took *reserve* to mean *at ease*, sir." Motioning toward the CP's situation map, Patchett added, "This overlay looks a little *too* neat, if you ask me. The terrain around here don't lend itself to no nice straight lines like they've got drawn. I reckon they don't have a clue where most of their troopers really are."

Jock stepped over to Eliason and asked, "What's your situation, Pete?"

"The gooks are everywhere," he replied, panic in his voice. "We're surrounded. Every company's in contact with them."

"It sounds pretty quiet right now, Pete. Any breakthroughs in your line?"

"I don't know, sir."

"Well, we'd better figure that one out real quick before we get some unwanted visitors here in your CP."

Sergeant Patchett had been studying the situation map closely. His fingertip began to trace two spots on the map along the gentle backslope the battalion occupied behind Hills 142 and 127. His finger stopping on one of the spots, he asked Colonel Eliason, "Y'all should have three Chaffees right about here, sir. That's where Sergeant Moon says he positioned them. I don't see them marked on this map anywhere. Did y'all move 'em?"

The blank look on Eliason's face was all the answer Patchett—or Jock—needed. He wasn't sure where those three tanks were or what they were doing. His excuse: "My radios don't even talk to the armor."

"Nobody's does, sir," Patchett replied. "But that ain't no surprise. We should have a liaison working with the tanks. One of your guys with a radio on your command *freq* is all it takes."

Then Patchett moved his finger to the other spot on the map. "I'm guessing this artillery battery is what the gooks want to knock out most. Have y'all set up security for it?"

Eliason replied, "Negative, Sergeant. The artillery can take care of themselves."

Jock took a dim view of that answer. "For cryin' out loud, Pete, that battery is supposed to be *inside* your perimeter. Are you even talking to them?"

Eliason's silence was as good as a *no*.

"Here's the way it's going to be, Colonel," Jock said. "I want you out of this damn CP and out in the weeds leading your men. Make sure you have excellent radio communications while you're doing it, too, because I want updates from you every ten minutes, starting ten minutes from right now."

Then he turned to Patchett and continued, "Top, make sure those tanks are doing Colonel Eliason some good. I'm heading over to the artillery battery."

Patchett found the three M24 Chaffee tanks right where Sean had positioned them, hull-down, within easy striking distance of the road. When the shooting started, they'd cranked their engines so they'd be ready to move immediately if necessary. The only problem was that once those engines were running, they couldn't hear much of the fight supposedly raging nearby.

Patchett told the tanker platoon sergeant, "Why don't you save y'all's gas and shut them noisemakers down now? You might hear what's going on that way...which, at the moment, is not a damn thing."

There was still that problem of their radios being incompatible with the infantry's. Patchett asked the tanker platoon sergeant, "Talk to any of the dogfaces from Second Battalion?"

"Yeah, Top. Some lieutenant came down from the ridge to ask what we were doing here. When I told him, all he said was *Good luck* and went back up the ridge. So we figure we're on our own keeping the gook infantry off our backs."

The tankers had set themselves up accordingly: they'd *circled the wagons*, orienting their tanks in a three-pointed star, the bows facing out.

Patchett said, "Well, I can see what y'all done...and it's good, for now. But it ain't gonna help a lick when some T-34s get behind us and come up that road from the south and they've got infantry with them. Y'all won't be able to handle both if you ain't got some dogfaces of your own."

The platoon sergeant looked surprised. "You don't really think we're going to see gook tanks popping up on the back side of this perimeter, do you, Top?"

"Let me put it this way," Patchett replied. "A bunch came at us from the north a while back, a few got their asses handed to them, and they pulled back. They could be working their way around to our back side right now."

"But they'll need roads, and the only other roads run through the regiments on our flanks, Top. They'd have to get through them first."

"And they just might, bubba. They just might. I'm gonna go have me a little chat with that lieutenant. Maybe I can convince him that by saving your ass he just might be saving his own ass."

When Jock broached the question of battery defense to Captain Swanson, the artillery commander was stunned to realize that providing protection for his unit hadn't been in Colonel Eliason's plans. But he felt confident his own plan for the battery would be more than adequate. He offered Jock the sketch of his position's defensive scheme.

After studying the sketch for a few moments, Jock asked, "What are you planning on doing if you get hit from the south, Captain?"

Swanson stammered his answer: "But, sir…the Koreans…they're coming from the north, aren't they?"

"Generally speaking, Captain, you're correct. But *tactically speaking*, they could be coming from *any* direction. I ask you again: what are you planning on doing if you get hit from the south?"

Swanson looked dumbfounded, as if being asked to ponder the imponderable. He finally managed to say, "I suppose we could reorient the howitzers and use them in perimeter defense."

"Damn right you could," Jock replied. "But let me ask you this: are your gun crews trained for that situation? And if they are, can they do it in the dark?"

"Well, sir…I'm sure that…no, I suppose that they've had some—"

"In other words, Captain, they wouldn't have any idea what to do, would they?"

There was no point trying to talk his way out of it anymore. Swanson replied, "No, sir. I don't believe they would."

"Well, they don't seem very busy right now. In fact, besides a couple of fire missions here and there, they haven't been very busy all night. So this is what you're going to do. You're going to draw up a simple plan for all-around battery defense right now and have all your section chiefs briefed on that plan within thirty minutes. Understood?"

"Yes, sir. Understood."

"Outstanding, Captain."

Sean Moon and his rocket teams had spent hours working their way back to the regiment. It had been slow going; the North Koreans always seemed to be blocking their path. They'd often been so close to the enemy that they could plainly hear them speaking, even laughing.

Soldiers only laugh when they think they're winning, Sean thought.

The darkness was their only friend. Had it been daylight, the GIs would've never been able to eventually slip through the Korean lines and scale Hill 142.

Assuming this even is Hill One-Four-Two, Sean

told himself. *We've been stumbling around in the dark for so long we might be someplace else.*

But if this really is the right damn hill, all we gotta do now is not get shot by our own guys.

The higher they climbed, the less confidence he had that they wouldn't attract friendly fire: *Those GIs gotta be jumpy as all hell. And they'll probably catch wind of us before we catch wind of them.*

But it actually worked the other way around. Sean spotted the dome-shaped silhouettes of GI helmets moving near the top of the hill. They hadn't seen or heard his team's approach. All he had to do now was call out the password.

But before he did, he whispered to the man right behind him, "Everybody bury his fucking face in the dirt, just in case this don't go right. Pass it on."

When he felt certain his entire team was hugging earth, he called out, in his best Brooklynese, "Hey, *youse guys*, the Cleveland Indians stink on ice!"

It seemed a safe bet: Cleveland was the password.

The reply from the top of the hill was a hail of bullets.

It lasted until the strident voice of someone—a sergeant, perhaps an officer—berated them to stop. As the last shot popped off, that voice said, "Did any of you fucking morons ever hear a fucking gook talk English like that?"

Okay...definitely a sergeant.

As they passed into the perimeter, Sean counted off his men.

They were all there, safe and sound.

Then he told the sergeant, "You guys better work on keeping your big heads down and your eyes open. I spotted your steel pots against the skyline way off. If I'd been a gook..."

It was just after 0200 hours when Jock Miles walked into the regimental CP and saw Sean. He'd been briefing the S2—the regimental intelligence officer—on what they'd encountered in their travels among the North Koreans.

After a recap for his benefit, Jock said, "So it looks like they're trying to work their way around our position, correct?"

"Sure looks that way, sir," Sean replied.

"I'm not surprised," Jock said. "We've already had some activity on the back side of the perimeter. But let me ask you something, Sergeant Moon...did you see any evidence of friendly units on our flank while you were making your way back?"

"Negative, sir. Not a damn bit of evidence."

Jock fell silent for a few moments, deep in thought. Then he said, "As if it's not bad enough trying to lead an outfit that's forgotten how to fight, I've got a nasty suspicion we're about to be a *cut-off* outfit that's forgotten how to fight."

Sean replied, "I'm wondering if *forgotten* is the right word, sir. It seems like most of these clowns never knew how in the first place."

"You could be right, Sergeant. But we've got to change all that, and quickly. By the way, you did a great job handling those T-34s. I take it those three point fives worked as advertised?"

"Affirmative, sir. Guys who never even saw one

before tonight killed two tanks right off the bat."

"Two? I thought you got three."

"Yeah, we did, sir, but I shot the third one myself, and I ain't no virgin. We gotta get a resupply of rockets like yesterday, though. Looks like we're fresh out now."

"Well, I'm damn glad you all made it back okay, Sergeant. We were really worried about you."

"We were pretty worried ourselves, sir. But if that damn radio hadn't crapped out, I could've given you a heads-up what was going on with them gooks a hell of a lot sooner."

"Scrounge yourself a new set, and then go have a look at those Chaffees. Sergeant Patchett's doing the best he can trying to integrate them into Second Battalion's perimeter, but we could sure use your armor expertise. Once you get there, tell him that I need him coordinating the mutual support between our units on the hills."

At 0315 hours, the shrill din of dozens of police whistles announced the start of the attack: North Korean pincers struck the 26th Regiment from the north and south. The force from the north attacked with infantry and heavy mortars. A sharp-eyed GI on Hill 142 spotted the dim flashes of the mortars firing from over a mile away across the rice paddies. Two volleys from the American 105-millimeter howitzers silenced them before they could inflict much damage.

Without mortar, artillery, or tank support, the Koreans attempting to scale Hill 142 faced withering fire from the troopers of 1st Battalion. Some GIs, however, still panicked and abandoned their dug-in positions at the first hint of pressure. When several squads broke and ran, the breach was only sealed when Patchett commandeered a *quad 50*—four .50-caliber machine guns mounted together and meant as an anti-aircraft weapon—and ordered its reluctant crew to tow it to the collapsing sector.

As bullets whizzed around them, the terrified gunner screamed to Patchett, "I CAN'T SEE WHERE THE HELL THEY ARE."

Patchett replied, "YOU DON'T GOTTA SEE NOTHING, SON. JUST LEVEL THEM GUNS AND PULL THAT FUCKING TRIGGER."

Once the quad 50 began spitting its industrial death into the Koreans swarming over the hilltop, Patchett yelled, "NOW JUST KEEP SWEEPING THAT BASTARD BACK AND FORTH LIKE CLOCKWORK. THERE YOU GO, JUST LIKE THAT."

But enough Koreans reached the top of the hill to ensure a series of confused and deadly skirmishes would continue until one side found itself with no one left to fight.

Across the highway, the North Korean attack on Hill 127—defended by 3rd Battalion—was far weaker, though as far as the GIs on that hill were concerned, they were up against the entire KPA. The battle quickly devolved into a confused melee of point-blank firing and hand-to-hand combat. Mortars and artillery would no longer play a part; bullets, bayonets, and sometimes fists would decide the outcome.

Fleeing wasn't much of an option when the enemy was right in their midst. A fight like this either quickly turned a man into a soldier or he quickly died.

Neither side could tell who had the upper hand. But after about five minutes of mortal struggle between shadowy adversaries barely visible to each other, the shrill sound of whistles pierced the night once again, this time long blasts quite different from the rapid staccato pattern that had begun the attack. The fight slackened and then stopped.

The GIs still held the hill. The only Koreans there with them were dead or badly wounded. The rest had heeded that primitive signal; they broke off their attack and retreated.

From the top of Hill 142, the sound of another battle raged behind them. The attack from the south possessed two things the one from the north had lacked: the growling of tank engines; the *boom* of their heavy guns. T-34s had entered the fight once again. Whether they were the same ones Sean had fought off hours ago or a different group, it didn't matter. What did matter was that they'd gotten around and behind 26th Regiment's position.

That meant there was no friendly unit protecting one—or maybe both—of their flanks.

The GIs who had fled the line on Hill 142 realized there was no safe place to go. A group of senior NCOs found most of them huddled near the battalion CP.

When one of the NCOs began bellowing a promise of a court-martial to *every yellow-bellied coward who quit his post*, Patchett pulled the man away so they wouldn't be overheard. Then he told him, "If we court-martial every swinging dick who gets *hisself* a case of the chickenshits, you and me gonna be standing on this hill by our damn selves in no time flat. Let's just do the jobs Uncle Sugar's paying us for and get them back into their fighting holes, maybe even firing their weapons."

As they walked back to the group of anxious GIs, a thunderclap of heavy weaponry from the south echoed through the night air.

"Besides," Patchett added, "sounds like we just might be surrounded, so there ain't no place to mosey off to, anyhow."

Chapter Seven

The attack from the south—straight up the highway from the opposite direction into 2nd Battalion's area—was the strongest of the night.

Sean had made only one change to the Chaffees' positioning, moving one of the tanks to a hull-down position a few hundred yards farther up the gentle backslope. "With her up a little higher," he told the tank platoon sergeant, "all three of your tanks have unrestricted fields of fire. You can shoot in any direction without being in each other's way, even if you have to shoot over each other's heads."

But Colonel Eliason didn't like it. Face to face, he told Sean, "I want those tanks spread out more, Sergeant…much more, dammit, so they can cover the entire west side of my position."

But there was no time to argue about it, however compelling Sean's reasoning might have been to keep the armor consolidated. The attack had begun…

And Colonel Eliason looked like a man racked with anxiety.

"We need illumination rounds right away," he said to his radioman.

Sean interjected, "Maybe we hold off on that, sir? The gooks are in the open, no shadows or nothing for them to hide in. Plenty of moonlight. Why ruin our night vision?"

Eliason fumbled for a good answer but couldn't come up with one.

"Besides," Sean continued, "your machine guns got *great* fields of fire on this easy slope. Hell, it's practically flat. Those guns interlock every which way. If you're gonna use artillery, let's have some HE airbursts. That oughta thin the gooks out real quick."

The colonel latched onto that suggestion, if for no other reason than it made him look decisive. Summoning his best command voice, he called the fire mission over the radio himself.

No sooner was he done than a mortar round landed less than twenty yards away, mercifully showering them with nothing but dirt. But it was enough to send Eliason scurrying back up Hill 142.

The noise of battle was constant now, with GI machine guns spraying bullets along their fixed fields of fire, creating a fence of invisible steel a man could only penetrate flat on his stomach. Over the machine gunners' objections, Patchett had insisted they perform the onerous task of removing the tracers from their weapons' ammo belts and replacing them with standard ball rounds. "Your gun's already fixed where it needs to shoot," he'd told them. "You don't need no tracers pointing a big, bright finger right back at you."

Sean thought the battlefield seemed eerie without tracers. He'd always felt that firing tracers brought a certain level of satisfaction—a confirmation of your efforts and your lethality—to a night fight. *But I'm looking at it as a tanker*, he told himself. *It ain't no secret where a tank is once she fires, and bullets don't bother her none, anyway. I guess a dogface sees it different. Once the bad guys figure out where he is, he's in a world of trouble.*

He knew that as long as Colonel Eliason's men didn't break and run, they would inflict serious damage on the exposed North Korean infantry trying to advance across open terrain.

It was the approaching tanks that had him concerned.

With the attack underway, Jock hurried to the artillery battery. He had little doubt Patchett was right: the North Koreans would like nothing more than to silence that battery and the far-reaching threat it posed. More importantly, it might be the last chance to see—and correct, if necessary—Captain Swanson's defensive plans.

When he arrived at the battery, Jock was impressed by what Swanson had done. The six howitzers in the battery had been pivoted 180 degrees and were firing the mission Eliason had called, delivering perfect airbursts over the North Korean infantry by using VT fuzes on the HE rounds. Developed late in the last war, each VT fuze contained a tiny radio unit that unfailingly delivered the desired burst height of 120 feet above ground with no need for corrections. Jock had never seen them used in combat before, and like everyone else who'd seen them in action, he was duly impressed.

The only problem was that the battery had just a handful of those fuzes left.

He told Swanson, "I like the changes you've made, Captain. Is it safe to assume that any gun can be spun around to fire in any direction now?"

"Affirmative, sir."

"Outstanding," Jock replied. "What's your ammo situation?"

"We're getting low on just about everything, sir."

Jock asked, "How low is *low*, Captain? Start with HE rounds."

"We've got a little less than two hundred left."

With all six guns engaged, that would mean they had roughly five minutes of continuous firing with HE remaining. The current fire mission could expend that lot easily.

"Cut off shooting HE when you're down to fifty rounds, Captain."

Swanson looked puzzled. "Why, sir?"

"There's a good chance you'll need it for the defense of your guns. How good are your men at direct fire?"

"We haven't had much practice, sir."

"Necessity is a great teacher, Captain...and I think class is about to be in session."

Lieutenant Colonel Eliason had—at the urgings of Jock and Patchett—moved his mortar sections to Hills 142 and 127, joining those of the other two battalions. Now clear of the fire crisscrossing the backslope below and nearly impossible to detect from the lower elevations, they'd been delivering effective support all night, first against the attacks from the north and now against the attack from the south.

But they were getting low on rounds, too. Like the artillery, they could only provide continuous fire support for a matter of minutes.

After the quad 50 had saved the day on Hill 142, Patchett had made it his mission—with Jock's blessing—to muster as many of the regiment's four quad 50s as he could. From the hilltops, they could throw their heavy rounds in a dense concentration to a range of four miles. It was just a question of how many of the weapons were still serviceable after the initial attacks and how much .50-caliber ammunition was still available.

The two quad 50s on Hill 142 were both serviceable but were very low on ammo, about one hundred rounds per individual gun.

A radio call to 3rd Battalion CP on Hill 127 was not encouraging: "No dice," the voice of a staff officer reported. "Both quad fifties here were badly damaged in the fight, *over*."

"Roger," Patchett replied. "How much ammo you got left for them?"

"Plenty."

"We'll come get it. Be there in about one-zero minutes."

"Negative. That requires *Wyoming Six* approval."

Wyoming Six: the commander of 3rd Battalion.

Patchett replied, "Negative, negative. We've got *Montana Six* authorization, *over*."

Montana Six: Jock Miles, the regimental commander.

Patchett's concluding transmission: "Stack it up. We're on our way. *Out*."

On the drive up Hill 127, one of the gunners with Patchett asked him, "Hey, Sarge, wouldn't it be better if we just gave them one of our quad 50s?"

"Not at the moment, son," Patchett replied, "because all the time we'd be dragging it up this hill, it wouldn't be shooting. And right now, that's what we need most. They can hit anything they need to from up on One-Four-Two."

Sean was counting his lucky stars that Colonel Eliason's scattering of the three Chaffees had been preempted by the North Korean assault. From their hull-down positions, the light tanks—with their low-silhouette turrets—had proved difficult targets for the T-34s. They'd even scored some hits against the Korean tanks, immobilizing one by damaging its track and bringing another to an unexplained halt in both firing and movement. It was a good thing, too; that was the closest enemy tank to their position, less than four hundred yards away.

"The crew's probably concussed and groggy from that hit against her turret, that's all," Sean told the tanker sergeant. "We didn't make no hole in her, but somebody had better finish her off real quick, while she's standing still."

The problem was that they'd be shooting at her frontal armor. As Sean had said, they hadn't—and wouldn't—penetrate it. The only weapons powerful enough to knock her out were the howitzers about a thousand yards away, shooting direct fire. When he called Colonel Miles on the command net, he was surprised—and happy—to learn he was at the battery.

Sean told himself, *How about that shit? I figured I'd have to go through a couple of relays to talk to the artillery. But I got me a direct line. This must be my lucky night...but it would be even luckier if I had some more three point fives to use on these damn gook tanks right now.*

Jock asked Captain Swanson, "Who's your best crew at direct fire?"

He could tell from the look on the artilleryman's face that the question was pointless: all his crews were equally inexperienced.

"I tell you what, Captain...let's give the honors to Number One. That gun's got the best angle on the flanks of those T-34s."

"Okay, sir," Swanson replied, "but should we keep the other guns firing the airburst mission?"

"Affirmative, Captain...until you're down to fifty rounds left, that is."

The section chief of Gun One, a buck sergeant just promoted from gunner a few days ago, seemed momentarily overwhelmed by the transition to direct fire. His orders to the gunner and assistant gunner only managed to confuse them.

As the section chief struggled to clarify the target identification, he forgot to tell his ammo handlers what type round, fuze, and propellant charge to prepare. They were starting to load a round prepared for the mission they'd been shooting only a few moments ago, one that would have fallen hundreds of yards short.

While Swanson corrected the ammo handlers, Jock identified the target for the gunner: "It's the tank farthest to the right. Sight down the tube...now go three fingers more to the right."

"Okay, got it," the gunner said. "But what's the

range, sir?"

"Put it just under the thousand-yard line in the scope. And I mean just barely a hair under."

Then Jock added, "Remember, you're firing *max charge* at low elevation. She's going to recoil like a son of a bitch. Don't get behind one of the trails unless you want your legs broken."

As the gunner adjusted his sight picture, he said, "I thought you were infantry, sir. You sure sound like you know this gunnery stuff."

"I am infantry," Jock replied, "but you pick up a hell of a lot when your life depends on it. Even about gunnery."

The assistant gunner began the chant:
Set...set...set...

And then the gunner replied: *Ready!*

With a jerk of the firing lanyard, the howitzer roared, jumping up and sliding backward a few feet from the recoil, its spades plowing the dirt just as Jock had promised it would. A few seconds later, they saw the flash of an impact. A few seconds after that, they heard the *boom* of the round's detonation.

"Did we get her?" the assistant gunner asked.

"No, we're a little short," Jock replied. "Bring the elevation up just a little...just a tiny bit on the wheel. There...that's good."

Another round was rammed into the breech.

The assistant gunner again began the chant:
Set...set...

"Hold up," Jock said. "Check your sight picture one last time. Ramming that round can knock off the aim just enough to miss."

After small tweaks that barely moved the traverse

and elevation handwheels, the chant began again.

This time, the assistant gunner only had to say *Set* once before the gunner responded with *Ready.*

And this time, they scored a direct hit.

Over the radio, Sean's enthusiasm was obvious: "Excellent shot. Don't know if you can tell, but you knocked the turret loose. She's gonna brew up in a second or two, I'm betting. Can you take out a few more?"

Gun One fired four more rounds of direct fire. Two missed. Of the two that hit, one shattered a T-34's track, immobilizing her.

The other hit didn't require a close observer to describe the damage. The tank's explosion was visible for miles.

Then Captain Swanson reported, "Fifty rounds HE remaining, sir."

Sean wasn't sure how many T-34s were part of this assault. Four had been knocked out so far by the concerted efforts of the Chaffees, the artillery battery, and a few courageous bazooka teams who—at his direction—set ablaze the two immobilized but still-firing Korean tanks with multiple point-blank shots, despite the inadequacies of their overmatched weapons. But the darkness had let them get close, simply *too* close to miss the T-34s' most vulnerable areas.

But he'd counted at least eight more tanks mounting a second wave...

And this time, their focus was the artillery battery. There seemed to be plenty of infantry with them, too.

The burning tanks had illuminated enough of the battlefield to get a rough count: it looked like hundreds of foot soldiers were advancing behind the tanks.

He tried to report that fact over the command net, but he got nothing but silence in reply. His radio was dead. The only working radios he had left—those in the tanks themselves—operated on a different band. They only spoke to each other.

Then one of the Chaffees was struck squarely in the turret by a round from a T-34. A momentary tongue of flame shot from each of her hatches, followed shortly by a string of internal explosions that spelled her—and her crew's—instantaneous death.

Hull-down as she was, with only her turret visible, she may have been a small target, shot at and missed countless times since this fight began. But some Korean tank gunner had finally found her. Whether it was skill or luck didn't matter.

The Korean force kept swarming toward the battery. Once the T-34 gunners could see enough of the artillery pieces to target them, they'd make short work of destroying the guns.

Sean grabbed a GI from a nearby fighting position and told him he was now a runner. "Get your ass to the battalion CP on the fucking double. Tell 'em Sergeant Moon says there's a shitload of infantry behind them tanks headed to the *cannon cockers*. Shift all the mortars onto them. Now say it back to me."

The GI repeated it verbatim. Then he said, "But I don't know where the battalion CP is, Sarge."

"How about your platoon CP? Do you know where the hell that is?"

"I think so."

"Good. Start there."

The runner on his way, Sean turned his attention back to the two remaining Chaffees. "We gotta hurt them T-34s before they can get a shot at the one-oh-five battery," he told the platoon sergeant. "We got a chance...the closer they get to them guns, the more they'll be broadside to us. As soon as you can hit one anywhere but the front, start shooting. Don't fucking stop until we've got as many burning as we can."

Sean's runner made it to the battalion CP as Colonel Eliason was being briefed by one of his mortar sergeants. The sergeant was experienced in target acquisition techniques. He'd had the chance to analyze several impact craters from Korean mortar rounds.

"We've got their azimuth of fire dead to rights, sir," he told Eliason. "I'd only be guessing at how far out they are, but judging by the caliber, I'd say it's about two thousand yards."

A staff officer interrupted. "Colonel, this man has an urgent message for you."

As soon as the runner's message was relayed, Eliason said, "Negative. Our mortars will continue to protect my battalion's position. Who the hell is making this request, anyway?"

"That master sergeant from Regiment, sir," the runner replied. "Moon, I think he said his name is."

"I see," Eliason said. "One of our new regimental commander's whiz kids. He's only been here a day, and already I'm getting a little tired of his senior NCOs telling me how to run my battalion. Private, you go back and remind Sergeant Moon that I don't work for him. Tell him he needs to coordinate his requests through Regiment."

"But his radio's dead, sir."

"That's not my problem, Private. Now, why are you still here?"

He turned to his mortar sergeant, adding, "With the data you've provided, our tubes are to immediately begin shooting counter-battery fire against those gook mortars. Good work, Sergeant."

With their first five shots, the Chaffees knocked out two T-34s. All the American tankers—Sean included—expected at least some of the T-34s to direct their attention back their way. But they all kept rolling toward the artillery battery.

"I'm telling you," Sean told the Chaffee crew he had joined, "these gook tankers fight just like the Russians. Once they get rolling, they can't communicate for shit. Half those tanks don't even know we're shooting at 'em. Get enough of 'em burning, though, they'll get the message, dammit."

"Do they really only have two guys in that turret, Sarge?" the loader asked.

"Nah, that's only in the real old models. These ones look to be *dash eighty-fives*, with a three-man turret. But it's still a tight little box they're cooped up in, and the tank commander's got bad communications and crappy visibility. Once a fight starts, he don't know whether to shit or go blind."

The Chaffee lurched as she fired another round. A

direct hit, it knocked out a third Korean tank.

And then her sister knocked out the fourth.

"Now things are getting interesting," Sean said. "We got their range cold...but if they turn toward us, we're screwed."

There were four T-34s still on the move. Suddenly, they stopped dead.

"Now ain't that the dumbest thing I ever seen?" Sean said. "Turn 'em inside out, boys."

In the next ten seconds, two more T-34s were in flames.

Of the remaining two, one began to pivot toward the Chaffees. Before it could get a shot off, it erupted in a flash of flame, struck by a direct-fire round from the artillery battery.

"Remind me to buy those cannon cockers a beer," Sean mumbled.

The last T-34 fired a shot at the battery. The men in the Chaffees couldn't tell if it had caused any damage; they were too busy trying to knock her out.

So far, they'd pumped four rounds at her without scoring a hit.

"She's farther than you think, guys," Sean said. "Up it another hundred yards."

The next shots missed, too.

"I didn't see no flash," Sean said. "We musta shot right over her. Split the difference."

They did...and still missed high.

Sean knew they'd find the range now without his help; they had her bracketed too well. But the North Korean infantry was still plodding toward the battery, rank after rank of men still unchecked.

Where the hell are those fucking mortars I called

for?

He climbed onto the turret roof and began to fire at the soldiers with the .50-caliber machine gun mounted there. It was an act of desperation, and he knew it; powerful as the weapon was, it was the wrong tool for the job, like trying to drive a pin with a mallet. One stream of bullets at a time—large-caliber bullets, at that—simply didn't have the scope to take down great numbers of well-dispersed attackers.

Even the tracers the tankers had left in the ammo belts failed to provide the satisfaction they'd always given Sean before. Watching them bounce off the ground a thousand yards or more away and then sail high into the sky was only enhancing his sense of helplessness.

Maybe the darkness was playing tricks on his eyes, but there seemed to be more than enough Koreans—even if they took heavy casualties—to overrun the artillery battery.

Those cannon cockers may be real good at a lot of things, but fighting off hordes of gooks in close combat ain't one of them.

The Chaffees let loose two more rounds at the last T-34. Both missed.

From atop Hill 142, Patchett saw Sean's tracers streaming from the Chaffee. He couldn't see the advancing North Koreans, but he felt sure of one thing: *Tankers don't waste their time engaging other tanks with machine guns. Whoever's shooting that thing is shooting at gook infantry headed toward that*

battery...and he's the only damn one doing it.

Looks like that boy could use a little bit of help.

He'd just finished repositioning one of the quad 50s. Since there'd been no time to remove the tracers from the newly acquired ammo belts, he'd made it a point to move one of the two gun sections fifty yards or so just as soon as they'd finished engaging a target. That way, a T-34 might return fire at the weapon with her deadly main gun, but she'd be targeting where it *used to be* just a moment ago. While one was being moved, the other would still be available to provide its devastating fire support.

He told the quad 50 gunner, "See where that Chaffee down there is aiming them tracers? Sweep that area real good while I get the other quad repositioned."

From the artillery battery, the cone of brilliant white tracers streaking down from the quad 50s on Hill 142, stirring the ground before them into a dust storm, looked like salvation from on high. It wasn't a minute too soon, either: the howitzers had done well against tanks but wouldn't be much use against marauding personnel. They couldn't even shoot high-angle airbursts against them; the attackers were much too close for that.

And no matter how many Koreans the machine guns from the hill stopped, some, the artillerymen were sure, were bound to enter their perimeter. There just seemed too many attackers for it to be any other way. Their howitzers would be useless to them; it would become an infantry fight, with rifles, machine guns, grenades, and bayonets.

Some of the artillerymen—perhaps an entire gun section or two—broke and ran when that one round from the T-34 sailed low over their heads. It impacted harmlessly well behind the battery, but to men gripped by panic, close calls offered no relief, only validation of their fears.

The others held their ground, taking some small comfort that Colonel Miles was still with them, calmly organizing them into defensive strongpoints that used the steel shields of the howitzers as bunkers.

To Jock, it was no different than those moments in the last war on Papua, New Guinea, Manus, or Biak, moments when he and his men were sure their life expectancy was being measured in seconds. But he'd never forgotten their lesson:

As long as we can keep them from surrounding us, we've got a chance.

And every second they continued to live made that life expectancy grow exponentially.

But this night, as those seconds ticked down, the enemy never emerged from that cloud of bullet-stirred dust. Instead, they heard shrill blasts from countless whistles…

And then the enemy evaporated into the night.

When the sun came up three hours later, they counted over two hundred dead North Koreans on the gentle slope to the south.

The one T-34 that had never been killed was just sitting there, silent, abandoned, yet untouched. After Sean examined it, he said, "The one bastard we couldn't knock out broke down all by herself. Ain't that some shit?"

Chapter Eight

Sunrise illuminated more than just last night's battlefield. Division headquarters was finally back on the radio, asking 26th Regiment for a status report. The man on the Division end of the conversation seemed startled to hear the regiment was not only still intact but in the same position it was yesterday. Then he said, "Wait one."

The *one* stretched into five minutes before Division transmitted again: "You'll have a visitor in two hours. Secure a suitable landing strip. *Out.*"

Two hours later, as promised, a light observation aircraft began circling over Hills 142 and 127. The regiment had placed panel markers along the south highway to mark a runway. The pilot inquired nervously about the tanks scattered near those markers.

"They're all dead and can't be moved," Jock's RTO told the pilot. "Wind is south at eight miles per hour. You're clear to land."

Everyone in the regimental CP had the same unspoken thought: *Speaking of dead, wait until they get a little lower and see a couple of hundred dead gooks lying all over the place.*

The little plane rolled to a stop. The division commander, a two-star general named Keane, stepped from her. As he looked around, he seemed startled by the scene greeting him.

Keane's first words: "It looks like there was quite a fight here. Tokyo will be very surprised to hear that. The word is that you couldn't have possibly been hit as hard as the other regiments."

Jock replied, "Well, as you can see all around you, sir, that wasn't the case at all."

The general's nod of agreement seemed somewhat grudging. Then he asked, "How long do you think you can hold this salient of yours, Miles?"

"Salient, sir?" Jock replied, surprised at the general's choice of terms. "The patrols I ran at first light tell me there are no friendly units to my left, right, or rear. We're not linked up with anyone, so this isn't a salient. We're an island in a sea of North Koreans at the moment."

"Call it what you will, Miles," Keane said, "but Tokyo is ordering us to consolidate our lines. We need you to pull back immediately."

"How far back, sir?" he asked the general.

"About ten miles, Colonel, just north of Taejon. That's where the rest of the division is regrouping, at the Kum River."

Regrouping...that's a polite term to describe the aftermath of a rout.

Keane continued, "I had a good look at the road south on the flight up here, Miles. It's clear. You shouldn't have any problem."

"Actually, sir, I have quite a few problems," Jock replied. "Without an immediate resupply of ammo, food, and medical supplies, we won't survive another fight." He motioned to the spotter plane, adding, "And I could use some of those *grasshoppers* to airlift out about forty of my wounded, like I asked for two hours ago, once Division actually came back on the air."

Keane shook his head. "We don't have those kinds of resources, Miles, and you know it. We can fly out a few, perhaps..."

"But the Air Force can certainly drop me the supplies I need, General. I've already radioed in the requisitions. I trust the G4 made those requisitions *top priority?*"

From the bewildered look on Keane's face, it was obvious he had no idea what the state of those requisitions was. "Look, Miles, last night was pure chaos," he said. "We had units getting thrown back, some overrun, all sorts of commo problems..."

Jock knew then that *pure chaos* couldn't adequately describe what had happened to 24th Division last night. Two regiments collapsed and ran; only his had managed to prevail on the battlefield. But the position they held now was an isolated bastion ill equipped to fend off one more assault.

Another foreboding thought crossed his mind: *When I was at KMAG, we always thought those initials really stood for "kiss my ass goodbye."*

But this is even worse.

Keane asked, "How about KIA, Colonel? What are your numbers from last night's fight?"

"Twelve KIA, sir. Five of them in one tank. Which brings up another question: when do we get the Shermans and Pershings we need so badly?"

"Just as quickly as the boat from the States gets here, Miles."

"That can't be soon enough, sir," Jock said. "In the meantime, when my men get on the road, will they at least have heavy artillery support?"

"Doubtful, Miles. There isn't much heavy artillery to go around. Most of it is being pulled back to Taegu. What guns we've got left are very low on ammunition."

"Well, that seals it, sir. I'm going to have to come

out by day, and I'm going to need plenty of air support to do it. Otherwise, it'll be like bringing a knife to a gunfight."

"I already told you the road is clear, Miles. Are you doubting me?"

"Will all due respect, sir, I think I've got a pretty good handle on what I'm up against here. We took a couple of prisoners last night, and they sang like birds to our ROK interrogator. They told him there are at least two KPA divisions between here and Taejon. They couldn't believe how much ground they were able to roll up last night. Their plan was only to take these hills around Chongju, but we gave them a lot more. A hell of a lot more."

Keane replied, "It sounds to me that if the KPA got farther than they expected, they've probably overextended themselves."

"Not likely, sir. Our POWs tell us they've got plenty of Russian trucks at their disposal. Ten miles isn't much of an *overextension.*"

"You're going to believe the fantasies of some little commie gooks over solid aerial intelligence, Miles?"

"After what I saw last night, General, I've got no reason to doubt their fantasies."

Major Tommy Moon didn't think much of the weather forecast over the Tsushima Strait between Japan and South Korea. The heavily laden F-51 Mustang fighter-bombers he'd be leading couldn't afford to fly so much as an extra mile. Having to skirt storms over the strait would eat up precious fuel…

And maybe even get us good and lost. Not one of us has flown over Korea yet.

He took comfort in the fact that the three other pilots in his flight—call sign *Banjo*—were, like him, combat veterans from the last war. Two of them even had considerable hours in F-51s, back in the skies over Europe when they were called P-51s by the Allies and a host of vile names by pilots of the Luftwaffe.

Tommy had racked up his wartime flying hours in the P-47 Thunderbolt— affectionately known as the *jug*—a sturdy, powerful aircraft that excelled at ground attack and wasn't a bad dogfighter in the right hands, either. Every man who ever flew that ship only had one complaint, though:

It's a good thing she can out-dive anything in the air because she sure as hell can't climb worth a damn. The late-model ones are a little better, but still…

At least the F-51 could climb, even ones as old and tired as theirs were. Tommy had never been impressed with them as fighter-bombers, though: the enormous coolant radiator slung beneath the fuselage was far too vulnerable to ground fire during low-altitude attacks. Once that radiator was punctured, the remaining life of the liquid-cooled Merlin engine was reduced to mere minutes. Those minutes had rarely been enough to get a pilot back to friendly lines in Europe, and they certainly would not get him back to Japan—over two hundred miles away—if he was hit over South Korea.

Banjo Flight were all volunteers, pilots who'd answered the call for experienced combat pilots in these early days of this sudden and confounding Korean Conflict. Tommy had been flying the F-84, a straight-winged jet fighter that, if the war still raged, would be posted to Korea as soon as sufficient logistical and maintenance support for turbine-powered aircraft in that country was in place. He'd liked that aircraft from the first time he'd climbed into her cockpit; like the P-47, she was manufactured by Republic Aviation, and even though he'd traded that throbbing radial engine and huge four-bladed propeller of the jug for a shrieking jet powerplant, he could feel that Republic lineage in her rock-solid handling with every movement of the stick.

Transitioning to the F-51 hadn't been quite as uplifting. Tommy didn't understand why his beloved Thunderbolts—now designated F-47s—weren't being sent to Korea despite still being in the USAF inventory. Nobody had any doubt they were the superior ground attack aircraft. But some general had mumbled something about *insufficient spare parts for F-47 combat operations and no money in the budget to buy them.* Ground attack aircraft hadn't been a priority for the brand new USAF in the post-WW2 era. That distinction went to the nuclear bomber force and the fighters to protect it. The F-51s, though well past their prime, had squeaked past the congressional red pen in that latter category.

Tommy's head was still deep in mission planning when the squadron operations officer told him, "Got something hot off the press for you, Major. Once you depart on this mission, don't come back."

That sounded like a bad joke, and Tommy wasn't in the mood for jokes—even good ones—at the moment.

"Hey, I didn't mean that like it sounded, sir," the ops officer said, genuinely contrite. "It's just that your flight plan has gotten changed by Tokyo. You're to terminate this mission at K-9."

"K-9," Tommy said, checking his map. "That's Pusan, right?"

"That's a big *roger*, sir. Ground support for the *'tangs* just showed up there. You'll be welcomed with open arms."

"What about our personal gear? How's that getting there?"

"Just stack it up here in Ops, sir, and we'll *red tag* it right over to you. It might even beat you there."

"That'll be the day," Tommy mumbled.

From a tactical standpoint, the rerouting had just improved the mission greatly. The fuel they would've needed to get back across the strait to Itazuke Air Base could now be burned loitering over the target area. As originally planned, they would've only had enough fuel for seven minutes of time over target. Now they'd have nearly forty minutes.

His big brother Sean had always told him how good it was for the ground-pounders to watch their air support loitering overhead, ready to swoop down and help at a moment's notice.

And for all I know, Tommy thought, *Sean's over there, somewhere. Last I heard he was with KMAG...and knowing him, he's got himself right in the middle of the shit.*

He asked the ops officer, "Nothing else in the order has changed?"

"Negative, sir. Proceed to the Taejon area, where target data will be provided by forward air control ships. Intel's saying there was a big fight around there last night. The area should have targets galore."

$$\star\ \star\ \star$$

At 1000 hours, Jock would assemble his commanders and staff to organize the regiment's pullback. Lieutenant Colonel Eliason, however, was ordered to report to the CP thirty minutes before that meeting.

Jock stopped him as he entered the van, leading him instead to a place where they wouldn't be overheard. Then he asked, "Colonel Eliason, why did you ignore Sergeant Moon's request for mortar fire on those KPA who were assaulting the artillery battery?"

Eliason seemed insulted by the question. "I didn't ignore anything, Colonel," he said to Jock. "I made a *decision* as to what was more important to my unit at the time."

"Define *your unit*, Colonel."

"My battalion, of course, sir."

"I see. And since you received this request by way of a runner, I assume you knew Sergeant Moon had lost radio communications?"

"Yes, I knew that, *sir*, but what does that have to do with anything?" He pronounced *sir* in a way that imparted little, if any, respect.

"It has to do with this, Colonel: you don't have any feel for how a battalion functions within a regiment. You're not an independent unit. In a position like this one we're in right now, what threatens one unit threatens us all. You had two choices—one good, one bad. The good choice was you could have passed that request over your working radio so the various needs for fire could be delegated among the several fire support outfits this regiment possesses. The bad choice was what you chose to do—ignore it. If it hadn't been for the initiative of another NCO—Sergeant Patchett—the artillery battery would have been overrun and, quite possibly, the rest of this regiment along with it."

"You don't know that, sir," Eliason replied. "That's merely conjecture."

"I beg to differ, Colonel. I know it too well—too damn well—because I was *at the battery* during the attack."

If that revelation surprised Eliason, he didn't show it. He replied, "Who's in charge of this regiment, Colonel? You, or some senior sergeants who seem to think they have license to run everything?"

"Let me guess, Pete," Jock said. "You were on MacArthur's staff in Tokyo before you took over this battalion, correct?"

"Yes, I was," Eliason replied with defiant pride.

"I figured. But let me answer your question now, Colonel. *I'm* in charge here, so I'll be the one relieving you of your command as of right now."

Disdainful but distressed, too, Eliason replied, "You can't do that. Not now..."

"I just did, Colonel. Major Harper, your XO, will take command of Second Battalion, effective immediately. You'll remain on regimental staff, performing duties as I see fit, until we get back to Taejon. Then I'm cutting you loose. And one last piece of advice...try listening to your experienced combat leaders, whether they're officers or NCOs. You'll probably live a lot longer if you do. That's something you'll never learn as one of MacArthur's errand boys."

Eliason started to say something, but Jock cut him off with, "You're dismissed, Colonel."

Jock had few delusions about the air-dropping of supplies: *If you end up with fifty percent of the stuff they kick out of the airplanes, you're lucky.*

He'd seen it too often throughout the Southwest Pacific campaigns of the last war. The aircrews meant well; they were brave men who took great risks to deliver the goods. But the dynamics and uncertainties of the process usually ensured a high error rate, with large amounts of the ammunition and supplies the receiving unit needed so desperately being dropped into the enemy's lap instead. Jock's men had done their part of the job, setting out the smoke markers delineating the drop zone.

Now all those flyboys have to do is hit the damn thing.

From his perch atop Hill 127, he was encouraged when he saw the size of the aerial armada headed their way; by quick count, there were at least fifty aircraft, mostly the ubiquitous C-47 *Gooney Birds* making up for their limited load-carrying capability with sheer numbers. The fact that the plane's crew had to kick the individual packages out the loading door one at a time guaranteed a strung-out line of parachuted supplies, even when that crew worked at peak efficiency. Hopefully, your unit's position lay somewhere along that line.

As he watched the first wave of C-47s approach, Jock asked Sean Moon, "Did you ever do much air-dropping in Europe, Sergeant?"

"Not really, sir. Pretty much everything came by truck. If it did come by air, the plane usually landed to unload. I'm guessing you did a lot of it in the jungles, though?"

"More than I care to remember, Sergeant."

Sean noticed them first; at the tail end of the aircraft formation were four much larger aircraft, strange-looking craft with twin booms supporting the tail and a boxy pod for a fuselage. He asked, "Are those things in the back what I think they are, sir?"

"If you think they're C-119 *Flying Boxcars*, you'd be right, Sergeant. I didn't think the Air Force had any of them over here yet. One of those babies can haul something like *eight times* what a Gooney Bird can...almost fifty thousand pounds."

Sean replied. "Swell. Let's hope we actually get some of it."

Jock watched uneasily as the first chutes blossomed from the C-47s. "I wish they were a little lower. Maybe they're skittish since we don't know much about the KPA's anti-aircraft capabilities."

"Good thing the gooks don't have much of an air force," Sean added. "Those crates they fly—that's the same old Russian crap we saw all over eastern Europe. My brother worked with the Reds a little, too. Even flew one of them planes of theirs."

"What'd he think of the Russians?"

"He hated their fucking guts, just like me."

Jock was right: the drop would've been much better if the C-47s had been lower. The south wind was pushing many of the chutes beyond the hills, into the rice paddies where Sean had battled the T-34s the night before.

"Ah, shit," Sean said. "Picking that stuff up looks like a great way to get your ass killed. There's gotta be gooks lying low out there. You want to use suppressive fire around the paddies, sir?"

"Yeah," Jock replied, "just as soon as all these airplanes are clear of the area. Tell the artillery to prep for high-angle fire on a rough azimuth of north-northwest."

The C-47s were done, their load distributed over several thousand square yards from the peaks of Hills 142 and 127, down their north slopes, and across the rice paddies. GIs were already collecting the bounty on the hills; the items dropped into the paddies were too far and too scattered to be collected on foot. They'd need trucks for that job.

As their mighty drones filled the air, the four C-119s lined up for their drop. Higher still than the C-47s had been, the *Boxcars'* loads toppled from their open rear fuselages as a series of net-covered pallets, each freefalling for just a moment until multiple parachutes blossomed to slow its descent. Even with the braking of the chutes, the pallets were on the ground within seconds, their weight obvious as the sparse scrub trees on the hills shattered beneath the impacts. Those landing on the steeper slopes began to tumble downhill; their retaining nets broke apart as they went end-over-end, littering the hillside with crates of ammunition and rations. The dozen or so pallets that landed in the rice paddies sent up geysers of mud as they touched down.

It could've been worse. Jock's assessment: "At least we can see all of it."

Patchett led the detail to collect the supplies from

the paddies: four deuces and twenty GIs. "Don't pay no mind to them artillery rounds," he briefed the detail. "That's suppressive fire—*friendly* suppressive fire—to keep the gooks off our asses while we scoop this stuff up."

"But Sarge," a nervous deuce driver said, "How are we going to know *friendly* from *unfriendly* fire out there? It all looks the same to me."

"It works like this, son," Patchett replied. "If it ain't landing close enough to hurt you, it's friendly. Don't matter none who shot it."

Nerve-racking though the close-in suppressive fire might have been to the men of Patchett's detail, it seemed to be doing the job. Unmolested by the KPA, they'd picked up just over a thousand crates of ammo, rations, and various other items, enough to fill the trucks three times so far. But there was still one truckload to be collected: a pallet and several small canisters that had landed the farthest from the drop zone, nearly a thousand yards from the base of Hill 142.

The suppressive fire had stopped. The sudden silence was as unsettling as the fire itself had been.

"The artillery's at *bingo* rounds," Jock advised over the radio.

Patchett knew that meant one of two things:

They gotta hold on to some rounds for an emergency...

Or they're just flat out of rounds. Either way, I ain't getting no more help from the cannon cockers until they get their share of what came in this drop.

He weighed his options: *Nothing's gonna do the job like them artillery airbursts. It's like a barbed wire fence all around those paddies the gooks can't cut through. The mortars are down to just about nothing, too.*

All we got handy is them quad fifties up on them hills. And they still got enough rounds left.

He glanced into the distance at that last pallet.

From what I can see, there's nothing but long white boxes on that pallet. Gotta be ammo. Maybe more of them three point five rockets Moon's been begging for. Or maybe more one-oh-five rounds.

He was ready to drive out there one last time.

"Ah, come on, Sarge," a deuce driver complained. "We don't want to go out that far. Let's forget it...it's just some more ammo, probably. We picked up plenty already."

Patchett gave him a look that would freeze gasoline. Then he said, "Son, let me tell you something. You can *never*—and I mean fucking *never*—have too much ammo."

They only needed one truck for this last run. As the GIs reluctantly climbed back on board, the walkie-talkie squawked.

The artillery FO atop Hill 142 was on the air, calling Patchett. "Relay from *Montana Six*...abort. Repeat, abort. We've got gooks in the open out there."

Montana Six: Colonel Miles.

Grabbing his binoculars, Patchett could see what the FO described: a group of men—maybe a dozen or more—were climbing onto the pallet, cutting free the netting. Then they started throwing crates off the stack to their comrades on the ground.

"Shit," he mumbled, "those little gook bastards are coming out of the woodwork to steal our stuff."

Then the quad .50s opened up, shooting at the

pallet itself.

On the third burst, there was a bright flash that quickly turned to steady flame.

Within seconds, it looked like every wooden box on that pallet was ablaze, as if someone had started a trash fire at the far end of the paddy.

Casually, Patchett asked, "Any of you men ever seen an ammo dump blow up?"

When the GIs all shook their heads, he said, "You're fixing to."

The first explosion blew so strongly that its rapidly expanding shock wave could be clearly seen rippling across the paddy, launching the KPA soldiers in its path as if shot from cannons.

Patchett's deadpan observation: "Kinda tossing them around like rag dolls, ain't it?"

The explosions continued as the hundreds of large-caliber rounds on the pallet cooked off in rapid sequence, each blast a brilliant orange orb more spectacular than the one before but lasting just an instant. The *boom* of each explosion arrived at the GIs' ears seconds later, a time-delayed soundtrack well out of sync with the visual fireworks.

It lasted a solid minute. It took a few minutes more for all the dust and debris to settle. When it finally did, there was nothing left of the pallet or the KPA soldiers who'd tried to claim it.

"At least we didn't give it away," Patchett told his men. "C'mon, stop gawking. We got plenty more work to do."

Chapter Nine

By 1200 hours, the supplies and ammunition from the airdrop had been distributed to the regiment's three battalions. Lieutenant Colonel Eliason, the relieved commander Jock had put in charge of the process, summarized the results to the assembled commanders and regimental staff:

"We're in good shape now with small arms ammunition, rations, and medical supplies. Still very short on artillery rounds, though...we received only ninety-six HE rounds and twelve WP."

Jock asked, "How are we stocked for fuzes for the HE, Colonel?"

"Seventy-two fuze quick, thirty-six fuze time, sir."

"No VT?"

"Negative, sir."

"Shit," Jock said. "All right, let's hear the rest of it. What about the tanks?"

"We received no rounds for the Chaffees' main guns, sir."

Jock turned to Sean and asked, "How many rounds do the tanks have left, Sergeant?"

"Eight per vehicle, sir."

"How much sustained fire does that give them?"

"About a minute and a half, give or take a couple of seconds."

"Let's make sure we don't waste it, Sergeant," Jock said. "While we're talking armor, how are we fixed for anti-tank weapons?"

"We picked up twenty-four of the three point five-inch rockets in the drop, sir," Sean replied. "Plus, they were nice enough to send forty bazooka rounds, for whatever good they'll do."

"Wait a minute," Jock said. "Didn't you say we killed a couple of T-34s with bazookas last night?"

"Yeah, we did, sir…but only because it was dark and we could sneak up right next to them. We won't be lucky enough to get away with that in daylight."

Lieutenant Colonel Lewis, the regimental XO, presented the operations order for the movement to Taejon. He'd only gotten a few sentences into it when Jock stopped him. "That's not what I wanted, Colonel. The infantry will not—repeat, *will not*—be riding on the road in vehicles or on top of the tanks."

Lewis said, "But sir, that's SOP for tactical motor marches."

"We're ripping that one up right now, gentlemen, because the KPA *knows* that's the US Army's SOP. They'd like nothing better than to ambush some more trucks overcrowded with GIs. And I'm sure Sergeant Moon would be glad to fill us in on why it's a bad idea to be riding on the tanks."

"Sure thing, sir," Sean replied. "First off, guys riding on top of the tanks are sitting ducks. If they're all you got for a short trip or hauling out wounded, go ahead and do it. But they ain't buses. For a long road march, forget it. Second, they fuck up the tank's ability to fight. Traverse the turret and you start knocking guys off the deck left and right. If they're lucky, they won't get run over. Last but not least, guys sitting on the aft deck block the cooling airflow to the engine…and all that heat just might set your trousers on fire, too."

An aged and portly lieutenant colonel named Bryant, the C.O. of 1st Battalion, rose to speak. "If I may, sir?" he asked Jock.

"The floor is yours, Colonel. What's on your mind?"

"Well, sir," Bryant began, "I've been in *this man's army* a long, long time and—"

Jock interrupted him. "Colonel, get to the point...or sit down."

"It's just that a foot march could take *hours*, sir, and—"

"Four and a half hours going cross-country, by my estimate," Jock said.

"Are you sure of those times, sir?" Bryant asked. "That seems a little fast to be—"

"Colonel Bryant, I've moved battalions that distance through thick jungle, so I've got a pretty fair idea how fast men can cross difficult terrain. Aside from some mild hill climbing, the terrain we're facing today isn't all that difficult."

"It's just not fair to my men," Bryant continued. "They've just been through a very tough night. They're dog-tired and a cross-country march would be—"

"All right, that's enough," Jock said. "Now listen up, all of you. First off, we're *all* dog-tired, Colonel, but that doesn't mean the KPA is going to cut us any slack. Second, this regiment repulsed a major attack last night because, for once, it didn't make the mistake of sticking to an SOP that was already a proven disaster. And we're not going to start making mistakes like that now."

He moved to the map, which covered the area between their current position and Taejon, ten miles to the south. "Our infantry will move to Taejon not on the highway but along this ridgeline, which runs almost two miles east of the highway. The KPA will most likely be strongest along the west side of the highway, where the high ground is only a few hundred yards distant. If we're forced to engage, and I expect we will be, we've been promised air support. We'll need it. Any questions so far?"

No hands went up.

"Outstanding. Now let's discuss our order of march. Colonel Brand's Third Battalion will lead the foot march." Nodding to Brand, Jock continued, "That puts you, Colonel, in command of the infantry element. Major Harper, your Second Battalion will be next in the line of march. Colonel Bryant, your First Battalion will be last but not least. You'll carry your light mortars and anti-tank teams with you. Your heavy mortar sections will ride in the truck convoy. Master Sergeant Patchett will be my liaison with the infantry element."

Colonel Brand asked, "Where does that put you, sir?"

"Overhead, Colonel," Jock replied. "I'll be keeping one of the spotter planes after it's done flying out our most seriously wounded men. A regiment's supposed to own a few aircraft anyway, so it only seems right. Once airborne, I'll be able to keep tabs on both the infantry going cross-country and motorized columns on the highway while performing scouting duties for both."

Turning to Sean, Jock asked, "I'd like your advice on this, Sergeant Moon. Since we've only got two tanks left, where should they go in the convoy?"

"Put one as the lead vehicle, sir," Sean replied, "and the other in the middle of the convoy. They're going to be the slowest vehicles, so putting one up front will keep everyone together."

"Okay," Jock said. "Sounds like a plan."

"Couple more things, sir?" Sean asked.

"Shoot, Sergeant."

"Request permission to mount the quad fifties on deuces. If we leave 'em as towed loads, it'll take too long to get them into action when we need 'em. Since them trucks won't be carrying any infantry, we can make the room, no sweat. I've scrounged up enough lumber to lift 'em onto the beds and secure 'em."

"Excellent idea, Sergeant. Permission granted. What else?"

Sean replied, "We salvaged enough of those shot-up quads to make one good one, so we got three now."

"Even better, Sergeant," Jock replied. "Got any more good ideas?"

"That's it, sir."

"Okay, then, let's talk about the schedule," Jock said. "For openers, Third Battalion will jump off in one hour."

He paused, expecting groans of protest. One hour was cutting it pretty tight, and he knew it.

But there were no complaints.

Sergeant Patchett smiled as he looked at the faces of the officers. Yesterday, those faces had shown nothing but skepticism. Today, there was only resolve. He told himself, *They all know damn well that if it wasn't for Jock Miles, they probably would've been killed or captured last night, along with most of their men. Now they're ready to follow him to hell and back...*

Just like me.

All the infantry battalions of 26th Regiment were on the move now, heading south toward Taejon. Their column stretched nearly two miles, over eight hundred men tactically dispersed in open terrain that offered little cover and no concealment. Colonel Brand's 3rd Battalion was in the lead, as specified in Jock's ops order; its command group was stocked with backpack radios covering a variety of frequency bands. They'd be able to talk directly with anyone in a five-mile radius except the tankers, whose radios remained incompatible with theirs.

Patchett led the five-man patrol scouting ahead of 3rd Battalion. He was hard-pressed to remember a time when he'd felt more exposed to the enemy: *At least we're on the back side of this ridge, so any gook to the west will have a hell of a time seeing us.*

Then he gazed warily at the mountains to the east, their bases some four miles away according to the map. *But they sure look a hell of a lot closer from where I'm standing. And if there's any KPA up there with even dime store binoculars, they can see every last one of us. It'd be just a question of which direction their artillery's gonna come from.*

But we ain't got no vehicles with us, so we'd be pretty hard to identify from that distance. Who knows? They just might think we're a gook outfit.

They'd traveled another half mile when he spotted a vehicle: an American-made three-quarter-ton truck. Unlike the GIs, the truck's nationality would be highly recognizable, even from several miles away. It was parked in a gully; Patchett could see only the top half of its unmistakable shape until the patrol drew much closer.

With hand signals, he told the patrol *get down on your bellies.* Then he summoned the RTO to him.

He called Colonel Brand and in hushed tones told him, "We've got contact. Hold up until I get a better look."

Brand immediately wanted a detailed situation report.

"Just ignore him for a spell," Patchett told the RTO. "He can find out all about it once it's over."

Then his patrol crawled to the edge of the ridge. From there, they could peer down into the gully with little chance of being seen.

The truck's bumper markings identified it as belonging to a sister regiment, the one that used to be on the right flank of the 26th.

But there was a KPA soldier lounging in the driver's seat, casually smoking a cigarette.

Three more KPA stood alongside the vehicle, laughing and pointing their rifles toward something—or someone—hidden at the bottom of the gully beneath Patchett's field of view.

"We're gonna move a ways over yonder," he whispered, pointing down the ridge. "I got a bad feeling what we're gonna find when we get there."

Peering over the edge of their new vantage point, they could see six GIs on their knees, faces to the gully wall, their hands bound behind their backs with wire.

Only four gooks…we can take them out easy…and make enough noise to attract the whole fucking KPA doing it, too. If there's more of them around, that is.

But those boys will be dead real soon if we don't

do something right quick.

For the moment, though, the KPA soldiers seemed more intent on tormenting their captives. With great delight, they'd teasingly place bayonets across the GIs' throats, going through the motions of cutting without actually piercing flesh. One had taken a pistol—unloaded, apparently—placed it against the head of a trembling prisoner and pulled the trigger. When the falling of the hammer made no more noise than an empty mechanical *clack*, the Koreans would erupt in mocking laughter.

I'm thinking these gooks are just a bunch of AWOL screw-offs having a little fun.

Still, even screw-offs can jerk a trigger. We gotta get our boys out of there.

That was easier said than done. Although Patchett and his men could view what was going on below them in the gully while prone and hidden, they'd have to rise up and expose themselves to fire their weapons. When they did, they'd be in plain view of the Koreans.

I can't guaran-damn-tee we'll get the first—or the best—shot once we expose ourselves.

We need a diversion.

Patchett paused once more to scan the terrain beyond for any sign of other KPA activity.

If there's a big unit out there somewhere, they couldn't hide any better than this regiment of ours. And I ain't seeing, hearing, or smelling nothing.

He unhooked a grenade from his shoulder harness. Then he whispered to his men, "I'm gonna fling this thing way the hell over there. When it blows, it should distract the gooks just long enough for us to pop up and cut them down before they can get off a shot at us or those poor bastards they got tied up down there. Don't *nobody* get jumpy and fire until this pineapple goes off, you hear me?"

He squeezed the grenade's handle, letting the safety pin drop out.

"Y'all ready?"

Laying on his back, Patchett released the grenade's handle, catching it in his free hand so it didn't make a sound bouncing off the ground. He began counting softly, *"One Mississippi..."*

If his GIs weren't jittery already, the live grenade in their sergeant's hand—just inches from their faces—was driving them crazy. Although it was just a fraction of a second, it seemed like a year had passed before he gave it a casual, low-angle toss, sailing it to a place down the ridge where it would threaten no one.

"Two Mississippi...three..."

Then, in what seemed an act of clairvoyant anticipation, he uttered the word *NOW* just as the grenade exploded, the always-disappointing *poom* that sounded more like a large firecracker than a weapon of war.

None of Patchett's men had to fire more than two rounds. The Koreans, who'd all suddenly turned toward the grenade's explosion, were cut down without a chance to return fire.

The shots were still echoing through the gully when Patchett said, "Let's go police up them GIs and high-tail it out of here."

Colonel Brand wasn't impressed by what Patchett

had just done. "You jeopardized this entire regiment to save half a dozen men, Sergeant."

"I don't reckon that *jeopardize* part is true, sir. But you're saying I should've left them for dead?"

"Do I have to remind you that the mission comes first, Sergeant, then the men? And they weren't even our men."

"The way I see it, sir, one don't have nothing to do with the other. Where I come from, we don't leave nobody behind. Feel free to press charges on me, Colonel...if you reckon it won't hurt this mission of ours none, that is."

Brand seethed quietly for a few moments. He knew that short of outright and provable insubordination, dereliction of duty, or murder, Colonel Miles would never consider charges against Sergeant Patchett.

And even if Patchett did commit any of those offenses, an old warhorse like him is crafty enough in the ways of the Army to never get punished for it.

"Speaking of the mission, sir," Patchett said, "shouldn't I be getting back to leading that patrol out in front?"

"Yes, Sergeant, you should," Brand said, conceding this round. "Dismissed."

Patchett took a moment to check on the GIs he'd just rescued. They'd overheard Colonel Brand's comments. One of them spit in disgust on the ground as he said, "That son of a bitch is just like the worthless officers we had. As soon as they heard the gooks were coming, they all piled into jeeps and drove away. Just left us there to die."

Patchett asked, "You think there are any other survivors from your outfit, son?"

"Ain't likely, Sarge," the GI replied, his glare of white-hot anger burning into Brand's back. "If I ever see any of those officers who ran out on us again, I'm going to kill them. Every last damn one of them."

Then he asked, "Sarge, you're an old-timer. I'll bet you know the score. Has it always been like this?"

"You mean about officers, son?"

The GI nodded.

Patchett replied, "Well, every now and then, we gotta skim a little scum off the top. But in this shithole, looks like we got ourselves a whole pot full of scum. Somebody'll come along to dump it out, though. Better be pretty soon, too."

Twenty-Sixth Regiment's convoy was four miles into the ten-mile drive down the highway to Taejon. It had maintained a steady pace of thirty miles per hour, just shy of the Chaffees' top speed. Sean Moon's only worry was at that sustained clip, the two tanks consumed so much fuel that they'd run out short of their destination...

Provided them transmissions don't burn up first.

The way Sean saw it, they'd driven through two choice ambush sites already, where the high ground to the west would've yielded perfect fields of plunging fire down onto the highway. But they'd had no contact with the KPA.

I get the feeling I'm whistling past the graveyard, he told himself. *The gooks gotta be somewhere.*

Jock Miles found that *somewhere* from his spotter plane. Two miles ahead of the convoy, he could see

KPA positions on the ridge to the west of the highway. *These guys don't know much about concealing themselves from aircraft yet. Even in the places they've tried to hide the guns and mortars, I can see tire tracks leading straight to them.*

The pilot asked him, "You think we're getting shot at, sir?"

"No," Jock replied. "That would give them away, for sure. They're hoping we haven't seen them so maybe their ambush isn't ruined."

Air support from a US Navy fighter unit was available, but he chose not to use it. *I'll save the flyboys for a big brawl, when it's worth the wait for them to get here. I believe we've got the firepower to take care of this one ourselves...and right away, too.*

Colonel Lewis, the convoy boss, had been annoyed when Sergeant Moon insisted the lead tank be given a walkie-talkie for communicating with the rest of the units on the road. He'd thought it a waste of critical communications gear. "After all," he'd argued, "I'll be in the vehicle right behind it. I can control the tank with hand signals."

"Them tankers ain't gonna be looking at you behind them, sir," Sean had replied. "They'll be looking out for gooks."

Jock's call for fire set off a flurry of activity within the convoy. "Range is short," he told Lewis, "so use the four-deuce mortars. Slow everyone else down to a crawl so you don't fall into the ambush zone while it's still alive."

Within ninety seconds, the mortar section trucks had pulled off the highway, set up their pieces, and had a round in the air. Nobody expected that first hastily aimed shot to be accurate. But a round right now, one which could yield quick adjustments to the target, was so much more valuable than an accurate one arriving too late.

As the convoy continued moving ahead, leaving the mortars by the roadside, Sean parked one of the deuces carrying a mounted quad .50 among them to provide protection.

That's the second thing Colonel Lewis can thank me for, he told himself. *If it wasn't for that walkie-talkie in the lead Chaffee, she wouldn't know to slow down, and we'd be losing her right about now. And if it wasn't for this quad, these mortar guys could get wiped out by a couple of gooks with Tommy guns.*

That first mortar round landed well behind the KPA emplacements. *The gooks probably didn't even see it,* Jock thought, *but they sure as hell heard it. Let's give them a correction of left one hundred.*

The next round was much closer...

And the fire for effect volley that quickly followed started the KPA soldiers who'd survived it running.

Jock shifted the fire onto the fleeing Koreans, giving them two more volleys.

That's enough, he told himself as the final rounds took their toll. *Time to get this convoy moving at full speed again.*

As the trucks raced through what would've been the ambush site, some KPA troopers on the ridge's front face opened fire on the vehicles with rifles and a few machine guns. They'd let the lead element pass by—the Chaffee, Lewis' jeep, and half a dozen trucks—before they began shooting up the next batch of deuces.

They didn't realize that among those deuces was one mounting a quad .50 until it was too late. As its heavy-caliber bullets riddled the KPA position, the tracers marked it clearly for the Chaffee in the middle of the column. Two rounds from its main gun silenced any further opposition.

Jock radioed to Lewis, "What's the damage?"

"Three wounded, not too badly. The medical section's picked them up already. Two deuces out of action, but nothing on them we can't live without."

"Then keep it moving," Jock replied. "Good job."

The next few miles of highway ahead looked clear, so Jock told his pilot, "Let's slide over and see how our boys on foot are doing."

They were only halfway through the turn when they saw the dust cloud billowing several miles farther east.

Dust means vehicles. Lots of dust means big vehicles—maybe tanks. And they sure as hell won't be ours.

Colonel Brand was calling Jock on the radio now, his strained voice sounding as if he'd just seen a ghost.

"KPA armored column," Brand said, "moving through our column from east to west."

"*Through?*" Jock replied. "Are you in contact?"

"Negative. But we've been split. Third Battalion and some of Second is south of the KPA column. The rest of Second Battalion and all of First is north."

Jock asked, "How many vehicles in this KPA column?"

"Ten T-34s, a couple of light trucks with machine guns."

They're traveling east to west, Jock thought. *That puts them headed straight for the highway...and my convoy. That's all we need—a strong broadside armored attack. I've got to stop them before they get anywhere near the highway.*

This is what I saved the air support for, I guess.

He told Brand, "Stay clear. Do not attempt to engage. Once they've passed, continue your column's move south without delay."

Then he told his pilot, "Get higher and do a one-eighty. I need to see everything."

The Navy flight answered his call for help immediately.

"We're three minutes out," the flight leader replied. "Be advised we're low on fuel and ordnance. It'll be rockets and machine guns, one pass only. Then we've got to get back to the boat. Any special requests?"

"Yeah. Come out of the east. Get the head of the tank column if you can. Be advised friendly infantry is *danger close*."

"Roger, copy the *danger close*. Can you give me smoke rockets where you want the stuff?"

Jock replied, "Negative. Don't have rockets. But you won't need the smoke. They're kicking up so much dust you can't miss them."

"Roger, we might be seeing it already. Are they on that north-south highway?"

"Negative, negative. Friendlies on the highway. Repeat, friendlies on the highway. Target column is presently two miles east of the highway, heading due west."

"Roger, copy that," the Navy pilot said. "Target identified."

As his spotter plane climbed higher—they were at 2,000 feet now—Jock had a grandstand seat for the unfolding battle. He could see his convoy still making good speed; if the GI vehicles didn't get slowed down again and the KPA tanks stayed on the same course—roughly perpendicular to the highway—they'd reach it just *after* the last vehicles had passed.

But if the T-34s shifted their course to the south, they could still engage the trailing elements of the convoy, which included the mess sections, the medical section transporting the wounded, and the artillery battery. The tanks would have to travel cross-country, but the terrain would permit it: the ground appeared dry and fairly level. If the T-34s could move fast enough—and if they had eyes guiding them to their quarry from the high ground to the east or west—intercepting the convoy was possible.

"One minute out," the Navy flight leader reported.

Jock could see the planes now, four dark blue Corsairs streaking across the mottled green backdrop of the mountains to the east as they descended for their attack run. He'd had no trouble identifying the type: the gull wings of these legendary Navy and Marine Corps fighters of the last war made them unmistakable, even from several miles away. They were in their last days as frontline fleet aircraft, already being replaced by the first jets that could operate from carriers. But just like the Air Force's F-51s, the sudden and unexpected need for close-support aircraft had pressed them into the fight one more time.

A stream of tracers rose up toward the spotter

plane; Jock's pilot did a quick turn and dive to dodge them. The bullets hadn't come from the T-34s; as Sean Moon had briefed him, the tanks weren't meant to fight aircraft. They usually had no flexible machine gun on top of the turret and the men inside would be far too busy to man it, anyway. The tracers had come from the wheeled vehicles mixed into the tank column.

"Okay, I get it," Jock said to his pilot. "They're starting to wise up to needing an anti-aircraft capability for their tanks. Let's see if we can keep them occupied. Maybe they won't even see the Navy coming."

"Occupied, sir? As in *draw fire*?"

"Yeah, that's exactly what I mean."

The pilot didn't sound crazy about the idea. He asked, "You ever done much time in one of these flimsy little kites, sir?"

"Plenty," Jock replied. "I did a stint in an L-4 over Papua back in Forty-Two."

"Did you try to draw fire then, too?"

"Only when necessary, Captain."

The Corsairs' attack was over in the blink of an eye. Jock counted eight HVARs fired, those being high-velocity air-to-ground rockets five inches in diameter. Two of them actually scored hits, causing two tanks near the front of the column to brew up spectacularly. The other six rockets only contributed to the dust cloud. Machine gun fire from the trailing Corsair tore up one of the wheeled vehicles, knocking its machine gun out of action.

"That's all we've got," the Navy flight leader reported. "There's an Air Force unit that just got into the area. Dial them up if you need more support. Good luck. *Out*."

Despite the two burning tanks, the attack hadn't slowed down their column at all. Eight T-34s were still bearing down on Jock's convoy.

Damn right I need more support.

He called for the Air Force unit.

Banjo Leader replied, "Roger, *Montana Six*. We're about two minutes out."

Then Tommy Moon—*Banjo Leader*—told his flight, "Gentlemen, welcome to the Korean Police Action."

Chapter Ten

The F-51s of *Banjo Flight* were over the target area at 4,000 feet. There was something in that fast-moving column of T-34s Tommy couldn't identify.

"*Montana Six* from *Banjo Leader*," he radioed to Jock, "what's that other vehicle behind the tanks?"

"It's a truck with a heavy-caliber machine gun."

"Copy. Has he been shooting at you?"

"Affirmative," Jock replied.

"Has he hit anything?"

"Negative."

"Roger, *Montana Six*. Any preference as to how we do this attack?"

"Negative, just so you keep them away from my boys on the highway and you do it real soon."

Mindful of that big coolant radiator hanging beneath the F-51s, Tommy quickly hatched a plan to take the truck with the machine gun out first.

"*Banjo Flight*, listen up," he broadcast. "Orbit over the friendly convoy while I get rid of that flak gun."

He smiled as he thought of what he'd just said: *flak gun.*

That sure dates me as some relic from the last war. Maybe I'm being too cautious here, but I'm really leery about low-level attacks with that radiator hanging under my ass.

That flak gun's got to go. If I come in from behind—out of that dust cloud they're raising—maybe he won't see me until it's too late.

Assuming I'll be able to see him through all that dust, that is.

He flew well to the east before turning back toward
the Korean column. Then he brought his ship down
practically to the deck and pushed her throttle forward.

*Good thing it's pretty flat around here. Altimeter
says 100 feet but I don't have a good baro
setting...could be a little more or a little less.*

It feels like a lot less.

*Just so I don't fly right into the back side of this
column.*

The dust cloud he was racing through was
thickening to where he could hardly see the vehicle in
front of his ship any longer.

Now, he told himself and squeezed the trigger,
letting a burst from her six .50-caliber guns fly.

A split second later, when the dark shapes of
vehicles became blurs slipping rapidly beneath him, he
released the trigger and banked away to the right.

*Don't go left. That's where Montana Six is. Don't
want to mid-air my spotter.*

Tommy clawed for altitude while flying a wide
circle, still unable to see the results of his run. He asked
Jock, "How'd I do? Did I get the truck?"

"Let's put it this way...it's burning and laying on
its side."

It would be a few more seconds until Tommy's
ship had turned enough to view the results of his gun
run. Once he could see it, he was satisfied:

*Well, that part of the job is over. Now let's see how
many of those tanks we can brew up. Sure wish we had
some five-hundred-pounders on the hook, though.*

He was referring to the bombs they would've been
carrying had they not left Japan with drop tanks on the
pylons instead. Those tanks had been emptied thirty

minutes ago and jettisoned into the mountains to become more scrap metal in the detritus of war. Alongside their now-empty pylons, each ship carried six air-to-ground rockets, HVARs just like the Navy Corsairs carried, along with the six .50-caliber machine guns in the wings.

"Banjo Flight from *Banjo Leader,"* he called, "join up on me. Attack in echelon right from their eight o'clock. That'll keep the dust out of our eyes. We'll target the lead tank and the three behind her on this pass. Two HVARs per pass."

Jock broke in, asking, "You're planning on more than one pass?"

"Yeah, why not? They're not going to be shooting at us anymore, right?"

"Looks that way, *Banjo Leader,"* Jock replied and then told himself, *I like working with this guy, whoever he is. He sounds like he really knows his onions.*

Sean Moon's jeep was equipped with an extra radio that covered the fighter control frequencies. He'd been listening with great interest to the aerial attacks on the Korean tanks, knowing every tank they killed was one less that would threaten the convoy.

But there was something about *Banjo Leader's* voice:

If that Brooklyn mouth ain't my brother Tommy, I'll be a son of a bitch.

Suddenly, the convoy began to slow. Within seconds, it had come to a halt. Sean had already pulled his jeep out of its slot near the tail end and raced to the front. When he got there, he saw why they were stopped: the highway was clogged from soft shoulder to soft shoulder with civilian refugees on foot, along with their livestock and wheeled carts, all trying to flee south, away from the KPA.

Banjo Flight's first run stopped two T-34s in their tracks. That left six more, which just kept racing toward the highway. They were less than a thousand yards from it now.

"Time for round two, boys," Tommy told his pilots. "Let's cut the approach tight. We don't have a lot of time."

As the spotter plane reversed direction to keep the attack in view, Jock noticed his convoy was stopped.

The T-34s must have noticed it, too. The tank now in the lead fired its main gun toward the highway.

Sean hadn't wasted much time at the head of the column. Colonel Lewis was standing there, impatient but doing nothing, as the ROK captain who was their interpreter tried to order the refugees to clear the road. He was having no luck.

"Colonel," Sean said, "didn't they ever tell you that a convoy doesn't stop for shit?"

"But...all these people," Lewis mumbled.

"Fuck 'em," Sean replied. "Run 'em over if they don't move. That's one of the reasons this Chaffee is up front. We gotta get going right fucking now or those gook tanks are gonna be on our asses in a minute."

As if to make his point for him, the round fired by the T-34 streaked over their heads, exploding against the ridge a hundred yards away.

"But the Air Force is taking care of those tanks," Lewis protested.

"They're just flyboys, Colonel, not miracle workers. If you want to live on faith, that's swell. But the rest of us gotta get outta here right fucking now. That guy only missed because he fired on the move. If he stops and aims…"

As if he'd just gotten the best idea in the world, Lewis offered, "We can just go around these refugees." Then he signaled the lead Chaffee to do just that.

"Hold up, Colonel," Sean said. "That ain't gonna work. You see how soft that fucking ground is? It's like every drop of water that drains off these hills ends up here. Looks like they built this road through what used to be a rice paddy. All the wheeled vehicles will sink up to their hubs the minute they leave the pavement."

Lewis dithered for another moment and then turned to the ROK captain. But the captain wasn't there; he'd fled into the crowd of refugees, running south as fast as he could. It had only taken one round from a KPA tank to motivate him.

"Ain't that fucking typical?" Sean said. "A couple more steps and he'll lose that uniform he's wearing, too, and blend right into the crowd. So what's it gonna be, Colonel Lewis? We move? Or we die?"

Banjo Flight's second pass netted two more T-34s. That left four still moving. Three were within six hundred yards of the American convoy; they'd turned parallel to the highway, driving south as if intent on getting to the head of the American column. The trailing T-34 had, for some inexplicable reason, stopped and then reversed course back to the direction from which it had come.

It would be nearly a minute before the F-51s were in position for another run. It would be their last one with rockets; each ship had only two remaining.

In that minute, the T-34s could be right on top of the stalled convoy.

The radio traffic had become a chaotic, non-stop stream of critical information. Sean thought he'd distilled it all to its essence: Colonel Miles wanted to integrate the air attack against the T-34s with direct fire from the howitzer battery and the Chaffees. But it would require careful coordination. They couldn't be engaging the KPA tanks at the same time; there was too good a chance of errant artillery fire downing one of the aircraft.

And if an HVAR from an F-51 sailed high over its target, it just might strike the convoy.

But if it was coordinated by someone who had his eyes on everything—like Colonel Miles—there wouldn't be much chance of friendly fire accidents.

Sean could hear it in Colonel Miles' voice: he was losing his patience with the artillery battery commander. They'd yet to fire a shot. Now, as the F-51s swung around for yet another pass, the window for artillery fire was closing.

Though it was still on the move, one of the T-34s fired again.

That round struck the gun mantle of the Chaffee in the middle of the column, knocking her main gun out of action and wounding three of her crew.

Sean slalomed his jeep through the line of stalled vehicles to get to the battery at the rear of the convoy. He didn't have to drive more than halfway down the line to see what the problem was: the battery's deuces had pulled off the road to position the guns for engaging the tanks. That involved making a tight U-turn in the mucky ground.

All six trucks had tried the move simultaneously, but none of them had made it through the U-turns. All six were stuck axle-deep in mud. The howitzers they pulled fared little better. Manhandling the mired howitzers in time to do any good was out of the realm of possibility.

"Forget the howitzers," Sean radioed to Jock. "One Chaffee knocked out, too."

Tommy Moon could imagine what the commanders of those Korean tanks were thinking:

If we stop to shoot accurately, we'll be easy pickings for the Yankee airplanes.

If we get too close to the Yankee convoy, soldiers will climb on our hulls and destroy us with grenades.

Since the T-34s were now running parallel to the convoy, it made aerial attacks on their flanks very difficult. Hitting them from the east ran the risk of launching HVARs or .50-caliber bullets into the GI convoy. Hitting them from the west involved a steep and sudden descent after clearing a ridge. Pulling out of that descent left almost no time to aim; you had little enough time to get a good sight picture even on a flat and stable approach to the target. And if your rounds went short, you hit the convoy.

That left only a head-on or rear approach to the tanks. Either one required another adjustment of *Banjo Flight's* position—and more precious seconds.

Think back to Europe, Tommy. How many tanks did you ever destroy in a head-on attack against their thickest armor?

He could never know the answer for sure. But he knew it was probably close to zero.

But an attack from the rear?

Everything about it, the thinner armor, the easier firing geometry, the lesser likelihood of being seen by your quarry, made an attack from behind the best choice.

"*Banjo Two* from *Leader*, you lead *Three* and *Four* in trail and hit them in the ass. I'll mop up anything you miss. Break on three. One...two...BREAK."

The convoy had started to crawl slowly forward again. That made getting back to its head difficult for Sean, who had to weave the jeep through a chain of vehicles whose spacing rippled like an accordion. When he was adjacent to the deuce mounting the forward-most quad .50, he saw her panicked crew taking aim at the T-34s.

Screaming at the top of his lungs, he tried to get

their attention: "DON'T FIRE. YOU WON'T DO SHIT TO THE TANKS AND YOU'LL SCARE OFF THE AIR FORCE."

The man on the trigger squeezed off a short burst before one of his crew, who'd had to lean over the moving truck's side rail to hear what Sean was saying, finally stopped him.

"*Banjo Leader* from *Banjo Two*, we're still a ways out but I'm seeing tracers bouncing all over the place. I'm fixing to abort."

Sean broke in before his brother or Jock had a chance to key their mike. "*Banjo Flight, Banjo Flight*, this is *Montana Four-Six*. Negative on the tracers. We turned them off. The sky is yours. Let them gooks have it."

Tommy had been in the middle of an orbit, trading space for time before beginning his mop-up attack run. He hadn't seen the tracers from the quad .50s.

But he'd certainly recognized his big brother's voice.

A feeling crept over him that he hadn't felt in five years, when in the skies over Czechoslovakia: *Today, I'm not doing this for anybody but my brother. Not God, not country, not flag, and not Mister Truman.*

It's just for Sean.

Banjo Two's rockets barely missed the lead tank.

The three T-34s plowed forward, turrets traversed right, firing their sporadic, poorly aimed main guns toward the convoy. They'd added rounds from their coaxial machine guns, too, but those were as off target as the main guns.

Then came *Banjo Three*. One of her rockets blew the trailing tank apart. A brilliant shot, it managed to penetrate her aft deck, igniting fuel and ammo simultaneously. The gun camera footage of her spectacular explosion would be one for the newsreels.

Banjo Four made her pass. Her rockets brought the second tank to a halt as she shed both her damaged tracks. Her crew promptly abandoned her and started running east, away from the American convoy.

The only T-34 still functioning pivoted hard left, centered her turret and proceeded to drive east, away from the highway. She slowed just enough for the crewmen of the disabled tank now on foot to clamber onto her deck. Then she accelerated away.

"*Montana Six* from *Banjo Leader*, looks like we've got two rust buckets still on the loose. Which one do you want me to take care of? Only got enough rockets left for one."

Jock replied, "*Banjo Leader*, take that one with the passengers. She's still too close for comfort. Keep an eye on the other one, too, in case she gets too close to my guys on foot."

"Roger," Tommy replied. "*Banjo Two*, you come with me. *Three* and *Four*, go make life miserable for that other runner."

Tommy led his wingman in a tight orbit around the T-34 closest to Jock's convoy. It was fleeing east at great speed; the crew that had bailed out was still clinging to her deck.

"She can run, but she can't hide," Tommy said. "I'm going to shoot her from the rear—try to put one of these rockets right up her ass."

He rolled out of the orbit and began to bear down on the tank.

Then she did something he wasn't expecting: a rapid deceleration.

"Dammit," Tommy said as he overshot his release point without launching his last rockets. "Clever little bastard."

Flying well behind his leader, *Banjo Two* had the best view of what transpired next. "She's stopped dead," he said. "And we've got runners. A bunch of them. Must be the crew on her deck as well as the gooks inside."

"Well, ain't that something?" Tommy said as he pulled his ship around for another look. "Maybe they threw their Russian tactics away and took a page from the old Wehrmacht book. Toward the end, the Krauts would usually ditch their tanks as soon as the jugs showed up."

"Yeah, so I heard," *Banjo Two* replied. "How do you want to handle this?"

"I'll finish her off," Tommy said. "You chase the track stars."

The *other runner*—the T-34 who'd fled the action a few minutes earlier—was having transmission trouble. It was getting harder by the minute for her driver to keep her moving. The only gears in which she could make steady forward progress were the two lower ones, which deafened her crew with the noise of the engine screaming at high rpm and produced a slow crawl of only a few miles per hour.

The crew hadn't dared to open their hatches with the threat of fighter-bombers still overhead. The lack of visibility in that buttoned-up tank accounted, perhaps, for why they'd driven straight into the midst of 26th Regiment's foot soldiers.

Just as they realized the vulnerability of their position—Americans were running in all directions around them; some might be on the hull already—the transmission failed with the piercing *crunch* and *clatter* of metal being fed to a shredder.

The T-34 lurched to a stop.

To the GIs, the fact that she stopped could only mean she was preparing to fire at them.

Instead, the T-34 exploded with a ferocity that knocked them flat. Every hatch blew open with a violence and speed that belied their heavy weight. Nothing but roaring columns of flame and smoke escaped those hatches.

As she lay burning from within, two F-51s streaked low overhead. They hadn't harassed the T-34 with their machine guns, the only weapons they had left. They'd watched her blow up through their gunsights from a thousand yards away, as if they'd simply willed her destruction.

Banjo Three reported back to his leader, "Somebody just blew her up. It sure as hell wasn't us."

It was Patchett who'd led the 3.5-inch rocket crews that blew up that lone T-34. When he'd seen her coming back toward them, he radioed Colonel Brand that he'd engage the tank, but Brand had balked. "A bunch of tanks passed through this column before. One can pass through it again," he'd replied. "Do not engage. Repeat, do not engage."

Patchett ignored him. He'd placed the rocket team with his forward scouting party after the initial parade of T-34s had passed through, cursing himself for not having them with him from the very beginning. When they saw the tank lurching back toward them, grinding her gears as if driven by a raw novice, he'd led them toward her down a narrow draw that offered some small amount of concealment.

As she came closer, they were amazed and thankful her buttoned-up crew hadn't seemed to notice them. They were less than twenty yards away when she'd driven past, and then—inexplicably—stopped.

The kill had been almost too easy.

There was no time to dwell on it, though. The column had to get moving again if it was to make Taejon before nightfall.

When Colonel Brand caught up to Patchett, he was livid. "You disobeyed my order, Sergeant."

"What order would that be, sir?"

"The one in which I told you not to engage. Actually, Sergeant, you disobeyed *two* orders: mine and Colonel Miles', too."

"Hang on a second, sir," Patchett replied. "Colonel Miles said *don't engage*. He didn't say *don't defend*. Were we supposed to let that tank run us over all she damn pleased?"

Before Brand could spit his irate reply, he was interrupted by his RTO. "First Battalion's on the line, sir. They've got a casualty."

"A casualty? From what?"

"From bad luck, apparently, sir. Colonel Bryant's collapsed. Might be a heart attack. The medics got him on a stretcher."

The regiment's convoy was moving again, but its average speed was less than before. It was necessary now and then to slow down and bulldoze off the road the carts and animals of refugees who still hadn't realized the Americans would do just that if they didn't yield.

The artillery battery wasn't with them anymore, either. Its mired deuces and guns were being hauled out of the roadside muck by other trucks using recovery cables. Two F-51s from *Banjo Flight* orbited over the rescue operation, acting as scouts who could turn into protectors at a moment's notice.

The other two aircraft of *Banjo Flight* flew a wide orbit over the convoy and the foot column, providing the same service as their sister ships.

Colonel Bryant was actually having a heart attack. It was Patchett who'd called Jock and advised that the man needed to be flown out or he'd never make it. That lifesaving thought had never occurred to Colonel Brand.

Jock's plane was getting low on fuel, anyway. He directed his pilot to land on a trail near the column, pick up Bryant, and evacuate him to the field hospital at Taejon. Jock would stay with the foot march. After refueling, the plane could return and pick him up again if sufficient daylight for flight operations remained.

As they watched the little plane fly away with the ailing Bryant, Jock asked Patchett, "Give it to me in a nutshell, Patch...how's it going?"

Patchett rolled his eyes. "In a nutshell, sir? Pretty fucking awful. You and me gotta have ourselves one hell of a talk."

The spotter plane returned a little over an hour later, landing near the column as the shadows of late afternoon grew long. The convoy—including the artillery battery—had already reached the division CP at Taejon. The foot column still had about three miles to go—an hour of walking.

Jock elected to stay with his men. He put the artillery FO onto the aircraft to act as airborne observer instead.

Patchett was about to ask him how his leg felt, but then thought against it. Jock was showing no problems with mobility. He seemed to relish the chance to be on the ground among his troops.

Maybe I'll just keep my damn mouth shut, Patchett thought.

There was only one more skirmish with the KPA. Mortar rounds began to rain down on the foot column, sending Jock's troopers scurrying for cover in terrain that had little cover to offer. The FO in the spotter plane couldn't immediately locate their firing position.

"I'd bet my life those tubes are just behind that hill over yonder," Patchett said.

Jock had no reason to doubt his sergeant's

instincts. He called for *Banjo Flight* to strafe the back side of the hill.

They did, and the mortar fire stopped.

There'd been a point in the afternoon when critical radio traffic had died off. Sean took that opportunity to confirm who *Banjo Leader* really was.

"*Banjo Leader* from *Montana Four-Six*," he called, "need a geography check, *over.*"

Tommy smiled; he knew who was doing the asking.

"What's on the northeast corner of Seaview and Remsen?" Sean asked.

"That's easy..the *DeeDee*. DiBennedetti's Deli. I guess you've been to Canarsie, too."

Sean said, "You bet I have. But I thought I told you to stay out of trouble, little brother."

"And I thought I told you the same thing."

Chapter Eleven

There was less than an hour of daylight left when the exhausted infantrymen of 26th Regiment dragged themselves across a bridge over the Kum River. Sean Moon was waiting for them; he'd been tasked by Lieutenant Colonel Lewis with leading the column to their designated sector in the division's defense of Taejon.

"These guys look like death warmed over," Sean said to Patchett, who didn't look tired in the least. "It was only a ten-mile march, for cryin' out loud."

Patchett couldn't agree more. "You should've heard some of the bellyaching about how they hadn't slept much in a couple of weeks. I told them that in the last war, we didn't sleep much for *a couple of years*. These boys got nothing but fat and stupid pulling occupation duty in Japan, that's for damn sure."

Then he added, "We're gonna have to sit on their fool heads all damn night to keep 'em awake so they don't get themselves bayoneted in their sleep."

The Kum River formed a natural barrier to the north, east, and west of Taejon, nestling the city's wooden sprawl in an inverted *U* that spanned forty miles at its widest point. The division would make its stand here, at the river's edge, seeking to maximize the obstacle the deep water would present to the advancing KPA.

Twenty-Sixth Regiment had been assigned the eastern flank of the defensive line, rugged country through which the river cut a meandering path, curving back on itself like a snake preparing to strike. Within those curves were numerous points which could be turned into dangerous salients by a determined attacker or bottlenecks by an equally determined defender.

"You ain't gonna think much of what Colonel Lewis got staked out for us, sir," Sean told Jock and Patchett. "All these things he calls *strongpoints* ain't nothing of the sort. They're all on low ground, right up against the riverbank. The gooks'll punch through 'em like tissue paper once they get across the river. And he's completely ignoring the high ground right behind us. That's where we should be."

Without even seeing the terrain Sean had described, they were inclined to agree. It was Patchett who replied, "I've got a hunch Colonel Lewis had a lot of help from Division thinking up this little gem, right?"

"Can't fool you *infantry types*, can I? But you're right on the money. General Keane gave him a personal tour when we got here. Practically painted lines on the ground for him. Even told him where we should dig the latrines. A real *hands-on* kind of guy. Too bad that ain't his job."

By the time they'd marched to their assigned area, there were only minutes of daylight left. Jock announced, "To hell with the darkness. We've got to get ourselves up into those hills right now. I'm not going to be stuck down on the low ground of that riverbank when the gooks start swimming across."

"I figured you might say that, sir," Sean replied, "so I took the liberty of setting up *guidelines* into the hills so our guys can climb 'em in the dark without killing themselves. Some of it's pretty treacherous even in broad daylight."

Patchett said, "Pretty good idea, coming from a tanker."

Sean ignored him and continued, "Had to do a hell of a lot of haggling with the locals to come up with the rope, but it didn't end up costing much."

"What'd you have to give them for it?" Jock asked.

"Nothing we can't live without, sir—a couple cases of fruit juice and a whole lotta cigarettes."

Jock asked, "What did Colonel Lewis have to say about it, by the way?"

Sean just shrugged and replied, "He pitched a fit, but he didn't try to stop me. Probably figured it was safer to pass the buck to you. Oh, and by the way, sir, General Keane wants to see you ASAP. I'll take you to his CP whenever you're ready."

"Sure," Jock said, "but give us a couple of minutes to get the lay of the land first. Once we've done that, I'll ask you, Sergeant Patchett, to dole out the assignments to the battalion commanders."

"Are you thinking two up and one back in reserve again, sir?" Patchett asked.

"You read my mind, Sergeant."

"That's my job, sir."

General Keane's CP was in the terminal building of the Taejon railroad station. As they pulled up in front, Sean relinquished the wheel, telling Jock, "She's all yours, sir. I've got something I need to check out over at the airfield."

"Won't you need a vehicle for that, Sergeant? It's quite a walk, isn't it?"

"Yeah, it would be, but I'm taking that deuce over there. I need the cargo capacity."

That brought a smile to Jock's face. "Oh? What are you looking to *appropriate* now?"

"Napalm, sir."

"What are we going to do with it?"

"Tank traps, sir. You've heard of *foo-gas*, right?"

Jock looked skeptical. "Yeah, I have. But have you ever used anything like that before?"

"No, but I've watched the engineers do it plenty. It's no big deal. And believe me, sir, the only thing a tanker hates worse than a round breeching his hull is his tank sitting in a pool of fire."

"I'll take your word for it, Sergeant."

Inside the CP, Jock had expected to find a beehive of frantic activity. Instead, he found just a few officers, their faces grim masks of defeat, pacing sullenly in front of large-scale maps hung on a wall. They were struggling to put some order to the hodgepodge of red and black lines sketched in grease pencil on the acetate overlays. A bank of GI radio and switchboard operators lined the wall opposite the maps; morose and beyond frustration, they repeated the same calls over and over again, seeking persons or units that would never reply. When one finally did get a response, he called with great urgency to the officers at the map, as if something thought hopelessly lost had miraculously been found.

Jock summed up the scene before him: *They're not sure where the hell most of their units are. And they don't know where the North Koreans are, either.*

No wonder this whole damn division's got bug-out fever.

General Keane was seated at a desk in a corner of

the room, looking very much the portrait of a man showing a brave face to the certainty of disaster. "Miles," he called out, "glad you're finally here. Are all your men across the river?"

"Yes, sir, they are."

"Good."

Keane summoned one of the officers at the map, telling him, "The Twenty-Sixth is across. Blow the bridges." That began a new flurry of activity for the radio and telephone operators.

The general turned his attention back to Jock, asking, "I assume you agree that our situation here at Taejon is bleak, Colonel?"

"It would seem so, sir," Jock replied. He wanted to say more but didn't. Maybe it showed.

"You hedge, Colonel. What is it you want to say?"

"I realize I'm the new guy here, sir, but a couple of things are painfully obvious. The KPA has us outgunned at the moment. Nobody's disputing that. But we're being routed repeatedly, even though we still have the capability to conduct an orderly delaying action. I think my regiment proved that last night."

Keane blew out a sigh of frustration. "We've already been through this, Miles. Your unit was subject to a much lighter attack than my other two regiments."

"With all due respect, General, I disagree. You saw the battlefield. There were at least two hundred KPA casualties around our position, and that's not counting the ones they were able to drag off. We destroyed nearly a dozen of their tanks, without having any capable tanks of our own. In my book, that indicates we absorbed—and beat back—a major assault."

"That's not the way Tokyo sees it, Miles."

"Then Tokyo better open its eyes, sir."

Keane paused, shuffling through a stack of dispatches on his desk. Finding the one he wanted, he said, "Well, maybe they have, Colonel. Let me share with you what they have in mind so you'll fully understand what we've been ordered to do here at Taejon."

Keane went on to describe MacArthur's plan to create a deep perimeter anchored around the port city of Pusan in the southeast corner of Korea, some 120 miles to the south of Taejon. Through that port—half a day's sail across the strait separating it from Japan—would flow the reinforcements to check the KPA onslaught. Holding that perimeter would prevent the American and ROK forces currently facing the KPA from being pushed into the sea. Ultimately, the perimeter would serve as a base for their counterattack.

"To ensure that the North Koreans don't get to Pusan before our reinforcements," Keane concluded, "we've been ordered to hold the line here at Taejon."

Jock didn't like the sound of that. Not one bit.

"Hold the line, General? For how long?"

"As long as it takes, Colonel Miles."

That sounds suspiciously like "at all costs," Jock told himself. He'd worked for MacArthur too long in the last war not to see the same denials of reality that made the early campaigns in Papua a living hell—and often a death sentence—for those serving under him. It was happening all over again here in Korea: the refusal to recognize an enemy's capabilities, especially if that enemy was Asian and thereby inferior in the minds of MacArthur and his sycophants; the careless throwing of his own poorly prepared troops into battle; the tactical plans based on political fantasies rather than situations on the ground; the refusal to take responsibility for the defeats that inevitably resulted.

Jock said, "I was in the fight for Buna, sir, back in the last war. It was a MacArthur fuckup just like his operation here in Korea. I still remember what he told the general in command: *Take Buna or don't come back alive.* Nobody doubted he meant it literally, either. So my question is this, sir: Are we being asked to make a *last stand* here at Taejon? Because if we try to hang on to this city to the last man, that man will be dead in less than a week and Pusan will be in the hands of the KPA before any reinforcements can step off the boat."

Keane was obviously rattled by the question. Jock thought he knew why: *It's not that I had the temerity to speak my mind. It's that General Keane never realized what the message between the lines of MacArthur's order was...*

Until just now.

But the general regained his composure quickly. "I've read your file, Colonel. I know how experienced you are. So I ask you, how do you propose we prevent a collapse like you describe from happening?"

"I think we need to employ mobile blocking forces, sir," Jock replied, "that can ward off attacks from any direction. The KPA has proved adept at getting behind our static positions time and time again. If each regiment uses its mobile reserve like I did with mine back at Chongju, we have flexibility to counter KPA breakthroughs, meeting force with force, and cover our own ass at the same time. We'll give ground for sure, but we'll do it at a more measured pace, one over which we have at least some control, and give Tokyo the weeks they need to build up Pusan."

"But mobility requires good radio communications," Keane replied, "and our commo capabilities are getting worse by the hour."

"Maybe so, sir, but if we keep the majority of the working sets with the mobile reserves and emphasize landline commo for the dug-in positions, we've got a chance to stay in touch with all our units across the board. Your RTOs and switchboard people won't waste so much time trying to contact units that have been knocked off the air or haven't been wired in yet."

"I see your point, Colonel," Keane said. "It's worth a try. But there's a few more things we need to talk about." Then the general lowered his voice, leaned in close, and asked, "This Colonel Eliason you've cut loose. As short of officers as you are, is that really what you want to do?"

"Affirmative, sir. He's not cut out to command a fighting battalion."

"Well, I'm assigning him to a staff slot in another regiment."

"I wish them all the luck in the world, sir."

"What about your Colonel Bryant? Heart attack, was it?"

"Yes, sir. He never should've been here in the first place. Wasn't fit enough."

There was a challenge in Keane's voice as he asked, "What about you, Colonel? That leg of yours?"

"My leg's fine, sir."

"All right, then…I'm counting on that to be true. Now one more thing…we've picked up some replacement troops. My adjutant has already assigned a contingent to your Colonel Lewis."

"Replacements, sir? Where'd they come from?"

"They come from Korea, Colonel. They're *KATUSA*."

Jock knew what KATUSA meant: *Korean Augmentation to the United States Army*. A few might be ROKs from a disintegrated unit, but most were untrained draftees. Supposedly, they all spoke enough English to be integrated into an American outfit. Without training, though, their immediate usefulness to that unit was about nil.

Even with training, Jock envisioned a host of problems absorbing them into American units, problems MacArthur refused to consider, no doubt, when he hatched this scheme.

Sensing Jock's resistance to the idea, Keane said, "They're warm bodies, Colonel, and right now, beggars can't be choosers. Any more questions?"

When Jock shook his head, Keane added, "Then I've got another one for you, Jock Miles. How do you rate the North Koreans as soldiers?"

"I rate them highly, sir. They're tough and highly disciplined. The Soviets taught them well, and so many of them have combat experience with the Japanese Army in the last war as well as the Red Chinese in their war against the Nationalists."

"General MacArthur would disagree with your assessment, Miles."

"I'm not surprised, sir. But with all due respect, our main problem is we're being led by a man who's never set foot on the Asian mainland yet considers himself the leading authority on all things Asian."

Jock paused, expecting a rebuke.

But he didn't get one, so he continued, "Getting

back to the KPA, sir, from what I can see, they have all the same command and control problems as the Russians."

"What do you mean, Colonel?"

"Their coordination in the attack looks pretty poor, sir. If the battle doesn't go exactly according to plan for them, cohesion between units falls apart quickly, as if subordinate commanders can't—or won't—take the initiative. Once we've got those units fighting individually, without mutual support, they can be defeated piecemeal...provided our troops don't give them a break by running away."

"Are you saying our men are cowards, Miles?"

"No, sir. I'm saying they lack combat discipline. It's never been trained into those GIs who joined postwar. Occupation duty in Japan was more a bunch of guys in green on a sightseeing tour than an army maintaining its readiness."

He paused, wondering if he'd gone too far; if occupation duty in Japan was a sightseeing tour, that would make General Keane one of the tour guides. Again, he waited for a rebuke that never came, so he added, "But now that they're stuck in the middle of this fight, they'll develop that discipline pretty damn quick...if we can keep them from bugging out at the mere sight of the enemy, that is."

It took Jock longer than he thought to drive back to his regimental CP. It was pitch black and the route was still new to him. He'd crept along in the jeep, its blackout lights providing just enough light to see a few feet of the dirt road in front of him. He cursed himself for not taking a driver; having to be both driver and navigator was forcing him to stop frequently so he could check the map. The process was eating up too much time.

And I haven't seen the first guidepost along the road pointing to the CP. Surely Patchett would've made sure they were set out properly. Nobody will find anything in a new position in the dark without them.

Have I not driven far enough yet?

Or did I miss the turn already?

After he'd driven another hundred yards or so, he was convinced he'd missed it. He was about to reverse direction when, just ahead, he saw the outline of something moving on the road, something big and boxy, visible only because its edges were just slightly darker than the envelope of night.

It's a truck...completely blacked out...moving real slow toward me.

Is it one of mine?

Is it even GI?

Taking the jeep out of low gear and letting it roll, he pulled his carbine from the floorboard and cradled it in his left arm, ready to fire if necessary.

There was a brief flash of red light just ahead of his jeep.

A flashlight...

And then the legs of two men walked through the tiny pool of illumination cast on the ground by the jeep's blackout headlight.

The red flashlight shone again, casting a momentary, ghoulish glow across the men's faces...

Their Asian faces.

Now the flashlight illuminated the carbine Jock had leveled at them. The men began to yell, "KATUSA! KATUSA!"

For good measure, they raised their hands high.

A much larger man was running toward them now, speaking in unmistakable Brooklynese, "You two numbnutzes better shut the fuck up before I plug you one. That you, Colonel Miles?"

"Yeah, Sergeant Moon, it's me." Then he slumped back in the driver's seat and blew a sigh of relief. "How many KATUSA do you have with you?"

"Six, sir. Been using them to set up those *foo-gas* tank traps I told you about. We're heading over to do the last one now."

"You do realize I nearly shot these guys, right?"

"Yeah," Sean replied. "I'm surprised it ain't happened already, sir. Nobody's too crazy that they're here. For openers, how the hell are we gonna tell them from the bad guys when the shit hits the fan? Whose bright idea was this, anyway? No, let me guess…MacArthur's, right?"

"Yeah, but we'll talk more about it later. I've got a more pressing problem…I think I'm lost. Did I miss the turn to the CP?"

"You sure did, sir, but it ain't your fault. I told Patch I'd put out the signposts on this road, but it took a little longer than I thought to get to it."

In precise English, one of the KATUSA added, "Yes, those barrels of gas are quite hard to move. Very heavy!"

"Did anybody ask you, pal?" Sean said. "You address this man as *sir*, you understand?"

"Yes, Sergeant. And I am so sorry, sir." He started

to salute Jock.

Sean battered his hand down. "Don't you never salute nobody out in the field. That's a good way to get your officers killed. You understand me?"

"Yes, Sergeant."

"Good. Now shut the fuck up when me and the colonel here are talking." Then he told Jock, "Sorry for the interruption, sir."

"No problem, Sergeant. As soon as I check in at the CP, I'll need to see these tank traps of yours."

Jock was glad to find only a few of his staff at the CP, all of them hard at work on the radios and field phones coordinating the defensive preparations of the three battalions. The rest of his staff, he hoped, were equally hard at work with the units in the field. Colonel Lewis gave him the detailed picture of how the regiment was now emplaced exactly how Jock had directed.

When he was done explaining the disposition of each battalion, Lewis said, "Note that there's no artillery unit in our position. All batteries have been brought under *Divarty's* control."

"Yeah, I heard," Jock replied without enthusiasm. "Division did it to make the most efficient use of the little ammo they've got. Consolidation does have one other advantage, too, if the division gets hit from only one direction. We'll be able to really mass fires on them."

"Do you think that's what the KPA will do, sir? Put all its eggs in one basket?"

"Not likely," Jock replied.

As they looked over the tactical map, Jock asked, "Do we really only have this one bridge across the Kum in our sector?"

"That's correct, sir," Lewis replied. "But according to Sergeant Moon's recon, the river's fordable by tanks at the southern end of our sector."

Jock zeroed in on the map's representation of that sector. The bank on the regiment's side of the river looked like a series of tight ravines. Drawn near each of them was a symbol he'd never seen before: a flaming arrow.

He asked Lewis, "These arrow symbols...they're the *foo-gas* tank traps?"

"Affirmative, sir."

"Can't wait to see them." Then Jock turned his attention to the other end of their sector, where the one bridge across the Kum lay, and asked, "Any evidence that this bridge blew up tonight?"

Lewis seemed surprised by the question. "No, sir. Was it supposed to?"

"General Keane ordered the blowing of all the bridges when I was up at Division. I think we would have heard if they did, don't you?"

"Affirmative, sir. What are they waiting for?"

Before Jock could offer a reply, the night was shattered by a series of thunderous explosions. But they hadn't come from the direction of the bridge; they'd come from the south, where the horizon had turned a brilliant crimson.

"Tell Division we've got contact," he told Lewis. "And get that damn bridge blown. I'm headed over to that blaze."

Chapter Twelve

Jock took his driver this time, a buck sergeant named Yarbrough. He'd be far more than a chauffeur; Jock would need someone just to help handle the slew of radio traffic on the command net. The transmissions were continuous; the division was getting hit from several directions.

When Jock returned to the jeep after checking a hilltop OP, Yarbrough told him, "Division just told the XO that the bridge in our sector has already been blown."

"What did Colonel Lewis have to say about that?"

"He told them they were full of shit, sir."

"In those words, Sergeant?"

"Pretty close, sir."

"Good," Jock replied. Then he told himself, *Maybe we'll make a fighting XO out of Lewis yet. Actually, we'd better make him a fighting XO. We've got no choice...the talent pool is a little shallow right now.*

The crimson glow in the sky had faded considerably by the time Jock found Sean Moon's makeshift bunker, which was dug into the front face of a hill overlooking the *tank trap* ravines. From there, he could see three T-34s still smoldering. Two blocked one of the narrow ravines completely. The third partially obstructed another ravine, channeling any further tank or vehicle traffic into a single-lane kill zone.

"You nailed them with your *foo-gas* contraptions?" Jock asked Sean.

"Yes, sir. Couldn't see 'em all in the dark, but I

figure there were at least six tanks that forded the river down this way. We set up *foo-gas* barrels in the three ravines in this sector, two per ravine. We smoked that first T-34, and then his buddy did us a favor and tried to drive around her. Smoked her, too. The two of 'em burning blocked the whole damn ravine. When that one over there tried to drive through the next ravine to the right, we torched her ass. Ain't seen any more of them since then...but the night's young."

"I think I understand the generalities, Sergeant, but give me a quick course in how these *foo-gas* things work."

Sean provided a *down-and-dirty* explanation: a sealed barrel of thickened, flammable liquid was dug partially into the ground like a mortar, its top aimed toward the kill zone. Napalm was convenient because it came ready-made in a jelly-like consistency, which ignited easily, burned prodigiously, and stuck to anything. If you didn't have napalm, about twenty pounds of laundry soap could be stirred into a fifty-five-gallon barrel of gasoline. The result was a flammable agent of similar properties.

An explosive charge was placed against the bottom of the barrel. When triggered, it hurled the flammable agent, now ignited, into the kill zone, which could extend as far as thirty yards from the barrel.

"What effect does that have on a tank and the men inside?" Jock asked.

"Like getting hit with a couple dozen Molotov cocktails, sir," Sean replied. "That burning shit sticks to the hull and gets into viewing ports, vents, hatches...anywhere there's an opening. The combustion can suck up all the oxygen, stalling the engine and suffocating the crew. Pretty soon, the ammo's cooking off, too."

"That's what happened to those T-34s?"

"Yes, sir."

"Did any of the crew get out?"

"Maybe. Couldn't tell too well, even with the flames lighting the place up like daytime."

Jock asked, "Any evidence of infantry attacking with the tanks?"

"Yeah, we think so. Once the tanks started cooking, though, they beat it. Ain't seen 'em since."

"What kind of explosive did you use to set the traps off?"

"We were gonna use grenades...they work okay in a pinch. But then I was able to bum some C-3 off the engineers. Didn't look like they had any plans for it."

"I see," Jock said. "How much napalm do we have left, Sergeant?"

"Well, sir, there are still three more barrels set up and ready to blow in the traps. I've got another four barrels in the deuce. But the airfield here at Taejon should be pretty cleaned out by now. The fighters they had flying out of there got pulled back to somewhere in a big hurry, so they had to leave a lot of shit behind. We split eighty cases of their fifty caliber with some scroungers from one of the other regiments, so the quads should be well-stocked for a little while, anyway." He pointed to the shadowy outline of one quad fifty on the crest of the rise, covering all three ravines below.

Jock asked, "You set those traps up just using the KATUSA?"

"Not exactly. Had a couple of GIs helping out, too.

But those KATUSA will dig all night for a pack of cigarettes. They're good laborers, I guess....but as soldiers?" His *thumbs down* gesture expressed his assessment of their military abilities.

"Good to know, Sergeant. Now tell me where our mortars are."

"Right behind these hills, sir. This is Third Battalion's sector, so we've got all their tubes. They're gonna be busy, too, because just between you and me, sir, I ain't expecting a whole lot out of the artillery. I wouldn't be surprised if the whole damn *Divarty* bugs out on us. They were looking pretty antsy when I passed them back by the airfield."

Satisfied that all three of the regiment's battalions were positioned as well as the darkness of night allowed, Patchett returned to the CP. Lieutenant Colonel Lewis had a new mission for him the moment he stepped into the van: find out why the bridge across the Kum was still standing.

"I can tell you that right off the top of my head, sir," Patchett said. "Seventeenth Regiment has a big chunk of its Second Battalion missing. Don't know whether they're captured or they bugged out. Most of the division engineers got farmed out to be infantry replacements for them. So if you're looking for someone to blow that bridge, sir, we're gonna have to do it our own damn selves."

Lewis pounced on that suggestion. "So I take it you're volunteering for that task, Sergeant?"

Patchett made a face like he was sucking lemons.

"I've been in *this man's army* more than long enough to know never to volunteer for nothing, Colonel. But I'm assuming you're giving me a *die-rect* order?"

"You assume correctly, Sergeant."

"Very well, sir."

Patchett had formulated a plan by the time he walked the few steps from the van to his jeep. He knew 2nd Battalion had scrounged up the hardware to mount one of its 75-millimeter recoilless rifles on a jeep. It could be easily driven to the riverbank, where it could shoot out a section of the arch bridge. The 75s might not have been successful against the frontal armor of T-34s, but they could certainly tear apart a bridge's stone and concrete structure.

The recoilless rifle gunners were less than enthusiastic about being ordered so close to the North Koreans just across the river. The crew chief whined, "Why can't the artillery do it, Sarge?"

"We ain't got artillery rounds to waste trying to land one square on some li'l ol' bridge," Patchett replied. "Saddle up, son. For once, we've got ourselves a job that's perfect for that lame weapon of yours."

One thing Patchett was sure of: as soon as they fired, they'd have to move to a different location—and quickly—because the muzzle flash would spoil the secret of their location. No doubt, KPA mortar and machine gun fire would rain down on them if they were foolish enough to stay put. He knew of three good firing positions for the recoilless rifle on the high ground near the riverbank. He told himself, *If we can't*

*knock the bottom out of that bridge with three shots,
we'd better start running and never stop.*

At the first firing position, the gunner asked,
"Where do you want me to hit that thing, Sarge?"

Patchett replied, "You see that center arch? Shoot
the keystone right out of the top of it."

"What do you figure the range is?"

"Just a pinch over four hundred yards, son."

"And the second we fire, we're hauling ass to the
next firing point, right?"

"Damn straight," Patchett replied.

The driver of the jeep with the mounted 75
millimeter already had the vehicle in gear, with the
clutch pedal to the floor.

"Whoa, son...let's not jump the gun," Patchett told
him. "Put her in neutral and let out the clutch. You'll
have a second or two to get yourself clear. Don't you
dare mess up his shot and start moving before you feel
that *whoosh*."

Then he told the gunner, "I'll be waiting for y'all at
the next position. Fire when ready, boys."

Patchett's jeep was halfway to that next position
when he felt the *whoosh* of the recoilless rifle's shot.
He was driving as fast as he dared in the darkness,
which wasn't very fast at all.

*Don't need to be in no hurry and drive myself right
off this damn cliff.*

But he was startled when he arrived at the next
firing position with the gun jeep right on his back
bumper. They'd wasted no time evacuating that first
position.

It took another five seconds before a KPA machine
gun began to riddle where they'd just been.

"See?" Patchett said, "Like I said, no need to rush. Now let's see what y'all did."

As the dust and debris settled, the center span of the bridge appeared still intact, standing defiantly in the moonlight reflected off the water beneath.

The gunner protested, "But I hit it dead on where you told me, Sarge!"

"I'm sure you did, son. Now settle yourself down and hit it again in the same damn spot. I'll meet y'all down the road apiece."

Once again, the gunner did exactly what he was told. But as they gazed at the bridge from the third—and last—firing position, its structural integrity seemed to be mocking them.

"What the hell?" the gunner wailed. "I swear I hit it right on the fucking keystone! Twice!"

"Probably did, son," Patchett replied, as the KPA machine gun fire shifted to the last place from which the 75 had shot. "Now do it one more time and then meet me just over the top of that next rise."

They didn't get a chance to shoot again. A T-34 had ventured onto the bridge, the first in what seemed a long column of tanks. When she got to the center arch, the structure seemed to hold for a few seconds. But suddenly, it began crumbling beneath her. The tank teetered as if on a seesaw for an agonizing moment, and then the roadbed gave way completely. Her bow rapidly pivoted downward and she joined the cascade of falling stone, plummeting headfirst into the roiling water below.

The center arch was now a gaping chasm. A second T-34 had rolled a short way onto the bridge. She stopped and then was quickly thrown into reverse, pulling back to the far bank.

"I guess I got it after all," the gunner said, sounding more amazed than certain.

"You got it started, that's for damn sure," Patchett replied. "Then a couple dozen tons of gook tank finished it off."

The gunner asked, "Did you know it was going to happen like that, Sarge?"

"Never doubted it for a minute, son. Now let's get you back to your platoon. This ain't near over."

As he drove through the darkness, Patchett laughed as he told himself, *Never doubted it for a minute...* *You're about as full of shit for these gray eyes of yours to turn brown, Melvin Patchett.*

★ ★ ★

There were three other bridges across the Kum above Taejon. Only the bridge leading into 33rd Regiment's sector—the unit holding the center of the division's line—was blown by the engineers. The remaining two, which led into 17th Regiment's sector on the left of the division's line, were essentially intact, despite a last-minute, ineffective attempt to demolish them with artillery fire. It was across these two bridges that the North Korean armor made its breakthrough, pouring across in seemingly endless columns that the GIs' sparse anti-tank weapons couldn't stem. Just after midnight, 17th Regiment collapsed. Its troops were in a headlong, chaotic retreat toward the city of Taejon.

Within minutes, the radio was blaring with reports of KPA armor and infantry swarming behind 33rd Regiment's sector, threatening to encircle both that unit and Jock's 26th Regiment. If the Koreans could succeed in doing that, the division's mission to delay them at Taejon would disintegrate, as would much hope of slowing their rush to Pusan.

"We're being ordered to block the North Koreans from reaching the city," Jock told his staff. "If we can move our reserve battalion into a position to start doing that, we'll have the KPA vanguard wedged between us and Thirty-Third Regiment."

Then he asked Colonel Lewis, "That force that broke through Seventeenth Regiment…what's their estimated strength?"

"Division suspects it's several battalions of infantry," Lewis replied, "with a company or two of tanks. But we all know how wildly wrong those estimates can be in the dark."

"Yeah, they're usually inflated like crazy," Jock said. "But speaking of the dark, moving our men rapidly at night is going to be one hell of a challenge, so let's keep the plan real simple. Major Appling, how long until your vehicles will be ready to roll?"

Appling, who'd succeeded the stricken Colonel Bryant as 1st Battalion commander, replied, "We can be ready in thirty minutes, sir."

Jock shook his head. "Can you make it fifteen, Major?"

The challenge didn't seem to daunt Appling. He replied, "We'll do it if that's what you need, sir."

"I needed it *yesterday*, Major, but fifteen minutes will have to do for now. Let's hope that's not too late. Now go and make it happen."

Jock liked the plan Colonel Lewis devised. It was just what he'd asked for, something *real simple.* Their reserve battalion—Major Appling's 1st Battalion—would take positions on the low hills astride the main highway that ran straight into Taejon. Those positions were closer to the city than Jock would've liked—only two miles north of its outskirts—but by giving up distance to gain some time, he hoped it would give the trucks carrying Appling's battalion the best chance of getting to that high ground before the KPA.

Jock had a special mission for Sean Moon: "Take the napalm you've still got on that deuce to First Battalion's new position on the highway. Put it to the best use you can find."

The *best use* would be one that stopped tanks, but when Sean reached the defensive line 1st Battalion was hastily cobbling together, Major Appling had a different take on how to use the napalm. "The pass through the hills is too broad to use the *foo-gas*, Sergeant," he told Sean. "Those bombs won't be able to throw the flames far enough to block even half its width. But I think my guys have found another place we can use the stuff."

He led Sean to the peak of what appeared to be a broad, smooth slope, steep but much easier to scale on foot than the craggy hills and gullies that flanked it. "If I was a gook infantry leader," Appling said, "and I had to storm these hills, I'd do it right here. It's an easy climb, especially if they can walk mortar or artillery rounds in front of them. This would be the place to penetrate…everywhere else looks like their forces will be canalized and easy to cut down."

"I see what you're getting at, Major," Sean replied. "But you realize we only got four barrels of the stuff left, don't you?"

"Yeah, I do. What's your point, Sergeant?"

"My point is that the napalm's gonna be a one-shot deal, sir. We may torch the first wave coming up the hill, but the fire's not gonna last forever."

"Who says we have to use it all at once, Sergeant? How about we set up two barrels near the base and the other two about halfway up?"

That idea had promise: those who managed to get past the first shower of flames would climb straight into another one. But setting it up was easier said than done. "Getting those two barrels up the hill's gonna be pretty tough, sir," Sean replied. "The slope's too steep for the deuce. We're gonna have to manhandle them into position. Maybe there's a way we could get the deuce on top of this hill and roll them down? That'd be a little easier."

"Doesn't look like it, Sergeant," Appling replied. "It's pretty rugged around here."

"Well, we'll give it a shot, Major. But we'd better set up the bottom two first, just in case we never get the top two where you want 'em."

Jock had given Patchett a special mission, too: "Now that Appling's battalion isn't right behind them anymore, make damn sure Second and Third Battalion are covering their own asses."

"Will do, sir," Patchett replied. "But maybe while I'm doing that, I take a recon patrol through that gap between Major Appling's boys and the rest of us? Might give us a better picture of what the hell we're up against."

"Good idea, Patch. Go ahead and do it, but do me one favor, too."

"What's that, sir?"

"Try to make sure our own guys don't start reporting your patrol as gooks in the gap. This night's going to be confusing enough without throwing in some friendly fire incidents, too."

"Amen to that, sir."

Sean and his team of KATUSA had two napalm barrels emplaced at the bottom of the slope in a matter of minutes. Now they had to run the wires from the detonators to the peak. One of the KATUSA grabbed a reel and started sprinting uphill.

Sean called him back. "Glad to see you're so fucking eager," he told the Korean, "but I'm here to tell you that you'll be shot dead as soon as you get near the top. No offense or nothing, but you don't look or sound even close to *American*. So hand that reel over to Smithers, okay? Let him take it up. He don't look like no Asian."

Then Sean assembled his Koreans and said, "Did you guys ever hear the story about the idiot who rolled some big fucking rock up a hill over and over again because it kept rolling back down on him?"

When he got nothing but blank looks, he said, "Well, after this fucking exercise, my friends, you'll know that story by heart, because you will have lived it."

Undaunted, the six KATUSA began to roll another barrel of napalm down the long wooden planks from the bed of the deuce. This would be the ninth one they'd taken off the truck that night.

It was, however, the first one that toppled from the planks. Every man there was sure the resounding *THUD* the barrel made as it struck the ground was the last sound they'd ever hear before the inferno consumed them.

But seconds passed and there was no flame, just the echo from that impact of metal with earth. The Koreans and GIs in attendance could do nothing but stare, open-mouthed, at the barrel as it lay on its side, fixated on the cremation from which they'd apparently been granted a reprieve.

They kept staring as Sean sauntered right up to the barrel and began inspecting it for leaks. Surprisingly, he even rolled the two-hundred-pound barrel a few inches—a one-armed push that seemed effortless—to check the complete circumference of the lid.

"The bastard's leaking a little," he announced, "so don't get none of this shit on you while you're pushing it up that hill. Even if it don't catch fire, it'll eat your skin right off."

Pointing to a large rock, he told the smallest KATUSA, "You...you just volunteered to be the *chock master*. When they gotta stop and change horses, stick that rock under the barrel so it don't roll away on you."

The Herculean task began. Slowly up the hill they went, five Koreans and one GI in two alternating teams, grunting from the extreme effort, rolling that leaking barrel. In its wake, it painted a thin, glistening ribbon of napalm along the slope.

Watching the team begin their ascent, Sean told the deuce's driver, "Move your truck a hundred yards forward."

"How come, Sarge?"

"Because, numbnuts, if that son of a bitching barrel comes rolling back down, it just might hit this fucking vehicle. And we might not be so lucky that it don't blow this time."

"But there's still one more barrel to unload," the driver said.

"So what? You can drive in reverse, can't you? When I give you three blinks of the flashlight, get your ass back here."

Chapter Thirteen

Patchett kept his recon patrol light: four men plus himself, with the heaviest weapon a BAR.

"Remember," he told his GIs, "this is a *recon* patrol. Who's gonna tell me what that means?"

The first GI to raise his hand was a Negro corporal named Potts, who replied, "It means we're just supposed to observe and report. We're not supposed to engage the enemy unless we have no choice."

"Very good, Corporal Potts," Patchett said. "That's exactly right. Any of y'all got a question about what the corporal just explained to you so well?"

When no hands went up, Patchett added, "So I can rest easy that no one's gonna start popping off rounds for no damn good reason and get us all dead, then, right?"

He didn't get any answers. He hadn't expected any.

Then he said, "I've gotta go check in with your battalion commander for a minute. Corporal Potts, you're top dog while I'm gone. Fill that time by doing a final check on every man's equipment before we head out."

As Patchett made his way back several minutes later, he was waylaid by one of the patrol's men, a PFC named Redfield, who asked, "How come you put that nigger *Pott-hole* in charge of us, Sarge? You and me both come from places where that just ain't right."

Locking him in a steely gaze, Patchett replied, "Oh, excuse me, *Private*, but I don't recollect you being the one who decides what's *right* in *this man's army*."

Redfield looked offended, as if Patchett had just

spoken sacrilege. "I never figured you for a nigger lover, Sarge," he said.

"I'm gonna cut you just a little bit of slack, Private, since you don't seem to know shit about nothing. But I'll give you a little *insight* into this sergeant standing here: *love* don't never come into it, because I ain't too fond of none of you whipdicks. Truth be known, I dislike you all, but since I pride myself on being a fair man, I dislike you all exactly the same. You'd better get one thing through your head, though, and damn quick: Uncle Sam put two stripes on that man's sleeve, and that's one more than you got, son. So if Corporal Potts tells you to lick shit, you'd best hop to it. Is that clear?"

Redfield grumbled his acquiescence.

Cocking an ear, Patchett said, "I didn't hear you, son."

"I said yeah, that's clear."

"That's clear, *what*?"

"That's clear, *Sergeant*."

"Outstanding. I think you and me gonna get along just fine, Private Redfield. Now let's knock off the chitchat and get our asses back to work."

Patchett's patrol didn't have to walk very far to find the North Koreans; they could hear the idling tank engines from half a mile away. The GIs crept closer, concealing their approach by duck-walking along a shallow ditch. They stopped when they heard voices shouting in Korean over the rumble of the tanks. A stand of scrawny trees was all that separated them from a massed force of KPA that didn't seem to be moving.

Alone among those trees, two Koreans were engaged in a heated argument. Even though he couldn't see their uniforms or understand a word they were saying, Patchett surmised they were officers.

Corporal Potts had crawled next to Patchett. He whispered, "What do you reckon they're arguing about, Sarge?"

"Don't rightly know. Maybe tactics, maybe a woman. But one thing's for damn sure: when the officers are arguing, it's a real good sign they're fucked up. And that just might be in our favor."

Potts asked, "How many KPA do you think are out there?"

Never taking his eyes off the silhouettes of the arguing men, Patchett replied, "I'm hearing a lot of tanks, so I'm guessing there's more than one company of armor. If that's true, there'll be at least two battalions of infantry, maybe a whole damn regiment. Funny thing, though...they're probably not real sure how many men they've got at the moment, neither. Moving fast in the dark does that to you."

"Maybe that's what they're arguing about," Potts offered.

"Could be."

There was no mistaking the body language now; one of the men was dismissing the other, sending him back toward the sound of the tank engines. But the superior officer didn't follow. Instead, he began to walk in the opposite direction, one that would bring him closer to Patchett and his men.

With a brisk hand signal, Patchett ordered his men to *stay down, don't move.*

Now clear of the trees, the Korean was standing at

the edge of the ditch some ten yards from the nearest GI but oblivious to their presence. He opened his trousers and began to urinate.

He never heard Patchett crawling up behind him.

The mortal wound was administered quickly and silently. As he hitched his pants, he was seized from behind; a hand over his mouth jerked his head back.

Then a bayonet sliced through his throat.

The Korean's strength ebbed as the blood gushed from the severed vessels in his neck. Patchett had little trouble forcing him down into the ditch.

He was dead in less than a minute.

Patchett released his grip and motioned his patrol to come closer. As they did, he could make out the horrified looks on their faces. They'd seen plenty of death in their short time in Korea, but this had been much different. Before, the killing had seemed so impersonal, random slaughter indifferently administered by a faceless adversary at a great distance.

But there was nothing random, indifferent, or impersonal in what Patchett had just done. They'd witnessed every moment of it, death as a cataclysm delivered by hand, not bullets, grenades, or shells.

And for some inexplicable reason, death was far more disturbing served up that way. In their minds, what they'd just witnessed wasn't combat; it was murder, plain and simple, in all its cold, primal fury.

"What are you touch-holes gawking at?" Patchett asked. "Hope y'all were paying attention, because that's how it's done when you gotta keep it quiet. Any old hand will tell you that. Corporal Potts, clean out this man's pockets. Treat any documents you find like they're hundred-dollar bills."

Then he took the handset from the RTO and called for artillery on the KPA units assembled beyond the tree line.

They were emplacing the last barrel of napalm on the slope when the first rounds of GI artillery whistled over their heads. "I hope to hell they know what they're shooting at," Sean said, looking up into the night sky. "They ain't got rounds to waste."

He gathered his team and told them, "Remember the leaking barrel? That son of a bitch left a trail all the way up from the base of this damn hill. We gotta break up that trail. Otherwise, when the bottom barrels blow, it's gonna burn like a fuse to these upper barrels and they'll blow too soon, while the gooks are still dancing around the fire down by the base. All your hard work getting these two up the slope's gonna be for nothing. Take the shovels and get to it, on the double."

Sean headed for the top of the hill. No sooner had his team started breaking up the napalm trail, the KPA attack began. All but two of Sean's men dropped their shovels and began a panicky sprint up the hill. The two who remained were KATUSA.

They continued their task, wielding their shovels with seeming indifference to the bullets flying around them. They didn't hear Sean calling them back; the sound of his voice was lost in the tumult of gunfire.

"I gotta go get those dumbasses, sir," Sean told Major Appling.

"The hell you will, Sergeant," Appling replied. "I'm not trading you for two useless gooks."

The rest of Sean's men—two GIs and four KATUSA—made it safely to the top of the hill just as illum rounds from 1st Battalion's mortars began to light the battlefield. KPA infantrymen were racing toward the base of the hill, firing their rifles and submachine guns as they ran. They didn't bother freezing in their tracks in the harsh glare of the flares, as well-trained soldiers normally would. They were too close now to their objective to worry about their movement giving them away; the GIs already knew they were there.

"Hit the *foo-gas*," Appling ordered.

With a quick twist of a detonator handle, the two barrels at the base of the hill flung their liquid fire across the path of the unsuspecting KPA soldiers, setting about a dozen of them ablaze. The rest—a number far too large to count—came to a halt.

"They don't know whether to shit or go blind," Sean said. "But they ain't running away, so I'm guessing they're figuring out a path through them flames."

The trail of napalm from the leaking barrel ignited at the base of the hill just as Sean thought it would. The two KATUSA had done their work well, though; the stream of fire stopped well short of the higher barrels.

But before they could start their escape up the hill, both men dropped from sight.

"Did they just get hit?" Appling asked.

Sean replied, "Who the hell knows, sir."

"We've got to blow those other two barrels in a couple of seconds," Appling said. "If those KATUSA are still alive, they're going to be right in the shit."

"I know it, sir. Fucking shame either way."

Then Appling said, "We've got this covered here,

Sergeant. I need you to get over to the highway and keep my anti-tank crews straight."

As Sean started to leave, Appling added, "I don't know how you motivated those Korean boys, Sergeant, but what we just saw them do was the greatest act of courage I've seen since I set foot in this shithole."

"Don't pin no medal on me, sir," Sean muttered. "All I did was get the poor bastards killed."

For all the world, he wished that wasn't true. But he knew better.

Sean met up with Jock Miles on one of the peaks overlooking the highway. "How the hell did you get here, sir?" he asked. "There must be a couple thousand gooks between here and the other two battalions now."

"I've been asking myself that same question, Sergeant. All I can say is, it's a damn good thing we made it before the sky got lit up like Christmas with illum rounds. Talk about being a sitting duck. But we've got a problem. A big one. Look over there..."

He was pointing to a tree line on the plateau well *behind* Major Appling's defensive positions along the high ground. "There are four or five T-34s hidden in there. With accompanying infantry."

Sean could see nothing but shadows. He asked, "How the hell did they get there, sir?"

"They drove right down the highway, right through the gap in the ridge. The KPA infantry managed to suppress our anti-tank teams. Our guys were only able to knock out one tank."

Sean could see that tank, partially hidden in

shadow where it had fallen off the roadway. Abandoned, with one track mired in a roadside ditch and its turret askew, it looked forlorn, like a wounded animal trying, yet failing, to hide.

"How bad did the anti-tank boys get hit, sir?"

"Pretty bad, I'm told. Most of the three point five teams got out okay, but we can pretty much kiss off the recoilless rifles. They got shellacked."

From its hide in the trees, a T-34 fired its main gun. The round struck the ridge in empty space about thirty yards from where Jock and Sean were crouched.

"That's the way it's been the last few minutes," Jock said. "One of them pops off a round, then you can hear their engines rev as they move around. Mercifully, though, those rounds haven't done anything but plow up some dirt, so far."

"Why ain't we putting some artillery or mortars on those woods, sir? Clean out that gook infantry, at least."

"We will, Sergeant, just as soon as those tanks present a more immediate threat. Right now, the artillery's working over that big mass of KPA well out in front of us while the mortars are hitting the ones climbing the slope. Speaking of the slopes, how'd the *foo-gas* do?"

"Slowed 'em down, sir. Cooked a bunch of 'em in the process, too..." He paused as another salvo of artillery streaked overhead, and then asked, "But how do we know that artillery's doing any good, sir?"

"Because Patchett's calling it, that's how. He's right on their tail...and he's going to get priority of fire as long as we can afford it. Every gook we hit in their assembly area is one less we'll have to deal with right here."

Sean couldn't argue with that logic. But one thing still puzzled him: "So they got four or five tanks with infantry support a thousand yards away down in those woods, popping off the occasional round at us. That don't sound like them...they usually come at you all hell bent for leather. I'm thinking there's only a few places in those trees where they've got decent fields of fire, and that's fucking them up. In fact, this whole attack of theirs seems a little fucked up, don't it?"

"Yeah, it does, Sergeant. But fucked up or not, they did manage to get behind us. Again."

"Wherever they are, sir, I can put some hurt on those tanks if we can sweep the gook infantry off 'em. Do you know where the three point five teams are now?"

"Yeah, they're just a little bit down this hill."

"If it's okay with you, sir, let me take the three point fives. As soon as Major Appling can see his way clear to cut loose a mortar section or two, he can turn those tubes around so they're firing behind us and—"

"I see where you're going with this, Sergeant, and it's a good plan. But we're still going to wait until I'm sure we're holding off the main element of this attack. We're sitting in a five-layer sandwich here, and each battalion of this dispersed regiment is, at the moment, technically surrounded. So we're going to eliminate the biggest threats first."

"I understand, sir. But I'd better get the rocket boys gathered up, anyway, just in case them tanks decide to come out of those trees. It wouldn't take long for their guns to rip First Battalion's position on these hills to shreds if they massed their fire. Infantry or no infantry, it's our only chance to stop 'em."

"Okay, Sergeant, you've made your point. Assemble yourself a tank-killer team, but leave several tubes to protect the highway pass, just in case more T-34s come out of the woodwork."

"Will do, sir."

Patchett heard them first, the incongruous clatter of small engines overhead. Then he saw them, dark silhouettes creeping across the night sky, visible only because they were backlit by the light of illum rounds reflecting off clouds. He felt as if he'd been propelled back in time; the slow-moving aircraft were biplanes, just like the first aircraft he'd ever seen over the trenches of France in 1918.

Then he remembered that the North Koreans were equipped by the Soviet Union; the biplanes were PO-2s, the same type the Russians had used for night interdiction missions against the Germans in the last war. And now their Korean allies would use these mass-produced anachronisms in the same role against the Americans.

The PO-2s operated only at night. In daylight, the low and slow flyers would be knocked from the sky like clay pigeons. But in the dark, they could sneak up on ground positions, sometimes killing their engines and gliding silently through their bomb run. Then they'd restart those engines and slip away. They couldn't carry much in the way of a bomb load, and the damage they inflicted was often more psychological than physical.

But they wouldn't be dropping any bombs here. They were headed south, toward Major Appling's blocking force.

Patchett interrupted the artillery adjustments he was calling in, switching frequencies momentarily to alert the regiment of the incoming aircraft.

Sergeant Yarbrough was exhausting himself running up and down the hill carrying messages to Colonel Miles on the peak. The commander's jeep—with all its essential radios—was parked far down the backslope, the only place Yarbrough could find in the darkness that seemed to offer some degree of cover for this critical vehicle. If it was knocked out, the loss to the commander's communications capability would be crippling.

As he handed the latest message to Jock—the one that said ground attack aircraft would be overhead very shortly—Yarbrough tried to catch his breath. "Sure would be great if I had a runner, sir," he said, "or at least a field phone link."

Too busy reading the message to look at his driver, Jock replied, "I hear you, Sergeant, but you know as well as I do there aren't enough of either to go around at the moment. You know what would be even greater? If we had a company or two of tanks and a few more artillery batteries."

The last time Yarbrough had run up this hill, the message he'd carried had been from Division. It was basically a warning that 33rd Regiment, the one supposedly in the center of the division line, was crumbling and might be overrun just like 17th Regiment had been.

Jock considered that message a harbinger of disaster:

That would put my regiment in the same position it was last night—an island in the middle of an enemy sea.

Does it even pay to trade lives to hold a few inches of ground around here? You end up withdrawing anyway.

And the artillery reports they're running low on rounds again. If their fire gets cut off, how many KPA will climb out of their holes and come swarming at us?

What the hell kind of half-assed operation are we running here?

It's just like 1942 all over again. MacArthur's underestimating his enemy abilities and overestimating those of his own troops He needs to be taught respect for his adversary all over again.

But the lesson hasn't gotten through that thick skull of his yet. Not even close, I'm afraid.

I'll be lucky if I get half my men out of this fiasco alive.

And now another threat was closing in on them. There was so little time to get out the word of the impending air attack. To keep the warning simple and direct, Jock had Yarbrough broadcast this message: "ALL AIRCRAFT HOSTILE. REPEAT, ALL AIRCRAFT HOSTILE."

Those who actually heard the message scanned the sky futilely. They couldn't see any aircraft, and the odds of hearing them over the noise of the ongoing battle were slim.

If those pilots are smart, they're above the burst height of the illum rounds, Jock told himself. *We'd never see them then.*

That was the trouble; everyone was looking *up.* The PO-2s were approaching from an altitude *below* the peaks on which the GIs were positioned, dodging the falling parachute flares, plainly visible now in their light...

If you were looking *down.*

The first signal the aged biplanes were upon them was when one crashed into the upslope just yards in front of one of Appling's machine gun crews. With a resounding *CRUNCH,* it crumbled like a broken kite against the hillside and immediately burst into flames. Burning gasoline from the wreck flowed downhill in narrow rivulets toward the attacking KPA, who ran through them like they weren't even there. When the fire detonated the four fragmentation bombs the plane carried, the only casualties were North Korean infantrymen.

The rest of the flight barely cleared the top of the hill, continuing southward into the darkness without dropping any bombs.

Sean had a theory on the PO-2's erratic arrival: "I think flying into the flares fucked up their night vision. They probably can't even see this damn hill."

He'd rounded up one 3.5-inch rocket launcher crew when another problem suddenly presented itself: the T-34s had begun to emerge from their hiding place in the woods. In the shadowy area behind the hill, shielded from the light of the illum rounds, they were forming a staggered, well-spaced line from which to batter Major Appling's men.

The 3.5 crew was led by PFC Curran, the man who'd loaded for Sean last night while killing the T-34 in the rice paddy. "You're the honcho now, Curran? What happened to Corporal Dowd?"

Curran shook his head. "He didn't make it, Sarge." He motioned toward some ground sheets rolled up like carpets. They could only be shrouds for dead men.

"Shit," Sean replied. "Too damn bad." Then he asked, "Are you up for a little more tank hunting?"

"That's our job, ain't it?"

Sean had been watching the movement of the T-34s, trying to figure out if they still had infantry covering them or not.

"Too fucking dark down there," he concluded. "I can't see shit, so let's assume the infantry's there."

"How are we going to knock out those tanks if there's infantry all around them, Sarge?"

"Carefully, Curran. Carefully. We're gonna have to move fast and move a lot. Where's your lieutenant? We need to take a thirty cal with us."

He pointed to the ground sheets again. "I don't think the lieutenant made it, either."

"So who the hell's running your platoon, Curran?"

"I'm not real sure, Sarge."

"Oh, that's just fucking swell. How about your company commander? Know where he is?"

"Yeah. Follow me."

The T-34s had been firing round after round at the hilltop for several minutes by the time Sean's team had moved into position behind the tanks. They now had with them the .30-caliber machine gun crew he'd wanted as well as another 3.5-inch rocket team.

They'd actually made good time getting behind the tanks, encountering no KPA as they moved briskly along the highway. Cutting across open ground, they closed the distance to the closest tank. Then they settled into a ditch for an easy rear-end shot.

"The infantry will be *behind* and *between* the tanks," Sean told his team. "No point of them having anybody in front...they'd probably just get run over in the dark. They'll be close to the vehicles but not too close. So after we shoot the first one, we'll cut *in front* of it and hit the next one with a flank shot. Then we'll see how long we can keep going down the line before they catch on...and when they do, we run for the hill as fast as we fucking can. Any questions?"

Curran, his eye against the rocket launcher's sight, had one: "What do you make the range, Sarge?"

"Two-fifty yards."

"Yeah. Me, too."

"Fire when ready, Curran."

He did. The first tank in the line shuddered, and then a red glow appeared at her hatches. Within seconds, those hatches were venting her internal explosions like a volcano.

In the light of her fire, Sean and his team could see men running, too many to be a tank crew. They weren't firing, just trying to get away from the burning T-34.

"Let's move, boys," Sean said. "Stay low and right on my ass."

He figured it would take about half a minute to get to the next firing position, one that would lay bare the right flank of the next tank in line. They were halfway there when a strange sound began to fill the air: a buzzing like angry insects.

Sean looked up to see strange winged shapes sweeping low overhead, like valkyrie seeking out the dead of battle.

Then the area around the T-34s erupted in a series of small explosions that more resembled a mortar barrage than a bombing run by aircraft.

It took a second to digest what had just happened: a flight of PO-2s—maybe the same one that had passed over the hill some ten minutes ago, maybe a different one—had bombed its own troops.

Perhaps the burning tank had acted as a beacon for the pilots…

Or they were just disoriented.

Either way, the fragmentation bombs they'd dropped decimated the KPA infantry around the tanks. The tanks had stopped firing at the hill as if they, too, were trying to sort it all out.

But Sean thought he knew what had happened: the tank commanders, exposed in their open hatches, had also fallen victim to the bombs. Their crews were now leaderless and confused.

His team killed two more tanks before the last two T-34s pivoted hard left to make their escape, spraying machine gun fire wildly into the night.

It was a risky maneuver, which exposed their flanks and rear ends to the 3.5-inch rocketeers.

Both tanks quickly met the same fate as their sisters.

Chapter Fourteen

Jock wasn't surprised in the least when, just before dawn, his regiment was ordered to pull back into the city of Taejon. There was little point in continuing to hold their blocking position; the two other regiments of the division had already fled into the city during the night's fighting, leaving Jock's 26th Regiment with no one covering its left flank and the dubious protection of a ROK division on its right. There'd been no contact with that ROK division. For all anyone knew, it was nothing but a little flag on the general's map table.

Sean Moon summarized everyone's feelings on the tactical situation: "If the ROKs are covering you, you're as good as surrounded."

Patchett's recon patrol of the past night had scored a double success. Not only did the artillery fire they'd directed disrupt the attack of the KPA forces, but the pockets of the North Korean officer he'd killed had yielded a gold mine of intelligence. Around 0400, once the North Korean formations he'd been tracking withdrew back across the Kum River, he'd come directly to the regimental CP with the captured documents.

The ROK interpreters had no doubt that the man Patchett had killed was at least a regimental commander, perhaps even a division commander. That would explain the quality and quantity of the documents he'd carried. Far and away, the most important piece of intel gleaned from those documents were the locations of the KPA forward supply hubs, the places from which all ammunition, fuel, food, and other essential supplies were dispensed. Those locations were in the hands of the Air Force before sunrise.

When Jock arrived at the Taejon railroad station, the division commander was incredibly upbeat. He couldn't imagine why.

"General MacArthur is very pleased with what this division achieved last night," Keane said.

"I don't understand that, sir," Jock replied. "Two of its regiments folded and ran. Our casualty rate is unsustainable. We're practically out of ammunition again. My men are exhausted from two straight nights of combat."

"There you go with that negativity again, Miles. The Seventeenth and Thirty-Third Regiments had a rough go of it last night, but they're regrouping in this city as we speak. Don't confuse a successful *retrograde operation* with a rout."

"Begging your pardon, sir, but I believe I'm being objective, not negative. Call last night's action what you will, but whatever respite we gained is only temporary. Even in the unlikely event that the Air Force wipes every last one of those KPA supply depots off the face of the Earth, they'll build them right back up and continue pushing us back. Sooner rather than later, too."

"That's where you're wrong, Colonel," Keane said. "We've gained critical time. All we've got to do is keep it up a little longer so the Pusan buildup can take effect."

"With all due respect, sir, we've bought ourselves a day, at best. They're prepared for this fight. We're not."

Jock had drifted toward the map table. Something on it didn't look right to him. When he got closer, he saw the problem clearly.

"General, you don't really expect to mount an urban defense in this city, do you? Our troops can't even fight effectively in advantageous terrain, yet you expect them to fight house-to-house? They don't have the combat discipline for chaos like that."

Keane seemed startled by the question. "What choice do we have, Colonel?"

"There's nothing within the city itself worth dying for, sir. For openers, it's a firetrap made entirely of wood. If we take up fixed positions, we can be easily burned out of them. To make it worse, they've got tanks. We don't. Their infantry will be protected behind those tanks while they function as both direct-fire artillery and bulldozers. Our soldiers will be cowering behind tissue paper walls."

"But the main highway and rail line to Pusan run right through it," Keane protested. "We must keep them out of the North Koreans' hands. We can defend them both at the same time if we hold this city."

"It would only take a properly emplaced battalion to block the highway anywhere you choose, sir. Same with the rail line. It doesn't have to be in the city itself. The only other thing critical to us in Taejon right now is the airfield. We need to keep that open as long as we can. That's the only fast, efficient way we're going to get resupplied. Short as we are on everything, if we don't give priority to the airfield, a platoon of Boy Scouts on bicycles could drive us out of here."

General Keane was unmoved. He fiddled with some of the markers on the map and then said, "Our orders are to conduct a delaying action here at Taejon, Colonel, and that's exactly what we're going to do. As far as the airfield you're so worried about, several ROK battalions are already assigned to its defense."

"Then may I make one suggestion, sir?"

"Shoot, Colonel."

"Let's beg the Air Force to fly in every last crate of ammunition they can today, because by tomorrow the airfield will be out of our hands."

"What's the matter, Colonel Miles? Don't you have any faith in our allies?"

"Afraid not, sir. As a matter of fact, the only ROKs I've seen in Taejon are mobbing this railroad station, looking to jump on any train headed south."

As Jock drove through Taejon to his CP in its northern outskirts, the city struck him as a place that had already fallen to the enemy, even though that enemy was still miles away across the Kum River. He hadn't been exaggerating when he'd described to General Keane the ROKs flowing to the railroad station, intent on escaping. Many had shed their weapons and uniforms to disguise themselves as civilians, but the odds were a young man of military age in this country was, in fact, a member of its military.

Then he saw a sight that sickened him: listless American soldiers wandering aimlessly, many without weapons.

Those GIs have to be from outfits in Seventeenth and Thirty-Third Regiments, where unit cohesion broke down completely.

I just hope to hell none of them are mine.

He told Yarbrough to stop the jeep by a group of unarmed GIs gathered on a street corner. Approaching the group, Jock said, "What unit are you men from?"

A lanky PFC replied, "We ain't got no unit, Colonel. Not no more."

"Who's your commanding officer?"

"Ain't got one of them, neither. He beat it out of here days ago."

"I see. Where are your weapons?"

"We lost them," the man replied.

Jock didn't need to reply. The half-smile, half-smirk on his face said it all: *Bullshit. You threw them down when you ran away.*

Sensing the inadequacy of his lie, the PFC tried to expand on it: "In the fighting, you know?"

Then he asked, "You gonna arrest us, Colonel?" He seemed ambivalent to the answer until he added, "A stockade back in Japan sounds like a pretty good deal to us."

"Sorry, but I don't have time for that right now," Jock replied. "But I'll tell you what, men...if you're interested in joining a *real* outfit and getting issued new weapons, report to Twenty-Sixth Regiment CP about a half mile down this street. We'll take care of you."

"Why the hell would we want to do that, sir?"

"Because we don't have enough transport available right now to ship every deserter to the stockade. And you won't last another day around here without a weapon. Think it over."

Then he got back into the jeep and told Yarbrough to drive on.

Jock had only been back at his CP a matter of minutes when a commotion erupted on the street outside. Sean Moon was arguing with a ROK captain leading a squad of military police. Against the wall of a building across the street was a lineup of Korean men. They were all middle-aged or older; that alone seemed to rule out the possibility they were AWOL soldiers hiding in street clothes.

"What the hell's going on here, Sergeant Moon?" Jock asked.

"These civilians showed up a couple minutes ago begging for help, sir," Sean replied. "They say the captain here's got plans to round 'em up and shoot 'em all."

One look at the men's faces confirmed that they had no doubt their lives were in imminent danger.

The ROK captain, who spoke excellent English, said, "They are communist dissidents. Teachers and such." He said *teachers* like it was a dirty word. "Our government has ordered their arrest. This is none of your affair."

"Arrest, *my ass*, sir," Sean said to Jock. "They're gonna kill 'em. The only reason they ain't done it yet is because we're watching. Don't want no witnesses, you know?"

The ROK captain repeated, "This is none of your affair. This is the business of the Republic of Korea. You Americans cannot interfere."

With a hearty laugh, Sean replied, "Now ain't that rich? You clowns didn't mind begging for us to *interfere* when your cousins up north lowered the boom on you. Now, all of a sudden, this is none of our business? I don't know, Colonel, but I never figured I'd be putting my ass on the line for some gook bastards who ain't good for nothing except killing their own people."

A crowd of GIs had gathered. There was no doubt they agreed with Sergeant Moon.

The ROK captain turned to Jock and said, "I demand this insubordinate sergeant be court-martialed at once."

Sean was done talking. He started for the captain, muttering, "Why I oughta wring your fucking neck, you little—"

It was Patchett who blocked his path, saying, "Easy there, *Master Sergeant*. I reckon we should let the brass hats handle this, don't you?"

"Let go of me, Top. This son of a bitch got himself a beating coming."

"Let's not be whooping up on Allied officers quite yet, okay?" Still with a firm grip on Sean, Patchett turned to Jock and asked, "So what's it gonna be, sir?"

Without hesitation, Jock replied, "It's going to be like this. These gentlemen"—he pointed to the terrified *dissidents* lined up along the wall—"will be granted safe haven inside our CP until we receive instructions from higher headquarters how to proceed." Turning to the ROK captain, he added, "Any problem with that?"

"You are making a grave mistake, Colonel," the captain replied.

The crowd of GIs took a menacing step toward the Koreans. One dissuading look from their colonel held them at bay.

"A grave mistake, eh?" Jock said. "We'll see about

that. Now why don't you and your men make yourself scarce?" Turning to the seething GIs behind him, he added, "I think my men will agree that you've worn out your welcome."

Major Tommy Moon's heavily laden F-51 finally broke ground from K-9's runway after a takeoff roll that had seemed to go on far too long. As her landing gear came up and she gathered speed and a modest rate of climb, he thought, *At least she's got herself a name now. And that little bit of extra paint didn't make her too heavy to fly, apparently.*

There'd been no time for fancy artwork, but the simple stencil job had still cost him a bottle of Tennessee sipping whiskey, smuggled over from the PX at Itazuke Air Base on Kyushu. It was worth it; the mechanic who'd become the proud and popular owner of that fine whiskey had done as he'd promised. Tommy's ship now bore the name *Moon's Menace V* on both sides of her fuselage just forward of the cockpit.

The mechanic, whose name was O'Flaherty, had told him, "I couldn't come up with a shamrock stencil on short notice, sir, so the closest I could come to the Irish theme you asked for was the green paint. I mixed in a little yellow with the O.D., so it's sort of Kelly green. I hope you like it."

He did. On every previous flight in this new mount, all he'd had to make her his own was the photo of Sylvie Bergerac tucked in the corner of the instrument panel. Adding the name *Moon's Menace*—the one

Sylvie had thought up back in Germany in the spring of 1945—made his bond with the ship truly complete, as it had with her four predecessors who'd borne the name.

As he trimmed the F-51 for the climb to 8,000 feet, he spoke to Sylvie's picture: *I got myself posted as near to you as I could, Syl. I've got to check the map...just how far is this place Vietnam from here, anyway? And why the hell would the CIA send you there?*

I'll stand on my head to see you. It's been way too long.

Forward airfield K-9 had been as disappointing as he'd expected. A relic of the Japanese occupation, this one-runway accommodation to necessity, nestled between rugged mountains and the sea, was barely adequate to the contemporary needs of the USAF. In its current state, that runway was too short to handle the heavy four-engined transports required to bring in the volume of supplies and equipment needed to resurrect the floundering defense of South Korea. It was also too short for the front-line jet fighter rushed to Korea—the F-80 *Shooting Star*—if that plane was to carry any meaningful ordnance load.

And my regular ship, that ground-loving F-84 named Moon's Menace IV...we can forget about flying her out of here until the engineers make that runway a whole lot longer.

The designation K-9 inspired the inevitable canine nicknames. Tommy had been having a rough time deciding which he preferred: *Dogtown, Dogville, The Dog House, Dog Shit.* No matter which one a man used, though, everyone immediately knew what he meant.

Tommy set a course for Taejon, some 120 miles northwest of K-9; a forty-minute flight. The other three ships of *Banjo Flight* had formed in echelon off the right wingtip of *Moon's Menace V*. Once over the city, they'd rendezvous with FAC aircraft—*forward air controllers*—working out of Taejon's airfield. The FACs would guide them to the targets for today: the KPA supply dumps across the Kum River that were feeding the drive against 24th Division at Taejon.

I know my brother's down there somewhere with the Twenty-Fourth. I talked to him the other day when we took out those KPA tanks for them.

Got to figure out a way to meet up with him.

But thoughts of reunions—with his brother Sean or with Sylvie Bergerac—would have to be set aside for now. This morning's mission involved several flights of F-51s from Korean bases. B-26 attack bombers and F-80s from Japan would follow up later to hit targets the Mustangs couldn't get to or that needed another dose.

Tommy rehashed the pre-flight briefing in his head: *Go for the fuel*, the intel officer had said. *Hopefully, the FACs will be able to figure out whether that fuel is in tanker trucks, barrels, or railroad cars.*

He'd cringed when the briefer said *Hopefully*. That was one of those ominously speculative words around which so many missions failed.

Hopefully the ground-pounders had called in the right target.

Hopefully that target wasn't obscured by smoke, haze, or clouds.

Hopefully a lucky triple-A gunner didn't knock you down before you even got there.

Hopefully you'd hit what you aimed at.

But *going for the fuel* sounded like the smartest idea he'd heard lately. It was the KPA's fast-moving mechanized attack that was chewing up the GIs and ROKs. Taking away their fuel could be a game-changer. At least for a little while.

He could see Taejon now, a wooden city of low brown and gray buildings sprawling across flat terrain ringed by rivers close in and jagged peaks beyond. The railroad tracks running through the city glistened in the mid-morning sun; *Banjo Flight* had followed those tracks from Pusan. The drab highways were harder to make out, only identifiable by the convoys of GI trucks kicking up dust as they made their way to and from Taejon.

"Good morning, *Banjo Leader*," a buoyant voice boomed from Tommy's headphones. "This is *Spectral One-Seven* with you at *angels six* at your ten o'clock. I'll be your host for this morning's fun and games. I'm the bright, shiny T-6 headed your way."

Tommy couldn't spot the FAC at first; the silver plane was lost against the shimmering backdrop of the Kum River. As she drew closer, though—just a few miles separating them—the broad wings of the rugged trainer-*cum*-forward air control ship gleamed with reflected sunlight.

"I'll pass below you as I come around to your heading," the FAC said. "Please be so kind as to orbit right one circuit so you don't leave me in the dust."

Even though the T-6 flew nearly twice as fast as the high-winged, fabric-covered Piper and Stinson ships which usually performed FAC duty, she was still designed to be a trainer of pilots, not a combat aircraft. But her rugged, fighter-like airframe, wide performance envelope, and high reliability made her a natural for spotting duties. When the need for such aircraft suddenly arose, the Air Force hadn't hesitated to fly some over from Japan.

"*Spectral One-Seven*, I've got one question, though," Tommy said. "Don't those low wings block your view of targets when you're down on the deck?"

"No problem," the FAC replied. "If the wings get in the way, you just stand her up on a wingtip for a couple of seconds. You've flown one of these birds, haven't you?"

"Sure," Tommy replied, "but way back in Forty-Three."

"Then you know what I'm talking about."

By the time *Banjo Flight* completed its orbit, *Spectral One-Seven* was well in front of them, flying north of the Kum River. Tommy slowed his ships as they began a descent to 5,000 feet.

"The triple-A will be heavy," the FAC said, "so I suggest you bring it in low. Don't give them too much time to track you. I'll mark what looks like the fuel storage now. When you hit it, we'll know right away if I got it right."

The T-6 rolled hard left and began a rapid descent, picking up speed for her target-marking run.

Tommy told his flight, "Get in trail and start S-turning. I don't want to have to orbit again if we can help it. Might lose the smoke."

Spectral One-Seven was right about the triple-A; anti-aircraft artillery of several calibers began to stream tracers into the air. But the gunners were having trouble tracking the fast-moving FAC plane as she raced by them at only a few hundred feet off the ground.

The T-6 bore down on a bowl-shaped depression framed by hills to the north and south. Her flight path would take her into the bowl from the east and exit to the west. Once down in the bowl, there was no other direction of escape.

Nearly there now, the FAC said, "Bingo! No doubt about it. We've got fuel in barrels and trucks. Tons of it."

Turning a few degrees to the right, he fired two smoke rockets. Then he pulled his ship's nose up sharply so she'd climb away from any explosion the rockets might cause as she streaked for that western exit.

As Tommy viewed it all from behind, the smoke rockets seemed to meander wildly on their brief trip to the target. He knew it was an optical illusion. The rockets were really flying straight as arrows; it was his tail-end view of their swirling exhaust trail, compressed by his distance from it, that gave the illusion of meandering.

There were two tiny flashes of brilliant light as the rockets struck home, and then thick clouds of white marking smoke began to rise from the points of impact.

"It's all yours, *Banjo Leader*," the FAC said. "Put your stuff right on the dot. I'll be out of your way to the south."

Banjo Flight's target run had already begun, with Tommy in the lead. As they raced closer, he could see what the FAC had described. There were big tanker trucks—at least a dozen of them—parked in a field of barrels. The white smoke of the marking rockets had begun to turn a dense black. The ground itself seemed to be on fire around the trucks.

Diesel's leaking out of something and already burning, Tommy told himself. *Let's see if we can finish this job.*

They were traveling faster and lower than the FAC plane had, making them even more difficult targets for the AAA gunners. Ignoring the tracers whizzing above his ship, Tommy put the pip in his gunsight on the target smoke. Satisfied he was close enough, he let two rockets fly and then immediately pulled up to let *Banjo Two* take her shot.

The fuel dump was burning ferociously by the time *Banjo Three* and *Four* added their rockets to the effort. Dense clouds of black smoke were rising high into the sky. The smell of burning diesel permeated the cockpits of the last two ships, as they had no choice but to fly through that smoke.

But once *Banjo Four* passed through that blackness, he knew he had a problem. "My Prestone temp's going off the scale," he told Tommy. "I felt some hits right before I fired. The triple-A must've got me."

The curse of the Mustang had descended on *Banjo Flight* already. As fine an interceptor as she'd been at altitude, the P-51—now F-51—had that critical vulnerability at low level. When Tommy eased *Moon's Menace V* alongside the wounded ship, he could see the thin, clear streams of engine coolant leaking from several punctures in the lower fuselage's radiator fairing.

"Dump your ordnance and head straight for Taejon," Tommy told him. "Keep her throttled back as much as you can. You may get a few more seconds out of the engine that way."

The FAC had one further piece of advice. "If you can't get your gear down, *please* don't belly her in on the runway. It's the only one we've got, and there's no recovery equipment there."

"Any place you suggest?" *Banjo Four* asked.

"Yeah, in the grass on the north side," the FAC said. "The ground's pretty firm there, so that belly scope may not dig in too badly."

Then, his voice expressionless, he added, "And maybe we can use her as part of the barricade."

The pilots of *Banjo Flight* weren't sure if he was trying to be funny or if he was dead serious. But considering the ruthless speed of the KPA onslaught so far, they decided it was probably the latter.

Something else crossed Tommy's mind, too. In the last war, if your flight had a damaged ship limping to an emergency landing, another aircraft would accompany her, providing protection to minimize her chances of being easy prey to enemy fighters. In this war, though, the North Koreans didn't have much of an air force. The little they did have—all prop-driven hand-me-downs from the Soviet Air Force—hadn't made much of a showing, especially as interceptors. Even though MacArthur's headquarters dismissed the idea out of hand, there'd been some fearful speculation among the American pilots of Chinese—or even Russian—jets and pilots joining the fray. That would increase the danger in the air tremendously.

But so far, it hadn't happened. Without airborne opposition, damaged ships limped home on their own.

The FAC made another pass over the target area, now an inferno. "*Banjo Leader*, I believe we're done here," he told Tommy. "Nice work. Let's go beat up some other gas station now."

The Korean civilians taking refuge at 26th Regiment's CP had gone out of their way all morning to make themselves useful. They'd carried supplies, erected barricades, dug fighting holes, and provided a wealth of information about the ins and outs of the city's streets and alleys, information that would come in handy in the urban combat that was sure to occur very soon.

Patchett had been resistant to the idea of allowing them to work. At this point, he didn't trust any Korean. In his eyes, they were all useless incompetents at best, potential saboteurs at worst. But Jock had convinced him of the wisdom and necessity of using their labor. His exhausted GIs needed to catch some sleep whenever they could; there'd been precious little of it since he'd taken command two days ago. With the Korean volunteers pitching in, preparing the headquarters for the inevitable attack could continue apace, even though a little more than half the GIs manning that headquarters were taking their turn to sleep, or at least trying to in the midst of the usual noisy and bustling activity of the CP.

But right before noon, General Keane arrived at Jock's CP. It was no surprise the general would be bearing bad news; right behind his jeep were vehicles transporting that same ROK captain from earlier with his squad of MPs.

"You've gotten my ass in a sling with Tokyo again, Miles," the general said. "MacArthur's HQ has directed that we are not—repeat *not*—to interfere in the political workings of the South Korean government. Any Korean civilians you're harboring are to be turned over to ROK authorities immediately."

As if those words weren't hard enough for Jock and his staff to swallow, the smirk on the ROK captain's face made them furious.

"This is bullshit, sir," Jock said. "These men are working their asses off to help us. They're no more dissidents then you and me. They're just on some government bigwig's shitlist."

Keane shrugged. "It's out of my hands, Colonel, and most definitely out of yours. Those are your orders. Don't let me hear of this again." Then he returned to his jeep and drove off.

Jock was sure he'd never forget the looks of betrayal leveled his way as the Korean *dissidents* were marched out of the CP by the ROK MPs. They weren't even loaded onto the truck waiting to transport them but marched down the street and around a corner.

Within moments, one volley of shots rang out, followed by a sickening silence. A disgusted Patchett broke that silence when he said, "If y'all never heard a firing squad before, I'm here to tell you that you just did."

Chapter Fifteen

It was near midnight, but there'd been no attack on Taejon. Despite the welcome quiet that blessed them this night, the defenders of that city knew that they'd only been granted a temporary reprieve. By all accounts, the day's airstrikes against the KPA supply depots had been successful. But nothing was ever one hundred percent effective, and fuel was portable. Unless USAF strategic bombers could pinpoint and destroy that fuel at its source deep within North Korea—a daunting and dangerous undertaking for the handful of B-29s in the Far East—it would quickly find its way south again.

And when the North Koreans reestablished depots in the vicinity of Taejon, the Americans probably wouldn't be lucky enough to have captured intelligence as to their location again.

In the years he and Patchett had served together, Jock had rarely seen Patchett sleep when their unit was in the field. This tour was proving no different. Having just risen from the one-hour nap he'd allowed himself on a cot in the CP, he found the sergeant at the regimental switchboard, checking in with critical emplacements throughout the regiment.

"Gotta let them know *somebody's* awake and on their ass, sir," he told his groggy commander, who took it for the good-natured ribbing it was intended to be. Then he added, "I've got Sergeant Moon paying surprise visits to the outposts, too. If that big Yankee *sumbitch* doesn't scare them awake, I don't know what will. He should be back real soon."

"It's all quiet, then, Top?"

"Pretty much, sir. Just one little personnel ripple over in Second Battalion. After Major Harper had to shuffle some people around, a few of the good ol' boys weren't too crazy about being teamed up with coloreds."

"What'd Major Harper do about it?"

"Followed your policy, sir. Read his NCOs the riot act. Reminded them that if they wanted to keep their stripes, they'd make damn sure their people were working together."

"Did that do the trick, Top?"

"About as good as anything else is right now, sir."

Patchett poured some coffee into his canteen cup and then settled onto a camp stool. In the harsh shadows of the lantern's light, his weathered face suddenly looked every bit of his fifty years.

"We're gonna lose this round, you know," he said to Jock.

"Looks that way, Top."

The weariness obvious in his voice, Patchett asked, "What the hell happened to this Army of ours, sir? It's like the brass don't remember a damn thing they learned beating the Japs and Krauts."

"You'd sure think that, wouldn't you? But this mess we're in right now is the result of one colossal high-level *snafu* after another, going all the way back to Forty-Five."

"So you're saying it's MacArthur's fault, sir?"

"You bet it is. He was so busy playing *king* in Japan he let the Army around him turn to shit. I was horrified by what I was seeing those months I was with KMAG. The entire Eighth Army became a nice, safe place to pick up some command time and get your ticket punched for promotion. So many of the light colonels and colonels around here are too old, too slow, and too locked in the past to move up in the real world. But in MacArthur's little fantasy kingdom, where all the usual standards got scattered to the winds, they got themselves a second chance."

Jock paused to rub his aching leg. Then he added, "And nobody, and I mean *nobody*, from the top on down, ever thought they'd actually have to fight here. Once again, MacArthur underestimated his Asian enemy."

Raising his canteen cup as if making a toast, Patchett replied, "Amen to that, sir."

But he'd watched Jock minister to his leg.

"How's it doing, that leg of yours?"

"It's okay, Top. Just the usual stiffness."

Patchett wasn't sure he believed him, but he let it go at that.

The sunrise found *Banjo Flight* back at full strength. Captain Pete Sublette, whose *Banjo Four* had been forced down yesterday, was back with them, flying an F-51 whose regular pilot had been stricken with dysentery. Sublette hadn't quite made it to an emergency landing at Taejon Airfield yesterday; the overheating engine seized while still three miles out. After belly-landing in a marsh, he'd slogged the half mile on foot to the airfield's perimeter, barely avoiding being shot by jumpy ROK soldiers defending the place. Hitching a ride on a courier flight back to K-9, he hadn't even missed supper.

Banjo Flight was ten minutes from Taejon when the call for air support spilled from their headphones. The airfield there was under attack.

"Here's the thing, *Banjo Leader*," the FAC radioed. "It's not an armored attack, just infantry, near as I can tell. We're going to have a hell of a time figuring out who's who on the ground."

Tommy knew what he meant. Few things were harder than sorting out the players in a ground combat action from a speeding aircraft. Everyone looks alike from the air. If your targets weren't clearly marked somehow, you were bound to hurt friendly troops.

When they arrived over the airfield, the opposing infantry forces—ROK and KPA—looked like several roughly parallel lines of ants all moving in the same direction, sweeping across the airfield from west to east. The FAC said, "I figure the easternmost group is the ROKs running away. It looks like a safe bet that the westernmost line—maybe a few of the western lines— are the KPA. Everybody in between, who knows?"

Tommy asked, "Any chance of the ROKs identifying themselves with smoke?"

"I've got pretty crummy commo with them," the FAC replied, "but I'll give it a try."

He asked the ROK elements to *pop red smoke*. Within ten seconds, *every* element on the ground had popped red smoke.

"Clever bastards, those KPA," the FAC said. "They're monitoring us, and they've probably captured more of our smoke grenades than we've still got on hand. Switch frequency to *tac six*. I'll try again."

It didn't help. Within seconds of his new request

for yellow smoke, all ground elements, friend and foe alike, complied.

"Your call, *Banjo Leader*," the FAC said. "How do you want to handle this?"

Tommy had been watching the flow of the battle intently. If he was interpreting it correctly, only the ROKs seemed to be using tracers in their machine guns. Those glowing rounds pointed like arrows to the KPA lines.

And those lines are the ones we'll attack.

I just pray this fight hasn't gotten so chaotic that anyone could be anywhere on that battlefield.

"Follow my lead, guys," he told his flight, "and give them the works."

A little over a mile away, in the northwest outskirts of Taejon, Sean Moon watched the F-51s trying to stop the attack on the airfield. He'd been checking on a quad 50 in the regiment's perimeter when the planes arrived, first orbiting, and then the four ships streaming down in column, firing their machine guns and rockets. The last plane to attack had even dropped both its five-hundred-pound bombs into the fray.

One of the gunners commented, "Looks like those *B-2s* are doing some good work over there."

"What do you mean, *B-2s*?" Sean asked. "They're P-51s. Oh, excuse me…we call 'em F-51s in this war."

"We know that, Sarge," the gunner replied. "It's just a joke around here. All the planes overhead have been friendlies, so when we see them, we say, *B-2 bad if they weren't ours.*"

"Okay, I get it," Sean said. But then he pointed out two more aircraft, much higher in the sky. "What do you figure they are? They don't look like no friendly aircraft to me."

None of the gunners could identify those ships. But Sean could; he'd seen them before, when the Russians flew them over Europe.

Big round engine, pointy wings, cockpit way back...they're Lavochkins, LA-7s.

I wonder if it's Russians or gooks in the cockpit?

The FAC had seen the LA-7s high overhead, too. He warned *Banjo Flight* of their presence.

In the middle of another strafing pass, a preoccupied Tommy asked, "Are they coming downstairs?"

"Not yet," the FAC replied. "But they did go into a half-assed orbit. Almost looks like they're trying to set up a Lufbery."

A *Lufbery*: named for the WW1 ace Raoul Lufbery, it was a maneuver in which two or more aircraft flew around the circumference of a circle so each could protect the tail of the plane ahead.

Tommy asked, "Do we have any interceptors in the area?"

"Negative," the FAC replied.

"How about an ETA on the flights coming to help out here?"

"Closest one's at least ten minutes out."

"Do we have any damn word from the ROKs if we're doing them some good here?"

"Not yet," the FAC said. "But from what I can tell playing *flak-bait* down here on the deck, you're hitting the KPA real good, but they're still coming."

Pulling out of the strafing pass, Tommy turned his ship hard left so he could observe the rest of his flight behind him. He could see the LA-7s above, too. They weren't in a Lufbery circle anymore. One ship had rolled over to begin her attack dive.

"Split into pairs," he told his flight. "Ted, you're with me."

Ted: First Lieutenant Ted Waleska, flying *Banjo Two*. He raced to Tommy's right wingtip as they flew east, staying low and building speed.

Banjo Three and *Four* broke in the opposite direction as they came out of their strafing run, completing the *split* Tommy had ordered. Both ships were flown by pilots who'd been in Mustang interceptors during the last war. They knew the aircraft's air-to-air combat capabilities better than Tommy or Waleska. Pete Sublette, flying *Banjo Four*, had three kills in P-51s against the Luftwaffe. Captain Al DeLuca, flying *Banjo Three*, had two.

Tommy told Sublette, "Pete, you and Al take the *Lavs*. Ted and I will keep up the ground attack."

"Roger," Sublette replied. "You sure you don't want one of them for yourself, boss? It'll get you one closer to *ace*."

"Negative. You guys have the experience. Ted and I will stay here and do what we do best."

"Roger," Sublette replied. "And thanks. We appreciate the opportunity."

Banjo Three and *Four* jettisoned the hanging ordnance still beneath their wings. They turned sharply so their flight paths were actually beneath the diving LA-7s and not viewable from their adversaries' cockpits. Then they began a brisk climb to gain height superiority.

"We're going to turn hard inside them," Tommy radioed. "They won't get a bead on us."

"Good plan," Sublette replied. "We'll be joining y'all down there before you know it."

Banjo Three and *Four* had gone *over the top*, reversing their direction of flight with a half loop. Once they rolled upright, it didn't take much of an adjustment to get on the tail of the trailing LA-7.

Tommy and Waleska went in for another strafing pass on the airfield. They no longer needed to elude the LA-7s, who now had big problems right behind them. The trailing ship—bracketed by rounds from Sublette's .50 calibers—dove for the deck. The lead ship broke left.

"These guys fight like Russians," DeLuca said. "At the first hint of trouble, it's every man for himself. Which one do you want, Pete?"

"I'll take the leader."

But the LA-7s had no interest in dogfighting. They opened their throttles wide—probably boosting their engines' parameters well past safe operating limits— and streaked away to the north.

"*Banjo Leader* from *Four*, should we chase?"

"Negative," Tommy replied. "Save whatever rounds you've got left to help out the ROKs."

Jock wasn't surprised when he heard General

Keane's jeep pull up to his CP. There was little doubt what the general had on his mind: the radio traffic had made clear that the fight for the airfield was going poorly. The reason why, though, was not encouraging.

"The ROKs say our planes are attacking *them*," the general said. "They're refusing to stay on the airfield. They claim it's too dangerous. It's a damn shame, too, because, by all accounts, our planes have driven the KPA back across the Kap Ch'on River."

Jock and his staff had watched the fight for the airfield from the roof of the building housing their CP. There'd been no shortage of American airpower. That first group of fighter-bombers had not only made pass after pass against the North Korean ground forces, they'd even chased away some enemy aircraft. After them had come more fighter-bombers—mostly F-51s but some F-80 jets—as well as what must've been a squadron of B-26 attack bombers. It wouldn't be uncommon to have some of that ordnance accidentally land on the heads of the ROKs.

As a result, Jock fully expected his regiment was about to be ordered to fill the gap created by the withdrawing South Koreans.

Patchett asked, "Are we sure that airfield's even worth holding anymore? With all the bombs our flyboys dropped, I wonder if they didn't chew the shit out of that runway. I thought the point was to keep the damn place open for business."

Keane replied, "Not to worry, Sergeant. The FACs report the runway received minimal damage."

Patchett tried not to smirk. He knew that what generals considered *minimal damage* often made the lives of ordinary soldiers a living hell. He remembered back to the last war, when the loss of landing craft during the amphibious assault at Hollandia, New Guinea, had been described as *minimal*. Unfortunately, most of one regiment's artillery had been on those craft that were sunk. The GIs denied that fire support certainly hadn't considered the loss of those guns *minimal*.

He imagined that a *minimal* number of bomb craters, properly placed, could render the entire runway unusable. But Keane was insistent: "The airfield will remain open. And I need you, Colonel Miles, to keep it that way for at least another forty-eight hours."

Then, as if twisting the knife, the general added, "You wanted that airfield, Colonel, and now you're going to have it."

"Fine, sir," Jock replied. "But I'll need an artillery battery attached to my regiment immediately."

"Impossible, Colonel," Keane replied. "You know how short of guns we are. Divarty will continue to prioritize requests for fire. But maybe I can give you something that'll be a big help. Two *Bofors* vehicles are on the road to us right now. They were intended for anti-aircraft defense around Pusan, but quite frankly, they don't see much use for them there at the moment. So they're coming to us."

Jock asked, "Bofors vehicles...you mean M19s, sir?"

"Affirmative, Miles. They'll give you a big boost in firepower."

The vehicle in question—M19 MGMC, for *Multiple Gun Motor Carriage*—was a Chaffee light tank chassis with the turret and its armament replaced by two quick-firing 40-millimeter Bofors anti-aircraft guns. Deployed to Europe late in the last war, M19s hadn't been needed against the crippled Luftwaffe but had proved very effective against soft ground targets. Jock would welcome their addition to his arsenal...

But they weren't tanks and they wouldn't stop an armored assault.

"I'll need your units in position by midday, Colonel," General Keane said. Then he stepped to the map and asked, "Show me how you propose to deploy your forces."

"There's not much choice there, sir," Jock replied. "Our only viable defense is to keep the KPA on the other side of the river. The Kap Ch'on is fordable along almost all of our western flank, and there are two bridges across it in that sector still standing. If they can put a strong force of tanks across, there's not going to be much we can do to stop them, I'm afraid, even with the M19s."

"Just do your best, Miles," General Keane said. "That's all I can ask. Now, are you ready for more good news?"

Jock wasn't sure he could stand any more *good news*. But he replied, "Of course, sir."

First Cav and Twenty-Fifth Division are offloading at Pusan as we speak. A Marine Corps regiment, too. They'll be out here with us in just a few days."

"That's great, sir," Jock replied. "But will they be bringing *real* tanks with them, like Shermans and Pershings? Not just Chaffees?"

"Let's hope so, Colonel. Let's hope so."

"One more thing, sir," Jock said. "Those two bridges over the Kap Ch'on in the airfield sector...do I have your permission to blow them?"

"Our engineer capability is extremely limited, Miles, I don't know how—"

"I don't mean using the engineers, sir. I'm going to have the Air Force do it."

"All right, whatever works, Colonel. Go ahead and blow them up."

As the general drove away, Jock told Patchett, "Get Sergeant Moon to recon some good positions around that airfield for those M19s on the double. We don't need them exposed on all that flat ground. They'll get shot up before they can do us any good."

"Amen to that, sir," Patchett replied. Then, grease pencil in hand, he stepped up to the map and asked, "How do you want to do this, sir?"

"Brand and Harper's battalions up, Appling's battalion back."

"Outstanding, sir," Patchett replied. "I'll get it written up for the S3 right away. Ops order will be out in thirty minutes."

Sean Moon walked into the CP. He seemed amused as he told Jock, "There's about a dozen of the most scraggly assed troops I ever seen standing outside, sir. They say you offered them jobs in this regiment."

Jock smiled; some of those GIs he'd come across in town yesterday—those who'd fled their units—were finally coming around. They'd thought it over and decided they had the best chance of staying alive with the 26th.

"Yes, I did, Sergeant," Jock said. "They're *late* of the Seventeenth and Thirty-Third, I believe."

"Yeah, that's what they told me, sir."

"Good. Let's put them to work. I'm sure Sergeant Patchett has a place for each and every one of them."

Patchett smiled and said, "Damn right I do, sir. And not a moment too soon. But since they ain't rightly ours, when do you want to inform the other regiments we got their stragglers?"

"Don't bother, Top. I already spoke with the other regimental commanders. Their attitude? *Save us the trouble and just shoot those deserters yourself.*"

Patchett let out a whistle, the sound of a bomb falling. Then he said, "I reckon I'll go ahead and list them on our morning report up to Division. Maybe then their mamas won't be getting no telegrams about sons who ain't dead yet."

Banjo Flight had refueled, rearmed, and was back in the air just after 1300 hours. They had their mission in hand before breaking ground: destroy the two bridges over the Kap Ch'on River immediately west of Taejon.

This was one of those times when Tommy really missed flying the P-47. Had he been in one now instead of this F-51, there was no doubt in his mind that his preferred method of attack against a bridge would be dive bombing. But the F-51's gunsight wasn't set up to double as a bombsight, as the P-47's was. Worse, there was no tech support in theater yet to make it so. Bridges were point targets; you needed to be very accurate in your aim if you expected to hit it. Without the help of that multi-role gunsight, you had little chance of a direct hit.

It's pretty ironic, too, Tommy thought, *since the Mustang airframe began life as the A-36 dive bomber. But once they replaced that Allison engine with a*

*Merlin, it became a whole different airplane, a badly
needed high-altitude, long-range interceptor that
wasn't about to be wasted doing ground attack when
the P-47s could do it better, anyway.*

So it's going to be five-inch rockets, Tommy told
himself, *fired from a hell of a lot closer than usual. I'm
not sure why we even bothered to load the bombs.*

Let's hope the triple-A isn't too bad.

Triple-A over the targeted bridges wasn't the big
problem; the dense clouds of smoke wafting across the
Kap Ch'on were. A just-finished airstrike against KPA
positions on the west bank had dropped so much
napalm that smoke from the resulting fires—propelled
by a northwest wind—was largely obscuring the river
and its bridges. The lower the ships of *Banjo Flight*
flew, the worse the visibility would be.

Tommy told his pilots, "Let's stay with the plan
and use the rockets. If you can't see the target well
enough to launch, then don't. Attack out of the north so
the span of the bridge gives the biggest target. Pete, you
and I will take the south bridge. Al, you and Ted take
the north one."

Coming out of their orbit over the Taejon Airfield,
they flew a few miles north. Tommy and Sublette broke
formation first, rolling hard left and then diving down
to begin their target run. DeLuca and Waleska began
their run twenty seconds later.

Following the river wasn't difficult, even through
all the smoke. The narrow ribbon of sparkling blue
water painted a vivid stripe through the colorless

landscape. But Tommy, flying lead, was startled when the north bridge suddenly passed beneath him. He'd never seen it coming.

Sublette was surprised, too, when he flew over that same bridge just seconds later. He asked Tommy, "How far out did you see that damn bridge?"

"I didn't, Pete. Couldn't see it until I was right on top of it."

The roughly three miles to the south bridge would click off in about a minute of flying. They were at 400 feet above the river.

"I'm going lower," Tommy told Sublette.

"You sure you want to do that, boss? In this pea soup?"

"No…but we don't have much of a choice if we plan on shooting that bridge."

Thirty seconds had clicked off the clock on the instrument panel. Tommy couldn't see the bridge at all.

Fifteen more seconds and I've got no choice but to abort.

Five of those seconds clicked off. Then a few more…

And then he saw the outline of the bridge, its span a gray line etched into the murk.

"I've got it!" he told Sublette.

Just need to nose down a little bit…

The center of the span slid beneath the gunsight's pip.

He fired four rockets.

Pulling up sharply, he told Sublette, "Rockets away. Clear."

He could feel his ship tremble as the rockets impacted the target.

Above the smoke now and turning back to the north, he could see Sublette's ship emerge above the dingy shroud obscuring the bridge.

"Did I hit it?" Tommy asked.

"I think you did, boss."

"How about you? Did you hit it?"

"Who the hell knows?"

At the north bridge, *Banjo Two* and *Three* were having better luck. "Yeah, it was smoky as all hell," DeLuca reported, "but it looks like we both got good hits. I think we shot out the center span."

Tommy asked, "Got rockets left for another pass?"

"Affirmative."

"Then do it again. Good luck."

As Tommy flew north to prepare for the next run, he could see the reason for DeLuca's optimism: the smoke from the napalm fires had thinned around the north bridge, greatly improving visibility. It certainly did look like they'd already rendered it useless.

"Wow, you can see stuff pretty good up this way," Tommy told DeLuca. "But that means the triple-A can see you, too. Change direction on your next run. Come out of the south. We'll hold until you're clear so we don't end up nose to nose."

"Roger, boss. You want us to unload these bombs, too? Do a little glide bombing, maybe?"

"Negative. You'll just be throwing them away. Save them...we might need them later."

Chapter Sixteen

The visibility hadn't improved around the south bridge. If anything, the smoke had gotten thicker. After their second low-level attack with rockets, Tommy and Sublette still weren't sure if they'd knocked out the bridge.

And now they were out of rockets. They were down to the two 500-pound bombs each aircraft carried and their .50-caliber machine guns.

But machine guns would not bring down a bridge.

"I'm going to dive bomb it," Tommy said. "At least from up high, I might get enough of a look at the damn thing to actually hit it."

Sublette replied, "Despite the paltry odds of success?"

"Yeah, despite the odds. Let's go upstairs."

They'd have to climb to 8,000 feet to begin a dive-bombing run. It would take almost four minutes and a lot of gas to get there.

Sean had selected several points on the airfield to deploy the M19 Bofors vehicles. Each provided a hull-down firing position with decent fields of fire covering not only a portion of the airfield but the river itself and its far bank. The firing points provided a defense in depth, too; the vehicles could pull back, if needed, to positions farther from the river, with minimal exposure while in transit. To ensure against their getting lost in the dark, the routes to those fallback positions were marked with signposts: crude arrows atop wooden stakes posted at regular intervals.

"Consider these bastards forty-millimeter machine guns," Sean told the first M19 crew as he led them to their initial firing position. "I got it set up so you and the other M19 will have interlocking fire across our whole front, once I get his ass on firm ground and into position."

"What's with all the smoke over the river, Sarge?" the gun chief, a staff sergeant, asked. "How are we supposed to see anything going on on the other side?"

"It's just napalm," Sean replied. "It'll burn off in a little bit. Don't sweat it. Nothing's gonna happen for a little while, anyway. The Air Force just kicked the shit out of the gooks. They gotta nurse their wounds."

Then he left the gun crew to retrieve the second M19. The driver of its transporter, a flatbed semi-trailer, had misunderstood the directions given him and missed a turn. The rig was now stuck fast in swampy ground just short of the airfield. If the M19 attempted to drive off the flatbed now, it would be mired just as securely; the regiment had no recovery vehicle capable of pulling a twenty-ton M19 out of the muck.

Before Sean had left to emplace the first Bofors vehicle, he'd organized a team to build a corduroy road leading out of the swamp using railroad ties they'd scavenged all around Taejon. Now, as he returned, the road they'd built—all sixty feet of it—was about to be put to the test.

"I don't know, Sarge," the three-striper he'd left in charge of the effort said. "I think the whole mess is gonna sink even deeper once the vehicle's on top of it."

"Not if you laid 'em like I told you, numbnuts.

Let's see what you did here."

Sean walked into the marsh along the wooden roadway, much of it awash beneath an inch or two of the muddy water. But he liked what he saw; they'd used two layers of ties, each layer at a right angle to the other. Even if it sunk another foot or two under the weight of the M19, it would still provide a solid if submerged road surface for the vehicle's tracks.

"You see what I mean, Sarge?" the three-striper said, kicking some of the brackish water above the ties. "It's sinking already."

Sean gave him a chilling look. "You ever done this before, pal?"

The man shook his head.

"Well then, my friend, you're about to learn something."

He signaled to the M19 driver to *crank her up*.

Moon's Menace V had reached 8,000 feet. Tommy tried to shake off the chill the climb had brought on; the sweat beneath his flying clothes now felt like an ice water bath.

He put her into a steep turn to look straight down at the bridge over her left wing.

Son of a bitch! I can see that bridge just fine, even with the smoke.

Now all I've got to do is hit the damn thing.

He told Sublette, "I'm going to swing around and come out of the west, right along the axis of the span. That'll give me a longer target, at least. Let me know if I score."

"Roger, boss. Good luck. Remember, you'll have the wind behind you."

One quick orbit put his ship at the IP—the *initial point*—of the dive.

He pushed her nose over and began the steep plummet.

From their firing point several miles away, the M19 crew had watched the two unidentified aircraft circling high in the sky.

"You got a make on those planes?" the gunner asked his chief.

The chief didn't answer. He wasn't sure.

He was the only man in his crew who'd served in the last war. But he'd only seen action in the Philippines, in an area where Mustangs were rarely, if ever, stationed.

To his eye, those circling planes could be anything, even Russian-made.

And then one of them started down in a screaming dive.

Holy shit! The bastard's coming right for us!

The dive to the release point at 3,000 feet would take less than a minute. In that brief time, Tommy tried to envision what the sight picture would look like had his gunsight been set up as a bombsight.

I've done this a hundred times before in the jug. When I was lined up right, it always looked like the bomb would drop well short of the aiming point.

The wind's behind me...and I've got to fudge the lateral acceleration of the bomb. I'll aim for the near end of the bridge...no, no, aim short of the bridge. You always underestimate the lead.

Okay, looks good.

Drop one bomb or both?

Dropping just one gives me another chance if I miss.

But dropping both at once gives me two chances to hit it simultaneously.

Passing through 4,000 feet, he flipped the salvo selector to *both*.

A few seconds after that, he pickled the bombs away.

He was surprised how much force on the stick it took to pull the Mustang out of the dive. For a ship that had been so agile in every other maneuver, now it felt sluggish—even reluctant—to regain level flight.

Live and learn, I guess. But I still wish I was in a jug.

Since he'd been so gentle on the stick at first, the pullout had taken longer and his ship sunk farther. Typically, you'd be level at 1,500 feet. *Moon's Menace V* was at 800 feet before her descent was halted, racing toward the airfield at over three hundred miles per hour.

Maybe if it hadn't been for the napalm smoke, the crew of the M19 might've realized there was a bridge just a little over a mile away across that river. Maybe they would've seen the bombs fall away from *Moon's Menace V* toward that bridge.

Maybe then they would've realized she was a friendly aircraft...

And they wouldn't have begun throwing up a barrage of 40-millimeter shells at her.

Tommy thought he'd flown into a wall. The force of the impact drove him hard against his seat harness, violently driving his chin against his collarbone. Had his tongue been between his teeth, he would've bitten it off. He felt like every inch of his body had just absorbed a colossal punch.

The shock lasted barely a second. Suddenly everything sounded so strange; the snarl of her Merlin engine was gone, replaced by the howl of a demonic wind. The instrument panel looked as if someone had been kicking it apart from the back side.

As he looked through the windshield, a dark line kept rapidly sweeping through his field of vision, like the shutter of a camera closing and opening. It took a moment to realize that the sweeping line was what was left of the propeller, its four blades reduced to just one windmilling survivor.

It took another moment to realize the canopy was gone.

At least the flight controls still seemed to work. But without engine power, there was nothing to do but sink rapidly to the ground below. The gear-up crash landing in the marsh was like a ditching, except the plane didn't sink more than a few inches. Once she slid to a stop on her belly, Tommy, with a calmness that only comes from experience, released his harness, put the gun switch to *safe*, switched off the ship's battery, retrieved the photo of Sylvie Bergerac from the shattered instrument panel, and started to open the canopy.

Then he laughed at himself as he remembered there was no need to open it; the canopy was already gone. Climbing out of the ship, he found where at least one piece of that canopy had gone: a chunk of plexiglass had penetrated the hard shell of his flight helmet, standing straight up from the top like the spike of a Prussian *pickelhaube.*

Had the sharp plastic penetrated the helmet another half an inch, it would've pierced his skull.

Several GIs in a jeep were shouting at him from the edge of the marsh. He was too far away to make out a word they were saying but started slogging toward them. Once within shouting distance, a sergeant yelled, "Holy shit, sir, are you okay?"

"Yeah, I'm just swell. Who the hell shot me down?"

"The guy who Sergeant Moon's killing right now."

"Sergeant Moon? Sergeant *Sean* Moon?"

"That's the guy, sir."

"Can you take me to him?"

"I don't think he'll need your help killing that idiot, Major."

"No, that's not the reason, Sergeant. He's my brother."

The first thing Sean said to his younger brother was, "We gotta get you outta here, *Half.*"

Half: a nickname Tommy hadn't heard in quite a while. Friends and family had called him that most of his life, with never a hint of negative connotation about it. It just seemed preordained that a very short kid—and now a short man—named Moon would have it hung on him.

But friends and family had been scarce the last few years. He wasn't as close to his peacetime squadron mates as he'd been to those during the last war. Trips home to visit family in Brooklyn were few and far between when stationed in the States and impossible while overseas. Sean had stayed on in Europe until Forty-Eight, three years after Tommy had left, and they'd only crossed paths once, very briefly, in those ensuing two years before this chance encounter on an airfield in South Korea.

Sylvie had never called him *Half* and never would. So in those years between wars, he'd simply become *Tommy*.

His first question: "Did I at least get that damn bridge?"

"Yeah, you did," Sean replied. "You flyboys knocked both them bridges down. My C.O.'s real pleased. But c'mon...get in the damn jeep, already. That crash left you looking like you been rode hard and put away wet."

"What are you, a cowboy now, Sean? The only horse you've ever been around was the one that pulled the junkman's cart up Flatlands Avenue."

"Standard expression in *this man's army*, Half. But really, ain't you a little shook up or something? With all due respect, *sir*, you look like shit."

"I'm okay, Sean. I've been through a hell of a lot

worse."

As they drove to the airfield's operations shack, Tommy said, "You don't have to be in such a hurry to get rid of me, Sean. I've been in combat on the ground before, remember?"

"Yeah, I remember all too well, Half. But this is different. Real different. The only place we need you is up in the air, shooting up these gooks all you can."

He cast a probing glance in Tommy's direction as he continued, "You do know what the score is here, right?"

"Of course I do, Sean. Everybody does. We're trying to fight a delaying operation with one hand tied behind our backs."

"Maybe it's one hand for you aviator-types, Half, but for us jokers down on the ground, it's more like both hands. We got nothing to work with here. Case in point—that dipshit who didn't know your plane from a Russian job."

Tommy asked, "But from where you sit, do you think we'll be able to pull the delaying action off?"

"It's gonna take a fucking miracle, Half. Just promise me you won't be stuck on the ground in Pusan when the gooks break through. Just get your ass back to Japan, okay?"

At Operations, Tommy came face to face with the pilot of the FAC ship named *Spectral One-Seven*. Captain Don Gerard was busy gathering his gear. "This airfield's as good as closed," he explained. "We've been ordered to pull back to K-2 at Taegu. I'll be glad to give you a ride that far, sir, but I have to fly a mission first."

"Mind if I come along on the FAC run?" Tommy

asked. "You've got a back seat in that T-6, right?"

"Yeah, sure. The more the merrier…and another set of eyes won't hurt. But are you sure you want to, sir, after just getting shot down and all?"

Tommy replied, "You know that old saying about getting right back on the horse, don't you?"

"Yeah, I know it," Gerard replied, "but you must've taken one hell of a beating, sir. There's a hole in the top of your helmet, for cryin' out loud."

Tommy stuck his finger through that hole and said, "Consider it ventilation. Now, are we going or not?"

The weather wouldn't give them much time for this FAC mission. Clouds were sweeping down from the north; a band of thunderstorms would arrive shortly. With Tommy in the back seat, Captain Gerard was piloting the T-6 over the small city of Kongju, located some twenty miles northwest of Taejon on the southern bank of the Kum River. At the junction of four major roads, it was suspected Kongju was being turned into a major logistics base by the North Koreans.

"After the way we hit their supply points yesterday," Gerard said, "I guess the KPA needs a few new places to stash their stuff."

Tommy cast a wary eye to the approaching storm. "If we find something, do we have anyone on station close enough to hit it before the weather socks in?"

"I'll give a call and see who answers," Gerard replied. "They should be on *tac eight* if they're there at all."

A B-26 flight responded, call sign *Stranglehold*.

They were fifteen miles to the east.

Stranglehold Leader said, "Roger, *Spectral*, but better make it quick if we're going to make it at all. I don't plan on being anywhere near that thunderstorm."

"No shit, Dick Tracy," Gerard blurted, careful to keep his comment confined to the FAC plane's interphone and not broadcast to the world. Then he asked Tommy, "How fast do you figure that storm's moving?"

"I think we've got about ten minutes."

"Damn, that ain't much to work with. You want to fly her a little while I get out the binocs?"

"Be glad to."

"Okay, your airplane," Gerard said, relinquishing the controls. "Hold us at three thousand feet, give me an orbit left over the city."

"Coming right up," Tommy replied.

The feel of the T-6 came back to him quickly. She'd been designed to handle like a fighter—and she did—but without the brute force acceleration of a fighter's powerful engine. Novice pilots had enough on their plate without having to worry about vicious prop torque flipping the ship on its back with a sudden advance of the throttle. He was proud of himself for not losing any altitude at all as he put her into the turn.

"How long did you say it's been since you flew one of these girls, sir?"

"Seven years," Tommy replied.

"Well, you ain't lost your touch, that's for damn sure. I just may take myself a nap."

After they'd orbited the city once, Tommy asked, "You seeing much of anything downstairs?"

"A couple military trucks, all going in different

directions. But that's about it."

Tommy said, "I'd say we've got one more orbit before the ground goes away and the ride starts to get rough."

Stranglehold Leader was back on the air. "We've got you in sight," he said. "What's the plan?"

Gerard replied, "Hold over that northern bend in the river just east of Kongju."

"Roger, *Spectral*."

In the few minutes it took to complete the orbit, long fingers of cloud had moved in below the T-6, partially obscuring the ground. It wouldn't be long before the burbling clouds at the storm's leading edge blocked their downward view completely.

"I've got a hunch that place is crawling with KPA," Gerard said, "but they know the storm's coming, too. They're just staying concealed until we can't see the ground anymore, the clever bastards. I'm calling this mission off and releasing *Stranglehold*. Maybe they can do some good someplace else."

As he made that transmission, the first waves of the storm's turbulence made the T-6 shudder.

Like a fiery orator, Gerard said, "Head east, young man—and quickly, before we get our brains beat in. You still okay with flying her, sir?"

"Yeah, I'm good."

"Then take her to K-2. We've got the gas. Heading one-one-five."

Trimmed in level flight, the T-6 flew practically hands-off. A few minutes into the half-hour excursion to K-2 airfield at Taegu, Gerard had gotten so quiet that Tommy began to wonder if he really was taking a nap.

"You okay up there?" he asked.

"Oh, yeah," Gerard replied. "Just enjoying letting somebody else do the driving. Hey, what's the latest rumors around Pusan, sir? Are we really planning on bringing the jets in?"

"Just as soon as we've got the runways and ground support for them," Tommy replied.

"I've got a few hours in F-80s, and I'd really like to get me some more jet time," Gerard said. "But I got stuck in C-47s, driving what boiled down to a delivery truck all over the Pacific Rim. I hoped volunteering for Korea would put me in a jet again, but I got FAC instead."

"Your chance may come," Tommy replied. "Sooner than you think."

"Maybe, maybe not, sir. I don't see why the Air Force is bothering with this buildup, anyway. The word we've been getting is MacArthur's going to put the gooks out of their misery by dropping a few A-bombs on them. Just a question of where to put them. Then that'll be the end of all this nonsense."

Tommy replied, "Funny, but that's not the word around Pusan. It's not just the Air Force building up, either. The Army and Marine Corps are shipping units over as fast as they can…two or three divisions' worth. There are a couple boatloads of helicopters on the way, too."

"I still think *the bomb's* a whole lot easier, sir. By the way, take a look straight up at nine o'clock."

High above, Tommy could see four weaving vapor trails. "Yeah, I've got them. What about it?"

"The contrails are from four F-80s," Gerard said. "I could only make them out through the binocs. Can you see what's right in the middle of them?"

It was only a silver speck almost five miles above the T-6, but it would've had to be a pretty big aircraft to be seen at all.

"Let me guess," Tommy said. "A B-29, right?"

"Exactly right, sir."

"Must be a recon ship with escorts," Tommy said. "Wonder where they're going and what they're looking for?"

Gerard replied, "If you ask me, sir, they're looking for places to drop *the big one*."

Chapter Seventeen

The storms that engulfed Kongju had moved southeast. Continuing throughout the afternoon, their heavy rain turned everything except the gravel runway on the Taejon Airfield to muck.

"Be a hell of a time for the gooks to start dropping artillery and mortars," Patchett said. "Every swinging dick in this outfit got his steel pot off, for sure, and he's using it to bail out his hole."

Jock hung up the field phone. He'd been talking to General Keane, who'd offered a suggestion: *Once it gets dark, drive those M19s I gave you around your position to make it sound like you've got a lot of armor at your disposal.*

He could tell by the look on Sean's face that his tank expert didn't think much of that idea.

"First off," Sean said, "you need at least a platoon of tanks to pull that little stunt off. Two vehicles driving around sound like nothing but two vehicles driving around, period. Second, as sloppy as the rain's made everything, the only place we'd dare do that is on the runway. Those tracks'll get bogged down in no time flat, otherwise. Kinda ruins the whole scheme, too, if that motor noise can't get spread out back and forth across our entire position. With that skinny runway running perpendicular to where the gooks are at, it'll sound like those tracks ain't hardly moving at all."

"I take it you've used this technique before, Sergeant?"

"Yes, sir. Used it on the Krauts a whole bunch of times."

Jock replied, "So in your expert opinion, we should respectfully decline the general's suggestion, Sergeant?"

"Well, sir, if that's the same as shitcanning it, then yeah, that's what I'm saying."

There was no doubt that KPA forces—as much as a division—were poised for attack just across the Kap Ch'on River. But there had been no sight of them. They'd been surprisingly quiet, too. Usually, the sound of massed tanks could be heard several miles away. But there'd been nothing.

Patchett said, "Been thinking, sir. How about I run a recon patrol across the river tonight to see where the hell those gooks are and what they got in mind?"

Jock wasn't warming to the idea. "Just how big a patrol are you thinking of, Top?"

"Something like the one we used back at the Kum breakthrough, sir. Just me and my choice of four savvy GIs."

"Count me in," Sean said.

"Negative, Sergeant Moon," Jock replied. "Absolutely not. I can't have both my senior NCOs out there. Besides, if we're going to be fighting tanks again tonight, I need you right here."

"Amen to that, sir," Patchett said. "You tankers make too damn much noise, anyway. Leave the recon patrolling to us infantry types. We know how to be real quiet-like."

As soon as night fell, Patchett and his patrol slipped across the Kap Ch'on, fording it at a point where the water barely reached their knees. The rain had stopped, but the ground was still a morass that clung to their sodden boots and trouser legs.

Picking up a trail on the far bank, they moved west as quickly as the boggy ground would allow, the only sound the faint smacking of mud that accompanied each footstep. They'd only gone a few hundred yards when they heard urgent voices and sounds of activity.

"Sounds like they're breaking boxes open," Patchett whispered. "I'm betting they're either fixing to eat or loading up on ammo."

But still they heard no vehicles. For the moment, he considered that encouraging news.

At 26th Regiment's CP, the switchboard operator yelled to Jock, "LP Baker's on the line, sir. Says it's urgent...they hear tanks coming!"

That made no sense. Listening Post Baker was on the road to Taejon at the back side of the regiment's perimeter, about as far as could be from the last known KPA positions. If there were suddenly North Korean tanks moving up that road to the airfield, there had to have been a KPA breakthrough beyond Taejon nobody had bothered to tell 26th Regiment about.

Jock told Sean, "Take an anti-tank team and get over there. Figure out what the hell's going on."

The closest 3.5-inch rocket launcher team was a half mile away from LP Baker. Sean gathered them up in a jeep and raced through the darkness toward the road. When the section chief asked, "Why the Chinese fire drill, Sarge?" he replied, "We got tanks at our back door. Nobody knows *whose* tanks. That's fucking why."

Still a hundred yards from the LP, they could see the silhouette of a tank on the road. It wasn't moving.

"If that ain't a fucking Chaffee, I'll eat my hat, Sarge," the section chief said. "But wait a minute…do you figure the gooks would use our captured tanks against us?"

Sean parked the jeep behind a derelict shack and shut the engine. "They'd be out of their fucking minds if they did," he replied. "And real desperate, too. A T-34 is five times the tank a Chaffee is. Take your team and set up in them trees over there. I'll figure out what the hell's going on."

LP Baker was nothing more than a shed with a scrap wood frame, sandbag walls, a tin roof, and a field phone. Two GIs were crouched inside, holding their weapons on a third man standing in the road with his hands up.

"Look, pal," the man in the road said, "I told you already…I don't know the fucking password. All I know is I was told to report to 26th Regiment. That's you, ain't it?"

Sean couldn't make out the man's face, but he thought he recognized his voice. "If I didn't know better," he said, " I'd swear that dumb sack of shit was none other than Sergeant Sal Nuzzi."

One of the GI guards asked Sean, "You *know* this guy, Sarge?"

"Unfortunately. Put your fucking hands down, Sal. What the hell are you doing here?"

"Well, as I live and breathe, it's Master Sergeant Sean Moon, greatest tanker that ever fucking lived,"

Nuzzi said as the two shook hands in the middle of the road.

"*Third* greatest, Sal, after George S. Patton and Creighton W. Abrams. I'd love to chitchat about old times, but we're a little under the gun here. So what are you, lost or something?"

They weren't lost, Tech Sergeant Nuzzi explained. His platoon had been ordered to provide whatever fire support it could to 26th Regiment.

"Be nice if somebody told us about it," Sean said. "I got guys in the bushes ready to toast you, you dumb shit. And where's this platoon of yours? I only see two Chaffees."

"We had four until about an hour ago. Two broke down almost as soon as they rolled off the flatcars. Fucking transmissions, you know?"

"Shit. Ain't that typical?" Sean mumbled. "The only one we had left burned up her engine last night."

"But if you don't want our company, Sergeant Moon, we can turn around and—"

"Not so fast, Sal. I got just the job for you. Climb back in that junk wagon of yours and follow me. Just let me tell the CP we're coming so maybe some other GI morons don't start shooting you up."

Patchett's patrol was a half mile past the river now, moving cautiously up the slope of a low ridge. At the peak, the usual odor of Korea—excrement used as fertilizer—was replaced by something far more stomach-turning: the stench of death. Among a group of shacks that once, no doubt, comprised a small village, they stumbled onto more corpses than they could count in the darkness. Most seemed to be ROKs, their hands bound behind their backs with wire, a bullet hole in the back of their skulls. But a few were civilians: men, women, and children.

One of Patchett's GIs—PFC Staley, the BAR gunner—hadn't seen much killing yet. He struggled to hold down the vomit he felt rising in his throat. But he'd rather swallow it than let the sound of his retching give them away. Then they'd be captured and executed by the North Koreans just like those unfortunate souls.

For all its horrors, the ridge proved an excellent vantage point. In a ravine to its north, they found the KPA armor assembling to attack. With their engines shut down, they loaded ammunition and refueled with hand pumps from barrels in near silence. Patchett counted twenty-eight tanks in the ravine; there might be more hidden in the folds of the foothills farther to the west.

Despite the USAF's efforts to deny them fuel, they'd found a way to get it to their tanks. The next KPA assault against the airfield wouldn't be infantry alone like the last one. It would be a combined arms action that would take a miracle to defeat.

"That's at least two tank companies, I reckon," he whispered to Corporal Potts, the colored trooper he'd handpicked as his second-in-command for this patrol. "Listen to how quiet those boys are. Excellent noise discipline. Puts our tankers to shame. They can't zip up their damn flies without making a ruckus."

He gathered his patrol close and said, "I reckon we've seen all we're gonna see. Let's head back toward the river. Once we're out of earshot, we can radio the bad news that their tanks are back in the game."

Potts replied, "Wouldn't it be a big help if we could tell them *where* those tanks are going to cross the river, Sarge?"

"You're reading my mind, Corporal. That's what we're fixing to do. That trail we came up on looks to be dead in the middle of the only place tanks can ford the river. Everywhere else around here seems too damn swampy. We need to know just how wide the avenue of advance of them tanks is gonna be. If they're canalized into a narrow column when they come at the airfield, they'll be a whole lot easier to defeat."

Sean led Nuzzi's two Chaffees to the middle of the airfield's runway. He climbed up to Nuzzi standing in the turret hatch and said, "This is where I'm setting you up. Your vehicles will be facing west, right down the runway."

The dim glow from the turret's interior lighting leaked up through the hatch, making it easy to read the look on Nuzzi's face. It said he didn't like that assignment one bit.

"But we're gonna sweeten the pot a little for you guys," Sean continued. "You're gonna get to build a big ol' barricade for yourselves. Look over there." He pointed to the mired semi-trailer that had been the second M19's transporter. "I dug up enough cables so you and your other tank can pull that wreck out without going in the muck. Drag that useless son of a bitch across the width of the runway and nestle in behind it."

Nuzzi seemed less than grateful. "That's all you

got, Sean?"

"No, Sal, I got plenty more. Look way over thataway." This time, he pointed to *Moon's Menace V*, now nothing more than a collection of scrap metal in the shape of an aircraft. "Feel free to use that hulk, too. Consider it a special gift from my flyboy brother. It used to be his airplane, until one of my zipperhead gunners shot his ass down. You remember my brother Tommy, right?"

"Yeah. Didn't he spend some time with us in France as an ASO?"

"That he did, Sal."

"So where's he now? I mean, is he okay after crashing that thing?"

"He's fine. Probably back in Pusan already, painting his name on a new airplane."

"Looks like you Moons are still pretty hard to kill. Hope it stays that way for you."

"Thanks, Sal. Same to ya. But you better get busy. It don't look like the gooks are gonna be coming for a while, but when they do, they'll probably try to push their T-34s right up this runway. It's about the only place the traction's good around here. Oh, and by the way, there's piles of logs and railroad ties behind that building over there. Hang 'em on your tanks for some extra armor."

Patchett's suspicions about the terrain proved correct. There was only one approach to the fordable part of the river that wasn't a quagmire. He estimated its width at about four hundred yards; around a quarter of a mile. They'd crossed to the American side of the river to radio their report; Patchett didn't want to do it from the KPA side. If they were found out, they would have had to flee across the open expanse of the river under fire and totally exposed. On the friendly side, they wouldn't be so vulnerable.

Once the report was made, they'd go back across to keep tabs on the enemy forces. As Patchett told his patrol, "A unit that big is like a mile-long freight train. It takes a while to get it all moving. But if we can give our guys just a couple minutes' warning that they're cranking up to come across, it could make a whole lotta difference in how the fight goes."

As they forded the Kap Ch'on for the third time, he still found it hard to believe the KPA hadn't put out any security along the riverbank. When they'd marveled at this earlier, Corporal Potts had said, "It's because they're damn sure we're not going to attack. We're the best security they've got."

Patchett knew all too well that Potts was right.

His plan was to return to the ridge overlooking the assembly area for the Korean armor. Halfway up the rise, though, the still-queasy PFC Staley suddenly became agitated. He was walking point—the lead man in the patrol's column—when he threw down the BAR, did an *about-face*, and started running back through the column toward the river, not caring how much noise he made.

Potts, the last man in line, tackled him. When Staley began to wail, the corporal pushed his face into the mud to silence him. Even then, his cries bubbled up through the ooze, sounding as if he was saying, *They're everywhere! They're everywhere!*

But the verbalized fears didn't last long; Staley was going to drown in the mud.

Patchett was crouched over both of them now, whispering in Staley's ear, "We'll let you up, son, but you gotta promise to shut the fuck up. Otherwise, your face goes right back in the shit. Squeeze my hand if you understand me."

Bullets were snapping over their heads before he could respond, first rifle fire, then a machine gun. The GIs seemed to be in the middle of a ring of gunfire, with rounds coming from every direction.

But no one was hit. Patchett noticed that no round had even splashed around them.

It's all over our heads. The damn gooks must be shooting at each other.

He and Potts grabbed Staley by an arm each and began duck-walking him toward the river as fast as they could. The other two men scooped up the discarded BAR and were duck-walking right behind them. By the time they reached the river, they were upright and on the dead run.

Staley was still babbling, "They're everywhere! I told you, they're everywhere!"

Reaching the other bank, they threw themselves into the concealment offered by a thicket to catch their breath. Looking back through the darkness across the Kap Ch'on, they could see clusters of brilliant muzzle flashes and the occasional tracer rounds flying in opposite directions between those clusters. It seemed certain that two KPA units were having a gunfight with each other, because there were certainly no other American units on that side of the river.

Staley, still terrified, had fallen silent. He was still

clamped in Potts' vice-like grip; the corporal was prepared to silence him once again, if necessary.

The gunfire across the river began to fade away, dwindling in a matter of seconds to random rifle shots whose echoes bounced around the hills as if trying to get the last word in a violent argument. Then it stopped.

"I told you they were everywhere," Staley said for what seemed the hundredth time.

"Yeah, you did, son," Patchett replied, "but that was a damn fool way you did it. Nearly got us all killed."

"You gonna have me court-martialed, Sarge?"

"The thought crossed my mind, Private, but I'm thinking now that I won't."

He motioned to Potts to release his hold on Staley.

Nobody said a word for a moment. Perhaps they were trying to understand Sergeant Patchett's sudden benevolence.

Finally, it was Potts who asked, "How come, Sarge?"

"Because we all fuck up sometimes, Corporal. And the way I look at it, the only harm done here was maybe a coupla gooks shot each other."

Potts said, "Yeah, but—"

"But *nothing*, Corporal. We got lucky, that's all. And I'll take a win any way I can get it."

Then, with a smile more chilling than a curse, he told Staley, "So, nice work, son…but don't you never fucking do something like that again, you hear?"

It was one of those rare moments when Jock found

himself alone in the CP. It would only last a minute, but it felt so strange, as if he was fighting the entire North Korean Army all by himself.

Physically, he'd reached the point he'd known in combat so many times before, where exhaustion had become the normal state of being. He'd slept so little since taking command of the regiment four days ago. He only hoped his troops were managing to get some rest before the fight began again. They'd need it more than him.

What he needed most right now was another cup of coffee. As he hopped off the stool, his bad leg buckled beneath him as if the muscles within had suddenly turned to rubber bands. He crashed to the floor face down.

I'm kidding myself if I keep thinking this leg will be even close to one hundred percent ever again.

But I can't let anyone see me flat on my face like this.

He'd struggled back to his feet just as the first man to return to the CP stepped inside out of the pre-dawn darkness.

Chapter Eighteen

The dawn brought a fog no one expected, its dense mist blanketing the Kap Ch'on River and most of Taejon Airfield. Back at the CP now, Patchett told Jock, "If they can find their way across that river, this would be one hell of a time for the gooks to attack. If I was them, and they got the numbers I think they do, I wouldn't even bother with the artillery prep or the tanks, just start coming real quiet-like out of that soup like a bunch of ghosts. We wouldn't see the bastards until they were right on top of us. I reckon most of our troopers would shit their britches sooner than fire their weapons."

But the KPA wasn't listening to Patchett's advice. He'd barely finished speaking when the CP rattled with the distant *boom* of artillery. It sounded like many pieces firing in near-perfect synchronization. With shouts of *take cover*, Jock and his staff at the CP hunkered behind walls stacked high with sandbags. GIs defending the airfield burrowed into their bunkers and fighting holes, counting the seconds to an impact they prayed they'd still be alive to hear.

Their prayers were answered, at least for the moment. The barrage fell well forward of the regiment's position. The impacts couldn't be seen through the fog, but based on the sound of the explosions, they were landing along the Kap Ch'on or, perhaps, farther west, closer to the KPA troops than the GIs dug in around the airfield.

"Now I get why the gooks didn't have any outposts along the river," Patchett said. "They don't trust their own artillery. Wanna give 'em a real wide berth."

"I wish we could see the flash from the tubes, though, Top," Jock said, peering through a firing slit in the sandbagged wall. "Then we could get some counter-battery fire on them. But this damn fog…"

Somebody yelled, "*Atten-hut.*" They all *snapped to* as General Keane dashed into the CP. "What's your situation here, Colonel?" he asked Jock. His tone was disturbing, sounding more like a question from a casual observer than the demand of a commander.

"My situation? That artillery you're listening to is pretty much it, sir," Jock replied.

"No attack by infantry or tanks yet?"

"No, sir, not yet."

"I wish I could say the same for the other regiments," Keane said. "By all reports, they're getting hammered."

The *other regiments*—the 17th and 33rd—were situated east of the 26th, centered two and five miles away, respectively, if you took the general's situation map as gospel. But if they were in a fight, Jock and company should've heard it. There'd been nothing over the division command net to indicate attacks in progress, either. That assumed, of course, that their consistently unreliable radios were still working.

It was Patchett who finally expressed the collective skepticism: "Well, sir, they must be fighting with swords and cudgels, then, because we ain't heard a damn thing. Are those boys holding their positions this time, at least?"

"As far as I know, they are, Sergeant," Keane replied. Then he asked Jock, "Colonel, where is that artillery landing?"

"Along the river, sir. They've shot several volleys, but nothing's hit the airfield yet. We don't think the KPA across the Kap Ch'on can see the impacts well enough to adjust them."

Patchett added, "And if they're trying to adjust by sound, they're doing a piss-poor job, sir."

"Well, let's hope they keep doing that piss-poor job," Keane replied. "Keep your heads down, men. I'll be back when I can."

Jock and Patchett locked eyes; they both knew what the other was thinking: *Golly, General, we'll be waiting with bated fucking breath.*

Once the general drove off, Sean said, "You know, there's another reason we might not be hearing anything from the other outfits."

Jock replied, "What's that, Sergeant?"

"Maybe the gooks are rolling tanks at 'em, and our guys just turned around and ran the second they showed up, like they already did a couple of times, right? Might be that not one damn shot got fired."

He had a point. Like it or not, that scenario was entirely possible.

One of the radio operators called out, "Colonel, I've got *Spectral One-Seven* on frequency."

"The FAC? Gee, he's up in the air bright and early."

"Says he's got those guns spotted, sir."

It had been a very early morning for *Spectral One-Seven's* pilot, Don Gerard. Flying an unarmed FAC ship, he'd been allowed to take off from K-2 before

dawn. Armed ships had to wait until sunup; it avoided
the possibility of the darkness causing a ground
collision or takeoff accident, either of which could
result in a daisy chain of catastrophic destruction on the
small, crowded airfield when armament detonated in a
post-crash fire. The smoke rockets his ship carried
weren't considered quite as capable of such devastation.

I can crash all I want, I guess.

When he was based at Taejon, close to the front
line, predawn takeoffs hadn't been necessary. But
flying out of Taegu now—almost one hundred miles
from the action—he needed to be off the ground almost
an hour before dawn to be on station when the sun rose.
That would give him roughly forty minutes to recon
and select targets before the fighter-bombers would be
in the area. Once they arrived, his T-6 would still have
enough gas to stay on station another two hours before
having to return to K-2 and refuel. Hopefully, another
FAC ship would be on hand to fill in while he was
gone.

Over the target area now, he couldn't wait for the
fighter-bombers: he'd spotted the guns firing at Taejon
Airfield. It was time to double as artillery observer.

"*Montana Six*, this is *Spectral*," Gerard replied
when Jock came up on frequency. "I have your problem
in sight, artillery in battalion strength four miles
northwest of the airfield. I don't have direct commo
with your guns. Can you relay?"

"Affirmative, *Spectral*. Send your fire mission."

In about a minute, the first adjustment round from
the American artillery landed. It was short of the KPA
guns.

"Add two hundred," Gerard radioed.

This time, it only took forty seconds for the next round to splash.

Shit, I'm still short.

He called in, "Add one hundred."

Listening at the CP, Patchett said, "Dammit, that flyboy's walking them rounds too slow. He still ain't got a bracket. Them gooks are gonna reposition themselves before he ever gets to *fire for effect*."

One more volley was fired by the Korean gunners. The twenty rounds actually landed on the western edge of the airfield, among the GIs of Colonel Brand's 3rd Battalion.

Orbiting well to the east of his target, Gerard watched as the next adjustment round landed just beyond the line of twenty guns, which were compactly emplaced hub-to-hub.

Finally! I've got the bracket.

"Drop five-zero, fire for effect," he transmitted.

But they better hurry up and get those rounds in the air...

Because Patchett was right; once they fired their last volley, the KPA gunners began to feverishly hook their weapons to the trucks that towed them.

Shit. Rare is the mobile target that stands still while you're adjusting fire on it.

By the time the American rounds struck, only a few of the KPA guns were caught in their impact. The rest had already driven well clear. Gerard lost sight of those that escaped as the road they traveled disappeared into the hills.

He called in the disappointing results.

"That's okay, *Spectral*," Jock replied. "We'll take whatever break we can get. If they pop up again, let us know."

Then Jock asked, "*Spectral,* do you see any KPA movement to the west of the airfield?" He was referring to the formations Patchett and his men had encountered during the night patrol.

"Negative, *Montana,*" Gerard replied. "Can't see much of anything. Still a lot of fog down there."

"How about to the east? Any movement over that way?"

"Stand by," Gerard said. "Give me a minute to get turned around."

Once he reversed direction, he reported, "Hard to tell. The early morning haze is taking its sweet time burning off today. Must've rained a lot yesterday."

The casualties from that last, on-target volley of KPA artillery had been mercifully light. "We got lucky," Patchett reported. "None killed; only a handful of men from Third Battalion are at the regimental aid station, none serious."

That was the end of the good news. Within minutes, the roar of KPA tank engines pierced the thinning fog, growing louder. They weren't waiting for their artillery to start firing again.

"They're coming," Jock said, "and by all reports, they're right where you said they'd cross the river, Top."

"You didn't doubt me, did you, sir?"

"Not for a damn minute."

That would put the tanks' axis of advance straight into Major Harper's 2nd Battalion. The width of that advance would be initially narrow; the boggy terrain would prevent the T-34s from widening their front until they'd penetrated deep into the airfield. Neatly centered on that narrow route of advance was the runway, with Sergeant Nuzzi's two Chaffees behind their makeshift barricade composed of the semi-trailer rig, Tommy Moon's wrecked F-51, and all the lumber they'd been able to move into place before the artillery barrage began.

The biggest threats to the T-34s were the 3.5-inch rocket launcher teams Sean had positioned close to the river and the fighter-bombers that *Spectral One-Seven* advised would be arriving within ten minutes.

Twenty-Sixth Regiment was as ready for attack as they could possibly be.

The division's other two regiments were not.

Radios in 26th Regiment's CP came alive with calls for artillery fire from 17th and 33rd Regiments. The voices spilling from the speakers had the shrill, high-pitched quality of men under extreme stress. The map plots of their fire missions were cause for additional alarm; the target coordinates were on the northern outskirts of Taejon, which was a good three miles *behind* the assigned positions of those regiments.

With one look at the map, Jock and Patchett agreed: those units were never where they were supposed to be in the first place. Patchett expressed the logic of that assumption simply: "They couldn't pull back that far that fast, unless they're all world champion sprinters."

Don Gerard in *Spectral One-Seven* added another chilling uncertainty: "Are there any GI tanks on the north side of the city? I can see real good now, and the place is crawling with armor."

"We're screwed again," Jock said. "Those other regiments are getting priority with the artillery. We're going to get shit."

He sketched a big red arrow on the map running due south from the airfield, skirting Taejon to the west, and ending on the far side of that city. "Start preparing a withdrawal order," he told his staff. Pointing to that big arrow, he added, "That's the route we're going to take. Get on the horn and tell Division we've got no choice. If we don't move real soon, we'll be surrounded. Again."

The KPA infantry attacked on a front much wider than that of their tanks. Their flanking units, hidden in the mist but without the T-34s to provide protection on the airfield's open terrain, were cut to ribbons by the M19s' 40-millimeter guns, plus the fire of heavy machine guns and mortars.

But none of those weapons could be depended on to stop tanks. Especially ones which could be heard but not seen.

To Sean Moon, this fight in the early morning fog seemed like so many others he'd survived in France and Germany during the last war. They'd all devolved to a series of isolated, close-quarters skirmishes between small units, where artillery and air power were of little use. More often than not, winning or losing hinged on the pivotal actions of just a few men.

He moved quickly from one anti-tank team to another. They'd scored some hits already; he could smell the diesel-fueled infernos consuming their victims. A 3.5 gunner told him, "When those sons of bitches pop out of the fog, they're so close a blind man could hit them."

But a few T-34s had slipped through and were on the airfield. Sean could hear their engines *inside* the perimeter.

"Come with me," he told a rocket team. Then they set off in the direction of the engine noise.

"I hear two vehicles," Sean said. "Anybody else got a different take on it?"

When no one disagreed, he pointed a quarter turn to the right and said, "Sounds like the closest one's that way. Let's haul ass and catch up with her. I think this fog's finally starting to burn off."

Sean was right about the fog; it had already cleared around Sal Nuzzi's tanks, allowing the crews to see the dark shapes of T-34s in the mist which still lingered near the river. One of them was presenting her vulnerable flank to the Chaffees. He told his number two tank, "Take her."

It took four rounds—all direct hits—from the Chaffee to set the T-34 ablaze. They'd aimed for her turret ring with their first shot, jamming it to prevent the main gun from being traversed toward them to return fire.

Sean and his team were about one hundred yards from the stricken T-34. Though still veiled in mist, there was no doubt she was brewing up.

"One down," he said. "Now let's find that other

bastard."

As if someone was turning a dial, the fog melted away in a matter of seconds. The T-34 they were tracking was plainly visible now, 150 yards ahead. She was showing them her front left quarter.

"I can take her from here," the gunner said.

"Nah, the angle's for shit," Sean replied. "Let's move over this way and hit her in the ass. Quick, into this gully."

They hadn't run fifty yards down the gully when they stumbled into another 3.5-inch rocket team. But the man aiming the rocket launcher wasn't an ordinary GI. It was General Keane himself.

The T-34 had seen them; the turret was traversing their way. Sean knew from hard experience that the tankers inside were frantic with the slow rate of the turret's movement. But he also knew that to the GIs in this ditch, it was moving with lightning speed.

General Keane still hadn't fired.

Time was wasting. Sean told his gunner, "Take the shot, right fucking now."

"No, I've got her," the general insisted. "She's all mine."

A split second later, the rocket roared from his tube. The sound it made penetrating her hull was the dullest of *clanks*, like a hammer against a distant anvil. The hole it left behind seemed impossibly small.

But then jets of flame erupted from her hatches. Only one man escaped. Ablaze from head to toe, he was able to run toward the Americans only because the pain receptors in his skin had already burned away. A few steps more and he would collapse and be consumed by his personal inferno.

Sean dropped him with one shot. "The gook was done for," he explained. "Did the bastard a favor."

General Keane was ecstatic, as if the act of killing this single tank was a pivotal moment in history. He kept pumping a victorious fist in the air while he gave and received backslaps of praise from the GIs around him.

Sean didn't think much of the display. It looked so wrong, this man wearing stars on his collar cavorting with common soldiers. But the meaning of it all was ominous:

The general's given up. He can't cut it no more. So now he's trying to be one of the troops 'cause he thinks that somehow it's gonna help keep morale up.

But it ain't gonna help shit.

If we ain't got a ringmaster for this circus, we're all as good as dead.

"Not to spoil the party or nothing, sir," Sean said, "and with all due respect, but do you realize that the other two regiments are bugging out again, and this regiment'll be pulling back just as soon as we get a little breathing space between us and the gooks?"

Keane didn't have to say a word. The stunned look on his face was damning evidence that he had no idea of this latest disaster befalling his division.

"And again, sir, with all due respect, I didn't spend those years fighting in North Africa and Europe just to buy it in some fucked-up Asian shitshow. So let me ask you, General...ain't there something more important you should be doing right about now instead of some private's job?"

General Keane's face went ashen. "The regiments...they're collapsing?" he asked. "How do you know that, Sergeant?"

"I just listen to the radio, sir." He hesitated, and then added, "Maybe you should, too."

He knew he'd just crossed a line. But maybe it was a line that needed to be crossed.

It might've been anger that flared in the general's eyes for just an instant, but it quickly faded, smothered by the catastrophe surrounding him. Finally, he said, "I'll do that, Sergeant."

But he seemed unsure how to go about it. After scanning the airfield, he asked, "Now where the hell is that jeep of mine?"

The answer must've come to him because he set off on the dead run.

Sean mumbled, "Good luck, General." It came out sounding far less sarcastic than he meant it to be.

Then he pulled the two anti-tank teams together. "You guys cover the flanks of the runway," he told them. "Don't let nothing or nobody get behind the Chaffees, you hear me?"

A section chief asked, "Where're you going to be, Sarge?"

"I gotta get back to the CP."

"Okay, but just so you know, Sarge, when the general court-martials you for smart-mouthing him, none of us saw or heard a damn thing."

Sean replied, "I appreciate that, pal. But I kinda doubt it's gonna come to that."

He knew all too well that things like court-martials were small potatoes when your life expectancy was being measured in minutes.

Though his regiment had managed to hold off the KPA assault so far, Jock knew they couldn't keep it up much longer. There were just too many enemy tanks. They would keep coming. Without a serious armor threat of his own, sooner rather than later the T-34s would break through, and their infantry would flood in behind them.

If the 26th didn't withdraw, it would find itself pinned between those Koreans and the ones who'd pushed the rest of the division into the streets of Taejon.

What happened next caught the regimental CP by surprise: the KPA tanks and infantry pulled back across the river. The battalions facing them, Colonel Brand's 3rd and Major Harper's 2nd, saw this as the perfect time to execute their withdrawal.

Jock stopped them with one transmission: "Negative. Repeat, negative. Stand fast and take cover. Expect enemy artillery on your heads momentarily."

"Damn right, sir," Patchett said. "That's all we need—two battalions running around in the open when the shit starts raining down. Now, how far out is that air support?"

Chapter Nineteen

Tommy Moon almost wasn't on this morning's mission. The flight surgeon wasn't going to return him to flying status after the battering he'd taken in yesterday's shoot-down and crash of *Moon's Menace V*.

"For cryin' out loud, Doc," he'd argued, "I've *already* been back in the air, flying that FAC T-6 to Taegu. And I was up in the air *again* in that liaison ship to get back here to K-9. So it looks like I can handle being upstairs, doesn't it?"

Afraid it might poison his argument, he hadn't said what was really on his mind: *My brother's in the shit down there and I've got to help him out.*

Better to keep that to himself; he'd seen too many pilots grounded when a surgeon knew of or suspected ulterior motives that were coloring a man's judgment of his own fitness.

Reluctantly, the surgeon had relented. As soon as dawn broke, Tommy was leading *Banjo Flight* back to the fight in a borrowed, *no-name* F-51.

The radio traffic en route to Taejon left no doubt a major battle was in progress. "Your target is four miles northwest of Taejon," *Spectral One-Seven* told Tommy, "but give yourselves a wide margin west of the airfield. A lot of lead in the air around there."

"Roger," Tommy replied. "What are we hitting?"

"Artillery, all nice and neat in a tight line running southwest to northeast. Coming out of the southwest should give maximum results. They're in the open. You shouldn't need any smoke from me to find them. They're making plenty of their own."

The Taejon airfield slipped by well off their right wingtips, covered in the smoke and dust of the KPA artillery barrage. If the pilots glanced at the right moment, they'd see the twinkling flash of explosions at impact and the rapidly expanding rings of their shock waves along the ground.

Tommy envisioned the trajectory of those rounds like the arc of an imaginary rainbow with his target at the distant end. He was still too far out to see the guns, their muzzle flashes, or their smoke, but he had a pretty good idea where they were.

"*Spectral* from *Banjo Leader*, I make the target west of the river and due north of the railroad intersection. Confirm?"

"Roger, *Banjo*. You've got it nailed."

"Outstanding. Any flak?"

"Not sure, *Banjo Leader*. They won't shoot at me. They're saving it for you, I guess."

"*Banjo Flight* from *Leader*, we'll do it in pairs. Come in low, guns only. Save the bombs and rockets for hard targets. On me, break on three..."

Tommy wished Gerard had only been joking when he said *They're saving it for you*. He could see the tracers from anti-aircraft guns rising up now as they bore down on the line of artillery pieces. But the triple-A scored no hits; *Banjo Flight* was too low and too fast to be easily tracked.

That looks like big-caliber stuff, Tommy told himself. *If it does hit you, it just might turn you inside out.*

The leading pair of F-51s—Tommy, with Ted Waleska on his right and slightly behind—raced across the closely spaced battery, its guns lined up as if on a parade field. The target was so compact they only had time to deliver two short bursts each before they were past it. As they climbed away, Waleska said, "That's pretty damn stupid, lining all those guns up like that. What a turkey shoot!"

"Like I said before," Tommy replied, "they use Soviet doctrine all the way. That's a couple of batteries' worth of artillery down there, probably a battalion. The only way they can coordinate their fire on one target is to line them up hub to hub, just like the Russians do."

The second pair—Al DeLuca and Pete Sublette— pulled up at the end of their strafing run, climbing to rejoin *Banjo Leader*.

Tommy asked, "Anybody get hit?"

Once the chorus of *negatives* was over, Tommy asked Gerard in *Spectral One-Seven*, "How'd we do?"

"Looks like an excellent job, *Banjo*. Still got a little bit of movement, though, like maybe they're trying to put a few guns back into action. How about another pass?"

"Roger, we'll give it another go."

He didn't want to attack from the same direction again, but the terrain gave him only two choices: hit them from the right, as they just had, or hit them from the left.

Or maybe we do both ways together, Tommy thought.

He brought the flight north, where hills would block the anti-aircraft gunners' view of what they were doing. Using the same pairs, he and Waleska split from the low orbit to attack from the left in a turning approach around the hills that would minimize their straight-in run and expose themselves to the triple-A as briefly as possible.

DeLuca and Sublette would buy time by flying one more orbit and then attack from the right with the same turning technique. By the time they were on their strafing run, Tommy and Waleska, having come from the opposite direction, would be clear of the target area.

"If we do this right," Tommy said, "we won't bump into each other head-on and mark the target with burning F-51s."

He'd meant it to be dark humor. He didn't expect any laughs.

Barreling around the last hill on his circular course to the target, Tommy saw what the FAC had been talking about: trucks were moving in the battery area. He lined up a group of three in his gunsight and started firing.

The bullet strikes were obvious; pieces of trucks were flying in all directions. Just before passing over his quarry, he could see men running away.

He was beginning the climb-out when his ship shuddered violently. It wasn't like being struck by anti-aircraft fire. He knew what had happened: a tremendous explosion in the target area was buffeting his plane.

Ted Waleska was on his gun run when the trucks Tommy had strafed exploded. He had no choice but to fly through the cloud of smoke and debris.

He could hear things hitting his airplane. It sounded like a stack of pots being dropped in a kitchen. The stench of explosives filled his cockpit.

As he pulled back on the stick to climb out, the ship's response was uncharacteristically sluggish. The engine sounded different, too. An unnatural vibration shook the aircraft as if she was trembling.

But he could deal with all that. Then he noticed the engine's coolant temperature rising.

"I just flew through a pile of crap," he told Tommy. "Those trucks must've been loaded with ammo. My girl's pretty banged up…and it looks like they got the radiator, dammit."

They were a long way from Pusan or Taegu.

And Taejon Airfield—the place that had been Tommy's salvation yesterday—didn't look like it was open for business anymore.

"Get as high as you can without red-lining the temp gauge," Tommy told him. "Let's figure out a safe place to set her down."

Spectral One-Seven had a solution. "Follow the west highway toward Taejon," Gerard said. "*Montana's* fixing to bug out from the airfield and head south. They'll be passing along there and should be able to pick you up. I'll let them know you're coming."

The sudden demise of their artillery must've caught the KPA troops attacking the airfield by surprise. They didn't relaunch their attack for ten critical minutes, allowing 26th Regiment to start pulling back. As the Korean tanks and infantry finally began storming across the river again, they ran into a delaying action by the two M19s and Sergeant Nuzzi's Chaffees.

That delaying action froze the attackers in place on the west end of the airfield just long enough for them to be pummeled by the bombs, rockets, and guns of *Banjo Flight*—down to three aircraft now—and the four F-51s of *Trombone Flight*, who'd just arrived on station from

K-9. Under the umbrella of this fighter-bomber protection and the flights that would relieve them when they returned to base to rearm and refuel, the regiment withdrew. Skirting the west side of Taejon, it would take up new positions on that city's southern outskirts. From there, they could block—at least temporarily—the main highway and the rail line, both of which ran south to Pusan.

But depleted as the regiment was, it would be spread thin covering both routes. Jock told his commanders and staff, "If the weather stays good and we can keep getting good air support, we might be able to hold out for a couple of days, until First Cav can get up here from Pusan and help us out." Then he asked his operations officer, "Do we have any idea where the other regiments are? And what about our artillery?"

The ops officer didn't know the answer to either question. But as the troops of 26th Regiment dug in along the highway and railroad, Jock's questions answered themselves: included in the steady stream of civilian refugees spilling out of Taejon were the disorganized remnants of 17th and 33rd Regiments as well as what was left of the division's artillery. When word passed down the column that they were approaching an organized roadblock of American forces, some GIs abandoned their vehicles in a panic and set out for the surrounding hills on foot to bypass it, afraid they'd be pressed into combat service with some other outfit.

Jock personally stopped the jeep of 17th Regiment's commander, an older colonel named Baldwin, who'd been intent on blasting right through the roadblock without even slowing down.

"We could sure use your regiment's help," Jock told him. "Especially along the railway. We're really strung out in the hills around there."

Baldwin was a man in a hurry. With great impatience, he replied, "I have no such orders, Miles."

"Nobody has *orders*, Colonel," Jock said. "We're doing this out of necessity."

"That may be your interpretation, Miles, but I don't take orders from you, that's for damn sure."

Jock tried a different tack, asking, "When's the last time you even heard from Division?"

Baldwin just shrugged and motioned to his driver to get moving.

"Hold on a second, Colonel," Jock said. "Last I heard, this division was conducting a delaying action here at Taejon. That means you, too, doesn't it?"

"Negative, Miles," Baldwin replied. "The only thing that makes sense is to withdraw until we meet up with First Cav. Staying around here is just going to get us all killed."

Jock replied, "Nobody's talking about conducting a suicide defense of Taejon, Colonel, just delaying the KPA for a little bit. We can do that if we pull our heads out of our asses and start using sound tactics to—"

Not liking the tone of that comment one bit, Baldwin interrupted, "Just who the fuck are you to decide what I should be doing? We could've all been safe and sound in Pusan already, but you're the one who's screwing everything up, always *pretending* to be standing tall and holding your ground, facing light attacks while the rest of us get hit with the brunt of the KPA."

Jock replied, "From what I've seen, you haven't

gotten hit any harder than my regiment."

"Don't kid yourself, Miles. You're running backward just like everyone else. Stop being such a show-boating buddy-fucker and face facts. You'll live longer that way. Now get out of my goddamn way."

Disgusted, Jock waved him through.

A few minutes later, the colonel commanding division artillery drove up in his jeep. Scattered back through the throng of refugees and fleeing GIs were a handful of trucks towing howitzers. Two had already passed through the roadblock.

Jock knew this colonel fairly well; his name was Mike Frost.

"Where you headed, Mike?" Jock asked.

"Any place but inside that fucking city, Jock. It's a slaughterhouse in there."

"How about setting up your guns about a thousand yards south of here? There's plenty of level ground for your guys along the highway."

"I'll be glad to, Jock, but don't get your hopes up. In case you haven't noticed, there's not much left in the way of guns. I can barely field two batteries. We just got another one overrun. And the guns that are left are getting really low on ammo. If we don't get a resupply in the next couple of hours, we're out of business."

"Welcome to the club, Mike. So I can count on you to back us up?"

"I guess so. Your regiment seems to be the only one that's got a grip on itself. Are you in contact with Division, by any chance?"

Jock replied, "Nope. Haven't heard from them since early this morning. And we've been trying, believe me."

"Do you really think we're going to be able to hold on here, Jock?" Frost asked.

"With the Air Force's help, I think we've got a chance in daylight, Mike. I'm not so sure about what's going to happen at night, though."

It was mid-afternoon at K-9. Three flights of F-51s—*Banjo, Trombone,* and *Oboe*—were being refueled and rearmed while another squadron provided air support for the beleaguered GIs at Taejon. There would be a change of armament for this mission: instead of the five-hundred-pound general purpose bombs they'd been carrying, they'd be dropping napalm instead. The intent was simple: try to turn the tinderbox city of Taejon into an inferno, incinerating the KPA swarming its streets.

The mission briefing brought *Banjo Flight* some good news. Ted Waleska was safely in the hands of the ground-pounders after his emergency landing. Riding with a supply convoy, he'd be back in Pusan sometime tomorrow.

"The lucky bastard," Pete Sublette said. "Some guys'll do anything to get a couple days off. But at this rate, we're going to run out of Mustangs real soon. Those fucking radiators hanging out down there..."

Sharing the truck driving them to their planes was the crew of a C-119 *Flying Boxcar* transport. The *Boxcar* pilot asked Tommy, "You guys heading up to Taejon, sir?"

"Yep. This'll be our third run up there today."

"Good," the pilot replied, sounding relieved. "You

know the way. Mind if we follow you? This is our first drop in that area."

"Sure, be my guest. What're you dropping?"

"Ammo, mostly artillery. Not real sure where they want it, though."

Tommy pulled a map from his flight bag. "We're going to be setting fires with napalm here, on the north side of the city," he said, his finger making a goose egg on the map. "So stay away from that area. I'm told there are no GIs or civilians left anywhere near there...they're all on the south side now." He sketched a line across the paper with his finger. "The Pusan highway runs south out of Taejon through this valley. Look for their panel markers in that area. If you can't tell where to drop, bring up the FAC on channel eight and ask for help. Maybe he can identify the good guys for you."

"Got it, sir," the pilot said. "I'll do that."

Tommy replied, "Good plan. And good luck. I've got a brother down there. I know he'll be real appreciative of your efforts. It's going to be a long night for those guys. They'll need that artillery."

The sun was ready to drop behind the mountain peaks to the west as Sean and Patchett took in the panoramic view from the regiment's hilltop CP. Below them was the southern highway. Three miles to the north, they could see the fires the napalm had started on the far side of Taejon.

"You think that fire's gonna burn the whole city down, Bubba?" Patchett asked Sean.

"Maybe, Patch. It's a lotta wood out there. Could use a little more wind to spread it, though."

"Yeah, I was thinking the same thing. The flyboys are saying they buried a lot of gook tanks under that napalm. What's your take on that?"

Sean offered one puff of laughter and said, "We love our flyboys...but they do tend to exaggerate from time to time."

"So you're still taking some of them rocket boys into the city with you?"

Sean replied, "Damn right I am, Patch, just as soon as it gets good and dark."

A mile south, they could see the artillerymen still gathering up the pallets full of ammunition the C-119s had dropped. Patchett said, "That gotta be about the best airdrop I ever seen. Looks like every damn chute landed where they could get their hands on it."

Then he glanced back toward Taejon and said, "Well, Bubba, where do you reckon the gooks are gonna come at us first?"

"We're gonna get hit by infantry that goes around the city and through the hills," Sean replied. "Probably on both flanks at the same time."

"Yep, that's how I figure it, too. The M19s and quad fifties are gonna be real busy tonight, I'm afraid. But what about their armor?"

"Unless they manage to come straight through the city, we ain't gonna see much in the way of T-34s for a day or two. Too many hills if they try to work the flanks with the infantry. They'll tear up their transmissions before they get anywhere near here."

They fell into silence for a few moments, until Patchett said, "But no matter what, there's still gonna be a lot more of them gooks than there are of us."

A jeep was driving up the hill to the CP. Even in the shadows of dusk, both sergeants recognized the man in the passenger's seat from a long way off. It was the assistant division commander, a colonel named Healy.

Patchett turned to Sean and said, "How about you and me mosey inside and give a listen to what the man's got on his mind?"

The news Colonel Healy brought seemed beyond comprehension at first: General Keane, the division commander, was missing.

This was something new. Some generals might occasionally be wounded if they got in the way of a bomb or a shelling. In rare cases, one might be unlucky enough to get himself killed.

But generals never went missing.

Until now.

Healy said, "I just got off the horn with General Walker at Eighth Army, Colonel Miles. For the time being, we're considering your regiment an independent regimental combat team comprised of your unit and whatever resources you can salvage from what's left of the other outfits in Twenty-Fourth Division. You are in command of this RCT. The mission to delay the North Koreans at Taejon falls squarely on your shoulders now."

Patchett leaned to whisper in Sean's ear: "Hell, ain't that the way it's been ever since we got here? Seems like Eighth Army's just now getting around to making it official."

Sean replied, "A day late and a dollar short, as usual."

Patchett replied, "Worse than that, Bubba. The way I see it, *this man's army* got itself a whole new definition of *FUBAR* going on here. Putting Jock Miles officially in charge is the only smart thing they done lately."

"Let's just hope it ain't too fucking late, Patch. But how much you wanna bet this is all just a smokescreen so some generals can beat the rap for losing a division? Or maybe this whole damn war?"

Lieutenant General Walton "Johnnie" Walker, commander of US 8th Army, finally had most of the American divisions currently assigned to that army on the ground in South Korea; they included 1st Cavalry Division, 25th Infantry Division, and what remained of 24th Infantry Division, an entity that, for the time being, existed only on *order of battle* charts. First Cavalry Division was moving northwest from Pusan toward Taejon. Its three battalions of armor—one per cavalry regiment—contained a total of just over one hundred tanks, mostly Chaffees but with a handful of WW2-vintage M4 Shermans. Twenty-Fifth Infantry Division was spilling off ships and aircraft from Japan into Pusan. It would take a few days to gather their equipment; once they did, they'd head northwest to positions on First Cav's right flank. The 1st Provisional Marine Brigade would be landing in a matter of days, as well, and—much to the displeasure of the Marine Corps' leadership—would fall under the command of

8th Army.

More Army divisions—2nd Infantry and 7th Infantry—were in transit to Korea. They'd be joining 8th Army within a few weeks.

Johnnie Walker was anxious to leave his Pusan headquarters and be out among his embattled troops near Taejon. He couldn't leave yet, however. He had a visitor: Major General "Ned" Almond, MacArthur's chief of staff. Even though Walker outranked him, Almond figuratively wore MacArthur's stars as if they were his own, relishing the power that came with his proximity and devotion to *the throne*. Talking to him was as good as talking to MacArthur. Pissing him off was as good as pissing MacArthur off, too, so Walker had little choice but to make time for Ned Almond.

Walker couldn't help but smirk as he remembered the nickname officers who'd served in Europe had bestowed on Almond: *Bidet*, as in the device found in posh restrooms on the Continent used to wash one's anus. The joke around Tokyo: *MacArthur never had to worry about wiping his ass after taking a shit because ol' Bidet would be there to lick it clean.*

As Walker tried to explain the disturbing details of the delaying action at Taejon, an obviously disinterested Almond waved him off. "We don't need any more of this negative talk," Almond said. "What we're witnessing is just another example of MacArthur's brilliance."

Walker was wondering if he'd heard the man correctly. "Excuse me, General? Are you really suggesting our current catastrophe is the product of *brilliance*?"

"Absolutely," Almond replied. "MacArthur is

waging a brilliant—yes, General, *brilliant*—retrograde operation against a numerically superior force that will result in the North Koreans being lured into his inescapable trap."

"What kind of *trap* are we talking about?"

Almond's face took on a sly smile as he said, "You'll find out, General. All in good time."

Walker shook his head in disbelief. "We don't have a lot of time, Almond...and I'm still not buying this *brilliance* song and dance. The only brilliance I'm seeing out there is the work Colonel Miles is doing. Without him, I fear the entire Twenty-Fourth Division would've been destroyed by now. For God's sake, the division commander is *missing in action*!"

"That's *General* Almond, *Johnnie*...and MacArthur doesn't wish to hear any more talk pumping up this Colonel Miles. He's acquainted with the man, who he considers just another colonel with an overinflated opinion of his own abilities. Disloyal, too, so I'd watch your back around him."

"I disagree, General. Completely. The man deserves to be wearing a star."

"Absolutely not, *Johnnie*. The man's got black marks in his file going all the way back to Pearl Harbor. The only reason MacArthur allowed him a regimental command is that we're very hard up for full colonels in theater at the moment. But his name will not be put forward for promotion. Is that clear?"

"Yeah, *crystal*," Walker replied.

But the words felt like dirt in his mouth.

Chapter Twenty

All Jillian Miles knew was that her husband Jock was somewhere in Korea; his exact location in that country was a mystery. The newspapers in California were reporting on a battle of epic proportions around the South Korean city of Taejon. The nightly news broadcasts on the radio were saying the same thing.

It all sounds like a bloody cockup, she told herself while dressing for her first officers' wives' tea at Fort Ord. *But wherever the fighting is, I'll wager that's where Jock is. He wouldn't want it any other way, the bloody mug.*

Wherever he is, though, I'd rather be there with him than sit through this ridiculous tea. But an officer whose wife doesn't attend gets a black mark on his fitness report.

We bloody well can't have that now, can we?

Resolved to the necessity of making an appearance, she loaded her children, Jif and Jane, into their Ford station wagon with the wooden side panels. It was just a short drive onto the post and the residence of General Jarvis Whitelaw and his wife, Priscilla.

Driving up to the smallish but stately Whitelaw residence in the most well-tended corner of Fort Ord, Jillian couldn't help but smile; she'd always felt at odds with the social hierarchy of the military. As she put it, *The wives might as well pin their husband's insignia of rank to their bloody bodice. All this "yes, ma'am" if her husband outranks yours or "fetch me a drink, dear...there's a good girl" if it's the other way around. It hadn't been quite so bad when we were still in*

Australia. It was my country. It was my home.

Everybody knew who I was, where I'd been, what I'd done...

And nobody gave me any shit.

Yanks were the outsiders then.

But here, I'm the outsider...and I'm starting from scratch.

As soon as they arrived, the children were shepherded off to play with the other young *army brats* in attendance under the supervision of the Whitelaws' teenaged daughters. The seventeen wives, wearing their white gloves and Sunday best, topped with stylish yet conservative hats and cashmere sweaters to ward off the coolness of a late July afternoon in Northern California, took their seats on the patio. Instinctively, each woman knew where to sit: cushioned rattan chairs for Mrs. Whitelaw and the colonels' wives, hard wooden folding chairs for the wives of the lower-ranking officers.

There was no doubt Priscilla Whitelaw considered herself a queen holding court. She steered the small talk through the usual laments of neophyte army wives: the pains of frequent relocation; the low pay; the poor choice of products available at the PX; the quality of the schools around Monterey. But Mrs. Whitelaw quickly grew bored of the repetitive drivel. She redirected the discussion to how hard it had been for the *veteran* wives like herself during the last war. While she threw inclusive nods to the few wives whose husbands had served overseas back then, it was clear to all that she'd be the only one allowed to wrap herself in the banner of sacrifice.

"It was just awful," Priscilla Whitelaw said. "Back in the *real* war, with mobilization in full swing, there was no housing available for dependents. They just gave you a paltry little housing stipend and kicked you into the street to find someplace decent to live. And believe me, ladies, there was no affordable, *decent* lodging anywhere. I was practically homeless and had to shuttle my children back and forth between my family and the general's for almost two years. And having to organize all those tiresome war bond and USO events! But that's the price we pay to live in the greatest country under God."

She paused for effect, her eyes making one sweep of the room to take in the sympathetic glances being cast her way. Somehow, she didn't notice the dismissive look on Jillian's face.

"But we won't have to worry about all that this time," Mrs. Whitelaw continued, "because there's no need for full mobilization. MacArthur's boys will take care of those little Asian *toy soldiers* in no time flat. Another feather in his cap for the elections in Fifty-Two, when this nation will elect the great man himself to the presidency and fix the mess our country is in, all caused by that little sales clerk Truman and his China-losing Democrats."

She leaned back in her rattan chair, soaking in the polite applause. But when she scanned the approving faces of her guests, she saw the look on Jillian's face; it was anything but approving. She wasn't clapping, either.

Mrs. Whitelaw stopped the applause with an annoyed wave of her hand. Fixing an iron gaze at Jillian, she asked, "I'm sorry, but I seem to have forgotten we have a newcomer from another land in our midst. Colonel Miles' wife…it's Jacqueline, isn't it?"

"No, it's Jillian."

"All right, *Jillian*. So you don't agree with my position?"

"I don't pay much attention to your American politics, but I do have some very clear memories of the last *little Asian toy soldiers* the Allies had to fight. It took us three bloody years to beat them into submission, didn't it?"

The American women might have been offended by the term *bloody* if they'd actually known what it meant in profane context. They'd just assumed she was describing the ferocity of combat.

But what did offend Priscilla Whitelaw was the challenge to her authority. This insubordinate Aussie upstart had to be put in her place, and quickly.

"I'm curious, Jillian…my husband spent some time in Brisbane during the war. He said it seemed that Australia didn't even think there was a war on. You people disrespected MacArthur, who should be revered for the god that he is, disrespected your own king…and you even had labor strikes! Workers actually refused to contribute to the war effort. That all sounds like you Australians are a terribly unpatriotic lot. You ladies *down under* were having yourselves a little party with all those fine American boys while the rest of the free world was sacrificing so much to win the war."

"Actually, ma'am, I would've loved to have been invited to that party. But, you see, I couldn't because I was a prisoner of the Japanese. So if you want to discuss *actual* sacrifice, I can tell you stories from now until Christmas."

In the hush that fell over the gathering, Priscilla Whitelaw refused to believe she'd lost the upper hand.

Her sense of entitlement wouldn't accept it. So, with all the false sincerity she could muster, she said, "Oh dear, one can imagine how terrible it was for you."

"No," Jillian replied, "one cannot, I'm afraid."

This time, it seemed nothing would be capable of shattering the silence. But then a voice—one of the Whitelaw daughters—called out, "They're ready, Mother."

As if handed a lifeline, Mrs. Whitelaw gushed, "Oh, wonderful! Let the parade begin!"

The Stars and Stripes Forever began to blare from an unseen phonograph. The back door of the house sprang open and the children—all twenty-eight of them—marched into the yard in single file. Boys and girls alike, they were in costume: paper replicas of army green uniforms complete with overseas caps. Each child carried a little toy rifle at *right shoulder arms.*

Jillian was the only one who didn't begin to clap with delight. She rushed to her children, removed the mock rifles from their shoulders, took them by the hand, and started for the door.

Before leaving the patio, she turned to face the rankled Mrs. Whitelaw and said, "My husband may be a soldier, ma'am, but my children will *never* be."

By the time they'd reached their station wagon, Jillian had removed the paper uniforms and torn them to shreds. She thought for a moment about picking up the scraps of paper now littering the Whitelaws' lawn.

Then she mumbled, "Bugger that…and bloody MacArthur, too."

She loaded her puzzled children into the car and drove away.

Chapter Twenty-One

As Sean assembled his tank-killer patrol, one of the members arrived at the assembly point toting a .30-caliber machine gun. Belts of ammo were crisscrossed around his torso. Sean laughed when he saw him and said, "Who the hell do you think you are, Pancho Fuckin' Villa? Get rid of that goddamn thirty. I said we're going in light tonight, didn't I, numbnuts?"

"Shit, Sarge...this *is* light. I wanted to bring a fifty cal."

"And I would've beat your brains in with it. When I say light, I mean fucking *light*. These carbines we got are almost too damn heavy, with all the rockets we need to be carrying."

"But I thought maybe we'd want a little...you know, *firepower*, Sarge? In case we've got to shoot it out with some gooks?"

Sean replied, "Let me ask you something, kid...you ain't never fought house to house before, have you?"

The gunner shook his head.

"Then take it from me. The only bad guys you're gonna shoot will be standing so close you can feel them breathing on you. And our job tonight is to kill tanks, not get into shootouts. You understand me?"

"Yeah, Sarge. I understand...I guess."

"Good. Now be back here in three minutes or less with a suitable weapon. We gotta get this show on the road."

The gunner was back in two and a half minutes.

Two 3.5-inch rocket teams comprised his patrol.

Sean told the teams, "All right, let's go over a coupla points before we head into Taejon. First, it's a safe bet the gook tanks are gonna move south through the city during the night. They wanna get as far as they can from that fire torching the north side. That'll put 'em in a better position to attack our line once the sun comes up. But if we can make good use of the darkness and the million hiding places the city's gonna offer, we can knock out some of 'em tonight, when they least expect it, and fuck up their plans big time. Everybody with me so far?"

Ten heads nodded as one.

Sean continued, "Outstanding. Now, we'll try to keep both teams in earshot of each other at all times."

A hand shot up. "So why are we lugging the walkie-talkies, Sarge?"

"To save your ass if everything turns to shit, dummy. If you need artillery or quad fifty support, how're you gonna call for it without a radio?"

"But the walkie-talkies don't have the range to reach the artillery, Sarge. They'll be three miles away, maybe a little more."

"You're getting ahead of yourself, pal," Sean replied. "LP Charlie is gonna relay for us. We'll never be more than a mile away from those guys. We'll do a commo check with the LP on our way out, just to make sure everything's working. We walk right by it. Any other dumb questions?"

Nobody had another question, dumb or otherwise.

"A coupla things to bear in mind," Sean continued. "The tanks that ain't on the move will try to hide themselves, maybe even *inside* buildings. Don't waste time and rockets on 'em if the only shot you got is at their bow. The ones moving down the streets give us a couple of engagement options. But whether we hit 'em from the sides or in the ass, make damn sure you got your escape route all figured out. If you miss a tank with your first shot, forget it and get the fuck outta there. If you stay put, you'll be dead before you get another shot."

Sean's anti-tank patrol had taken a little over an hour to creep to the center of Taejon. It was 0130 hours now, and they'd yet to see or hear a T-34. As they huddled in the darkness in what looked and smelled like a butcher's shop, Sean said, "The fire up north's dying out. The damn wind ain't spreading it too good, so I guess there's no big rush for the T-34s to move south."

One of the gunners asked, "So what're we going to do, Sarge?"

"We're gonna go find those bastards and see what we can do to fuck up their night."

"But if we go much farther north, we'll be out of radio range with the LP."

"Yeah. Too bad about that," Sean replied. "Now let's get moving."

They'd crept a few blocks deeper into the darkened city when Sean suddenly pulled his men inside a building. "I smell diesel," he said. "Only things in this whole fucking country that run on diesel are Russian-built armor. All of you, get real quiet and listen. If they're fueling tanks around here, they gotta make a little noise eventually."

He moved to the far side of the building, across an

interior space cluttered with crates, as if it might be some sort of warehouse. Crouching beneath a shattered window, he heard that *little noise* he'd expected: the *shush-shush* of a hand pump. When it stopped, he could hear voices speaking Korean and then the sound of a motor cranking up.

Sean dared to take a peek through the window. Not more than thirty yards down the street, a small tractor was towing a fuel bowser. He could make out the silhouettes of the driver and three men walking beside it. When the bowser stopped, the men dragged the long hose connected to it into an alleyway. He couldn't see what type of vehicle they were in the process of fueling.

"Looks like maybe they got tanks parked between the buildings across the street," Sean told his men. "We gotta figure out which way they're facing." He pointed to one of the loaders and said, "Mendoza, come with me. We're going for a little walk. You're gonna cover my ass. The rest of you hold tight right here."

☆ ☆ ☆

Crossing an alleyway, Sean and PFC Mendoza snuck into the building on the other side. The moment they entered, they were struck by the strong odor of fermentation. They could make out the shapes of a dozen vats lined up across the floor, each like a giant wooden barrel with sides that came to a man's chest. Sean took a look inside one; it was empty.

"Looks like somebody beat us to sucking down everything in this brewery," he whispered to Mendoza. "Too bad for us, eh?"

Actually, Sean considered himself lucky. If they'd

entered the brewery first instead of the warehouse, the smell of diesel might've been masked by the enticing aroma of Korean beer. Robbed of that clue, they might've blundered into the street—and right into the KPA tankers.

They were about to move toward the side of the building facing the refueling operation when he heard more noises. These were coming from *inside* the brewery. They sounded very close.

Too close.

It was coming from the other side of the vats: the sound of men snoring.

Even though Sean needed desperately to look out the window and see what was parked in those alleyways, he didn't dare walk around the vats. There was no guarantee that *everyone* behind them was asleep.

Grabbing Mendoza by his web gear, Sean pulled him back out of the building the same way they'd entered. Once outside, he whispered, "Let's have ourselves a look from that next alley."

Entering that alley, they found it occupied by an empty flatbed truck. It didn't have military markings, but that didn't mean it wasn't being used by the KPA. There were no Koreans around it, though, and the truck gave good cover for surveilling the opposite side of the street.

From his perch on the truck's running board, Sean realized three things. First, there were six T-34s parked across the street, each nestled in her own alley. Second, the bow of each tank was facing him. Third, there were KPA soldiers in the building to his left, too—lots of them—and they weren't asleep like their comrades in the brewery to his right.

Silently retracing their steps through the brewery, he and Mendoza rejoined the rest of the GIs in the warehouse.

"Here's the deal," Sean told his men. "We got six T-34s across the street, parked with their bows facing us. We gotta get behind them. Be aware that every building from here north looks like it's got gooks in it, so we're gonna backtrack a little, cross this street, get behind 'em, and put a rocket up the ass of all six of them bastards."

He'd expected the uneasiness he saw in their faces, so he quickly continued, "Now, before you get your panties all in a bunch, this is how it's gonna work. With only two tubes, we can't kill 'em all at once, right? So we're gonna start from the north end. *Team Able* will kill the tank on that end, then run like hell to kill the *third* tank in line while *Team Baker* kills the *second* tank in line. We leapfrog like that twice and then get the hell outta here. Just remember—if you miss, forget it and move on to the next target. But if you do miss, you gotta be the biggest fuckup in *this man's army*, because we're gonna be pretty fucking close. Everybody load their tube right now."

One of the gunners spoke up. "But if the tube's hot, Sarge, and it's dark and shit and I trip and fall, it just might—"

"Then don't fall down, numbnuts. Now hurry the fuck up. Let's get this over with before sunup, okay?"

Once in position behind the T-34s in the alleys,

Sean's gunners dispatched the first three tanks in just under two minutes. By the time Team Baker was lining up on the fourth tank, though, the initial surprise and confusion gripping the KPA troopers had worn off. They'd figured out where the tank-killing fire was coming from. They started shooting their rifles and submachine guns down the street from which Sean's teams were staging their attack.

Even though he was behind the cover of a building, Team Baker's gunner was rattled by the gunfire. The rocket he launched at the fourth tank—less than a hundred yards away—sailed past her turret, crossed the next street, and struck the brewery.

Stunned by the miss, the gunners seemed frozen in place. Sean yelled, "MOVE OUT, GODDAMMIT! YOU KNOW THE DRILL. NEXT TARGET."

The KPA gunfire slowed the teams' leapfrogging from one firing point to the next. Just a minute ago they'd simply run down the street; now they were seeking cover as they moved, ducking through or around buildings. It took extra time. Too much time.

The fifth tank was blown up just like the first three. But when the leapfrogging Team Baker got to the sixth and last tank, she wasn't in her alleyway anymore. They couldn't see her, but they could hear her bellowing engine beyond the buildings on the parallel street.

It sounded as if she was moving south, intent on cutting off the GIs' escape.

"She's gonna turn down one of these alleys and come straight at us," Sean said. "We gotta cross the street and get behind her, or at least broadside to her."

As he marshaled his teams for the dash across the

street, he did a quick headcount. It came up two men short.

Sean asked, "Where the hell's Mendoza and Culp, for cryin' out loud?"

Nobody had an answer.

But there was no time to wait, no time to search for them.

Sean and his men bolted across the street. Despite the KPA's random gunfire, they all made it safely and kept going down the alley toward the next street. They were halfway there when they heard another roaring engine; the T-34 they'd shot at and missed was moving down that street they were running toward.

The tank rolled past the alley and then braked to a sudden stop. Her commander, high in his turret hatch, had spotted the GIs.

As he shouted orders to his crew, the tank began to back up as her turret slowly traversed toward the alley.

Dumb move, pal, Sean thought. *You should be pivoting her on her tracks instead of trying to spin that turret around. Takes too fucking long. In the meantime, you're showing me her bad side.*

"Take her," he told Team Baker's gunner. Then he yelled to the men bunched in the alley behind the tube, "Clear the backblast, dammit!"

The rocket struck low on the center hull between two road wheels. There was that agonizing split second when nothing seemed to happen.

Don't tell me it's a fucking dud...

Then there was a dull *thud* from within her. Flames shot from every hatch. No one got out.

She was dead and so was her crew.

But the tank still alive was at the other end of the

alley now. She hadn't made her late sister's mistake and driven past it.

Instead, she'd turned right into it, her two machine guns blazing.

The GIs had already slipped into an adjacent building. They raced through a near pitch black maze of machinery and rubble in what seemed to be a textile mill. There was only one clear path they could take: straight across the building to the opposite side.

When they reached it, they could find no way out. No doors, no windows. Just a solid brick wall.

"Ain't this some shit," Sean said in frustration. "We're in the middle of a wooden city, trapped behind the only brick wall in the whole fucking place."

In the alley, the T-34 had come to a halt, but the GIs weren't sure exactly where. They could only hear her, not see her.

A few seconds later, the mystery of her location was solved by the snapping sound of wood being torn apart. The muzzle of her main gun was suddenly inside the building, protruding through the shattered wooden wall, swinging slowly toward the GIs. In a few seconds more, that gun would be pointing right at them.

Team Baker—the team who'd just killed the tank in the street—was frantically trying to reload their tube.

Team Able's 3.5 was ready to fire. But her gunner wasn't.

"Where the hell do I aim, Sarge? I can't see shit!"

There was no time to reply. The T-34's main gun was almost on them.

Sean grabbed the rocket launcher from the gunner's hands, stood straight up for a better angle through the splintered wall, and fired right where he felt sure her turret ring would be.

The cloud of dust and debris that resulted reduced visibility in the mill to almost nothing. But there was no doubt he'd hit the tank. With a shriek of torn metal, the turret's traverse ceased abruptly.

Congratulations for the fortuitous shot would have to wait. Damaged or not, the tank was still blocking their only path of escape from the building.

And she wasn't dead; the clatter of grinding gears made that obvious. The driver, at least, was still able to function and trying desperately to shift the transmission into reverse. But her main gun was still jammed through the wall. It would have to tear through the rest of that wall to free itself.

From the sound of the tank's screaming engine, the extrication wasn't going well.

Sean tossed the empty 3.5 back to Team Able's gunner. Then he yelled to Team Baker, "Knock a hole in that fucking brick wall. Everybody else, hug yourself some floor."

Heeding his own order, he threw himself prone, thinking, *Let's hope that with that fucking tank trying to rip down one wall and us shooting out another one, this whole shitty building don't fall down on top of us.*

If the first *whoosh* of a 3.5 firing at the tank in an enclosed space hadn't deafened the GIs, the second one firing at the wall finished the job. They were blind now, too; the multi-layered veil of darkness, smoke, and dust saw to that. They made their way out of this black void by feel alone.

The rocket had punched a hole in the brick wall big enough to drive a jeep through. Choking, gasping for air, they stumbled into the alley. Although his throat felt like he'd just swallowed a sackful of sand, Sean managed to speak a hoarse command: "This way, dammit. Follow me."

The wild revving of the T-34's engine was replaced by the steady rumble of lower rpm, as if she was finally finding it easier to back out of the alley.

Sean's plan was to move around the building, positioning his teams to kill the crippled tank from behind. In a matter of seconds, they'd left the alley, crossed the street, and had the rear end of the tank in their sights.

But neither of the 3.5s had had a chance to reload. Frantic hands shoved rockets into each tube while struggling to hook up the ignition wires.

"Take it easy, boys," Sean said, "but hurry the fuck up."

Team Able was loaded first. Just as the gunner was about to pull the trigger, the silhouette of a man appeared in the alley right behind the tank, running slowly toward them. He wasn't alone; he was carrying someone on his back.

"Shit, I think that's Mendoza," Sean said.

The man on his back had to be Culp.

Then three more men appeared in the alley, running around the tank.

Sean yelled to Mendoza, "GET THE HELL DOWN."

Mendoza did as he was told. He took cover behind the corner of the building, shielding the wounded Culp with his body.

Just as the other three men got to the rear of the tank, it lurched backward, knocking down all three. Two of them slipped beneath the tracks and were crushed.

Sean told his gunner, "Fire, goddammit. NOW."

He did.

His rocket was still in flight when Team Baker fired, too.

Within seconds, the T-34 was ablaze from within.

Mendoza picked up his wounded buddy again and struggled across the street to rejoin the rest of the GIs.

Culp was conscious but hit in the leg, the wound bleeding badly. Sean took him from the winded Mendoza and hoisted him onto his shoulders in a fireman's carry.

"Party's over, boys," Sean said. "Time to get the hell outta here."

He told Mendoza, "See if you can get a tourniquet on his leg while we're on the move. If we stop, we might all get dead."

Using his GI belt, Mendoza managed to get the job done, but he worried it wasn't good enough. He said, "It ain't perfect, you know."

Sean replied, "Nothing ever is, pal."

On the way out of Taejon, they heard a few more vehicles but only caught a glimpse of one—yet another T-34—several streets away. Thirty minutes later, they crossed the American line at LP Charlie. They'd radioed ahead; the medics were waiting to take care of Culp. Barely conscious, he'd lost a lot of blood during the escape. That didn't stop him from saying, with the faintest of smiles, "At least I didn't get run over by my own tank like those gook bastards."

As the GIs flopped to the ground trying to catch their breath, Sean had one lament: "We had six rockets left, dammit."

Chapter Twenty-Two

As he watched the morning's aerial attack on
Taejon from his hilltop CP, Jock Miles knew that
further nighttime raids by his armor sergeant weren't
worth the risk. While they'd done an amazing job last
night, killing what amounted to more than a platoon of
KPA tanks, the pickings would be slim in the city from
here on out. The Air Force was systematically reducing
it to a gigantic pile of charred lumber. Soon there
wouldn't be many North Korean troops or tanks left in
the city, just enough to guard against the Americans
slipping through it to get behind the main body of their
forces. That *main body*, he was sure, was already taking
to the hills east and west of Taejon to continue their
relentless march south to Pusan. Once KPA tanks and
infantry were hidden in those hills, air power wouldn't
be much help rooting them out.

Jock wasn't kidding himself: *I can delay them
another day or two, but there are just too many of them.
They've probably still got plenty of armor…*

And we've got zip.

*Maybe once First Cav moves up here, we've got a
little bit of a chance.*

But I'm not going to hold my breath.

Patchett emerged from the CP tent with some
dispatches in his hand. He told Jock, "Says here that
aerial recon counts about a company's worth of gook
tanks killed inside Taejon itself, sir. Looks like the
credit for about a quarter of that goes to our own Bubba
Moon. The rest goes to the flyboys."

"That's all the armor they said was in the city? Just

a company—about twenty tanks?"

"Affirmative, sir."

Jock turned his binoculars to the hills that flanked the city. "That means there are probably still a couple of battalions of T-34s out there somewhere," he said.

"Affirmative again, sir. But as I live and breathe, ol' Bubba needs to get decorated for what he did last night. I mean, what does a man gotta do to get a medal around here?"

"I hear you, Top. Draw up the paperwork. Put him in for another bunch of oak leaves on that Silver Star of his."

"Roger, sir. Now, one more thing. Got a dispatch from Eighth Army saying General Walker just might be dropping in on us this morning. I reckon we ain't gonna like what he has to say."

"Why's that, Top?"

"It's simple, sir. Bad news comes over the horn. *Real* bad news gets delivered in person."

Jock was about to counter with *Maybe it's good news…*

But he knew better.

The air attacks on Taejon had swelled the flow of civilian refugees heading south from the city. A lieutenant at LP Charlie—the American roadblock on the Taejon-Pusan highway—noticed something strange about a particular column of approaching refugees; dispersed among the old men, women, children, and animal-drawn carts were men of military age. True, they were dressed in civilian clothes and carried no visible weapons…

But something isn't right, the lieutenant told himself. *There are just too damn many of them, even though they're trying to string themselves out.*

He ordered his men at the roadblock to detain the first group of young men trying to pass. Then he got on the landline to 3rd Battalion CP.

"I need the gook interpreter down here, right fucking now," he told the CP. "Better send another platoon for prisoner duty, too. We might have ourselves a bunch of infiltrators."

Third Battalion reported the lieutenant's suspicion to Regiment. Jock told Patchett, "Go down there and check it out."

"Okay, sir," Patchett replied, "but what if the ROKs want to start executing gooks they don't like again?"

"We're not supposed to stop them, remember? Just make damn sure that none of our men are on that firing squad. I don't want our boys to have that hanging around their necks."

"Amen to that, sir."

Patchett arrived at LP Charlie just moments after the ROK interpreter. The extra platoon the lieutenant requested had a dozen of the young "civilian" men in custody. They were seated together on the ground alongside the road as if enjoying a summer picnic.

"Better separate those prisoners, Lieutenant," Patchett said. "Spread 'em out so they can't whisper to each other like they're doing."

"But the interpreter says they're okay, Sergeant," the lieutenant replied.

"You gonna bet your life on that, Lieutenant? Take

a real good look at what's going on over there."

He pointed to the interpreter, a ROK captain. He was talking to three young men at the roadblock.

"Watch their hands real close, Lieutenant," Patchett said.

Quick as a flash, one of the young men slipped something into the ROK captain's hand. Whatever it was in his hand, the ROK captain pocketed it in the blink of an eye.

Patchett asked, "You saw that, didn't you, Lieutenant? I reckon they're bribing him. And he's taking it, too, the gook son of a bitch."

He walked up behind the ROK and ripped the pockets out of his fatigue trousers. Packets of South Korean *won*—the local currency—spilled to the ground.

"I suggest you arrest this captain immediately, Lieutenant," Patchett said. "Better round up all these KPA bastards, too. And search every one of them wagons."

Somebody screamed, "GRENADE!"

Patchett looked down to find a GI hand grenade at his feet, white smoke wisping from its fuze.

He kicked it toward the group of young men who, until just a moment ago, were lounging by the roadside. Now they were all flat on their faces. The appearance of the grenade was apparently no surprise to them.

Then Patchett hit the deck like everyone else.

The explosion killed two of the KPA infiltrators outright and wounded half a dozen more. When Patchett raised his head, he saw the men who'd just bribed the interpreter running back toward Taejon. They were in good company; all the other young men farther back in the column were running away, too.

With three shots from his carbine, Patchett took down the closest three. He would've emptied his magazine, but he didn't have a good bead on the others anymore.

A few of the other GIs started to fire at the fleeing KPA men, too.

"Cease fire," Patchett said. "You ain't gonna hit 'em. Save your ammo."

A search of the carts found two in the middle of the column loaded with weapons, which were concealed beneath sacks of refugees' belongings. Several dozen weapons were Soviet issue, but another dozen were American. There were more GI grenades still in their shipping crates.

"This is what happens when a unit throws down its weapons and bugs out," Patchett said as he rummaged through a cart. "You become your enemy's supply depot."

The ROK captain was running away, too, trying to mingle with the refugees. A GI tackled him.

"Tie that captain's hands behind his back and put him in my jeep," Patchett said. "We're gonna have ourselves a little *military justice* later on up at the CP."

A few of the GIs were picking up the packets of money that had been torn from the captain's pockets. The lieutenant seemed unsure whether to stop them or not.

"Better grab some of that dough for yourself, Lieutenant," Patchett said, "before your boys get it all."

But the lieutenant didn't touch the money.

"Ah, very good, sir," Patchett told him. "Always take care of your men first."

After assigning some of his soldiers to guard the ROK captain, the lieutenant said, "You know, Sergeant, I swear that grenade had the longest fuze in history."

"Three and a half to five seconds, sir," Patchett replied. "That can be one hell of a long time. The difference between life and death, you know?"

Walking to his jeep, Patchett knew the lieutenant still had something on his mind. Hesitantly, it was put into words: "I need...I really need to thank you, Sergeant. I messed up back there. But I've got to ask you, do you think any of those genuine refugees were in on it?"

"If they were, they were forced to, that's all. I reckon we should let them go on their way, Lieutenant. We scared them enough."

"Yeah, okay. But I still feel like a horse's ass for missing what that ROK was up to."

"All's well that ends well, sir. But remember, just because you and another guy are fighting the same enemy, that don't make you friends. Now don't let them KPA bastards you got rounded up over there get away. We're gonna need to have a real long chat with them."

General Walker's plane—a single-engined Stinson L-5—touched down in 26th RCT's position just after 1100 hours. She'd had to land along the highway behind the artillery's position; it was the only safe place to avoid all the *friendly* rounds in the air. A waiting jeep whisked the general the mile to Jock's hilltop CP.

"I like what you're doing here, Colonel," Walker

told him as he scanned the area around Taejon through binoculars. Do you think you can hold this position another four days?"

"No, sir, I don't."

"Then how long *do* you think you can hold it?"

"Two days at most, General. Unless I get some serious armor support, their armor will break through in that time."

"But Tokyo says the Air Force is doing a fabulous job knocking out their armor, Colonel. Is that not the case?"

"Well, sir, it *is* the case—in daylight. Until we get aircraft that can find and destroy armor in the dark, though—or tanks that can kill a T-34—our stay here will be very short."

"Tokyo is convinced the KPA doesn't have the capability for large-scale armor operations at night, Miles. Are you telling me they do?"

"No, sir, I'm not telling you that. It's absolutely true they don't have the capability for *large-scale* night operations, just as we don't. But they're perfectly capable of *small-scale* operations…and a few of those strung together will break through our line and run wild. Once that happens, this position—and this unit—is as good as overrun."

"How can I help you make sure that doesn't happen, Miles?"

"Give me tank support from First Cav, sir. Put them on the road direct to here today. How about a couple of battalions?"

"But they're *already* supporting you, Colonel. Within twenty-four hours, they'll be relieving you of the job of holding the Taejon-Pusan railway."

"Negative, sir. That's not the type of support I'm talking about. They'll still be twenty-five miles away. I want some of their tanks here *tonight*. Preferably Pershings or Shermans."

"Hardly any Pershings or Shermans have landed in Korea yet, Colonel. You know that."

"All right, sir, I'll take Chaffees if that's all you've got. They'll be sacrificed, make no mistake about that, but I can buy the time you want if I have them."

General Walker fell silent. He was a short, squat man—like a bulldog, some said—and the figurative weight of the world on his shoulders only made him look more so. Jock thought he knew the calculation going on in the general's mind:

He's afraid if he divides his forces, they'll all be destroyed piecemeal. But if he keeps First Cav intact, at least they'll have a fighting chance to survive.

The Twenty-Sixth, on the other hand...we're all that's left of a shattered division.

We're here to be sacrificed.

All I can say to that is "over my dead body."

Let's hope it doesn't come to that.

Walker snapped from his contemplation and said, "I'll give you a battalion, Colonel. That's the best I can do at the moment. But I still need you to keep this highway blocked."

Jock replied, "Very well, sir."

The general looked at him quizzically, because he'd smiled when he said it.

Men just handed an impossible task rarely smiled.

Maybe he would've understood if he knew what Jock was thinking:

Patchett was right, as usual. Real bad news gets

delivered in person.

Two flights of F-51s—*Banjo* and *Trombone*—were attacking the KPA in the hills east of Taejon while a squadron of B-26s bombed the city itself. The F-51s' objective was to keep the North Korean armor away from the rail line that ran to Pusan. They'd already derailed a southbound train hauling twenty-one T-34s on flatcars. Once derailed, the entire train had slid down an embankment. Most of the flatcars were now overturned, as were the tanks they were carrying.

"Pretty nice of them to try to move that train in daylight," Tommy told the other two pilots in *Banjo Flight*, Al DeLuca and Pete Sublette. Ted Waleska, the flight's fourth pilot, who'd been forced down yesterday, was safely in GI hands but hadn't made it back to K-9 yet.

Tommy's flight had done the lion's share of the attack on the train; as a result, they'd expended all their rockets. Down to bombs and guns now, they went looking for other targets. The FAC thought he'd found one for them: an artillery battery tucked into a valley.

"*Banjo Leader*, this is *Spectral*," the FAC radioed. "I see four—maybe five—SPs trying to get under camouflage netting. Looks like a battery. They're between hills so it'll be a steep approach to target. I'll mark them for you. Get south of me so you can see the big picture."

Tommy positioned his flight as requested. He caught a glimpse of one SP—a self-propelled artillery piece—still in the open. When he glanced again a moment later, it was gone.

"Looks like it's an SU-76," Tommy said. "Standard Russian war surplus. But it couldn't have gone that far that fast. He's still there but hidden under a net, that's for sure."

Spectral One-Seven asked, "You still need the smoke?"

"Affirmative. Couldn't hurt."

"This run will be with bombs, right?"

"Affirmative again," Tommy replied.

"Okay, I'll mark the south and north ends of their position. Drop your eggs between the markers."

Pete Sublette asked, "How do you want to do it, boss? High or low?"

"Let's make it low," Tommy replied. "We'll waste too much time and gas climbing up to *angels eight* for a dive-bombing run."

"Roger," Sublette replied. "Looks like I'll be closest once *Spectral's* done marking. Want me to lead?"

"Affirmative," Tommy said. Then he told DeLuca, "Al, you follow Pete. I'll be tail-end Charlie. We'll hit them from the southeast. That should keep us out of their line of fire."

As *Spectral One-Seven* rolled into its target-marking run, Tommy's flight orbited both to observe and buy time before they turned toward the KPA artillery battery themselves.

The tense voice of *Trombone Leader* burst from their headphones: "We've got *bandits*—lots of them—straight above. We're getting out of here."

Tommy could see the enemy aircraft. He counted twelve, well above the American ships, probably at

10,000 feet or higher.

They're Lavochkins...LA-7s, he told himself.

They didn't worry him. Not yet.

Tommy could see the four ships of *Trombone Flight* a few miles to the east, too. Not only had they made a rapid turn to the south—and the relative safety of American airfields—they were jettisoning their bombs on nothing in particular. The five-hundred-pounders looked like black specks falling toward barren mountains to be wasted.

How much you want to bet they unload what's left of their rockets, too? Why the hell are they running so scared?

"*Trombone,* this is *Banjo.* Where the hell are you going? Those bandits can only come at us from one direction, and as long as we can see them, we can handle them."

"Negative, *Banjo.* I'm not taking on the whole gook air force."

Tommy's thoughts: *Twelve fucking ships...hardly "the whole gook air force."*

I wasn't too impressed the last time we came up against their Lavochkins, either.

But if they want to come down and play, we'll cross that bridge when we come to it.

He kept an eye on the LA-7s overhead while watching Pete Sublette roll into his bomb run. Pete used the cover of a low hill for his approach to the artillery battery. Once he'd popped over that hill, his glide bombing run was over in a matter of seconds. His two 500-pound bombs fell right between the smoke markers *Spectral One-Seven* had put down. Several secondary explosions quickly followed the initial blast.

"I'm clear," Sublette reported. "Feel those secondaries? I must've hit something good. Don't think I took any triple-A, either. You still watching those bandits upstairs?"

"Affirmative," Tommy replied. "No problems from them yet."

Al DeLuca rolled into his attack run. He employed a different approach, passing between a gap in the hills to fly even lower over the target than Sublette had. His bombs fell just as accurately.

Tommy radioed, "You guys did so good, I don't think you even need me. I'm going to hold on to my eggs for another target."

Sublette asked, "Unless we get into a fight with those bandits, right?"

"Goes without saying, Pete."

Spectral One-Seven came back on the air. "I've got what looks like another battery, south-southeast of last target, about two miles. They're shooting, too. I saw their smoke and that's about all. By the way, we've got no interceptors in the area, repeat—no interceptors."

"Figured that," Tommy replied.

As *Banjo Flight* regrouped and turned to the new target, DeLuca reported, "Ah...we've got action from our friends on high. Four of them are peeling off and heading downstairs. It looks like they're going to come at us from the northwest."

"Yeah, I see," Tommy replied. "You know the drill. We'll meet them head-on."

"So you're going to dump your bombs?" Sublette asked.

"Not yet."

"You sure, boss?"

"Yeah," Tommy replied. "The US Air Force already wasted enough ordnance this morning."

He hoped *Trombone Flight*—now almost fifteen miles away—had heard his last transmission because it was meant for them.

The four LA-7s came at the F-51s spread wide in line formation. The encounter went exactly as Tommy expected: they closed head-to-head at frightening speed, exchanged poorly aimed gunfire briefly, and nobody was hit. Staying low, *Banjo Flight* turned hard left while the Koreans clawed for altitude.

"Dammit," DeLuca said, "I'd love to be chasing their asses right now."

"Yeah, but that's not our job," Tommy replied. "Let's set up for a pass at this other battery. I'll go in first and unload these eggs. You guys cover me and then follow up with a gun run."

There was great urgency in *Spectral One-Seven's* voice as he said, "You might want to reconsider that, *Banjo*. Looks like a whole bunch of *Lavs* are coming down. I've got to make myself scarce for a little bit."

A quick glance over his shoulder told Tommy that the FAC was right: the eight LA-7s that had stayed at altitude were diving down now. The four that they'd just tangled with were turning hard to join their comrades.

Shit, Tommy told himself as he pickled the five-hundred-pounders away to fall on nothing but barren landscape. *But I've got no choice now...got to lighten the ship up if we're going to dance for real with those Lavs. Three against twelve are pretty shitty odds.*

Push comes to shove, we can outrun them.

The bombs gone, Tommy led *Banjo Flight* in a

tight turn to engage the LA-7s head-to-head once again. Watching the Koreans form for the attack, he told himself, *Just like I figured...they formed a line straight across. Russian tactics all the way. But that's good...spread out like they are, only a couple of them can even come close to getting their guns on us.*

"Stay together, guys," he told Sublette and DeLuca, "but leave us some room to bob and weave. Don't go off by yourself to chase somebody."

"No chance of that, boss," Sublette replied. "Safety in numbers, right?"

Once again, the engagement was over with blinding speed. Sublette got lucky: an LA-7 pulled up too early, giving him a momentary look at her belly and a much bigger target. He pulled up, too, while spraying a quick burst for the LA-7 to fly through. The twinkles of bullet strikes along her lower fuselage were obvious. As *Banjo Flight* turned hard left once the encounter was done, they watched the LA-7 pitch up, stall, and then spin to the ground like a falling leaf. There was no parachute.

The line of Korean ships split apart, some turning north, some climbing; two turned south into the path of *Banjo Flight*.

"They're making this too fucking easy," Sublette said as he maneuvered for a deflection shot on an LA-7 almost directly in front of him. He fired off a long burst.

But the kill wouldn't be his; his rounds never found their mark. DeLuca had the better angle; with three short bursts, he sent the Korean ship tumbling to the ground.

When he'd tried to squeeze off a fourth burst,

nothing happened. His guns had gone dry.

After that long burst, Sublette's guns were dry, too.

The Koreans, less their two downed comrades, were scattered across the northern sky. Maybe they were regrouping for another attack.

Maybe not.

Checking his counter, Tommy saw he was down to forty-eight rounds remaining, just twelve rounds each in his four inboard guns. The outer two were already dry.

It was time to go home.

That second artillery battery—the one that had just escaped being pummeled from the air—continued to pour its fire onto the positions of the 26th RCT.

Chapter Twenty-Three

Captain Don Gerard, flying FAC ship *Spectral One-Seven*, could tell *Montana Six*—Colonel Miles—was angry, even though his voice over the radio remained controlled and professional. But the colonel had good reason to be angry: North Korean artillery was pounding 26th RCT in broad daylight and the USAF was doing nothing to stop it.

Gerard tried hard to keep his own frustration from his voice as he explained, "All attack ships are dry and returning to base. There'll be no flights on station for approximately six-zero minutes." He didn't dare mention that one flight of F-51s—*Trombone Flight*—had decided to flee the threat posed by enemy aircraft while still fully armed to attack ground targets.

Jock knew that in another *six-zero minutes* of this pounding, there was a good chance his regimental combat team might suffer so much destruction—and so many casualties—that it might cease to exist as a combat-effective unit. The only thing that would save his men was how deep they'd dug themselves into the ground.

In the absence of aircraft to direct, Gerard turned his attention to acting as aerial observer for 26th Regiment's artillery. But that effort came up empty, too. The Korean artillery—SU-76 assault guns—had parked themselves just beyond the maximum range of the American batteries. Even though the SU-76 fired smaller shells—76 millimeter versus the American 105 and 155-millimeter rounds—they could shoot them farther. Smaller shells, delivered with accuracy and in sufficient quantity, killed you just as dead as larger ones. Even though the FAC had pinpointed the location of the Korean guns, the American artillery commander knew that attempting counter-battery fire was futile; the Korean guns were simply a mile out of range, and in the confines of the mountainous terrain, there was no way to position the American guns closer. Until friendly attack planes reappeared, the only hope was that the Korean guns would run out of ammo.

"They gotta have an OP on one of them hills to the west," Patchett told Jock as they scanned the surrounding terrain with binoculars. "We knock that out and we take their eyes away, at least. Maybe keep those guns from doing too much damage."

"Yeah," Jock replied, "and it's got to be high ground that they can't see our artillery positions from."

"How do you figure that, sir?"

"Because if they could adjust fire on our gun positions, they would've hit them first damn thing. As it is, they haven't come anywhere near the artillery yet."

"I see your point, sir," Patchett said, "but I'm getting worried about that forty-millimeter buggy of ours in Third Battalion's sector. I'm betting the gooks can see it plain as day. Dug in or not, they chipped some paint off it a coupla times already. Want to move it? Get it behind this hill until we need it?"

"Yeah, Top. Get on the horn and do it."

Jock went back to studying the hills for the likely Korean OP. *I need something, some clue,* he told himself. *A glint of sunlight off a lens...an antenna...or maybe somebody moving around in the open.*

He ruled out the two closest hilltops, sitting like the breasts of a woman lying on her back, a little more than two miles away. His GIs had come to refer to them as *The Tits.* Officially, though, they were known as *The Twins.*

Those hills have line of sight on our artillery, for sure, so the OP's not there.

He shifted his focus to the hill farther north, rising above the western outskirts of Taejon. The GIs called this one *The Balcony.* It was a mile farther from 26th RCT and its elevation was lower than *The Twins.*

It seemed a likely location, high enough to get a good view of the front side of 26th RCT's position but little, if anything, behind it. Anything not concealed on that front side would be in plain sight of anyone with even cheap optical equipment. It had more trees on its sides and peak, too, allowing troops to hide on it far better than on its taller but more barren sisters.

Patchett hung up the field telephone. They held their breath as the M19—with its deadly twin 40-millimeter cannon—backed quickly out of its defile and raced for cover, because anything moving in plain sight was a choice target.

But the M19 made it safely to the backslope of the hill. The few rounds that impacted the position during its dash came nowhere near it.

"It's that one," Jock said. "*The Balcony.*"

"Yeah, I was coming around to that myself, sir," Patchett replied. "And it's even inside a li'l ol' one-oh-five howitzer's range. Give 'em a dose of their own medicine?"

"Affirmative, Top. Good thing we've got those hills registered in. Go straight to *fire for effect.*"

As Patchett called in the fire mission, Jock kept his binoculars fixed on that hilltop. At first, he thought he'd imagined it: a glint of sunlight reflecting off something.

But then it happened again. A glint came and went as if someone was playing with a mirror.

Patchett's binoculars were back to his eyes now. Seeing the flashes, too, he told Jock, "You sure called that one, sir."

From the call of *shot, over* to the *fire for effect* volley's impact, that intermittent glint continued, flashing out an indecipherable message like an Aldis Lamp in the hands of a drunk.

When the smoke and dust of the explosions settled on *The Balcony's* peak, they could see through the shattered trees the smoldering carcass of a small utility truck, a type used by the KPA.

"That son of a bitch had been there all along," Patchett said. "Just couldn't see him through them trees, except for them reflections he was dumb enough to keep making. Want to give him another volley?"

"No, let's save it, Top. We're going to need it."

A few minutes went by without another Korean artillery round landing in 26th RCT's position. Patchett said, "I reckon we shot their eyes out, sir."

"Yeah. Let's hope it stays that way for a while, Top."

Jock checked his watch; there were four hours until sundown and the inevitable attack the night would bring.

Patchett asked, "You heard anything from ol' Bubba, sir?"

"Not a word, Top."

Then Patchett said, "You know, sir, I told him if he don't come back with them tanks, he'd better not come back at all." He gazed off into the distance, and then added, "Even though I was just pulling that big Yankee's leg, I wish to hell I hadn't said it now."

It had taken Sean Moon almost three hours to drive the thirty miles to the village of Yongdong along the Taejon-Taegu highway, where he was to meet up with 1st Cavalry Division. Supply convoys running to and from Taejon and the ROK units east of that city had clogged the highway; if he'd been driving anything larger than a jeep, he wouldn't have been able to leapfrog the slow-moving vehicles. But he'd made it by late afternoon, knowing that if he hadn't arrived at Yongdong until after dark, his chances of finding 10th Tank Battalion would've been little better than zero.

Asking directions from any American around the village, even officers and NCOs, had been an exercise in futility. Nobody seemed to know the location of any unit other than his own, and a number of lower-ranking enlisted men weren't even too sure of that. By the time an MP sergeant had steered Sean toward 10th Tank's bivouac, he had four of that unit's lost and confused troopers hitching a ride with him. The only indication he'd arrived at the battalion's area was the unit markings on the vehicles. The CP had to be the tent surrounded by all those jeeps with antennas; they were obviously command and staff vehicles.

He hadn't taken two steps inside the CP when the voice of the battalion commander, Lieutenant Colonel Roy Parker, boomed, "Well, holy shit! Master Sergeant Sean Moon! If you ain't a sight for sore eyes. How the hell are you doing, *Crunch*?"

Sean winced when he heard the nickname *Crunch*. He'd hated it when it got hung on him in France back in 1944. During the Normandy breakout, he'd sometimes found it necessary to run his Sherman down trenches and roadside ditches full of German soldiers. Some smart-ass NCO thought it a fitting name.

He'd promptly put a stop to enlisted men calling him that, by his fists if necessary. Nobody had dared call him *Crunch* to his face in six years.

But I guess the colonel here is kinda swept up in the moment. We haven't seen each other since Forty-Five, and he'd just made major then. I'll just ask him real nice to knock it off if he fucking says it again.

As they shook hands in the middle of the tent, Colonel Parker announced to his staff, "I want you all to meet the finest fighting NCO in Patton's Third Army. So what brings you here, Sergeant?"

Sean wasn't sure if that question was meant to be funny or not. Not being in the mood for jokes, though, he asked, "You mean you don't know, sir?"

Parker had never been much of a poker player, so the look of confusion on his face had to be genuine.

"Know *what*, Sergeant?"

"Your battalion has been detailed to Twenty-Sixth Regimental Combat Team, sir—*my* outfit—at Taejon. We need armor support in the worst way."

"You mean you don't have any tanks, Sergeant? How can that be?"

"We got two Chaffees left, sir. Never had more than a platoon to begin with."

Shocked, Parker asked, "What the hell happened to them? Did they break down or..." His voice trailed off, not wanting to say the other possibility out loud.

"It's mostly the *or*, Colonel," Sean replied.

Parker said nothing, but he looked like a man grasping at straws, wanting desperately to believe the orders to join 26th RCT were anything but real. While he knew from hard experience that Sean was a champion bluffer, this wasn't a poker game. Sergeant Moon was dead serious.

"Look, sir," Sean said, "you and me have been in this army long enough to see plenty of fuckups like this. Now I know you need orders before you can roll, but I'm here to tell you what those orders are gonna be. We need to get this sorted out, because we gotta get rolling real damn soon. If we don't, the 26th might not be there no more. I know the way to Taejon like the back of my hand, so I'm here to lead you there because the route's pretty damn tricky in the dark."

Much to Sean's surprise, Colonel Parker issued a warning order to his commanders and staff on the spot, before he'd even confirmed his new orders with Division. "This is your lucky day, Sergeant Moon," Parker said, "because we were fixing to move north a ways tonight, anyway. We might as well just follow you all the way to Taejon. We're all fueled and loaded up. I just need the magic word from my boss."

It took almost three hours to get 10th Tank Battalion on the road to Taejon. An hour of that was confirming the order attaching the battalion to 26th RCT. Another hour was spent briefing the company-level leaders on the details of this new mission. The final hour was clearing the colossal traffic jam that developed on the Taejon-Taegu highway just north of Yongdong as the battalion column became ensnarled with a ROK convoy moving—Sean referred to it as *fleeing*—south toward Taegu. Unable—or unwilling—to understand the commands of the American MPs attempting to direct traffic, the ROKs refused to yield right-of-way until Colonel Parker ordered a tank platoon to force their lead vehicles off the road.

Once the battalion was finally on the move—all forty-two tanks and twelve wheeled vehicles of it—Sean had a radio message relayed to 26th RCT, estimating their arrival time at Taejon as 2300 hours.

Let's just hope we get there in time to do some good, he told himself.

Tenth Battalion was understrength, like just about every other American unit in Korea. Worse, it was equipped almost exclusively with M24 Chaffee light tanks; only one platoon in Able Company—3rd Platoon—was equipped with medium tanks, the M4A3 Sherman. Sean had lobbied—successfully—to have that platoon at the head of the column. He would take command of the first Sherman in column and lead the battalion to Taejon. Colonel Parker, in his Chaffee, would be several tanks back.

They weren't twenty minutes out of Yongdong when a Chaffee broke down. Parker radioed for the column to halt. Reluctantly, Sean complied.

Hopping off the lead Sherman, Sean ran back to confer with the colonel. "We really shouldn't be stopping, sir. A bunch more are gonna break down before we hit Taejon. You know that as well as I do. We can't pull over every time that happens."

"I won't leave any of my men out here

unprotected, Sergeant," Parker replied.

"You don't have to, sir. When they break down, they just pull the machine guns and the breech block from the big tube and hop on one of the Service Company trucks that's trailing us for just that reason. Everybody else keeps moving. The trucks can catch up easy enough."

"That's all well and good, Sergeant, but what about the main gun ammo? We can't just leave that out here."

"We got no choice, sir. It would take forever to unload that stuff into a truck, and without boxes to put it in, it's more dangerous rolling around loose in the bed of a deuce than leaving it behind."

While Parker took a moment to mull that over, Sean prodded, "So, we can get moving, sir?"

Reluctantly, the colonel replied, "Yeah, go ahead."

Rolling in the Sherman again, Sean thought, *Why is it some of these officers forget everything they learned in the big war the minute they show up in this shithole? Colonel Parker's no novice. He was no fireball, but he led a tank company through some pretty rough shit in France and Germany. Back then he'd never do anything as stupid as what he just did. He's got the same delusion as MacArthur, like this ain't real combat because it's just a bunch of gooks we're up against. Too many of these fucking officers are thinking like that, like they forgot how hard it was to beat down the last bunch of gooks—excuse me, nips—this army had to fight.*

Talking to some First Cav guys, I finally got a reason how come the entire Eighth Army got almost nothing but these little toy Chaffees for tanks: the bridges in Japan were too narrow and flimsy to support the bigger models, so the whole damn Army of Occupation was equipped with lightweight Chaffees. What'd they need bigger tanks for, anyway? They thought it was all for show. Nobody was ever going to actually fight, right?

But the bridges...that gotta be the biggest crock of shit I ever heard in my life. All across Europe, I musta watched combat engineers build about a hundred bridges—each one in a coupla hours—that could support any damn vehicle we had.

The only reason they couldn't do the same in Japan was because MacArthur only cared about putting on his little show, with him being the star and the nips throwing flowers at him...what'd they call those things, Chrysanthemums or something? But he couldn't give a shit less about something as trivial as combat readiness.

It was 2200 hours now, and 10th Battalion's column was less than ten miles from Taejon. The crew of the lead Sherman had never been thrilled with Sean's presence in their tank since it put them at the head of the column. But they'd loosened up a little in the last hour, just enough to ask this master sergeant in their midst some questions.

The gunner asked, "You really fought in Shermans back in Europe, Sarge?"

"Yeah," Sean replied, "went through a whole bunch of 'em. They're pretty good vehicles if you use 'em right. Not perfect, mind you, but pretty good. They need more armor and a bigger gun, but if you made 'em any heavier, they couldn't get out of their own way."

There'd been no point in Sean asking this crew if they were combat veterans. It was obvious they weren't. They knew the basics of how to operate the tank well enough, but he knew they didn't have the experience yet to jell as a team and become one with the Sherman when the pressure of combat tried to crush them. *When the shit hits the fan, they're gonna get all clumsy and shit and start screaming at each other because they're scared out of their fucking minds. That fear stops them from doing their jobs right.*

If they can work through that—and get a round off before the other guy—they just might live.

If they don't, they're cooked meat...

And so am I.

Sean told the crew, "In a minute, we're gonna hit the village of Kumgu-ri. If you blink, you'll miss it. Right on the far end of that village, the highway's gonna split. We wanna take the left fork. Understand?"

"Yeah, Sarge," the driver replied. "I've got it."

The gunner asked, "What happens if we go the other way, Sarge?"

"We drive straight into *Gookville* and get shot to shit, that's what happens."

The gunner continued, "When we started out, didn't you think it was kind of strange that ROK convoy was on the road, screwing everything up? I guess none of the brass knew they were coming. And it sure seemed like they were bugging out or something."

Sean replied, "It wouldn't be the first time, pal."

"Something else I've been meaning to ask you, Sarge," the gunner said. "How come you made us load the main gun with a WP round? Our SOP says it should be HE."

"Your SOP is written by dumbshits, that's why," Sean replied. "It's nighttime, remember? So dark you can't hardly see past your fucking headlights. So if you gotta engage, I guarantee you ain't gonna see much of what it is you're shooting at. The *willy pete* starts a fire that lights up the area for you while it's torching the target."

"But in training we always used illum rounds from artillery and mortars to light up targets, Sarge."

"Let me tell you something, pal...by the time we get an illum round out of 'em—*if* we get an illum round out of 'em way out here in the middle of fucking nowhere—we'll all be dead. Believe me, I done this shit before."

"But you just heard it on the command net, Sarge...Colonel Parker is talking with the guys at Taejon. Can't their artillery support us now?"

"Sure, if we got plenty of time on our hands. You realize the guns at Taejon are about eight miles away as the crow flies, right?"

"Yeah, so?"

"Do the arithmetic," Sean said. "By the time we put in a call for fire, the cannon cockers compute the firing data, and the shit flies eight miles out and about two miles up, you're talking almost two minutes, and that's if everybody's on the fucking ball. We'd already be dead about a minute and fifty seconds by the time the rounds got here."

They were just a few hundred yards from the fork in the highway when the driver's voice filled their headsets, yelling, "Heads up! I think we've got more

ROK deuces coming our way!"

The *deuces* were barreling down the other leg of the fork, the one Sean had said would take them to *Gookville* just a minute ago. They were driving in column without lights, which was a good thing; it allowed Sean to clearly see their dark shapes as they lumbered toward the lead Sherman. Sean could count three trucks. There might've been more masked behind those three.

"Kill your headlights," he told the driver.

As the approaching trucks followed the curve that led to the fork, their broadside silhouette told him they weren't GI or ROK: *The hoods are too long, the fenders are too square, and they got those stood-off headlights like on them Lend-Lease Studebakers Uncle Sam gave the Ivans back in the last war.*

Mounted on each of their cargo beds was the unmistakable shape of a long-barreled gun: *Probably Russian forty-five-millimeter anti-tank guns.*

Seen a shitload of them in the last war, too.

Sean ordered the driver, "Turn into them, head-to-head, dead on. Then stop."

Then he told the gunner, "Put that *willy pete* right through the first truck."

The driver promptly did what he was told.

The gunner promptly froze.

Sean didn't waste time repeating his order. He jerked the gunner from his seat and took it himself. Training the main gun on the lead truck, he called out, "ON THE WAY."

And then he fired.

Before the tube had even completed its recoil, amidst the cloud of acrid smoke that filled the turret and the chaos of ringing ears, he told the loader, "Put another *willy pete* up, right fucking now."

The impact of the WP round on the gun truck was everything Sean had said it would be. Not only did it rip the vehicle apart, it started a fire that lit up the Korean column.

"UP," the loader shouted.

A split second later, Sean said, "ON THE WAY."

This round ripped the third truck in line apart. It started another blaze, which illuminated yet a fourth gun truck.

Sean grabbed the gunner off the turret floor and said, "You ready to do your job now? I've got her all warmed up for you. Take out that truck at the back end."

The gunner screeched, "Are they even shooting back?"

"Are you fucking complaining? *Fire the gun,* dammit."

In moments, the fight was over. Three Korean gun trucks—the first, third, and fourth in the column—were shattered and burning, their ammo stores beginning to randomly cook off. There was no need to shoot the second truck; her crew had abandoned her and run off into the night. The bow gunner of Sean's tank hit her with a burst of machine gun fire anyway.

"What do we do now, Sarge?" the driver asked.

"We get moving," Sean replied. "The fork's right up ahead. Shouldn't have any trouble seeing it now with them fires burning."

Rolling once again, Sean radioed Colonel Parker, "Might want to get our ass-end Charlie to drop a coupla thermite grenades in that abandoned gun truck. No point wasting any rounds on her. We're gonna need 'em before you know it."

Even though he'd killed the fourth truck, the gunner still hadn't come to grips with the whole affair. His voice trembled as he asked, "How the hell do we know we didn't just kill a whole bunch of friendlies, Sarge?"

"Let me put it this way...if they were dumb enough to be driving around in Russian vehicles with Russian weapons, they deserved what they got."

"But they never shot at us."

"That's the name of the game, pal. Get 'em before they get you. Didn't they teach you clowns *anything*?"

Chapter Twenty-Four

Sean's lead Sherman was two miles beyond the fork in the highway when Colonel Parker came on the radio, ordering the column to halt once again. Then he called Sean back to his command tank.

"Just got word from your boys at the Twenty-Sixth," Parker told him. "They're getting hit...*hard*. We'll be walking into a cauldron if we keep—"

"Hang on just a second, sir," Sean interrupted. "With all due respect, are you thinking about *not* helping them?"

"We're bumbling into a fight in the dark, Sergeant Moon. It sounds like suicide to me. Hell, you're the only guy out here who even knows where he's going."

Before Parker could respond, the radio squawked again. This time, it was *Clipboard Six*—the commanding general of 1st Cavalry Division—on the air.

Sean watched as Parker pressed the headset closer to his ears so as not to miss a single word. As he listened, the colonel's face grew more tense. The radio exchange came to an end as he said, "Roger, *Clipboard*. Solid copy. Will advise. *Out*."

He told Sean, "Division wants us to press on to Taejon."

"That's good news, sir."

"I'm glad you think so, Sergeant. Now, do me a favor." Parker handed the headset to Sean. "Talk to *Montana* at Taejon and figure out where they need us. You know the terrain, so maybe there won't be any misunderstandings."

"Gladly, sir."

Sean's communication with Colonel Miles took less than a minute. When it was done, he laid his map on the turret roof of Parker's tank and said, "We need to split into two teams, sir...one that continues up this highway and cuts the gook armor off just east of Taejon. The other team needs to backtrack a coupla miles and then cut across the hills. That'll bring it around the back side of the Twenty-Sixth so it can stop the armor rolling down the west side of the city."

Parker was shaking his head. "I'm not real crazy about splitting my battalion, Sergeant. That's asking to get cut up piecemeal and—"

"Sir, we're not applying force piecemeal here. We're performing a *double envelopment*, just like we used to do all the time back in the big show. It's just a little trickier in the dark. But I got a plan for that, too."

Sean went on to explain how *he* would lead a company of tanks through the hills to get to the west side of the battle. Colonel Parker would take his other two tank companies and continue up the highway to interdict the KPA on the east side.

"You keep the platoon of Shermans with you, sir," Sean said, "because you're gonna need 'em. Just leave me the one I'm already riding in."

After a moment's hesitation, Parker replied, "Oh, all right." To Sean, it sounded like the most unenthusiastic acceptance of a plan he'd ever heard.

"Let me take Baker Company with me, sir, since they're already at the rear of the column. That'll make the backtracking easier, so we ain't bumping into each other."

The colonel replied, "Fine," with that same lack of

enthusiasm. Then he laid a fingertip to the map and said, "But I've got one question. What do I do if I get to this T-intersection at the end of the highway and there are no gooks there?"

"Even better, sir. Just turn left toward Taejon until you roll up on 'em...and then you kick 'em in the ass. With any luck, I'll be coming from the other direction and we'll trap 'em but good."

As he navigated the lead Sherman along the trail through the hills, the driver said to Sean, "Now I see why you only took a company down this trail...less tanks to fall into ditches and throw tracks."

Of all the technical things that could go wrong on this trek of fourteen lumbering armored vehicles through steep hills in the darkness of night, roadside ditches weren't Sean's biggest concern. This was: *A driver's gonna try to stay right on the ass of the guy in front of him so he don't get separated...and that's fine, until he gets too close or too far away from that guy when they're on a hill. Then he panics, downshifts real hard and sudden, and blows his transmission. Narrow as this trail gets sometimes, there may be no place to push a broke tank out of the way...and then everybody behind him gets stuck.*

Apparently, Lieutenant Bradshaw, the Baker Company commander, had the same concern; he kept slowing his column of Chaffees to put as little strain on the transmissions as possible. But they were dropping far behind the lead Sherman now, so far that Sean could barely make out their blackout lights.

"Might want to step it up a little," Sean urged the lieutenant over the radio. "We need to get there sometime *tonight*."

"Just trying to get as many of us there as possible," Bradshaw replied. He was in the process of abandoning a broken-down Chaffee as they spoke. Her crew were cramming themselves like sardines into other tanks.

Sean's reply: "Amen to that. Let's just try to do it a little quicker, okay?"

They were coasting down out of the hills now, getting closer to the Taejon-Pusan highway. Looking north, they could see the luminous signs of a night battle raging: the momentary orange pinpoints of dazzling light that were artillery and mortar rounds bursting; the tracer rounds like brilliant dashed lines arcing across the sky; the vivid flames of shacks and vehicles set alight. From a distance, it seemed breathtaking, almost beautiful.

But that distance would dissolve quickly...

And so would the illusion.

"Nobody's shooting illum," the gunner said. "I wonder why?"

"Because it's probably a close fight," Sean replied, "and when you're close, illum lights you up just as good as it does the enemy. Better off without it."

He got on the radio and advised *Montana Six* that they'd be at 26th RCT's perimeter in just a few minutes.

The reply: "Outstanding. Come up the highway and block the pass between *The Twins*." Sean recognized the voice: Sergeant Patchett. Then he laughed as he thought, *I'm surprised that old cracker didn't name that pass The Cleavage, with it being between The Tits and all. I would've known what he was talking about, that's for damn sure.*

Watching the light show going on in the sky to the north, the driver said, "Oh, man...I don't like the looks of this."

"Don't sweat it, pal," Sean replied. "It's your lucky night. You're about to lose your virginity."

The driver was surprised that Sean could crack wise while the rest of the crew were on the verge of soiling themselves. He asked, "C'mon, Sarge, aren't you scared, too?"

"Sure I'm scared," Sean replied, "but at the moment I'm more scared of you clowns getting me killed than the gooks doing it."

Colonel Parker's column lost a Sherman and three Chaffees to breakdowns before reaching the T-intersection. Like Sean and his crew, he could see the lights of a battle in the distance. The only difference was that he was viewing them from the opposite side.

But those lights were all Parker's column could see. There appeared to be nothing ahead of them, not KPA tanks, vehicles, or troops; not even the road intersection. He was pretty sure they should have reached that intersection by now. He could think of nothing else to do but stop the column to get his bearings.

They were closer to the T-intersection than Parker realized. He was climbing out of the turret when, in the distance ahead, a brief glint of dim light caught his attention. Whether it was a struck match, a carelessly handled flashlight, or the flare of an engine backfire, he couldn't tell. But in that glint he caught the shadowy outlines of blacked-out tanks moving down the intersecting roadway toward Taejon. It was like watching a parade through a nearly opaque filter; the evenly spaced vehicles rolled along as if passing in review. The parade appeared endless.

He'd taken Sean's suggestion and put his two still-serviceable Shermans at the front of his column. His Chaffee was third in column behind them.

It was off the glacis plate of the lead Sherman that the first shot from a KPA tank ricocheted, showering it and the tank behind it with shell fragments when it exploded a millisecond later.

And then many more Korean tanks were firing at the stalled American column, like warships outgunning their foes in a classic *crossing the T*. The Americans strung along the base of the *T* could only return fire with the few guns at the front of their column; the guns farther back were masked by their own vehicles. The Koreans along the top of the *T*, however, all had unobstructed fields of fire. They only had to traverse their turrets toward the American column to bombard them at will.

The next round that hit the first Sherman was no ricochet; it penetrated the hull low on the bow and set it ablaze. Methodically, the KPA tank gunners worked their way down the American column. Within thirty seconds, Colonel Parker had lost nine tanks, including his own.

Taking command of a Chaffee still untouched by the onslaught, he radioed his column to withdraw. Most of his tanks didn't bother to turn about by pivoting; they threw their vehicles into reverse, hoping to keep their thickest armor toward the KPA guns.

But they could only make half their top speed while driving in reverse gear. The T-34s chasing them down the highway had little trouble running them down, picking off the American tanks one by one.

Five miles north of Yongdong, the Koreans broke off the engagement. By that time, Parker had lost eight more tanks. The companies comprising his column, Able and Charlie, had left Yongdong with twenty-eight tanks between them, manned by 112 men.

When they returned to Yongdong, their serviceable tanks numbered seven.

On the way out, they'd managed to rescue a number of crewmen, but around sixty of his tankers were missing.

As near as Colonel Parker could tell, his unit had killed no KPA tanks.

He wasn't sure if any of them had even fired their guns.

As they rolled into 26th RCT's perimeter, Sean brought Baker Company's column of tanks to a halt for a private conference with its commander, Lieutenant Bradshaw. "I'll make this real quick, Lieutenant," Sean said. "We need to put the tanks into *diamond formations* in column now, so we can cover each other's asses while we engage gook tanks. Once we're beyond the Twenty-Sixth's perimeter, diamonds will be the easiest way to do that, plus it'll give us the best all-around firepower."

"Okay by me," Bradshaw replied. "How should we

set it up, Sergeant?"

"We got thirteen vehicles, so each platoon makes a four-tank diamond. My Sherman's the extra guy, so I'll ride in the middle of the lead diamond."

"Sounds like a plan, Sergeant. Where do you think I should ride?"

"Put yourself in the second diamond, Lieutenant. Preferably at the ass end."

"Got it."

Sean continued, "But a coupla questions before we move out. All your vehicles got the frequencies for the Twenty-Sixth, right? They only got a few radios that can actually talk to us, so make damn sure you're on the right *freq*."

"Yeah, we're all set on that, Sergeant. Got those *freqs* written in grease pencil on the turret walls, just like you suggested."

"Outstanding, Lieutenant. Now, last but not least...your guys ain't shy about *dusting each other off*, are they?"

"You mean shooting at each other with our machine guns to knock sappers off our tanks?"

"Exactly right, sir. What I'm asking is if your guys are gonna watch each other's backs."

Bradshaw hesitated before replying, "They've never had to do that, Sergeant. But I'm sure that once they're buttoned up they'll—"

"That ain't good enough, sir. That's just *faith*, but we need to be fucking certain. Once they're buttoned up, they won't see shit unless they know to look for it. Tell you what... while you get 'em organized into the diamonds, I'll give 'em the song and dance about *dusting* procedures."

✯ ✯ ✯

Once beyond 26th RCT's perimeter, Sean was surprised to find they weren't as blind as he'd thought they'd be. The darkness was eased slightly by dozens of fires burning brightly; there'd obviously been quite a fight here already, and the fires were detritus of that fight. The carcasses of several T-34s still smoldered, the victims, no doubt, of audacious anti-tank teams.

If those tank killers are still out here, let's just hope that in the dark they know us from the gooks.

The driver called out, "Hey, I got something in the road right in front of us. Baker One-Two just drove right by it. She almost ran over it."

He slowed the Sherman so as not to run over whatever—or whoever—it was. But buttoned up, they still couldn't identify it.

"Turn the headlights on for a second," Sean said.

"You sure you want to do that, Sarge?"

"Am I talking English here? I said turn the fucking headlights on, numbnuts."

"But isn't that going to give us away?"

Sean replied, "Are you shitting me? You think it's any secret this bellowing beast is here? Especially after that lead foot of yours shoots flames out the exhaust every time it stomps on the gas? Now turn those fucking lights on."

A quick flash of the headlights was all it took. What had looked like just a satchel—or perhaps a duffle bag—was two men lying next to each other. They might've been dead...

But maybe not.

"Straddle 'em," Sean ordered the driver. "Put the

escape hatch right over 'em."

"But what if it's a trap, Sarge?"

"Might be," Sean replied, "or it might be two wounded GIs. We're gonna find out."

He told the assistant driver—a PFC named Rapp—to open the emergency hatch in the bottom of the hull below his seat. Then he told Rapp, "Have your pistol ready if they turn out to be gooks. But if they're GIs, pull 'em in."

"What if they're dead, Sarge?"

"Then the adjutant don't have to list them as *missing*, and their families don't have to suffer through none of that false hope bullshit."

The men were beneath the tank now as it slowed to a crawl.

"Okay, stop," Rapp said.

The first thing he could see was their GI helmets. His pistol in one hand, he reached down through the hatch with the other and gingerly removed the helmets.

The men were definitely Americans. They were wounded and terrified, but both were conscious. "They're GIs," Rapp yelled as he began hauling the first of them up through the hatch and into the tank.

"Hey," the driver said, "we've got action outside!"

"Yeah, I see it," Sean replied. He'd been scanning all around through the commander's periscope. He could just make out the shapes of men running around the tank to get to its rear end.

As soon as those shapes got close to the vehicle, they dropped from sight.

Sean's first impulse: *Get Baker One-Five to dust us off. But wait...they'll probably shoot the poor bastards we're trying to rescue. So let's do something different.*

"They're trying to get underneath," Sean said. "Back the fuck up and pivot hard left."

"But Rapp's got one more guy to pull in."

"So let him keep pulling. But do what the fuck I told you right fucking now."

With a sudden lurch, the Sherman leapt backward and then spun left. With the second wounded man half in and half out of the tank, Rapp could barely hold on to him through the violent maneuver.

But somehow, he did. No sooner was the man fully inside the tank than Rapp saw yet another man's arm in the hatch...

And this one was holding a grenade.

Rapp slammed the hatch closed just as the grenade was tossed. It bounced off the hatch cover and fell back under the tank. He managed to lock the hatch just as the grenade exploded.

"Nice move," Sean told him.

Then he told the driver, "Back up a couple yards more. Let's see how many gooks we just ran over. Flick the headlights back on for a second."

It looked like four bodies lying on the ground: two that seemed to have been blown apart by their own grenade and two that got caught under the tracks as the Sherman pivoted.

"Good job, all of you," Sean said. Then he asked Rapp, "Those guys we picked up...how bad are they?"

"Aw, they're more scared than wounded, Sarge. I'll patch them up for now. They'll be okay."

"Outstanding," Sean said. "Now catch up with our diamond. We don't want to fall too far behind."

As they plowed toward *The Twins*, Sean told himself, *Dammit, I hate running over people with a*

fucking passion. But it's kill or be killed, right? And it don't matter how you do the killing part, neither.
But if I hear that fucking name Crunch again...

As they approached *The Twins*, Sean was delighted to find he'd been right; he'd only seen this area through binoculars from 26th RCT's CP, but he was sure he'd seen a big fold in the open terrain just to the south of the peaks. That fold would provide Baker Company's tanks the ability to go *hull-down* as they formed their blocking position.

He knew they were almost there when his driver reported, "Okay, Sarge, I'm having to ride the brakes a little. We're definitely going downhill now. This must be the *hull-down* spot you were talking about."

As his Sherman slowed to a stop, Sean radioed to the company, "Stay in your diamonds, but put 'em on line with mine in the middle. Just remember we're on our own out here. We got gook tanks *and* infantry to worry about now."

Then he told his crew, "I'm gonna have a look outside my hatch. The rest of you stay buttoned up."

His head wasn't outside the turret but a few seconds when a sniper's round *pinged* off the hatch ring. Dropping back inside, he slammed the hatch closed. "We got gook infantry around here," he radioed the company. "Watch your back...and your buddy's back, too."

The pass between *The Twins* had looked like a light gray notch between the black mounds when they first arrived. Now, that notch was darkening as if an artist working in charcoal was gently shading it. Sean knew what he was looking at: *It's dust kicked up by vehicles. Gook vehicles...probably T-34s.*

Looks like they're coming back for another round.

Baker Company's gunners couldn't see individual vehicles, but they didn't have to; they just needed to fire at the base of the notch between the hills. It was only wide enough to accommodate two or three vehicles abreast. Knock out that number and the pass would be blocked.

"Let 'em get a little closer," Sean said.

Artillery rounds began to impact between the pass and the American tanks.

"Who the hell's shooting?" the gunner asked.

"It ain't our guys, that's for damn sure," Sean replied. "It's *prep* for the gooks' next assault. They're gonna walk it right over us, I'll bet."

"Ah, shit, Sarge! We've got to get out of here!"

"No, we don't," Sean replied. "You're in a tank, remember? She's gotta have a direct hit on her to get hurt."

"But what if we *do* take a direct hit?"

"Then it's been nice knowing you, pal. But look at the bright side...as long as gook artillery is raining down, there won't be no gook infantry on our backs."

As Sean predicted, the Korean artillery salvo swept over them and continued toward 26th RCT's perimeter. "Okay," he said, "everybody's reporting they're still up and running. But shit...now we gotta worry about sappers again."

Then he told his gunner, "Wait a minute...I got an idea. Our cannon cockers don't sound like they're too busy right now. Tell the company to stay buttoned up while I talk to *Montana.*"

He proceeded to call in a fire mission on his own position. "Keep it all airbursts," he told the CP. "Target is infantry in the open. Don't worry about us. We're all buttoned up."

The gunner asked, "Are you sure there's a whole mess of gook infantry out there, Sarge, and not just that one sniper?"

"Yeah, I'm sure as I can be. Now get your fucking sight picture on that notch."

"I can't see shit in the sight, Sarge. It's too dark out."

"Then sight down the damn barrel, for cryin' out loud. When you think you've got it where you need it, crank the tube up another quarter of a turn."

"I've...I've never done it like that before, Sarge."

"School's in session, my boy. Live and learn. Or rather, learn...and live."

Twenty-five seconds later, the shell fragments from the American artillery's airbursts began to *clank* against their hulls like spasms of hail on a tin roof. A few seconds after that, all thirteen of Baker Company's tanks began to pour fire into the notch between *The Twins.* Even though being buttoned-up limited their fields of vision to the little they could see through periscopes and viewing ports, they could still see the brilliant flash when one of their rounds struck steel.

"We got to keep banging the shit out of 'em," Sean said, "because one round of ours ain't gonna go through the front of a T-34. But if we hit that same tank a whole bunch of times, we gotta be fucking something up."

It took a few minutes of firing to *fuck something up.* In that time, the T-34s got off some shots of their own. It was nothing like the volume of fire Baker Company was delivering, but it was enough to knock out three unlucky Chaffees, who took deadly hits to their turrets, the only part of their hull-down tank that was exposed.

"One of them T-34s is breaking through, dammit," Sean said. "He don't know where he's going, though...stupid bastard's showing us her side."

He told his gunner, "Take her."

"I can't see her, Sarge. Guide me in."

"Bring the tube right ten degrees," Sean said as he stared down the barrel through the open breech. "Slow down now...little more...HOLD IT."

The loader slammed in an HE round, slid the breech closed, and then yelled, "UP."

"She's all yours," Sean told the gunner.

When the smoke vented from the turret, Sean could see they'd missed. The T-34 was still plowing diagonally across their front, getting closer.

"Gotta lead her a little more," he said as the gunner eased the traverse farther right.

"There," Sean said, pulling his head away from the breech. "Try that."

Before they could load another round, the T-34 fired while on the move.

Sean and his men could sense the round hurtling just inches past their turret. They couldn't hear the *swoosh* as it passed, not over the clatter of the Sherman's engine, but they felt that momentary bump in air pressure from its shock wave.

But a miss is a miss. "Fire on the move, you won't hit shit, you dumb gook bastard," Sean said.

Another HE round was in the Sherman's tube now.

"Tweak it a little to the right," Sean told the gunner. "She's gotta have moved a little more than we figured by now."

It was an excellent guess; the round went right through the side of the T-34. She blew up spectacularly, lighting the battlefield just long enough to get a glimpse of the carnage they'd caused.

"Holy shit," Sean said. "There must be five dead T-34s piled up in the notch. They won't be coming through there tonight."

Calling *Montana* on the radio, he told the CP, "*The Twins* are blocked. Shift the artillery into the notch so they can't unblock it for a while. We're coming in…and we've got wounded."

Chapter Twenty-Five

The dull gray light of a new day brought nothing but bad news. The fog that had settled across 26th RCT's position in the predawn hours showed no hint of burning off anytime soon.

And when there's fog, Jock Miles knew, *there'll be no air support.*

After last night's clashes, the battalion of armor he'd requested had been whittled down to Sean Moon's ten tanks. The rest of Colonel Parker's 10th Tank Battalion—and that *rest* consisted of only seven tanks after the rout on the Taejon-Taegu highway—was licking its many wounds back at 1st Cavalry's bivouac in Yongdong.

Despite Jock's renewed request for armor, he was advised that 1st Cav would not be sending any more tanks to support his delaying action at Taejon.

If there was any hint of a silver lining in last night's decimation of 10th Tank, it was that KPA forces conducting that decimation were diverted from any further attacks on 26th RCT. After their initial probes from both the east and west—the actions that precipitated the splitting of 10th Tank Battalion into two forces—the only follow-up attacks from the Koreans had come from the west. That was the attack Sean's force had repulsed.

But last night's page in the history books had already gone to press. Today's page was still waiting to be written.

Patchett had more bad news to deliver: "The artillery just reported in, sir. They just reached your cutoff point for *final protective fires*."

Sean asked, "And that means they gotta stop firing into the notch now, don't it?"

"Affirmative, Bubba. And if that ammo convoy don't show up real soon, we're up shit's creek without a paddle."

"Son of a bitch! They'll have them shot-up tanks towed out of the way before I can scratch my ass. Then I get to fight 'em all over again. Ain't like that never happened before, though."

"Amen to that, Bubba. But listen up…we got ourselves a plan cooking."

"Yeah, we do," Jock joined in. "Until this fog lifts, the KPA will be as blind as we are. But we've still got a slight advantage: we're up on the high ground with all their avenues of approach covered one way or the other." He looked to Sean and added, "But there's still one problem."

"Yeah, I know what you're gonna say, sir," Sean replied. "If they force enough tanks down the highway, we ain't got the muscle to knock 'em all out."

"Right, Sergeant. And once that starts to look inevitable, we're going to have to fall back immediately. If for some reason we can't withdraw south down the Taejon-Pusan highway, we're going to have no choice but to escape into the hills to the east and try to link up with First Cav. My question is, how do we make the best use of the few tanks we've got?"

Sean replied, "First off, sir, the tanks gotta be able to move. None of this using them as fixed fortifications, okay? And we gotta keep them together, too, to maximize their firepower, which individually is gonna be pretty shitty."

"But where should we position them?" Jock asked.

Sean pointed to a spot on the map. "We start off right here, sir, at that village that's stuck on the back of this hill we're on. The one the guys are calling *Calvary*."

Jock smiled; he hadn't yet heard that nickname for the village of *Kao-ri*. He asked, "Sounds ominously biblical, doesn't it?"

"Maybe so, sir," Sean replied. "But from there, the tanks can move real fast to cover an attack from either flank—or one coming straight outta Taejon. The terrain's real good for tanks, too, unless we get a lot of rain and it all turns to muck. Most important, it's a closer run to the east highway, where the gooks who kicked Tenth Tank's ass last night are probably assembled to attack us today. I'm guessing that's where our biggest problem's gonna come from."

Jock looked to Patchett. "You agree, Top?"

"Affirmative, sir."

"Okay, that's decided, then," Jock said. "But one more question, Sergeant Moon. These tankers from First Cav…how good are they?"

"Let's put it this way, sir…the ones working with me are a hell of a lot better now than they were yesterday morning. But they still got a lot to learn. A hell of a lot."

"I understand their company commander was one of the badly wounded we evacuated early this morning," Jock said. "Who's in command of Baker Company now?"

"I guess I am, sir, if that's okay with you. They ain't got no other officers out here, and I'm *waaay* senior to every NCO they got."

Patchett chipped in, "And a damn sight more experienced, I reckon."

Sean laughed and replied, "That gotta be the understatement of the year, Patch."

"It's settled, then," Jock said. "Congratulations, Sergeant Moon. You're now the acting commander of Baker Company, Tenth Tank."

The steady casualty rate had elevated many a junior NCO to a leadership role far exceeding the stripes on his sleeve. Corporal Potts was now an infantry squad leader in 3rd Battalion of 26th RCT, a position usually filled by a staff sergeant. The fact that he was a colored man leading an otherwise all-white squad didn't make the job any easier.

Potts' squad was dug in along a ridgeline, providing protection for one of the M19 gun carriages. Contact on this foggy morning had been light so far: two probes by KPA infantry had been chased away by bursts from the M19's twin 40-millimeter guns. After the latest probe, Potts crawled along his squad's five fighting holes, checking for casualties and ammunition status.

There was a man missing.

Potts asked the man who shared the hole, "Where's Simpson?"

PFC Redfield replied, "He's off this morning."

"What do you mean, he's *off*, Private?"

"It means it's his turn to sleep in, *Pott-hole*. He'll wake up if we need him." He paused, as if considering his next words. Then he delivered them: "We play by white man's rules around here."

"I got news for you, Private…we play by gook rules around here, where there ain't no such thing as *the morning off.* You're on report, Redfield. Now where the hell is your buddy?"

Redfield smirked. The threat of discipline— especially from some Negro corporal—meant nothing to him. "I'm on report, am I? What're you gonna do? Send me to fucking Korea? Besides, you ain't got that nigger-loving Master Sergeant Patchett to protect your black ass now."

"Where's Simpson? I ain't gonna ask you again, Private."

Redfield waited a few moments before answering, that same smirk still plastered on his face. Once he figured he'd pushed the corporal far enough, he replied, "Behind that ammo trailer over yonder."

Before Potts could take two steps toward the trailer, a mortar round blew it to pieces. If it hadn't been empty, the resulting explosion of the ammo within would've killed them all. As it was, it just killed the napping Simpson.

Then it rained mortar shells for a few seconds.

Potts had thrown himself into the hole with Redfield, who'd dropped his M1 and was cowering in the bottom. "Move your ass, *cracker,*" Potts told him. "You're covering up the grenade sump."

As soon as the mortar rounds stopped falling, KPA infantry came charging up the rise again, emerging like gray ghosts from the fog once they got to within fifty yards of the peak.

Nobody was shooting at them, not his squad, not the M19 behind them. The mortar barrage had sent the

40-millimeter gunners diving off their piece. The small arms fire snapping all around them was keeping those gunners flat on the ground.

Potts could see the heads of his men stealing peeks over the rims of their holes. None of them began shooting at the attackers, though. A few climbed out and started running to the rear. Those who stayed dropped back into their holes.

When Redfield tried to run away, Potts decked him with an uppercut to the jaw. Then he thrust the M1 back into the private's hands and said, "You ain't dead yet, so you better be firing that damn weapon."

Then Potts started climbing out of the hole.

His eyes wide with terror, Redfield screeched, "Where the hell you going, boy?"

"To get those forty millimeters firing, that's where."

The KPA infantry was cresting the rise when Potts opened up with the twin 40 millimeters. It chopped down the first wave like an invisible scythe.

It did the same to the second wave.

By the time the third wave emerged from the fog, the 40-millimeter guns were out of ammo...

And all of Potts' men had fled.

Sean had been right: the major thrust of the KPA armor was coming from the east, the same force that mauled Colonel Parker's column last night. Using the fog as a screen, he would attempt to interdict their column a mile outside 26th RCT's perimeter, positioning his ten tanks broadside to the much larger

enemy force. To fire, his tanks would advance through
the fog toward the Koreans until they could see the
outlines of the opposing T-34s. Then they'd quickly
pick a target and shoot before withdrawing in reverse
gear back to the concealment of the mist.

A stream with marshy banks that would mire a tank
would keep the opposing forces separated, ensuring
they would get no closer to each other than several
hundred yards.

Still, Baker Company—with Sean as its acting
commander—would be badly outgunned. Their only
hope was to inflict as much damage as they could on
the enemy tanks while hiding in the fog as much as
possible.

"Remember," Sean told his tankers, "all we're
trying to do is keep the gooks away from the Twenty-
Sixth. Disabling a T-34 out here on the highway is just
as good as blowing it to kingdom come. If you just
knock off a track or jam her turret, that's as good as a
kill."

To make it seem that his force was much larger
than it was, he'd deploy only a pair of his tanks forward
at a time across a wide front. His Sherman would be in
the first pair, just to see firsthand that his concept of
engagement was sound.

It went well for the GIs—for the first few minutes.

But when the third pair emerged from the fog to
take their shots, some Korean gunners must've
anticipated their approach. Both Chaffees took multiple
hits and were quickly turned into smoking hulks. Only
four of their ten crewmen managed to escape, running
back into the fog and the dubious safety of the other
American tanks.

Rather than allowing another pair to venture forth and be sacrificed, Sean revised his plan. "Stay in the fog and fire blind," he told his tankers. "Set the range to four hundred fifty yards. Spread your shots in a twenty-degree arc. Keep shooting until I tell you to stop. Then we get the hell outta here."

The Koreans decided to *fire blind*, too. But the fewer American tanks, spread farther apart, proved difficult to hit. Only one Chaffee was knocked out in a shootout lasting almost two minutes, which seemed an eternity. Engagements like this were usually over in a matter of seconds.

When Sean withdrew his tanks—now down to seven—he had no idea how many T-34s they had hit, if they'd hit any at all.

The gooks couldn't see shit, too, so they won't know how many they hit, neither.

The loss of the 40-millimeter guns made it clear that 3rd Battalion was on the verge of being flanked and overrun. By the time Jock had arrived at the battalion's CP, Colonel Brand, the battalion commander, had readjusted his lines to check the KPA's incursion. But the situation was far from under control.

"It looks like we've lost the high ground on our left flank," Jock said to Brand. "Is that the case, Colonel?"

"We lost just a part of it, sir."

"Yeah, I can see that," Jock replied, "but the *part* you're talking about gives the gooks a clear route to the back side of our perimeter, and once this pea soup clears, a bird's eye view of about half our positions.

What are your plans to retake that ridge, Colonel?"

His silence was all the answer Jock needed.

"So you have no plan, Colonel Brand?"

"Well, sir…we are putting mortar fire on them."

"The gooks can dig holes for cover just as good as we can, Colonel. In fact, I'm sure they're using the ones your people already dug for them. You need to take back that ridge immediately."

"Sir, if I move any of my units, I'll just create new weaknesses for the gooks to exploit. I've got no reserve. I just don't have the people anymore."

Jock knew there was no point arguing about manpower; casualties had taken their steady toll, making every commander's headcount perilously low. With no hope of replacements, 26th RCT's combat effectiveness was in bad shape. *Barring a miracle,* he told himself, *we'll be pulling back from this position very soon.*

Studying 3rd Battalion's situation map, Jock pointed to a spot and asked, "Is your entire *Item Company* covering this area here?"

"Yes, sir, they are."

"Hell, Colonel, a platoon with a machine gun could cover that gap. Pull *Item Company* from the line and have them do the counterattack. I'll slide the boundary between you and First Battalion over so they can cover the hole."

Just then, an artillery round impacted near the CP, knocking everyone to the ground.

When the dust settled, no one had been seriously hurt, but the CP's radios were destroyed, torn apart by shell fragments.

"I'll see if I can scare up another radio for you,"

Jock said as he headed for his jeep. "In the meantime, warm up your runners. I'll need to know ASAP when you've taken back that ridge."

Outside the CP, he was surprised to come upon a Negro corporal huddled behind a pile of sandbags. "Potts, isn't it?" Jock asked.

He only had a handful of colored GIs in the RCT. Their names had stuck with him. Especially Potts, who was the only NCO among them and a man Patchett had classified *a good troop*.

"Yes, sir. That's me."

"What're you doing just sitting out here, Corporal?"

"I'm under arrest, sir."

"For what?"

"Assault, sir. One of my peckerwood privates is pressing charges. Says I hit him." With a forlorn laugh, he added, "Ain't that some shit? We're fighting for our lives here, and the colonel's talking about putting my ass in Leavenworth. I got a whole damn squad of white boys that cut and run. Nobody's talking about putting them in no stockade."

"Get in that jeep, Corporal," Jock said. "I'll be right back."

Back inside the CP, Jock asked Brand, "What's the story with Corporal Potts? You're bringing him up on charges?"

"Damn right, sir. Bad enough we've got to live with these coons, but I'm not going to have them assaulting any of my boys. Fucking Truman and his *integrate the services* shit. The world's going to hell, sir."

"It sure as hell is, Colonel, when my battalion

commanders are taking combat-experienced men out of action in the heat of battle for what sounds like petty bullshit. I'll tell you what…Corporal Potts is coming with me. Consider him transferred out of your battalion, effective immediately."

"But I'll still be bringing him up on charges, sir."

"I'm afraid that's in my hands now, Colonel. And in case I didn't make myself clear before, I'd better hear by 0900 hours that you've taken back that ridge."

When Jock returned to his CP, Patchett told him, "Ain't looking too good, sir. Bubba Moon did what he could, but we still got an armored force of unknown size sitting a mile to the east. He's down to seven tanks now. The ammo convoy ain't even left Taegu yet, so we ain't gonna be seeing it any time soon. You still want to hold to the artillery shooting *final protective fires* only?"

"Yeah, I do. The weather forecast change any?"

"No, sir. Once this fog burns off, say about 1000 hours, we're looking at solid overcast until late afternoon."

"Man, you're the only ray of sunshine around these parts, aren't you?"

"I do what I can, sir. Third Battalion going to hold up?"

"Could go either way, Top."

"Want me to go see what I can do to help out over there, sir?"

"Yeah, and if you can dig up another *Angry Nine*, bring that with you. Their CP radio just got shot to hell."

"Will do, sir," Patchett replied. Then he noticed Corporal Potts standing in a corner of the CP. "You lost, Corporal?"

Potts explained how he'd come to be there.

"Any witnesses to this assault?" Patchett asked.

"Don't think so, Sarge...unless they could still see with their heads up their asses."

Patchett dropped off the radio at 3rd Battalion's CP and then drove his jeep to where Item Company was assembling for the counterattack on the ridge. Along the way, he came across several GIs wandering the trail. With one look, he knew what they were up to: *These touch-holes are fucking off. They ain't where they're supposed to be, doing what they're supposed to be doing. That's for damn sure.*

He recognized one of them: PFC Redfield, the trooper who'd called him a nigger lover during that recon patrol a few nights back and the man who'd accused Potts of assault.

"Climb in, son," Patchett said. "You and me gonna have ourselves a little chat, one cracker to another."

He drove behind a thicket of trees where he was sure nobody could see them. Climbing from the jeep, he said, "C'mere, Private...I wanna show you something."

Once Redfield was standing before him, Patchett sent him to the ground with a punch so quick the private couldn't even flinch in anticipation, let alone block it.

As the stunned Redfield sat on the ground rubbing

his aching jaw, Patchett said, "Ain't no witnesses, you yellow-bellied dumbass. Your word against an NCO's ain't never gonna mean shit, *irregardless* of whether that NCO's white, brown, blue, or purple. Now pick yourself up because you're coming with me. I need me an RTO, and you just got yourself *volunteered*, boy."

When they reached Item Company's assembly area, its commander, a green second lieutenant, was briefing his platoons on his plan to take back the ridge. He returned again and again to the combat principle behind his plan: the double envelopment.

But to a combat-seasoned infantryman, his plan sounded like a debacle in the making.

"Begging your pardon, Lieutenant," Patchett said, "but maybe we'd be money ahead if we threw an element of *surprise* into this attack of yours."

"I'm not sure what you mean," the lieutenant replied.

"It's simple, Lieutenant. Basically, you're just planning to walk straight up that ridge like lambs to the slaughter. It don't make no nevermind that you're splitting your force so it sorta *looks* like a double envelopment because your zone of advance is too damn narrow. Y'all will look like just one lump of GIs coming at them, and they'll eat y'all for second breakfast."

"You have a better idea, Sergeant?"

"Yeah, I believe I do, Lieutenant. How about I take your lightest platoon around this ridge and come up the other side? They probably won't be looking out for that. With any luck at all, we'll send half of them to commie heaven before they even know what hit 'em. Then the rest of y'all can come charging up this side and maybe actually make it to the top. Now that's a *real* double envelopment."

"But what if there are KPA all over the place on the other side of the ridge, Sergeant?"

"This fog's pretty damn thick in the low-lying areas, Lieutenant. We could probably walk right past 'em and nobody'd be the wiser."

Patchett read the lieutenant's face. He could tell the man didn't like being shown up by an NCO. But on the other hand, that NCO's plan was suddenly sounding a hell of a lot better than the one he'd been forced to concoct on the spur of the moment.

And if it goes to shit, the lieutenant told himself, *I've got somebody else to blame for it.*

"All right," he told Patchett, "take Second Platoon. It's got no officer, just sergeants, so there won't be any leadership conflicts."

"What happened to their platoon leader, Lieutenant?"

"He bought it a couple of days ago, Sergeant."

It took Patchett and 2nd Platoon fifteen minutes to walk to the other side of the ridge. They saw no one except each other. "Just remember," he told the three squad leaders, "when we get to the top, y'all go on line and just start walking straight across it. Shoot every *sumbitch* you see that's in front of you."

Then they began the climb to the peak, a long, thin column with Patchett at its head. He turned to Redfield, who was right behind him carrying the backpack radio, and said, "Don't you dare get separated from me in this fog, boy. Hang on to my belt if you need to. We gotta tell the rest of the company to start coming at just the right moment so the gooks don't get no chance to recover."

Halfway up, they could see the silhouettes of men coming down the slope toward them. There were five of them, and they weren't making a sound. On their heads were the unmistakable shapes of GI helmets.

Redfield whispered, "They're GIs! They must've taken the hill already."

Patchett muttered, "Bullshit." He leveled his carbine at them and fired off two quick bursts on full automatic. Every one of the approaching men was taken down.

"Shit, Sarge, what'd you do that for? They were…"

Redfield couldn't finish the sentence. The shock of what he'd just seen made the words catch in his throat.

"Keep your fucking voice down," Patchett hissed. "Get on that radio and tell the lieutenant to start moving."

When Redfield didn't immediately do what he'd been told, Patchett added, "I mean right fucking now, boy. Or don't you understand English no more?"

As each squad emerged in turn out of the mist, Patchett pointed them to their attack position.

"Now move quick, dammit," he told each squad leader. "Don't give them gooks a chance to figure out what all just happened."

He pulled Redfield to his feet and together they resumed the climb. It was only a matter of yards before they came upon the men who'd just been shot dead. Viewed up close, their uniforms were obviously KPA.

Redfield stared at the bodies with disbelief. He'd

been so sure they were GIs.

The helmets. The fucking helmets.

Beside each corpse was an American Thompson submachine gun, too.

Redfield steadied himself against a tree. This was all too much for him, as if he'd been thrust into a new game with rules he didn't understand. Patchett grabbed him and began pulling him up the hill.

But Redfield had one question that couldn't wait: "How'd you know, Sarge? I mean...they didn't...I couldn't..."

"It's simple, son. Them Thompsons...they got a shape like nothing else. And you ain't never seen that many GIs all carrying 'em at once, have you? The only way these KPA gooks got 'em is they picked 'em up after some ROKs dropped 'em, because there sure as hell ain't no ROKs around here."

"But the helmets, Sarge..."

"Fuck the helmets. Steel pots are laying around all over this fucking country. Ain't no big thing to scoop one up."

There were a few crazy seconds of continuous gunfire. Then it stopped; 2nd Platoon could find no more Koreans to shoot. They milled around the twin 40-millimeter gun carriage still parked there. The bodies of two KPA soldiers were slumped across the weapon, as if they'd died in a futile attempt to fire it.

Second Platoon had suffered just two casualties of their own. Neither wound looked to be life-threatening.

Patchett warned the GIs, "Y'all best find some cover now so your buddies coming up the other side don't shoot your asses."

A minute later, the rest of Item Company came

charging up the slope from the opposite direction, firing at any shadow that even vaguely resembled a human form.

It took a few moments of frantic beseeching by the GIs of 2nd Platoon to get them to stop.

When they counted the KPA bodies on the ridge, it came to fourteen, including the five Patchett had shot on the slope.

"Well, Lieutenant," Patchett said, "we sure had them gooks outnumbered. Good work. Are you gonna consolidate your position up here now?"

"Yeah, Sergeant. That's the plan."

"Okay, then...I'm headed back to Regiment. I'll see what I can do about rounding you boys up some more ammo for that forty millimeter over yonder."

Although it was combat on just a small scale, retaking that ridge was the first victory over the KPA any of the GIs had ever seen.

But it wouldn't change the big picture.

Chapter Twenty-Six

The fog cleared at 1000 hours, as if on cue. But there'd still be no air support; the solid overcast was so low that those at 26th RCT's hilltop CP swore they could reach up and touch it. From that hilltop, there was now enough visibility to look across several miles of surrounding terrain. The view wasn't comforting. In Patchett's words, "I think I liked it a whole lot better when we couldn't see what-all we were up against. There are just too damn many of 'em, sir."

"If only this sky would clear," Jock said. "The Air Force could do us a world of good right now. Look at how bunched up the gooks are in those assembly areas. A couple of napalm runs would thin them out real good."

"They know the score, sir," Patchett replied. "Ain't no secret we ain't getting no air support. And the fact that our artillery ain't shooting…they gotta know we're low on rounds. Those fucking ammo drivers must've gotten themselves good and lost. So the plan is we're still not shooting them guns until you call for final protective fires?"

"Affirmative, Top. Not until they get close, real close…so it'll give us a fighting chance to pull out of here with as few casualties as possible."

"Let's damn sure hope so, sir."

Jock was busy scanning the forces arrayed against him through binoculars. "Sergeant Moon was right about that notch between *The Twins*," he said. "The gooks cleared that roadblock he made. Look, Top…there's a column of tanks coming through right now."

"Yeah," Patchett replied, "but there ain't that many over that way, sir. Six at most, I reckon. All the rest of their armor is still to the east, smack dab in front of Bubba Moon. That boy got a real taste for shit, don't he?"

Sean's seven tanks—six Chaffees and the Sherman he rode—were tucked behind a railroad embankment just one mile beyond 26th RCT's perimeter. As *hull-down* positions went, this one was a gift, the best Sean had found since coming to Korea.

But we're still outgunned, he knew, *and there ain't anywhere near enough of us.*

Best we're gonna do is stall 'em a little bit more.

It all went to hell very quickly. Just before 1100 hours, the North Korean artillery—which had been hurling rounds for the last thirty minutes uninterrupted by American counter-battery fire—stopped shooting. To the sound of shrill whistles, their infantry assault on the hills began.

Colonel Brand's 3rd Battalion collapsed first. The flanking ridge Patchett had reclaimed just two hours ago was the first piece of the regiment's high ground to be taken by the KPA. Worse, the ammunition Patchett had scared up for the twin 40s had arrived just a few moments before the assault began. There wasn't even time to unbox it before it fell into Korean hands. Within minutes, the M19 was being deployed against other

American positions with devastating results. It hadn't taken the KPA troopers long to figure out how to use it.

At the regiment's CP, a tease of hopeful news spilled from the radio: the Air Force reported they were in the air, gambling that breaks in the cloud cover would develop, allowing strikes against the KPA onslaught. The fighter-bombers would arrive overhead in twenty-five minutes.

"They're loaded with napalm, sir, just as you requested," the radioman told Jock.

"Twenty-five minutes will be too damn late, sir," Patchett said.

"Dammit, Top…tell me something I don't already know."

Then, like a poker player asking for his final card, Jock said, "Shoot the *FPF*."

The radioman had more news. "Eighth Army's on the horn, sir. They're asking what your situation is."

"Tell them I'm shooting my *final protective fires*. That's my fucking situation."

Suddenly there was too much to do and too many questions demanding answers. Within the next minute, men throughout the regiment would be burrowing deep into the ground, praying they wouldn't be killed by the *friendly* artillery that was about to *protect* them by landing on their heads.

And hopefully, that same artillery fire would sweep the KPA from the hills just long enough for the GIs to make their escape.

Patchett asked, "Which withdrawal plan are we gonna use, sir?"

"*Able*," Jock replied. "We'll be using Plan Able. The XO will lead."

A staff officer said, "But the XO is down with First Battalion, sir."

"That's all right. It doesn't matter where Colonel Lewis' ass is at the moment, as long as it's under cover."

Turning to Patchett, he said, "Go ahead and execute *Plan Able*, Top."

The radioman again: "*Adonis Six* wants to talk to you, sir. Immediately."

Adonis Six: the call sign for General Walker, 8th Army commander.

"Tell him we're too fucking busy."

The radioman looked like he was about to be sick. "I can't...I can't tell him *that*, sir."

"Then just tell him to wait, Corporal."

Once all three battalions had acknowledged *Plan Able*, Jock made his way to the radio. He recognized the voice; he was surprised it was General Walker himself.

"I need you to hold your position, *Montana*," the general said.

"No longer possible, *Adonis*."

"I can't make myself any clearer, *Montana*. I need you to hold."

"I know you do, *Adonis*. I'm sorry. *Montana Six*, out."

He put the microphone down and returned to the daunting task of conducting a withdrawal while in contact with the enemy. As soon as the final protective fires were lifted, the men lucky enough to have survived them would execute *Plan Able*, the ceremonious name for their great *bug-out* south to Pusan.

★ ★ ★

Sean got the word that *Plan Able* was in effect just a little too late. They were already engaging the lead elements of the KPA armor.

"Son of a bitch," he said, "they couldn't have told me that a minute ago, so we coulda just turned around and gotten the hell outta here? Now we gotta disengage somehow without getting our asses roasted."

But he had a plan.

He radioed the tank on his company's right flank. "*Blue Two-Four*, take out that bridge to your right."

"I've got to move to do it, Sarge. Got no line of sight. This embankment's in the way."

"Then go ahead and move, dammit," Sean replied.

Then he told the tank on their left flank, "*Blue Three-Two*, start leading the column back to the highway, but take out that bridge way out to our left while you're at it."

"Shit, Sarge," *Blue Three-Two* replied, "that bridge is a mile away."

"It's nine hundred yards, give or take. Well within range. Start moving and shooting."

Sean's gunner was confused. He asked, "What's the big idea, Sarge? Shouldn't we be shooting tanks instead of bridges? Better yet, shouldn't we just be getting the hell out of here?"

"Getting the hell outta here is exactly what we're doing, pal. And as long as we got that railroad embankment between us and the gooks, we're bad targets. To get a clean shot at us, they gotta get across that fucking muck, and they need the bridges to do that.

If we can shoot those two out, they gotta go all the way into Taejon to cross it."

Blue Two-Four took its bridge out in five shots.

Blue Three-Two took eight shots to collapse its bridge. At its greater range, two of the rounds had missed completely.

By the time they were finished, the rest of Baker Company was rolling behind the embankment, headed to join the rest of 26th RCT on the highway going south.

"How's our gas?" Sean asked his driver.

"Down to a quarter of a tank, Sarge."

If his Sherman was down that low on fuel, the Chaffees were in even worse shape.

If we can't beg, borrow, or steal some gas real soon, we all just joined the fucking infantry. Damn shame, too…we still got about half our ammo load.

While the railroad embankment provided excellent cover for the hulls of Sean's tanks, their turrets were still exposed. That's why Sean had insisted that while they were traveling parallel to the Korean tanks, they keep their turrets pointed at them—perpendicular to their direction of travel—even though they no longer had plans to stop and shoot.

"We show 'em our turrets' thickest armor that way," he explained.

Heavy machine gun fire frequently bounced off the turrets as they moved to the highway. But if a T-34's main gun had fired a shot at any of them, it had missed by a wide margin.

"Hey, take a look at this," Sean said. "One of their tanks is trying to ford the stream."

None of his crew took him up on sticking their heads out and seeing it for themselves, preferring

Sean's commentary from the turret's cupola to a head wound.

"Whoops, she didn't get far," Sean reported. "She's stuck. Them tracks are just spinning, throwing mud like a fire hose."

They were almost to the highway now. Sean could see smoke from the impacts of the final protective fires ahead.

Then he saw something he hadn't figured on: KPA infantry running toward them.

A Chaffee commander's frantic voice was on the radio, asking, "Should we engage them?"

"Hell, yeah," Sean replied. "Knock 'em down."

Within seconds, the lead Chaffees were raking the KPA soldiers with their bow machine guns.

Then the Koreans surprised him again. In small groups, they turned and began swarming the American tanks. Each group seemed to have a specific vehicle picked out.

"These clowns ain't too scared of tanks, are they?" Sean said as the KPA troopers tried to clamber onto their decks.

"Dust 'em off, boys," he ordered. "Traverse your turrets as necessary. Forget the T-34s for now."

The nerve-racking clatter of bullets bouncing off their hulls and turrets began as the tanks defended one another. Those that weren't at the ends of the column were cleared of KPA sappers in seconds.

Those at the ends, though—*Blue Two-Four* and *Three-Two*—had a problem Sean was well aware of:

Them gook bastards on those tanks are only getting shot at from one direction. They can hide behind the turret and there's nothing you can do about it, unless...

"*Two-Four* and *Three-Two*, spin your damn turrets all the way around, right fucking now," Sean said over the radio. "Knock 'em off you with the tube."

Three-Two succeeded in doing just that. Once the two sappers were swept off her foredeck, the tank behind her gunned them down.

Two-Four wasn't so lucky. Her crew hesitated to traverse the turret. It gave the three sappers on her aft deck an extra moment to stuff grenades down her engine vents. By the time the tube pivoted around to sweep them away, they were gone, fleeing toward the stream and the Korean tanks.

Two-Four's engine faltered, damaged by the grenades. Then she burst into flame.

Her crew abandoned her and scurried to crowd into other tanks.

Sean's Baker Company was down to six tanks—five Chaffees and his Sherman.

When they'd left Yongdong yesterday, they'd numbered fourteen.

★ ★ ★

As they approached the pass just east of 26th RCT's position, the final protective fires began to fall right in front of Sean's tanks. "Hold here," he told his crews. "The FPF is sweeping the whole area. It'll move away in a couple of seconds. When it does, blast right through to the highway."

Just like he said, the fires quickly shifted west. The tanks began to plow through the pass.

Sean's Sherman was at the rear of the column, its main gun facing aft in case any T-34s tried to overtake them. *Better a Sherman's gun than a Chaffee's*, he thought. *Neither one's gonna kill 'em with a head-on shot, but a Sherman will at least give 'em a bigger headache.*

The others had cleared the pass now. As the Sherman started through, the driver said, "Hey, Sarge, get a load of this."

There was a lone GI standing in the middle of the road. He was pointing his M1 at the Sherman.

The driver asked, "What do you want me to do, Sarge? Go around him? Knock him down?"

"No. Just stop when we're close enough so I can yell at him."

When they'd closed the distance to about two hundred feet, the GI fired a shot from his M1. It *pinged* harmlessly off the turret.

"WHADDA YOU WANNA DO THAT FOR, PAL?" Sean said. "WE'RE ON THE SAME FUCKING SIDE HERE."

But the GI was pacing frenetically in a small circle, ranting words Sean couldn't hear. Alternately, he'd point his rifle at the tank and then pump it back and forth across his upper body, as if performing a crazed and repetitious close order drill between the positions of *port arms* and *right shoulder arms*.

"Get a little closer," Sean told his driver.

The Sherman creaked to about one hundred feet from the raving GI. Now Sean could make out what he was saying:

"FUCK ALL THESE GOOKS. I AIN'T DYING FOR THEM. I AIN'T DYING FOR NOBODY, SO FUCK MACARTHUR AND FUCK TRUMAN, BECAUSE I'M GETTING OUTTA THIS STUPID

GODDAMN WAR AND THIS FUCKED-UP ARMY,
TOO. IF I GOTTA WALK ALL THE WAY HOME,
I'M GONNA DO IT. IF ANYONE TRIES TO STOP
ME, I'LL SHOOT THEM DEAD."

Sean leaned forward in the turret hatch, unfazed
and relaxed as he rested his forearms on the hatch ring.
He'd seen men go crazy in combat before, so afraid of
dying that their fevered minds lost all grasp on reality.

But this guy's redeemable, he told himself. *As long
as they're talking—even if it's total bullshit—you can
bring 'em back to their senses.*

*It's once they clam up and start that fucking
staring into the distance—that thousand-yard stare
shit—then he's fucked up for life.*

"C'mon, pal," Sean said, "why don't you get into
this nice safe tank and we'll get you outta here."

"Safe, my ass," the GI said, his eyes wild. "Don't
bullshit me. That ain't nothing but a rolling coffin."

Sean tried a different approach. "You know, you
must be a real lucky son of a bitch. You must've been
walking around while all that artillery was coming
down, and you didn't get a scratch, did you? Me and
my crew could sure use some of that luck rubbing off
on us right about now."

The GI looked at Sean as if he didn't know what he
was talking about.

"But everybody's luck gotta run out sometime,
pal...and that artillery just might be coming back this
way, so I think you better climb aboard. We're gonna
drive up to you real slow and—"

The GI leveled his M1 and fired again. This shot
didn't do any harm, either, bouncing off the glacis plate
next to the driver's viewing port.

"This guy's getting on my nerves, Sarge," the driver said as he slammed his hatch closed.

"Take it easy," Sean replied. "That pissant M1 ain't gonna hurt you or this vehicle none."

The GI stood defiantly in the middle of the road, rifle at the ready, a sentry guarding nothing but his own madness.

"C'mon now, pal...nice and easy...climb up her nose and—"

Sean sensed the shell coming. There was nothing to hear when you were on the receiving end; the round traveled faster than the *swoosh* it made as it streaked through the air. He'd felt it too many times before, that feeling in the split second before impact that something was suddenly amiss in the universe.

He ducked into the turret.

There was no telling which side had fired the round. It impacted close to the bow of the Sherman, the shock wave of its explosion making her shudder. Shell fragments *clattered* against her hull like brief but vicious steel rain.

When Sean peered out of the turret again, the raving GI had been erased from the face of the earth.

Slamming his hatch closed, he told his crew, "Stay buttoned up and let's get through this pass lickety-split, before any more of that shit comes down."

As they roared ahead, he mumbled, "Well, that poor bastard got his wish, anyway. He's out of the fucking Army now."

The FPF lasted only a few minutes, but to the GIs

of 26th RCT, it seemed so much longer. When the explosions of the impacting rounds finally ended, there was no silence. Instead, there were the sounds of officers and NCOs bellowing orders to control their rapid withdrawal; the injured wailing for their mothers, the medics, or God to save them; the disappointing snarl of aircraft, undoubtedly American but invisible and impotent above the solid overcast.

There'd be no formal account of the GI casualties from the FPF for now; there was too much else to do to ensure this *tactical withdrawal* didn't devolve into a rout. At least it had accomplished its intended purpose; the only KPA troops still in the American position were dead. Now the GIs had a few precious, uncontested minutes to clear the hill and retreat down the highway toward Pusan.

Jock had mandated they'd take their dead with them. Everywhere he looked, he could see the bodies of his GIs, hastily shrouded in ground sheets, being loaded into utility trailers. Each dead man was another knife to his heart, another marker in the cemetery of his mind at which to mourn the rest of his life. There would always be that question: *Were their deaths inevitable or unnecessary? Could I have done something better—something different than the FPF—to save them?*

Many would offer their opinions in the days and weeks to come, for senior officers were experts at dispensing blame. They weren't burdened by the need to be correct, only decisive. Jock knew there'd never be an objective answer to his question.

But right now, he'd swear on his children that there was nothing else he could've done but rain friendly fire down on his own position.

★ ★ ★

Sean's six tanks met up with 26th RCT's retreating column a few miles down the highway. The gas truck he'd asked for was nowhere to be seen.

"It's empty, Bubba," Patchett told him. "They all are. Wasn't enough to go around as it is."

"So when are we gonna get more, Top?"

"There's supposed to be a refuel point down the highway at Kumsan."

"Shit," Sean replied, "that's almost twenty miles from here. The tanks'll never make it. They're practically dry already."

"Then you're gonna have to abandon 'em all and put 'em to the torch with thermite, Bubba."

"Yeah, but I got a better idea. Colonel Miles wants us covering the ass end of this column, right?"

"Affirmative," Patchett replied.

"Good. Then we can sit here for a while and pump out the driest Chaffees. That should give us enough to get the Sherman and one or two Chaffees to Kumsan. We'll torch the rest."

Patchett nodded. "Sounds like a plan. You got a big-ass hand pump to transfer that fuel?"

"Sure do, Top. How do you think we get the shit outta fifty-five-gallon drums?"

Laughing, Patchett replied, "From what I seen, a buncha big bubbas like you just manhandle the drums onto the deck and dump 'em right into the fueling port."

"You gotta be pretty fucking desperate to do it that way, Top...or pretty fucking unprepared. Besides, if you gas up like that, I guaran-damn-tee you you'll end up with a fire on your deck before you know it."

"So that's your plan? Rob Peter to pay Paul?"

"Damn right, Top. You do want at least a coupla tank guns covering your ass, don't you?"

Patting him on the back, Patchett replied, "I like the way you think, Bubba. You're pretty damn clever for a tanker...and a Yankee."

Jock would be the last man off the hill. He needed to be sure his RCT was leaving nothing—and no one—behind.

Checking 3rd Battalion's sector with one of its staff officers, a glimmering object attracted his attention. It was hanging on a tree which had been denuded of leaves and scarred by shellfire. As he walked closer, he recognized what it was: a GI's dog tag.

Stepping forward to grab it, his bad leg betrayed him and he fell flat on his face. As he went down, a bullet smacked into the tree trunk behind him.

Had he still been standing, that bullet would've struck him in the chest.

Struggling to his knees, he reached up and snatched the dog tag. Then he and the staff officer—a captain—stumbled to the cover of the backslope.

"You must be clairvoyant, sir," the captain said. "If you'd been standing, that sniper would've taken you out."

"Yeah, I know," Jock replied. "But believe me, Captain, clairvoyance had nothing to do with it."

Making his way back to his jeep, Jock thought, *And all these years, I've been cursing this damn leg...*

Chapter Twenty-Seven

For almost two weeks, 26th RCT conducted a fighting withdrawal along the sixty miles of highway to Pusan, protecting the western flank of the retreating 8th Army. The weather had been mercifully good, allowing air support to inflict considerable punishment on KPA forces during daylight hours. But at night, the GIs were forced to survive on nothing but their wits.

Far too many didn't.

On the morning of 1 August 1950, the retreat of the 26th ended as they crossed the Naktong River and entered what was now called the Pusan Perimeter. It was a rectangle of territory measuring one hundred miles by fifty miles, with its back to the sea in the southeast corner of the Korean peninsula. Three US divisions and four ROK divisions—all battered and badly understrength—occupied the perimeter along with the fresh 1st Provisional Brigade of the US Marine Corps. These units comprised the sum total of 8th US Army forces in Korea.

"Welcome to the Pusan Perimeter, gentlemen," General Walker had told Jock Miles and his regimental cadre soon after crossing the Naktong. "The Eighth Army, along with its ROK allies, is now well consolidated within this perimeter and powerfully massed to repel the enemy. Very soon, more United Nations forces will be joining us. This is where we'll begin the annihilation of these North Korean savages. The Naktong will be the last river you'll ever have to fall back across, I can promise you."

Patchett howled with laughter when told of the

general's bravado. "I guess the general's finally took *hisself* a look at a map. We done run out of rivers to fall back across. Next time our feet get wet, we'll be swimming in the Sea of Japan."

"By the way," Jock told his assembled commanders and staff, "we're no longer Twenty-Sixty Regimental Combat Team. That designation is hereby retired. We are once again the Twenty-Sixth Infantry Regiment, one of three regiments comprising the resurrected Twenty-Fourth Infantry Division."

"Resurrected, sir?" Sean Moon asked. "You mean they're coming back from the dead?"

"More or less, Sergeant. The MPs have been real busy rounding up all the stragglers from Seventeenth and Thirty-Third Regiments."

"*Stragglers*, sir?" Sean said. "Ain't *deserters* a more accurate term?"

"Let's just say that a lot of sins are being absolved for the sake of making headcounts look good, Sergeant. But let's not kid ourselves. This regiment—this entire division—took a serious beating. The Twenty-Sixth's manpower is only slightly better than fifty percent of authorized strength, yet we're the strongest regiment. If you put every outfit in this so-called *division* together, you'd end up with the manpower of one real flush regiment."

Patchett said, "Well, sir, that's what happens when a buncha starry-eyed generals believe their own bullshit. They throw *route-step* rookies into combat against an enemy they're underestimating real bad, and them rookies get their asses handed to 'em. But it ain't nothing we ain't seen before."

When the murmur of agreement died down, Jock

continued, "Until replacements start arriving from the States, we'll be getting a lot of KATUSA to augment our numbers. I don't have exact figures yet, but I expect every platoon will get half a dozen or so. The first group arrives today. Sergeant Patchett, you're to see that they're distributed to the battalions as necessary."

"Will do, sir," Patchett replied.

Major Appling, 1st Battalion commander, asked, "What about those UN forces General Walker was talking about, sir?"

"All I know about them is that they're on the way. Don't have an exact arrival date yet, but it's supposed to be within a few weeks. Looks like they'll function as intact battalions, not replacement personnel, and be assigned to existing US regiments. The biggest numbers will be coming from Great Britain and the Commonwealth."

As the meeting broke up, Colonel Brand asked Jock, "A word in private, if I may, sir?"

"Sure. What's on your mind, Colonel?"

"I request that my battalion doesn't get assigned any of those KATUSA gooks, sir."

Jock regarded him coolly for a moment. Then he replied, "Colonel, you'll get whatever your commander decides, is that clear?"

Jock drove the three miles to Division HQ to inform his commander, the newly promoted Brigadier General Healy, that he was relieving Lieutenant Colonel Brand as 3rd Battalion commander, effective immediately. But he didn't expect he'd be announcing it with General Walker in attendance, as well.

"Are you sure that's what you want to do, Colonel?" Healy asked when Jock delivered the news.

"Affirmative, sir."

General Walker looked up from the folders he was thumbing through and said, "You realize what that'll do to his career, don't you, Miles? Being relieved of a combat command is a stain you can never wash out."

"I care more that my men have effective leadership, General. They deserve it, and that's more important than any one officer's career."

"I see," Walker replied. "Well, this is General Healy's show, so I'll stay out of it."

Healy asked, "How do you propose to replace him, Miles?"

"The battalion's XO, Major Hopkins, is more than ready to assume command, sir."

"Wouldn't a lieutenant colonel be more befitting to lead a battalion, Miles? We certainly have enough of them floating around here. I don't have any privates, dammit, but I've got more light colonels than I know what to do with."

"To be honest, sir, I'd put a captain—or even a lieutenant—in charge if he knew how to properly lead a combat unit. My other two battalions are commanded by majors, and I have no complaints with either of them. They've done excellent jobs in some pretty terrible circumstances."

Healy asked, "So what am I supposed to do with Colonel Brand?"

"I'm sure he'll make someone else an able staff officer, sir. But he's just not an effective combat leader. His decision-making skills leave a lot to be desired. I want him gone."

Healy wasn't happy about it, but he said, "Well, then...so be it, Colonel Miles. I'll have my adjutant cut orders immediately."

Then General Walker added, "Have Brand assigned to my headquarters. I know the man—he's worked for me before. I'll make good use of him."

Jock tried not to smile. Not only was he getting rid of Brand, but now he understood the basis of the man's uncooperative attitude, too: *He's in Johnnie Walker's pocket. No wonder that surly son of a bitch thought he could make his own rules.*

Walker wasn't finished. "Your problems with Brand wouldn't have anything to do with that Negro trooper of yours who assaulted a white man, would it? I'm told you let him off the hook."

Damn, word travels fast, Jock thought. *I wish my supply requests moved up the chain as quickly as political bullshit does.*

Jock replied, "I prefer to think I put the issue into proper context, sir, and dealt with it accordingly."

"Well, just remember, Colonel, that even though the official Army policy is one of *integration* in the ranks, we can't let these darkies think they can do whatever the hell they please, like they're back in Harlem or one of their other shitholes. That would be terrible for morale, don't you think? This isn't the first bit of racial trouble that's flared up in Eighth Army. Rest assured I'll be doing something about it very damn soon."

Then General Walker went back to studying the reports.

Healy asked, "Anything else you need to discuss,

Colonel Miles?"

"No, sir."

"Then you're dismissed."

Jock was just about to walk through the door when General Walker called him back. "Speaking of morale, Miles, how's yours?"

"I'm holding up just fine, sir."

"That's good, because I've got to ask you, do you think your *wife* is happy with Army life?"

The question stunned him. It'd been only three weeks since he'd left Jillian and the children to return to Korea. That wasn't even enough time to receive a letter from her. Whatever Walker was alluding to, he had no idea.

"General," he replied, "my wife has survived more combat than most of the soldiers in your Army and came back stronger each time. I don't think her morale will ever be an issue."

"I certainly hope you're right, Colonel," Walker replied. But he sounded decidedly skeptical.

After Jock was gone, Walker pulled a folder from the pile he'd been perusing and placed it on the desk in front of Healy. It was Jock's personnel file.

Flipping the file open, Walker tapped a *buck slip* fastened to it with his fingertip. Written on the slip were the words: DO NOT PROMOTE THIS OFFICER.

"This comes from the man in Tokyo himself," Walker said. "Consider it *gospel*."

Then he added, "Now let me fill you in on this *big thing* MacArthur's got planned. But remember, this is *top secret*."

★ ★ ★

During the entire drive back to 26th Regiment, Jock's head was filled with speculation about why General Walker had brought up his wife, a woman the general didn't even know. But MacArthur knew her, and Jock had no doubt the *king of Japan* hadn't forgotten the contentious dealings he'd had with both Jock and Jillian in the last war. They'd rejoiced when circumstance finally got them out from under the general's thumb. But now they were beneath it again and nothing had changed: MacArthur still considered himself a god—a vindictive one, at that—and Jillian didn't suffer fools easily. Especially fools in Army green.

Stepping into his CP brought Jock back to tangible matters quickly. Patchett had a laundry list of things on which to update him. "First off, sir, I see you succeeded in firing Colonel Brand. His new orders beat you here by a couple minutes."

"Where is he now, Top?"

"Gone. Didn't waste no time. He's headed to Pusan…on one of them newfangled helicopters, yet. Major Hopkins done took over Third Battalion already."

"Outstanding. What else?"

"I need to fill you in on a little racket I just busted up, sir. Seems some GIs took it upon themselves to *employ* KATUSA for their personal use. I found a bunch I'd assigned as ammo bearers digging holes instead. These GIs were paying the gooks a buck apiece to dig their fighting holes for 'em. Had to put a stop to that bullshit right quick."

"Damn right, Top. How'd you do it?"

"Put those GIs on the ammo detail. They started crying that they'd take their dollar back and dig their own holes...anything not to haul ammo. But I told them *a deal's a deal*, so pay up and start fetching. Don't reckon we'll be seeing much of those shenanigans again."

"Excellent. What's next?"

"Got all the artillery registration points along our stretch of the Naktong fired in, sir. It'll be a simple shift to the bridges if them gooks try to come across."

"Very good. Are we absolutely sure the river's not fordable anywhere along our front?"

"Absolutely, sir. I put Corporal Potts and his recon squad on it. They confirmed it—that water's too damn deep for men and vehicles."

"Potts is working out okay, then, Top?"

"Affirmative, sir. He's the best recon man we got in this regiment...besides me, of course. Kinda reminds me of that good ol' Cajun boy we had with us back in the last war. Potts has all the right instincts for sniffing things out, just like ol' Bogater Boudreau. Only darker. And Potts is from *Loosiana,* too. Don't that beat all? I reckon it's about time to hang another stripe on him."

A runner came into the CP and handed a message to Patchett. As he read it, Jock could see the anger building in his face. Without saying a word, he handed it to Jock.

The message was a communiqué from 8th Army HQ, ordering all Negro troopers to be immediately reassigned to segregated battalions being formed at Pusan.

"I'm a little confused, sir," Patchett said. "I thought

we done *de*-segregated the whole damn military back in Forty-Eight."

"Yeah, Top…that was the policy *officially*. But they never said it all had to be done right away."

"*Right away*, sir? We're talking two fucking years here, ain't we?" He threw up his hands and added, "I been thirty-two years in *this man's army*, and if there's one thing I learned for sure, it's this: if you expect men to fight just because you asked 'em to, you better not keep changing the rules on 'em. A man's gotta know where he stands, no matter what shade of skin he's in. This *one minute, we're all one color—Army green*—and then the next minute, we're *back to ol' Jim Crow*…that shit just ain't gonna fly, sir. Them coloreds will never trust us again."

"You're absolutely right, Top. But there's something else I'm sure your thirty-two years have taught you: there isn't a damn thing you or I can do about it right now."

"I'll give you a real big *amen* to that, sir."

As Patchett headed out of the CP, he added, "Oh, by the way, sir, ol' Bubba Moon's a l'il bit put out with me. Turns out one of our new KATUSA is named Moon, too. I asked Bubba if they were kin. Just joking, of course…but he didn't see no humor in it."

"I assume you smoothed it over, Top?"

"Didn't get the chance, sir. He high-tailed it down to Pusan to get us some more armor. Hitched a ride on that helicopter with Colonel Brand, in fact."

It was just after 1200 hours when Major Tommy

Moon and *Banjo Flight* returned to K-9 at Pusan. They'd just flown their second mission of the day, another strike against the Taejon-Taegu railroad line, attacking trains resupplying the KPA forces arrayed against the Pusan perimeter. "Better we wipe out their logistics along the main route—the railroad—before it gets distributed to the trucks that'll supply the individual divisions," they were told at the pre-mission briefing. "As you can see, the Pusan Perimeter's pretty big, so the more we can consolidate our interdiction efforts, the better off Eighth Army will be."

That seemed to be exactly what they'd been doing. They'd found six trains along a fifty-mile stretch of track leading to the perimeter and left each one in flames. "Kind of surprising to find so many of them moving in broad daylight," Tommy said at the debrief. "Makes you think the KPA's getting pretty desperate for their beans and bullets. Or maybe I should say *rice* and bullets."

As the debrief wrapped up, the squadron commander arrived with startling news. "Major Moon, you need to pack your bags. You're going to Yokota."

"Tokyo, sir?" Jock asked. "What the hell for?"

"Your jets should be arriving in the port of Yokohama as we speak, Moon. They've got to be unboxed, reassembled, and test flown. They need an experienced F-84 jockey to oversee all that. You sound like just the man for the job, so you've been *volunteered.*"

"Shit. When do I leave, sir?"

"Your flight's in four hours, Major."

✯ ✯ ✯

Four hours in combat would seem an eternity. But when you had only four hours to find your brother in the mayhem that was the five-thousand-square-mile Pusan Perimeter, it seemed like mere seconds. But Tommy had to try.

Surprisingly, it took him only ten minutes to get through to 26th Regiment's CP on the landline. They gave him some encouraging news: his brother Sean was actually at the port of Pusan, picking up tanks for 24th Division.

The port was just a few miles from K-9, a quick drive in a jeep. He changed into khakis, packed his kit bag for the trip to Japan, and set out to locate Sean.

It took less than an hour to find him, directing a team of GIs who were checking out tanks just unloaded from the ships.

"I figured you was around here somewhere, *Half*," Sean said as he wrapped his little brother in a bear hug. "But I ain't had time to look for you yet. Just got here this morning, in fact. You look a lot better now than the last time I saw you, after that crash landing at Taejon."

"I feel a hell of a lot better, too, big brother. I don't have much time myself, though. I'm going back to Japan to pick up some jets in a couple of hours."

"Jets, eh? You think that's part of MacArthur's *big thing*?"

"What are you talking about, Sean? What *big thing*?"

"You mean you flyboys ain't heard? MacArthur's got something cooking. Something *real* big. Nobody seems to know exactly what it is yet, though."

"This is all news to me, Sean."

"Maybe you'll get the lowdown when you're in Japan, Half. If you ask me, I'm betting we're gonna drop *the big one* on the gooks."

"Are you talking about the atom bomb, Sean?"

"Yeah, whaddya think I'm talking about?"

"That doesn't make any sense. There aren't any targets concentrated enough to waste an atom bomb on in that whole damn country."

"Oh, pardon me, *sir*," Sean replied, bowing irreverently. "Didn't realize you got promoted to G2."

"Cut the shit, Sean. If MacArthur's really got a *big thing* in the works, I'll bet it has something to do with all this armor you've got here."

"Yeah, maybe, Half...but I'd hate to think that's true because they're sending us the wrong vehicles." He pointed to a tank that had just been hoisted from a ship to the wharf. "See that monster? That's an M26—a Pershing. You ever seen one before?"

"Yeah, back in Europe, I think. But they all look pretty much alike from the air."

"Yeah, you told me that a long time ago. We didn't use Pershings in Third Army when they showed up in late Forty-Four. Patton didn't want 'em. From what I've seen of 'em since, he was right. They got problems, especially in a place like this."

"Like what?"

"Well, the ninety-millimeter gun's real good and the armor's the thickest we got, but the thing's too damn wide for a lot of the roads around here. And as heavy as they are, they're underpowered as hell. We'll have a fuck of a time getting 'em up hills."

Tommy pointed to a line of Shermans across the

wharf. "So you still like the *Zippos* better, Sean?"

"They may be old as hell now, but at least we know what we got with a Sherman. Won't be too many surprises. They got half a chance against a T-34...as long as you get the first good shot. Hey, you hear anything from Mom and Pop lately?"

Tommy shook his head. "I haven't gotten a stitch of mail since I've been in this damn country. I guess that part of the admin chain isn't up to speed yet."

"So you ain't heard nothing from that French girlfriend of yours, neither?"

"Hey, Sylvie's an American citizen now. Works for Uncle Sam, too."

"Yeah, I know that, Half. But what's she been doing for *you* lately?"

"Not a whole lot, Sean. She's been posted to Vietnam the last few months."

"Figures," Sean replied. "That's *Frenchy* territory, right? She'll fit right in."

Tommy had no doubt that's why the CIA had sent her there. The agency couldn't ask for a better liaison with the French.

Sean continued, "That ain't too far from here, right? You got a plane...why don't you pop in and say *hi?*"

"It's over two thousand miles, Sean."

"So what? You ain't walking it."

"You've got a point, big brother. Believe me, if the opportunity presents itself, I'll take advantage of it."

"Love'll find a way, right?"

"Something like that."

"*Something like that*, my aching ass, Half. You been in love with that tomato for the last six years." A devilish smile crossed his face as he added, "Still ain't figured out what a *split-tail commando* like her sees in a choirboy like you, though."

"I guess European women just know quality when they see it, Sean."

"You are so fulla shit, Half."

The brothers talked about everything under the sun for another hour, neither wanting their time together to end. But the clock kept its relentless progress toward the departure of Tommy's flight to Tokyo.

As they said goodbye, Tommy said, "You don't really believe all that shit about dropping the A-bomb, do you, Sean?"

He just shrugged. "Why not? Nothing about this war makes a lot of sense. The way I see it, anything's possible. I ain't alone thinking like that, neither...and you can take that to the bank, brother."

Chapter Twenty-Eight

As darkness fell over that first night on the perimeter, the music began. A symphony was blaring from loudspeakers on the far bank of the Naktong, drifting across its waters toward the men of 26th Regiment. Some might have considered it beautiful if it hadn't seemed so eerily out of place.

"What on God's green Earth do you make of that, sir?" Patchett asked Jock. "This ain't the evening's *entertainment*, is it?"

"I doubt it, Top. Maybe the KPA are using it to signal instructions to their units like they do with those damn whistles. Or maybe they're trying to use it to mask some other noise they're making."

"Yeah," Patchett said, "like the noise of vehicles moving up to the far bank."

"Who's leading the recon teams across the river now that Potts is gone, Top?"

"A sergeant named Karpinski, sir. He's the best I could come up with on short notice."

"What's he telling us?"

"Not a damn thing yet. I reckon he'll get real talkative, though, if vehicles do start moving toward the river."

Jock said, "I just hope his guys can hear anything at all over that damn music. It must be pretty loud on the other side. I'd hate for them to get jumped because they couldn't hear the gooks coming. They did take some KATUSA with them as translators, right?"

"Negative, sir, and I'm real pissed off about it, too. I didn't find out until after they left, but Karpinski had

hisself a fit when he found some of them gooks
chowing down on some roast dog. We GIs like our
dogs, you know, sir? Shit like that ain't making it any
easier to work with them Koreans. Maybe we oughta
outlaw the consumption of canines?"

"Yeah, Top, I'll get the doc on it. That way, we can
say we're doing it for hygienic reasons." He paused and
then added, "But you're right. He should've taken a
KATUSA or two with him, anyway, dammit."

The music stopped abruptly at 2345 hours. Within
seconds, automatic weapons fire erupted in 2nd
Battalion's area on the regiment's left flank. As Jock
drove toward a sky filled with tracers and the flashes of
explosions, he could hear that battalion's artillery FO
calling in a fire mission over the radio.

Don't tell me they're shooting an FPF, Jock
thought as he fumbled for his map. But the location of
the fire mission's target—*left two hundred from
Registration Point George*—plotted on the river itself, a
narrow but unfordable stretch of water nowhere near a
bridge. And it wasn't an FPF; the target description was
vehicles in the open.

That puzzled him: *The North Koreans can't
possibly be crossing the river there...or are they?*

When Jock reached 2nd Battalion's CP, he found
the battalion commander—Major Harper—in a
whirlwind of activity, a commo handset pressed to each
ear. Harper was a study in controlled fury, not letting
his anger with being taken by surprise impede his
ability to deal with it.

"They're driving gun trucks right across the goddamn river, sir," Harper told Jock. "All our intel says the river's not fordable. Something's wrong somewhere. At least the artillery seems to be stopping any more from coming over."

"Where are they hitting you, exactly?" Jock asked.

Harper dropped one of the handsets and pointed to an arc on the map. "They're here, sir, in Easy Company's position. About half a dozen of those gun trucks busted in while that fucking music was still playing and started spraying machine gun fire all over the place. My guys couldn't hear the trucks until they were right on top of them. It looks like we got chewed up pretty bad for a minute or so, but then we got the twin forties zeroed in on them. Blew half those trucks to kingdom come right away. We're trying to track down and kill the rest before they can get behind us. Thank God we haven't seen any gook tanks yet."

Jock asked, "What's your reserve company, and where is it?"

"That's *How Company*, sir." Harper pointed to the map again, adding, "They're on *Topeka Trail*, moving to block anything trying to get behind us. They've got a quad fifty with them. That should cut the KPA trucks to ribbons. I've told them to stay on the east side of the trail so maybe I won't have my companies engaging each other by accident."

"Good plan," Jock said. "I'm going down to the river to try and figure out how the hell they got across. If they did it here, they can do it again someplace else."

"I know how it happened, sir," Harper replied. "Our recon guys didn't do a very good job scouting the river. The intel they provided was for shit."

If that was true, it was a condemnation hurled at Corporal Potts, the man who'd led the recon effort and was now abruptly gone from the 26th, reassigned to a colored battalion.

And if it was true, it would be the first time Jock could ever recall Patchett's assessment of a soldier's abilities to be in error.

"Let's not jump to conclusions, Major. The night plays tricks on all of us."

"I know, sir," Harper replied. "But are you sure you want to be going down to the river right now? My men are really on edge. Walking around in the dark sounds like a great way to get the wrong guy shot."

"Tell me something I don't know, Major. Just swear to me that all your guys know the password."

Jock figured he was halfway to the river when he heard the *whoosh* of a rocket. He never heard the subsequent explosion that knocked him and his RTO off their feet. They landed in a fighting hole occupied by two GIs and a .30-caliber machine gun. The men might not have known Jock's name, but they had no trouble identifying the silver eagle on his collar in the dazzling light of the fire now blazing about thirty yards to their left.

"Hell of a way to drop in, Colonel," one of the men said. "Are you guys hit?"

"No, we're okay," Jock replied, "and sorry about that entrance, but can you tell me what the hell just happened? I heard a rocket, and that's all she wrote."

"A bazooka beat us to it and wiped out one of those

gook gun trucks, sir. Even with all this racket going on, we could hear that truck coming. Have a look for yourself."

Peering over the edge of the hole, Jock could see the vehicle, aflame in a pool of burning gasoline. The silhouettes of several heavy machine guns mounted on the truck's bed were plainly visible. They all looked like Russian weapons.

"Keep an eye on that truck, men," Jock said as he dropped back into the hole. "The ammo from those machine guns on its bed will probably start cooking off pretty soon."

Then he began to crawl out of the hole. His RTO—a PFC named Baum—was right behind him.

The machine gunner asked, "Where the hell are you guys going, sir? You just said it ain't safe out there."

"We've got more important business someplace else, I'm afraid. Thanks just the same for the hospitality."

"Can I ask you one thing before you go, Colonel?"

"Sure, but make it quick."

"You *are* going to get us out of here, right, sir?" He asked it with all the youthful sincerity of a child seeking reassurance from a parent. In the gunner's voice, Jock could hear his five-year-old boy asking that same question.

"I'm doing my damnedest, son."

Reaching the bunkers overlooking the river, Jock exchanged challenge and password with a jumpy lieutenant who kept shining a flashlight in their faces.

Jock said, "Point that light at me one more time, young man, and you'll be prying it out of your ass.

Now tell me what the hell's going on here."

Before the lieutenant could say a word, a flare arced across the river, illuminating for a few seconds the strange scene beneath it: a tank, its turret askew at a crazy angle, was sitting in the middle of the river as if walking on water. Only the lower half of her road wheels were submerged.

"I believe that tank took a direct hit from the artillery, sir," the lieutenant said. "But how could she be sitting up there like that? We watched one of her crewmen struggle onto her foredeck and jump over the side. He went down like a rock, like the water was over his head. We never even got a chance to shoot at him."

"Well, one thing's for sure, Lieutenant," Jock replied. "Tanks don't float...not without one of those big inflatable *donuts* around them, anyway. There's some kind of submerged bridge beneath her, that's for damn sure."

An artillery round struck the water directly in front of the tank. By the time the geyser it caused finally collapsed, the tank had slid deeper into the river. Only the top of her cockeyed turret and the muzzle of her main gun protruded above the surface.

"I think we just wrecked their underwater bridge," Jock said.

"What if they've got more of them, sir?" the lieutenant asked.

"Then we've got ourselves more problems, Lieutenant. Listen close. You hear that?"

In the silence between spasms of gunfire and artillery rounds landing, they could hear the faint sound of vehicle engines from across the river. Some of that sound was the deep-throated rumble of idling tanks.

For the moment, at least, Jock was fairly sure they'd cut off the Korean's path across the water. There was no point shelling the river itself anymore. Any KPA still waiting to cross were probably bunched up on the far bank.

He told Baum, the RTO, "Call Major Harper's CP and tell them to shift the artillery off the river. Target is vehicles and armor. Give them a correction of *add two hundred, shell white phosphorous, repeat fire for effect.*"

After calling in the data, Baum said, "Major Harper says he thinks he's got a couple of those gun trucks cornered near Hill One-Oh-Two. But there are groups of gook infantry everywhere."

Jock replied, "Tell him we're headed that way."

"Shouldn't we go back to the CP and get the jeep, sir?"

"No. We'll do it on foot. With everybody looking to shoot at vehicles, it's probably safer that way."

Jock and Baum stumbled slowly in the darkness up the shallow slope. They could hear a fight going on well in front of them and see the flashes from weapons of all sorts. Baum asked, "All that shooting…is that where Hill One-Oh-Two is, sir?"

"Looks like it," Jock replied. "The compass says we're headed the right way, and it's pretty hard to get turned around when you're going uphill."

"But those flashes…those tracers…they all look so close, sir. One-Oh-Two's got to be almost a mile from here, easy. Maybe a little more."

"Here's a little field wisdom for you, Baum," Jock replied. "When you're looking up, everything seems closer, especially at night."

"So if we were on top of this rise looking down, everything would seem farther away, sir?"

"Affirmative. You catch on fast, Private."

"Well, sir, one thing I haven't caught on to are these gook gun trucks. What's the point of them? It's not like they're armored vehicles or anything."

"True, they are pretty vulnerable," Jock replied, "but they're a good way to get a lot of heavy firepower around quickly. Hell, we've done it, too. We mounted our quad fifties on deuces, didn't we?"

"Yeah," Baum said, "but I sure hope when we did that, we didn't give the gooks the big idea."

"I doubt we did, Private. They're quite capable of figuring it out for themselves." The voice in his head added, *Maybe too damn capable.*

On the ridge that formed the base of Hill 102, they could see the shadowy figures of men—five, maybe six—moving in roughly the same direction as they were. Two of those men were lugging what looked like long pipes.

"A rocket team," Jock whispered as he dropped to a prone firing position. Baum quickly did the same.

"Theirs or ours, sir?"

"Let's find out. Is your weapon on full auto?"

"Affirmative, sir."

"Well, get ready to use it if we don't get the right answer."

Jock called out, "Hey, any Red Sox fans over there?"

The immediate reply: "Fuck the Red Sox. I'm a

Tigers fan."

Then the GI from Detroit added, "You in the mood for some *pale* ale?"

That would make no sense unless you knew that *pale* was the day's challenge word.

"Only if it's *spring*, my friend," Jock replied, *spring* being the current password.

As Jock and Baum got up off the ground and joined the rocket team, the gunner caught the glint from his eagle. "Holy shit, sir," he said, "you're Colonel Miles, aren't you?"

"Last time I checked, son."

"What the hell are you doing wandering around out here, sir?"

"Same thing you are…trying to kick some gooks in the ass."

"Well, looks like you're in the right place, sir. There are supposed to be some of those gun trucks around here somewhere."

They could just make out the hill rising above them, its deep gray outline one shade darker than the night sky framing it. The gunner identified himself as Corporal Bifulco and added, "If those gook trucks get up that hill, they'll be able to spray every swinging dick down on this ridge."

Jock replied, "Our guys are still on top, Corporal, and that's a pretty steep climb for a truck. My guess is they're hiding behind the hill, trying to figure out what to do next."

"Any word on gook tanks in the area, sir?"

"The only one I saw got blown up trying to cross the river. These gun trucks are probably a reconnaissance force for their armor, trying to find an easy path through our perimeter."

"So if the trucks get blown up, they won't send the tanks?"

"Let's hope so," Jock replied.

"We keep hearing there's gook infantry all over the place, sir. You seen any?"

"No, Corporal. Have you?"

Bifulco shook his head.

"We'll take that as a gift, for now. Let's go find those trucks."

But the trucks found them before they'd walked fifty yards. Two large vehicles the size of deuces were moving slowly down a trail along the top of the ridge, headed their way.

"Move right," Jock told the team. "We'll set up a little bit down the slope so we can get good flank shots."

They could barely see the trucks as their dark shapes blended into the mass of the hill behind them. But their sound was unmistakable.

"Those are GI deuces, sir," Bifulco said. "Just listen to those General Motors engines!"

Jock replied, "They may be our deuces, but it's not our guys driving them."

"I don't know about that, sir. With all due respect, I'm not shooting friendlies."

"You won't be, Corporal. See those guns on the beds?"

Bifulco strained to make out the shape of the machine guns in the darkness.

"Those aren't GI guns," Jock continued. "They're Russian—*dushkas*. We don't have anything shaped like that or pedestals like that to mount them on. Look at the flash suppressors on those guns, for cryin' out loud. That's not GI stuff."

"So what do we do, sir?"

"Shoot the trucks. Hit them right in the gas tank."

For a moment, nothing happened; even in the face of imminent death, a man could wrestle with questions of right and wrong, hesitating as his uncertainty hid behind a curtain of righteousness. Jock was about to add *That's an order, Corporal* to his instructions, but suddenly it wasn't necessary; with a double *whoosh*, two rockets—one from each tube—became glowing dots streaking toward the trucks.

A few armed men who'd survived the rockets' impact leapt from the burning trucks and began running toward Jock and his men.

There was no uncertainty this time as bullets from the GIs' carbines cut them down, with one qualification: Jock was sure he heard a GI wail, "God, forgive me," as he let loose with a burst of fire.

And then it fell quiet except for the crackling of the flames incinerating the deuces.

"There'll be cook-offs," Jock said, "but we've still got a minute. Corporal, come with me."

Together they low-crawled to the nearest body. Even in the darkness, there was no doubt the dead man was KPA.

Bifulco asked, "Were you just guessing, sir? I mean, playing the odds?"

"No, Corporal. I was pretty certain from the get-go."

"But *how*, sir? I mean, the trucks…the dark…"

"Let's just say that this isn't my first dance," Jock replied.

As silence settled in along the Naktong, that dance was over for now.

Sunrise provided answers the darkness would have never revealed.

A quick examination of the charred markings on all six of the destroyed gun trucks showed they'd been captured from ROK units. "They probably got lots of GI vehicles to use as decoys," Patchett said. "I guess it never occurs to them ROKs to destroy equipment they're gonna abandon. Seems like they're always in too big a hurry to skedaddle."

Jock replied, "Those trucks could've just as easily come from an American unit, Top. GIs were abandoning stuff like it was going out of style, too, remember?"

"You got a real good point there, sir. Unfortunately."

The burning question, however, was this: how did a submerged bridge across the Naktong get built right under the noses of the Americans?

It didn't take much investigation of the crossing site to understand the bridge's construction. Sandbags had been piled across the river bottom and topped with weighted planks tied together to form a concealed roadway two feet below the water's surface. Short poles protruding above the surface at regular intervals guided men and vehicles across the invisible pathway in the darkness. Building it would've been a Herculean task that could only be accomplished in the secrecy of night...

And it would've had to happen *last* night.

"It was that damn loud music," Patchett said. "They could've had a thousand *coolies* toting them sandbags into place, and we never would've heard a thing. Wouldn't've seen nothing from our positions on the high ground, neither. But if someone was standing real close…"

He was glaring at Karpinski—the recon sergeant—as he spoke the word *someone*.

Jock picked up the questioning. "There must've been quite a crowd at that crossing site while they were building it," he said to Karpinski. "If you were patrolling the area you were supposed to, how do you account for not coming across them?"

"We did come across a bunch of gooks," Karpinski replied, "maybe twenty or so men and a couple of women. But they were *civilians*, sir."

"What makes you so sure, Sergeant?"

"They weren't in uniform or anything…and they didn't carry weapons. They looked a hell of a lot more like refugees than soldiers."

Patchett interjected, "They coulda used civilians to haul them sandbags, sir. Maybe that's who he ran into—a civilian labor party."

Jock said, "Show us on the map where you encountered them, Sergeant."

Karpinski pointed to a spot on the far side of the river, a fair distance north of the submerged bridge site.

Jock continued, "I understand you didn't bring any KATUSA with you, so I'm assuming you couldn't talk to these Koreans. Am I right, Sergeant?"

"I can't trust anyone who'd eat a dog, sir, so I didn't take any of them with me."

"And in not doing so, you fucked up, Sergeant. But we're getting off track here. Did you have any sort of communication at all with these Korean *civilians*?"

"Just a lot of hand signals, sir. They were real worked up about something. Kept pointing north while they jabbered away. I figured they were trying to tell us where the KPA were. So that's where we went looking for them—north. Then the music stopped and all hell broke loose across the river. We heard that call for artillery fire, so we got the hell out of there, jumped in the rubber boat, and came home."

"Which way were these *civilians* going, Sergeant?"

"South, sir."

"In other words, Sergeant, *toward* the site of the submerged bridge."

"How was I supposed to know that, sir?"

"It's not what you were supposed to *know*, Sergeant. It was what you were supposed to *find out*. That's what recon does, remember? You didn't cover half the area you were supposed to patrol. Instead, you retraced your steps north, across ground you'd already covered and found no trace of the KPA. You never set foot in the southern part of your patrol area…and I've got a big problem with that."

Patchett added, "And you didn't radio in none of this while it was happening, neither, like you're supposed to. Put this all together and we damn near had a breakthrough on our hands."

"Sergeant Patchett is right," Jock said. "We could've stopped them on the other side of the Naktong if we had some idea they were planning to cross there. You could've—*no*, you *should've*—been the one to tell us that. Have you got anything else you want to say?"

Karpinski's voice quavered as he replied, "Yeah, I do, sir. You're trying to hang this fuckup all on me, but that ain't fair. I did what I thought was right under the circumstances. I couldn't help it if—"

Jock cut him off. "No, Sergeant, you *could* have helped it. All you had to do was follow your ops order. Now report back to your unit. You're dismissed."

Patchett escorted Karpinski from the CP. Once they were outside, he said, "You really fucked the dog on this one, boy. You're damn lucky the colonel ain't looking to bust your ass."

As he watched Karpinski walk away, Patchett muttered, "That whole circus wouldn't've happened if ol' Potts had been running that patrol, that's for damn sure. At least that man had *hisself* a lick of sense."

Back inside the CP, the S2 began his report on the interrogation of the four KPA prisoners the regiment had captured during last night's action. "This is what the ROK interpreters learned from the POWs," the intel officer began. "They're a pretty ragged lot. They don't appear to have eaten in days. Doc says they're weak and dehydrated."

"For a *pretty ragged lot*, they're sure causing us a lot of trouble, Captain," Jock said. "What else did you learn?"

"Quite a bit, sir," the S2 continued. "Once we fed them, they spilled their guts. It seems the KPA are running short of everything—food, ammo, gasoline, medical supplies, spare parts...not to mention people. But their officers remain intent on pressing the attack and are severely punishing malingerers. We suspect their supply lines are badly overextended now and taking a terrible beating from our air attacks. In this regiment's sector, we're facing elements of a depleted division, which is at no more than half-strength."

Jock asked, "How many troops is that?"

"We estimate about two thousand, sir."

"Two thousand," Jock said at almost a whisper, "against our five hundred."

"But their combat effectiveness appears marginal, at best, sir."

"I hope you're right about that, Captain. What's the estimate of their artillery and armor capabilities?"

"In bad shape, sir. Our POWs say they haven't had effective artillery support for over a week—again, it's taken a pounding from air attacks—and a large part of their armor has either been destroyed in combat, suffered mechanical breakdowns, or is just flat out of fuel."

"What do they know about that submerged bridge?"

"Not much, sir. Apparently, soldiers didn't construct it. Our POWs suspect that was done by impressed labor. They said they knew nothing about it until told to cross the river. They were sure they were going to drown but were very surprised when the water never got above the wheel hubs."

"Yeah, we were pretty damn surprised, too," Jock replied.

Chapter Twenty-Nine

Hurry up and wait…

It's a dish as old as the military itself, and it doesn't matter what rank you are; if you're lower than general grade, you'll taste of it frequently. Major Tommy Moon was handed a hefty helping of it as soon as he stepped off the plane at Yokota Air Base, Tokyo.

Shouting over the noise of the busy airfield ramp, a captain told him, "The jets aren't here yet, Major Moon. The ships have been delayed. Bad weather in the Pacific. We don't expect them to dock in Yokohama for at least another forty-eight hours. Then they'll have to be uncrated and reassembled, of course. That'll take a while."

Tommy resisted the urge to fling his flight bag at the captain, an Air Force logistics officer overseeing the shipment of the F-84s. If they'd bothered to send word to K-9 about the delay, he could've kept flying missions against the KPA for a few more days.

And maybe I could've spent a little more time with my brother.

"So what the hell am I supposed to do until then?" he fumed. "Cool my heels?"

"Tokyo offers many delights, sir," the captain replied.

"Yeah, I know about the *delights*. I've been here before. Just give me a ride to the transient officers' quarters so I can get my gear squared away."

After securing his room—a glorified closet with just a bunk, a rack on which to hang clothes, a small desk, and a single window which offered a depressing view of the base's scrap yard—Tommy wandered to the officers club for a late supper and nightcap. He was surprised that he didn't know a living soul in the place, but he struck up a conversation with another major who was nursing his beer at the bar.

Introducing himself as Case Cantrell, the major hoisted his pilsner glass and said, "Only one for me. I've got an early hop in the morning."

Tommy asked, "What do you fly?"

"A C-54. I've got to do the diplomatic shuttle."

"Diplomatic shuttle...what's that?"

"Just like it sounds, Tommy. We fly *diplomats*— and by that I mean CIA *spooks*—all over the Philippines and Indochina. Their secret cargo, too. Supposed to be real *hush-hush*, but the plane's still got US Air Force markings plastered all over it."

The mention of Indochina piqued Tommy's interest. "Indochina...you mean like Vietnam and places like that?"

"Damn right. We'll be touching down in Vietnam late afternoon tomorrow...Hanoi, to be exact. We lay over there for a day and then do it all in reverse the day after that."

Tommy asked, "Do you have room for one more passenger? I might have a little bit of business in Hanoi."

Cantrell smiled and said, "Oh, yeah? What's her name?"

When Tommy told the maintenance squadron commander—his temporary boss during the acceptance checks of the F-84s—of his request to take a three-day *joy ride* on the diplomatic shuttle's airplane, the colonel just shrugged and said, "Well, Moon, it's not like I've got anything for you to do around here for the next few days. Just remember to get yourself put on the crew manifest and bring some civvies, unless you want to live on the damn aircraft. You don't want to be wandering around civilian areas in uniform in any of those countries."

"Already got the civvies packed, sir."

"Well, then, see you in a few days, Moon. Have a nice trip."

After a stop in Manila, the diplomatic shuttle was headed west across the South China Sea toward Hanoi. It was mid-afternoon; the leg from Tokyo had been a long and boring eight hours. This leg to Hanoi would consume another six hours.

Slouched in the aircraft commander's seat while his co-pilot flew the ship, Case Cantrell said, "If we didn't have to make that stop in Manila, we could've cut some time off this Hanoi run by going nonstop. The old girl's got the range and then some. But you fly awfully close to Red China. A couple of our guys had to dodge chink fighters on that route, so the brass said to knock it off. They didn't want any *international incidents* while we've got this mess in Korea going on."

Tommy asked, "Really? How the hell does a slow ship like this dodge anything?"

"It's simple…just head straight out to sea. Those chink fighter jocks don't seem too thrilled about flying way out over open water, so if you go *farther* out…well, you know what I mean. You fly single-seat ships." Cantrell pointed to the rear of the cockpit, where the navigator was hunched over the chart table, deep into his calculations. "Without somebody like ol' *Whiz Wheel* there, it's real easy to get lost when you're over the drink."

"Yeah, you've got that right," Tommy replied.

"You sure you don't want to get a little stick time?" Cantrell asked. "She handles like a real pussycat."

"Thanks, but I'll pass. She's a little tame for my tastes."

Tommy made his way back to the cabin. The only other passenger after the Manila stop was a middle-aged CIA man named Whitechurch who had slept the entire leg from Tokyo. He was wide awake now, though, and while pretending to read some papers was giving Tommy a surreptitious once-over.

"I thought you were a pilot," Whitechurch said, "but I don't see you doing any flying."

"I'm just along for the ride, sir."

"No need to call me *sir*, Major Moon." Yet everything about Whitechurch—his bearing, his cropped, graying hair, his command voice—labeled him as one who once wore a high officer's rank. "It's just you, me, and all these crates full of *foreign aid* sitting in this cabin. We can be informal, right?"

"If you like, sir."

"Please, call me Howard."

"Sure. My name's Tommy."

"I know. I read the manifest."

"These crates, Howard…this stuff you call *foreign*

aid. It's really weapons, isn't it?"

The CIA man replied with just a knowing smile. That was all the confirmation Tommy needed. But that smile sent a chill up his spine all the same.

Whitechurch asked, "Why are you going to Hanoi, anyway, Tommy? It's not the place American officers usually go to relax. And there is a war going on there, you know."

"Yeah, I know," Tommy replied. "The French, the Viet Minh...just another guerrilla uprising."

"Oh, it's far beyond that, Tommy."

"Maybe you'd better fill me in, then."

Once again, Whitechurch replied with only that disquieting smile.

Tommy shifted in the hard bucket seat, fighting a losing battle for physical comfort. Thanks to his fellow passenger, he'd already lost the battle for emotional comfort as fear for what Sylvie was doing in Vietnam took hold of him all over again.

"Why *are* you going to Hanoi, Tommy?"

"I have a friend there working for Uncle Sam. Well, she's more than a friend..."

"Really!" Whitechurch replied, sounding almost bubbly. "A woman working for the US government! She must be with the agency, then, correct?"

Tommy got the sinking feeling that he'd already revealed too much. If he'd learned anything from his time with Sylvie, it was that you never—*never*—revealed the identity of an operative.

Whitechurch persisted. "You're talking about *Frenchie*, aren't you?"

Now he *knew* he'd said too much. He'd never been a convincing liar. Or even an unconvincing one. But he needed to slam the door shut on this line of questioning immediately.

"Look, Howard...Mister Whitechurch...I don't know any *Frenchie*, okay?"

With an approving nod, Whitechurch replied, "All right then, Moon, not badly played. Not entirely credible, but..." Then he went back to studying his papers.

For Tommy, the thunderous silence that fell between them drowned out even the numbing drone of the C-54's engines. That silence persisted for over an hour, until the CIA man said, "By the way, good luck even *finding* Sylvie Bergerac. She spends most of her time at the French outposts in the north, near the border with China. That's a combat zone, you know. Getting there could prove quite a difficult—and dangerous— proposition for you."

It was just after 2100 hours when the flight crew cleared the French military checkpoint at Hanoi's Gia Lam Airfield. Then they piled onto a French Army truck for the quick ride across the Red River to the hotel where they'd spend the night. Tommy had little intention of staying in his room, though. In civilian clothes now and armed with a crumpled Michelin street map, he set out to find Sylvie's flat at *127 Rue Paul Bert*.

He was relieved to realize the address was just a few blocks from the hotel. As he walked briskly down broad boulevards still crowded even at this late hour, the sound of people speaking French was everywhere.

He rubbed shoulders with Vietnamese, French civilians, and soldiers of the French Foreign Legion enjoying an evening off duty. Some were casually strolling, others relaxing in the many bars and restaurants. Taking in the architectural style, cloaked in the mysteries of night but still resplendent with its ornate facades and balconies overhanging the sidewalks, he felt he could've been walking down a street in any number of cities in France, or even the French Quarter of New Orleans.

This place feels just like France, he told himself, *with a lot of Asians thrown in.*

But there was one big problem: he couldn't find a number 127 on Rue Paul Bert. Number 125 was the last building before an intersection. Beyond that intersection, the buildings began with number 131.

He approached a lone legionnaire on the street corner. In the rusty French he'd barely used the last few years—and then only when he and Sylvie wished to have a private conversation in the midst of Americans—he asked, "Where can I find number One-Two-Seven Rue Paul Bert?"

In English, with the accent of one from the American Midwest, the legionnaire asked, "New York or Jersey?"

"New York. Brooklyn. It's that obvious?"

"The moment you opened your mouth, pal."

Then he took Tommy to the entrance of number 125. The door opened to a long corridor, a passageway through the building's first floor. "Try going all the way through," the legionnaire said. "They number things real crazy around here. One-Two-Seven is probably just the back side of One-Two-Five."

"Gee," Tommy said, "you think they'd put up a

sign or something."

"Nah, that would be too easy. You know how the French are. They like to be… *qu'est-ce que c'est? Mystérieux.*"

Tommy thanked him and headed down the corridor. The legionnaire called after him, "Hey, what are you, anyway? Army? Navy?"

"Just a tourist."

"Bullshit. But you have a nice night, anyway, whoever she is. Hey, one more thing…watch your ass on the street. The *Minh* aren't just up in the hills, you know."

Number 127 was right where the legionnaire said it might be. There were four names printed on the wall at the bottom of a narrow staircase. One of the names was *S. Bergerac, chambre 3.*

That's her.

Climbing the stairs, he could feel his heart pounding and his breath growing short. Every step closer heightened the dread that disappointment would be the outcome of this impulsive trip. He couldn't stop telling himself, *If that Whitechurch guy is right, she's probably not even here.*

But as he stood before the door to *chambre 3*, he could hear music playing softly.

American music. That's Nat King Cole, for cryin' out loud.

His hand quivering, he knocked with more force than he'd intended.

Shit. That sounded like cops getting ready to raid the place.

A few seconds later, her strident voice demanded, "*Identifiez-vous!*"

Identify yourself.

He'd barely gotten out the words, *"C'est moi,* Tommy," when the door flew open and the pajama-clad Sylvie pulled him into the tiny flat with one hand and kicked the door shut with her bare foot.

In her other hand was a snub-nose .38-caliber pistol; he didn't realize it was there until their deep kiss and vice-like embrace finally ended. By that time, Nat King Cole had long finished singing *Nature Boy* and the phonograph needle was scratching over and over again across the record's play-out grooves.

Still clinging to him, she spoke softly into his ear: "What on earth are you doing here, Tommy?"

"Aren't you happy to see me?"

"Of course I am, silly boy. How long do you have?"

"Two nights, one day. But what's with the gun?"

If she had her choice, she would never want him to know just how dangerous a place Hanoi—in fact, all of Vietnam—could be. But the pistol had given her away.

"A girl can't be too careful, you know," she said. Then she smothered his mouth with hers, praying it would be enough to flush his fears away…

At least for tonight.

It worked; there would be little talking that night. There was simply no need for words.

He hadn't noticed them in the shadows and passion of last night, but they were impossible to miss in the light of morning: hanging on the wall were garments that looked very much like safari clothes. Or military fatigues, perhaps.

From the cut of the cloth, they were something a man would wear. Just like the pair of workman's boots stashed in the corner.

"Of course they're men's clothes, Tommy," Sylvie replied after he'd seized on their presence, casually deflecting his implied accusation that a man might also reside in *chambre 3*. "But they're mine. I have no choice. There is no such thing as women's utility gear around here."

That only explained one of the burning issues on his mind. He asked, "Since when do you wear a uniform, Syl? Is the CIA part of the military now?"

"Tommy, have you ever seen rural Vietnam?"

"Of course not."

"Then trust me. It's not a very pleasant environment. Quite primitive, in fact. And very dirty. There's shit everywhere, animal and human. Those clothes are the only practical things to wear. Even if I need a belt *and* suspenders to hold up the trousers."

He saw something on the shirtsleeve that made him bolt from the bed for a closer look. It was a smear of blood.

"It's not mine," she said, as if that simple statement would end his sudden obsession with it.

Then she rose from the bed, snatched the shirt from his hands and threw it, along with the rest of the soiled clothes, into a pile near the door. "We'll need to drop these at the laundry on our way to breakfast," she said.

"Does that pistol come with us?"

"*Mais oui*," she replied.

But of course.

If it hadn't been for the Vietnamese waiters, the café would've seemed exactly like the many places they'd shared meals in France during the last war. The clientele was exclusively French, equal parts civilian and military. Many of them knew Sylvie; they wished her *bonjour* while curiously eyeing Tommy.

She could tell he had a million questions to ask her. Most could never be answered.

"I'm so glad Sean is okay," she said. "Give him my best, please." She paused and then asked, "Does he even know you're here?"

"Nope. This was a real spur of the moment opportunity."

"I see. And you met my colleague Whitechurch on the airplane. He was an old Asia hand in the OSS. His life in the agency now revolves around the conviction that losing China to Mao's communists was the greatest calamity ever to befall the United States."

"So I guess that's why you're here, Syl? To help prevent the communists from taking over Indochina?"

"Of course. It's all part of the same mistake that's sent you to Korea."

She was glad they were seated away from the other patrons. Conversations such as this one, whether in French or English, were best not overheard.

He leaned close and asked, "Are the French winning against the Viet Minh?"

Looking around to make certain that no one could hear, she replied, "Winning? No. But they're not losing at the moment, either. They're asking for more serious military aid from the US now—airplanes, artillery, and such. Without it, they'll lose in less than a year. With it, a French defeat is still inevitable but will take a little longer."

"Why would it be inevitable if they're getting US support, Syl?"

"Why? Because the French are desperately trying to cling to an empire they no longer have the means or the will to oppress." Her eyes swept the café as she added, "Look at all these deluded fools, thinking they can turn back time merely because they will it."

Her voice took on an exasperated tone. "Paris— and most of Washington, too—doesn't understand their struggle with this breed of Asian communism. It's not merely a political fencing match like it is in the West, where the goal is to take control of existing power structures. Here, it's an umbrella beneath which nationalists of many stripes gather to demolish the imperialist power structures they'd lived under for decades. Fighting them is like trying to make water flow uphill. So yes, the French will leave Indochina in defeat. And then the Americans will come and take their turn trying to beat down the communists."

"Like we're trying to do in Korea?"

"Like you're *failing* to do in Korea, Tommy."

"Gee, Syl…is that really the CIA line?"

"It's *my* line, Tommy. Case officers like myself merely observe and report. Politicians decide the policies. Usually badly. I'm not in Korea, of course, but I see all the same mistakes being made there."

It was hard for him to imagine her as one who *merely observed and reported.* Not Sylvie Bergerac, the ex-French Resistance fighter, ex-French Army agent of the *Affaires Civiles* in Germany during the war's closing months, ex-OSS operative for the Americans in the early post-war days, and a CIA operative ever since. She was more a warrior than most of the soldiers he'd known.

And she was in the fight again. The blood on the sleeve had been an ominous reminder.

He was still totally in awe of her.

And in love with her more than ever.

"Do you have to be somewhere today?" he asked.

"No. I'm at your disposal, Major Moon."

As they strolled back to her *chambre* along the noisy, teeming *rues* of Hanoi, he said, "There's talk all over Pusan that MacArthur's gearing up for some *big thing* to turn the tide against the KPA. A lot of GIs— my brother included—think he's going to drop an atom bomb in Korea."

Disagreement was written all over her face. "Don't be ridiculous, Tommy. Washington would never allow it. There'd be too much of a chance of drawing China, and maybe even Russia, into the war. That would turn the miscalculation in Korea into a catastrophe of colossal proportions."

"Okay, I'll buy that, Syl. But what's your take on the *big thing*?"

She considered her answer for a few moments. Then she said, "I don't know MacArthur well, but he strikes me as a carbon copy of de Gaulle, who I'm *very* familiar with. They're both self-absorbed actors pretending to be God. Whatever his *big thing* is, it'll be all theatrics and hubris masquerading as strategic brilliance."

She paused before adding, "But in the long run, it won't change a damn thing."

Chapter Thirty

For 26th Regiment, their second night on the Pusan Perimeter brought more attempts by the KPA to attack across the Naktong River. Unlike the night before, none of those attacks took the Americans by surprise.

And none of them had resulted in a North Korean foothold on the river's eastern bank.

As the new day dawned, Jock and Patchett stepped outside the CP, surveying the Naktong valley winding below them. After a few moments of pensive silence passed, Jock said, "Our guys did a pretty good job last night. But I think a lot of credit goes to you, Top. I suspect you had the locations of the KPA assembly areas figured out damn near perfectly. Our artillery must have screwed them up badly before they could even think about getting their feet wet."

Patchett shrugged it off. "Hell, sir, figuring out where they're gonna be assembling ain't no step for a stepper. After all, we *have* been fighting these gooks for over two weeks now. If you ain't learning, you're dying."

"So I guess you're not finding it too worrisome anymore that we're supposedly outnumbered four-to-one in this sector?"

"Worrisome for who, sir? Them or us?"

Jock expected to see that brief, tight-lipped hint of a smile that meant his old friend was joking. But there wasn't any smile, just the enduring scowl of a man who'd suffered the fantasies of one high command or another for a long, long time.

"No, I'm serious, Top. What's your assessment of

our situation?"

"I think you and me have been in worse scraps, sir. And I ain't so much worried about the gooks as I am about ol' MacArthur thinking up new and exciting ways to get us all killed." He paused, scanning the river valley once more. Then he said, "I reckon this Pusan Perimeter is a little too big for the headcount we got at the moment, sir. But I like seeing all that heavy artillery of ours that's showing up and them airplanes that kick ass when the sun shines. Once Bubba Moon gets back with some *real* tanks, well…things just might start to get a whole lot different around here."

"I'm glad to hear you say that, Top. I'm thinking the same way."

Patchett wasn't finished, though. "Of course, the replacements we get are gonna be even more useless than the dumbasses we already got."

"Wait a minute, Top. I think we've turned a lot of these men into decent soldiers in the last few weeks. Last night was a good example."

"Maybe so, sir. But something's different about these boys than the ones we had in the last war. They think if they don't feel like being a part of this, they don't have to be… and the stupid bastards don't feel no shame in that. It's like nobody ever told 'em, *Cowards die many times before their death. The valiant never taste of death but once.*"

"Well, I'll be a son of a bitch, Top. I didn't know you read Shakespeare."

"I ain't never read any of that shit, sir. But Shakespeare? He said that?"

"Yeah. Where did you think it came from?"

"From some captain back in the first war who was

trying to light a fire under a bunch of us scared-shitless doughboys."

"Did it work?"

"Not at the time, sir. That man couldn't knock a hole in the wind with a sackful of hammers." But then that hint of a smile finally crossed Patchett's lips as he added, "But I reckon with a little more head-banging, we can convince the greenhorns to see the light."

"We'd better, Top, because there's something else Shakespeare said: *Hell is empty and all the devils are here.*"

* * * * *

Don't Miss Book #2 in the
Jock Miles-Moon Brothers
Korean War Story

Available Summer 2019

Sign up to be added to the Mailing List for New
Release Announcements at
wpgrasso@cox.net, with Mailing List as the
Subject

Connect with the Author on Facebook
https://www.facebook.com/AuthorWilliamPeterGrasso

Follow the Author on Amazon
https://amazon.com/author/williampetergrasso

More Novels by William Peter Grasso

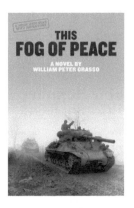

This Fog of Peace
Moon Brothers WWII Adventure Series
Book 4

The Moon brothers know all about the fog of war—
they've lived in its obscurity as the Allies fought their
way across Europe. Now that Germany has been
defeated, a new obscurity envelops them—a fog of
peace—as the Western Allies clash with the Soviets in
a series of provocations, blunders, bluffs, and deadly
confrontations. To these battle-hardened veterans, the
"peacetime" occupation of postwar Europe in 1945
feels little different than being at war.

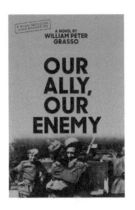

Our Ally, Our Enemy
Moon Brothers WWII Adventure Series
Book 3

Allies can be your worst enemies.

1945. The war may be going badly for the Third Reich, but they continue to develop "super weapons" to throw against the Allies. As the Moon brothers—fighter pilot Tommy and tanker Sean—struggle with the myths and realities of defeating the new technologies, a new threat appears: their Soviet allies are intent on dominating Europe. But a game-changer still looms: in the mountains of Bavaria, the Germans are preparing a super weapon against which there is no defense.

Fortress Falling
Moon Brothers WWII Adventure Series
Book 2

France, October 1944: Fort Driant may be a 19th century
anachronism, but it proves itself an impregnable obstacle
to Patton's forces as they fight to seize the city of Metz,
a gateway to Germany. Another fortress—a Flying
Fortress—may be the key to the fall of Fort Driant. The
Moon brothers are in the thick of the battle as Tommy
volunteers for Operation Aphrodite, a gambit that turns
unmanned heavy bombers into radio-controlled flying
bombs of enormous power. But as zero hour for
Aphrodite approaches, his brother Sean is trapped in the
tunnels of Fort Driant, with the Germans just inches
away behind armored doors. It's a race against time for
the GIs to take Driant—or escape before the Flying
Fortress falls.

Moon Above, Moon Below
Moon Brothers WWII Adventure Series
Book 1

France, August 1944. In this alternate history WW2 adventure, American and British forces struggle to trap and destroy the still-potent German armies defending Normandy. But the Allies face another formidable obstacle of their own making: a seething rivalry between generals leads to a high-level disregard for orders that puts the entire campaign in the Falaise Pocket at risk of devastating failure—or spectacular success. That campaign unfolds through the eyes of two American brothers—one an idealistic pilot, the other a fatalistic tanker—as they plunge headlong into the confusion and indiscriminant slaughter of war.

Operation Fishwrapper
Book 5
Jock Miles WW2 Adventure Series

June 1944: A recon flight is shot down over the
Japanese-held island of Biak, soon to be the next jump in
MacArthur's leapfrogging across New Guinea. Major
Jock Miles, US Army—the crashed plane's intelligence
officer—must lead the handful of survivors to safety. It's
a tall order for a man barely recovered from a near-
crippling leg wound. Gaining the grudging help of a
Dutch planter who has evaded the Japanese since the
war began, Jock discovers just how little MacArthur's
staff knows about the terrain and defenses of the island
they're about to invade.

The American invasion of Biak promptly bogs down,
and the GIs rename the debacle *Operation Fishwrapper*,
a joking reference to their worthless maps. The infantry
battalion Jock once led quickly suffers the back-to-back
deaths of two commanders, so he steps into the job once
again, ignoring the growing difficulties with his leg.

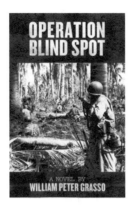

Operation Blind Spot
Book 4
Jock Miles WW2 Adventure Series

After surviving a deadly plane crash, Jock Miles is
handed a new mission: neutralize a mountaintop
observation post on Japanese-held Manus Island so
MacArthur's invasion fleet en route to Hollandia, New
Guinea, can arrive undetected. Jock's team seizes and
holds the observation post with the help of a clever
deception. But when they learn of a POW camp deep in
the island's treacherous jungle, it opens old wounds for
Jock and his men: the disappearance—and presumed
death—of Jillian Forbes at Buna a year before. There's
only one risky way to find out if she's a prisoner
there…and doing so puts their entire mission in serious
jeopardy.

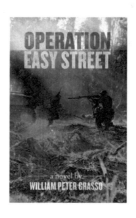

Operation Easy Street
Book 3
Jock Miles WW2 Adventure Series

Port Moresby was bad. Buna was worse.

The WW2 alternative history adventure of Jock Miles
continues as MacArthur orders American and Australian
forces to seize Buna in Papua New Guinea. Once again,
the Allied high command underestimates the Japanese
defenders, plunging Jock and his men into a battle
they're not equipped to win. Worse, jungle diseases,
treacherous terrain, and the tactical fantasies of deluded
generals become adversaries every bit as deadly as the
Japanese. Sick, exhausted, and outgunned, Jock's
battalion is ordered to spearhead an amphibious assault
against the well-entrenched enemy. It's a suicide
mission—but with ingenious help from an unexpected
source, there might be a way to avoid the certain
slaughter and take Buna. For Jock, though, victory
comes at a dreadful price.

Operation Long Jump
Book 2
Jock Miles WW2 Adventure Series

Alternative history takes center stage as Operation Long
Jump, the second book in the Jock Miles World War 2
adventure series, plunges us into the horrors of combat
in the rainforests of Papua New Guinea. As a prelude to
the Allied invasion, Jock Miles and his men seize the
Japanese observation post on the mountain overlooking
Port Moresby. The main invasion that follows quickly
degenerates to a bloody stalemate, as the inexperienced,
demoralized, and poorly led GIs struggle against the
stubborn enemy.

Seeking a way to crack the impenetrable Japanese
defenses, infantry officer Jock finds himself in a new
role—aerial observer. He's teamed with rookie pilot
John Worth, in a prequel to his role as hero of Grasso's
East Wind Returns. Together, they struggle to expose
the Japanese defenses—while highly exposed
themselves—in their slow and vulnerable spotter plane.

Long Walk to the Sun
Book 1
Jock Miles WW2 Adventure Series

In this alternate history adventure set in WW2's early days, a crippled US military struggles to defend vulnerable Australia against the unstoppable Japanese forces. When a Japanese regiment lands on Australia's desolate and undefended Cape York Peninsula, Jock Miles, a US Army captain disgraced despite heroic actions at Pearl Harbor, is ordered to locate the enemy's elusive command post.

Conceived in politics rather than sound tactics, the futile mission is a "show of faith" by the American war leaders meant to do little more than bolster their flagging Australian ally. For Jock Miles and the men of his patrol, it's a death sentence: their enemy is superior in men, material, firepower, and combat experience. Even if the Japanese don't kill them, the vast distances they must cover on foot in the treacherous natural realm of Cape York just might.

Unpunished

Congressman. Presidential candidate. Murderer. Leonard Pilcher is all of these things.

As an American pilot interned in Sweden during WWII, he kills one of his own crewmen and gets away with it. Two people have witnessed the murder—American airman Joe Gelardi and his secret Swedish lover, Pola Nilsson-MacLeish—but they cannot speak out without paying a devastating price. Tormented by their guilt and separated by a vast ocean after the war, Joe and Pola maintain the silence that haunts them both...until 1960, when Congressman Pilcher's campaign for his party's nomination for president gains momentum. As he dons the guise of war hero, one female reporter, anxious to break into the "boy's club" of TV news, fights to uncover the truth against the far-reaching power of the Pilcher family's wealth, power that can do any wrong it chooses—even kill—and remain unpunished.

East Wind Returns

A young but veteran photo recon pilot in WWII finds the fate of the greatest invasion in history--and the life of the nurse he loves--resting perilously on his shoulders.

"East Wind Returns" is a story of World War II set in July-November 1945 which explores a very different road to that conflict's historic conclusion. The American war leaders grapple with a crippling setback: Their secret atomic bomb does not work. The invasion of Japan seems the only option to bring the war to a close. When those leaders suppress intelligence of a Japanese atomic weapon poised against the invasion forces, it falls to photo reconnaissance pilot John Worth to find the Japanese device. Political intrigue is mixed with passionate romance and exciting aerial action--the terror of enemy fighters, anti-aircraft fire, mechanical malfunctions, deadly weather, and the Kamikaze. When shot down by friendly fire over southern Japan during the American invasion, Worth leads the desperate mission that seeks to deactivate the device.